THEY COURTED DANGER
AND DESIRE. . . .

Richard took her hand and kissed it, a courtly gesture all the more touching on that soldierly man.

"Dark times are ahead," he said. "It is good to know there is a friend at your back when you are facing your enemies. I know that you and your family will hold true."

They parted then and went to their chambers. Eleanor lay in her bed, and her thoughts tumbled around in her head like stones in a whirlpool. Then she rose and stole softly along the passage to pause before his door. Her hand rose to the latch, but before she could touch it, the door opened silently. Their eyes met.

"I knew you would come," he said.

THE
FOUNDING

Cynthia Harrod-Eagles

A DELL BOOK

Published by
Dell Publishing Co., Inc.
1 Dag Hammarskjold Plaza
New York, New York 10017

This work was first published in Great Britain
by Futura Publications Ltd.

Dell ® TM 681510, Dell Publishing Co., Inc.

ISBN: 0-440-12677-0

Printed in the United States of America
First U.S.A. printing—February 1982

For my parents

"Let man wear the fell of the lion,
woman the fleece of the sheep."

William Blake: *The Marriage of Heaven and Hell*

FOREWORD

Until the 1950s, the fifteenth century was almost totally neglected by historians, and this fact, together with the scantiness of contemporary sources, and the unreliability of sixteenth-century treatment of the period, made the fifteenth century seem as remote as the dark ages.

There are now, however, a number of works which offer clear and reliable information to anyone who wishes to read more about this period. Professor S. B. Chrimes's *Lancastrians, Yorkists & Henry VII* is very good for the earlier part of the century; on the Yorkist period Cora Scofield's *The Life and Reign of King Edward IV* is a brilliant and detailed study, while Paul Murray Kendall's *Richard III* is a vivid and readable work on both Richard III and Edward IV.

For the social history of the period G. M. Trevelyan's invaluable *English Social History* still cannot be bettered.

The main books in addition to these which I have found useful are as follows:

Original Sources: York Civic Records
   Warkwarth's Chronicle
   The Croyland Chronicle and Continuations

The Cely Papers
The Paston Letters
William of Worcester's Annales Rerum
Anglicarum
Memoirs of Phillipe de Commynes

Historians' Works: Chrimes, S.B. *English Constitutional Ideas in the C15th*
Costain, T.B. *The Last Plantagenets*
Derry, T.K. & Blakeway, M.G. *The Making of Britain*
Kendall, P.M. *The Yorkist Age*
Laver, James. *A History of Costume*
Quennell, M & C. B. M. *A History of Everyday Things in England*
Rowse, A.L. *Bosworth Field*
Turner, Sharon. *History of England During the Middle Ages*
Wilkinson, B. *The Later Middle Ages in England*
Williams, C.H. *England: The Yorkist Kings*

Note from the Author

My initial researches for the Morland Dynasty series were attended by such good luck that I could easily believe it was all meant to be. I decided to base my fictional family in the north of England, and almost at random I chose the city of York.

What a lucky choice that was! I was to discover that York was the second capital of England, and anything that didn't happen in London happened there. In the course of many visits I have fallen helplessly in love with this beautiful city, rightly called the White Rose of the North. It is one of the few surviving medieval walled towns, and its walls are in a remarkable state of preservation—it is possible to walk around three quarters of them along the paved parapets where the soldiers stood guard.

Within those walls is a storehouse of architectural treasures, buildings from every period I shall be writing about, beautifully preserved and still inhabited by ordinary people, who seem to think nothing of coming home from work to let themselves in through a fourteenth-century nailed-oak front door.

My second piece of luck occurred when I was holidaying in Wales while researching *The Founding*. On a country walk I saw a signpost marked "Ancient Monument," and following it down a winding, narrow lane I came upon Tretower Court: a fourteenth-fifteenth-century fortified dwelling-house, a perfect and very rare example of late medieval domestic architecture.

It was all there—the Great Hall, the solar, the inner court—everything I had been reading about. As I walked through its rooms, so well preserved and so magically full of atmosphere, the fifteenth century came alive to me, vividly and for the first time. By the time I left, some hours later, Tretower Court had become Micklelith House, the Morland family's first home.

Watermill House, which will appear in my second novel, was another lucky find. It is a Kentish hall-house (in the village of Benenden, where Princess Anne went to school) and belongs to journalist and critic Felix Barker. His father found the house in a sad state of disrepair and lovingly restored it over a period of some twenty years, using only such materials as the original builders would have used, such as fully-seasoned oak, and wooden pegs instead of nails. I fell in love with it, and was delighted to receive permission to use it in the forthcoming *The Dark Rose*.

Perhaps the most moving experience I had while researching was a visit to the Battlefield of Bosworth, where Richard III, the last English King of England, lost his throne and his life. The battlefield has been thoughtfully preserved and marked with sensible, unobtrusive notices showing how the battle was fought. The actual place where King Richard fell is now a small paddock, lush and green, with a little brook running by and trees all around, and the peace is disturbed by nothing but birdsong. On the gate a notice exhorts the visitor to treat the place with "the respect due to a great King and a brave and good man." Standing on the spot where Richard fell, like all the other pilgrims to that place, I wept.

It has been amusing to discover how real the Morlands have become to my family and friends as well as to me. When I took my sister to see Tretower Court, she greatly puzzled the curator by referring to it throughout as Micklelith House and asking to have pointed out various places mentioned in *The Founding*. A friend, having visited York on holiday, telephoned me, bubbling with excitement, to tell me that she had been to look for the place where the fictional John Butler and Helen Morland were supposed to have lived, and found *the original house still standing*!

I entered fully into her excitement. For me, the Morlands *are* history, and each new volume is a chance for me, as well as for my readers, to find out what really did happen next.

Cynthia Harrod-Eagles
London, England

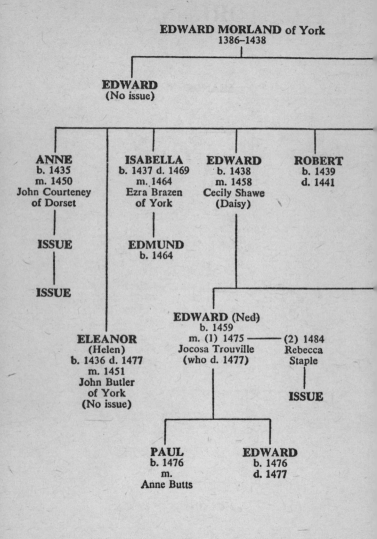

EDWARD MORLAND of York
1386–1438

EDWARD
(No issue)

ANNE
b. 1435
m. 1450
John Courteney
of Dorset

ISSUE

ISSUE

ISABELLA
b. 1437 d. 1469
m. 1464
Ezra Brazen
of York

EDMUND
b. 1464

EDWARD
b. 1438
m. 1458
Cecily Shawe
(Daisy)

ROBERT
b. 1439
d. 1441

ELEANOR
(Helen)
b. 1436 d. 1477
m. 1451
John Butler
of York
(No issue)

EDWARD (Ned)
b. 1459
m. (1) 1475 ———— (2) 1484
Jocosa Trouville   Rebecca
(who d. 1477)   Staple

ISSUE

PAUL
b. 1476
m.
Anne Butts

EDWARD
b. 1476
d. 1477

THE MORLAND FAMILY

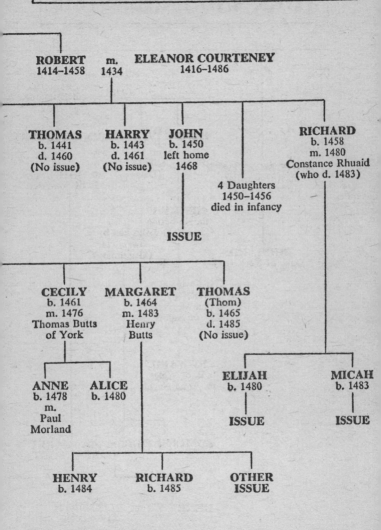

ROBERT m. **ELEANOR COURTENEY**
1414–1458 1434 1416–1486

THOMAS
b. 1441
d. 1460
(No issue)

HARRY
b. 1443
d. 1461
(No issue)

JOHN
b. 1450
left home
1468

4 Daughters
1450–1456
died in infancy

RICHARD
b. 1458
m. 1480
Constance Rhuaid
(who d. 1483)

ISSUE

CECILY
b. 1461
m. 1476
Thomas Butts
of York

MARGARET
b. 1464
m. 1483
Henry
Butts

THOMAS
(Thom)
b. 1465
d. 1485
(No issue)

ELIJAH
b. 1480

MICAH
b. 1483

ANNE
b. 1478
m.
Paul
Morland

ALICE
b. 1480

ISSUE

ISSUE

HENRY
b. 1484

RICHARD
b. 1485

**OTHER
ISSUE**

THE HOUSES OF
YORK AND LANCASTER

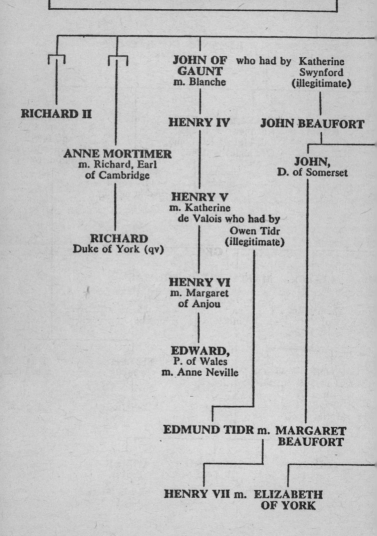

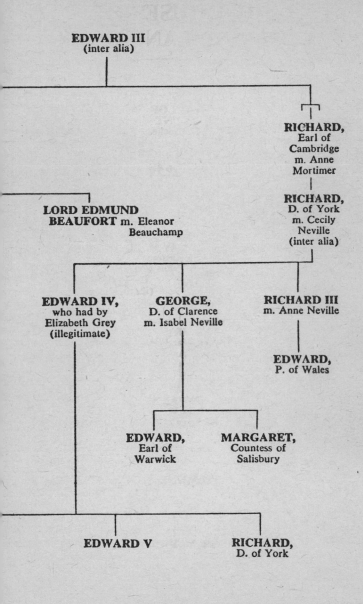

BOOK ONE

THE
WHITE
HARE

CHAPTER ONE

"We leave before dawn tomorrow," said Edward Morland through a mouthful of mutton. He was a tall, gaunt man of uncompromising aspect who had acquired manners too late in life for them to sit entirely easy on him. His movements as he helped himself to supper at the high table had a barely controlled violence about them, and, but for his evidently expensive clothes, a casual observer might have been forgiven for thinking he had strayed by accident to the high table from the low.

His son Robert, the only other occupant of the high table, since his wife and elder son had died, was quite different. Tall, like his father, and thin, and still with the gawkiness of youth upon him, he had an air of refinement about him: a gentler cast to his features, a quietness to his movements, an appearance of ease with the social aspects of eating. He was his mother's son, though he could hardly remember her; Edward Morland more coarsely said that he should sit to the distaff side of the fire—he resented, as far as it was possible to resent the ways of the Almighty, that it was the elder son that had died of the belly-gripes, and not the younger.

And now Robert looked up with that typically vague gaze and said to his father, "Why such an early start? Where are we going?"

"We take the road to Leicester, my son. We are going

south, and you know what the roads are like at this time of
year. If we get stuck behind a wool train, we'll be a fortnight on the road."

"South?" Robert said in perplexity. "South? What for?
Not with the clip—?"

Morland smiled sardonically. "No, not with the clip, boy.
The clip will take care of itself. No, we are going south to
get you a wife."

Robert's mouth opened at that, but he could find no
word to say.

"Well may you look surprised, boy," Morland went on
unkindly. "For all the interest you've shown in women, I
might as well have found you a husband as a wife. Why
God in his wisdom took my son and left me a daughter I'll
never know."

Robert stiffened and clenched his teeth at the familiar,
cruel words, but bore them in silence as he must. He
wanted to ask a lot of questions, but he was afraid of his
father and could only wait and hope that they would be
answered without his prompting.

"You don't show much interest, boy," Morland said irritably. He flung a scrap of fat to his dog, but the dog was
too slow and the scrap disappeared under a welter of
flying, growling bodies. "Don't you want to know who it is
I've managed to get for you?"

"Oh, yes, of course, Father—"

"Yes, of course, Father," Morland imitated. "You've got
a bleat like a eunuch. I hope you can manage to do your
duty by this girl at any rate. Perhaps you'd better go and
practice on the ewes." He laughed heartily at his own joke,
and Robert forced a sickly grin to his face, knowing that if
he didn't appear to laugh he would be cursed and perhaps
cuffed for being sullen—and being cuffed by his father
was rather like being kicked by a horse. "Well, I'll tell you,
since you press me so hard," Morland went on when he
had wiped the tears of laughter from his eyes. "She's the
ward of Lord Edmund Beaufort—a girl called Eleanor
Courteney. She's an orphan—one brother—estate encumbered. She hasn't a groat by way of dowry, but she brings
Lord Edmund's patronage, and she's cousin to the Earl of
Devon. Do you understand?"

"Yes, Father," Robert said automatically, though he didn't, quite.

"Think, boy, *think*," Morland prompted him. "The girl's got family and patronage. I've got money. It's a fair exchange, isn't it? Lord Edmund's trying to raise money for the wars, and he wants to keep on the good side of me. And I—well, I've got plans."

Robert understood. It was the way of the world he lived in. Edward Morland had made a lot of money during the wars under King Harry the Fifth, as had so many people who followed the young King into battle. He had bought up land and stocked the land with sheep, and he was now one of the biggest sheep farmers in Yorkshire, and one of the richest. And on the throne was a boy king, while the kingdom was ruled by his uncles, my lord of Bedford, and the good Duke Humphrey.

And among the powerful men who helped to rule was the great Beaufort family, also kin to the King. To them had fallen the task of carrying on the war they had inherited from the former King; not a profitable war anymore, but a very expensive one.

These great men needed money: Morland had money. It was the Earl of Somerset himself who suggested to his brother Edmund that his young ward would make a suitable wife for Morland's son. The marriage would ally Morland to one of the great families of the land, and would give him the right to the protection and patronage of the Beaufort family—the "good-lordship" as it was called. On the other side, it would hitch Morland and his gold firmly to the Beaufort wagon, give them the right to his money and service whenever they needed it. That's how bargains were made: that was what marriage was for, as both Robert and the unknown Eleanor Courteney had been aware since early childhood.

"Aye, I've got plans," Morland went on. He banged his wooden cup on the table, and at the signal one of the kitchen boys who did duty as page ran to fill it again with ale. "I'm a rich man. I've got land, sheep, and gold. And I've one son, just one son. What do you think I want for that son, eh, boy? Do you think I want to see him a rough country farmer like me? Do you think that's what your

mother—God rest her soul"—he crossed himself piously
and Robert followed suit automatically—"what your mother
wanted? No, lad; no, Robert. It's too late for me—but before I die, I'll see you a gentleman."

"A gentleman?" Robert said.

His father cuffed the side of his head, but gently. "Stop
repeating everything I say. Yes, a gentleman. Why do you
think I've chosen this girl for you, instead of a rich farmer's daughter to bring me more land? Because this girl will
bring you family." He mused for a moment, and then said
with unwonted gentleness, "Aye, and maybe it was for the
best it was you who lived. You can read and write and play
music. Edward couldn't. Mayhap you'll make a better gentleman than he would. Your sons will be gentlemen born.
Too late for me—you can't make a silk purse out of a
sow's ear. Your mother did right to teach you to read."

"Lots of gentlemen can't read, Father. And lots of yeoman can."

"Well, well," Morland said impatiently. He didn't like to
be comforted by his own son. "Anyway, this girl can read,
so I'm told. So you'll have a lot to talk about. But never
forget where your wealth came from." Robert knew what
was coming next. His father would quote the little rhyming
tag dear to the heart of all sheepmen. " 'I thanke God, and
ever shall; it is the sheep has payed for all.' "

"Yes, Father," Robert said dutifully.

There was a frost in the night, first sign of the declining
year, and Robert shivered as he was waked in the dark by
William, the butler. Robert's little truckle bed was under
the window, and the shutters were not tight, and let in a
dribble of cold air. His father slept in the big bed, and that
had curtains that drew right round it. He would have slept
warmly.

Breakfast was waiting for them in the hall—bacon
cooked in oatmeal, and ale and bread—and by the time
they had eaten, the horses were tacked up and waiting in
the inner yard. There were six of them: five riding horses
for Robert and his father and three servants, and a packhorse to carry their own gear and the presents for the bride
and her guardian. Seeing his father was not in sight, Robert

hurried across to one of the tackle sheds and was greeted as he ducked inside by a gentle whine. His bitch, Lady Brach, was in there on a bed of straw with her new family—though the family was not so new now, and Brach often deserted them to their own devices to follow at her master's heels. The whelps ought by rights to be weaned now, he thought. He missed Brach's padding sound behind him.

"Robert! Where in heaven's name is that boy?" It was Morland's voice out in the yard.

"I have to go," he said to his bitch, and she beat her tail against the ground at the sound of his voice. "I wish you could come with me, Lady Brach, but it can't be. Still, when I come back there'll be a new mistress for you to love—and I hope you won't be jealous and snarl at her."

"Robert!" The voice was growing irate. He caressed the bitch's head hastily and got to his feet, and then paused. A wonderful idea had come to him. In a frantic hurry now he stooped and felt about amongst Brach's litter, and picked out the biggest and strongest of the whelps: he would take it as a present to his bride-to-be. He pushed the puppy down inside his shirt for the warmth and ran out into the yard just as he was about to be called for the third time.

A minute later they were trotting out on to the road in a dark only just tinged with gray. At this time of the year—the time of the summer shearing—there were wool trains every day loaded down with the county's clip and heading south for the great market and port of London. The trains were sometimes a hundred or two hundred horses long, and they moved barely at foot-pace, filling the road with their bulky, swaying bodies and raising behind them such a dust that anyone traveling behind could scarcely breathe. There were in fact people who waited for the wool trains and rode with them, those travelers who wanted the company or felt they needed the protection of numbers. The Morlands were not travelers of this kind. Five men, armed and well mounted, were not likely to be attacked. The wool trains started out at dawn; the Morland party must set off before dawn if they were to get on the road ahead of them. When the first rim of the sun appeared over the horizon, they were already more than five miles from home.

* * *

Eleanor Courteney sat on the carved oak window seat in the south window of the solar, trying to get the last of the good light on the embroidery she was doing. It was a shirt for her master, and the delicate frocking at the neck needed the finest white silk and the tiniest needle. When the light grew too bad she would put it aside and take up some plainer work. From time to time she lifted her head and gazed out of the window. It was a perfect late summer day, and all around her, under the inverted blue bowl of the sky, were the rolling green hills of the Isle of Purbeck.

She loved it here at Corfe, the summer castle. She had lived all her life within sight of those hills and she could not imagine ever leaving. Across the room from her, sitting on a stool by the unlit fire, was her mistress, another Eleanor: once Eleanor Beauchamp, now Lady Eleanor Beaufort, wife of Lord Edmund Beaufort, and nicknamed Belle for her fair beauty. Belle was pregnant again and hoping for a son this time. The summer's heat had tired her, and her hands moved slowly among the colored silks. Eleanor would probably finish the task for her. Many a time when they had been girls together Eleanor had done double her task of spinning or weaving to keep Belle out of trouble.

The two girls had been brought up together from the time Eleanor's parents died. Belle was two years the elder, but Eleanor was forward and well grown, so they never felt the difference, and together they had been taught to read, to write, and to reckon; they had learned French and Latin and dancing and music; they had learned to use the needle and had done their daily task of spinning and weaving. Belle, small and fair and pretty, was generous and kindhearted and lazy. Eleanor, taller and dark, was energetic, sharp and clever. They had perfectly complemented each other.

When Belle had married Lord Edmund she had begged to take Eleanor with her, and the plea had been admitted, and Lord Edmund had bought her wardship from Belle's father. To Eleanor it had seemed to seal her fate. She would stay here forever, tending poor fretful Belle through her interminable pregnancies and later, she hoped, become lady-governess to the results of those pregnancies. That was the summit of her ambition. She hoped for nothing more.

No, that was not quite true. There was something, something she longed for and hardly dared to hope for, something over which her mind plunged and soared from wild hope to deep despair and back again, so that she hardly knew any longer whether it was a hope or the most distant of dreams. As she thought about it, her busy fingers, all unknown to her, slowed and stopped and lay idle in her lap. Her eyes went again to the window and gazed out, over the little stone houses of the village with their lichen-gilded rooftops, past the outfields and common land and the fringes of woods to the great wild hills, where the wind bent the trees and snatched the clouds into fronds.

His name was Richard. He was twenty-three and unmarried, a soldier, with a soldier's broad shoulders and light step. He was not tall, and rather stocky, broad-chested and strong; he had a square, good-humored face, sun-bronzed, and fair hair burnt white as barley at the front from the weather. His eyes were blue and had a piercing gaze that seemed to see into your soul. He didn't smile often, not because he was dour but because he thought deeply about things; but when he did smile, it lit his whole face and made you feel that the sun had come back after a long winter. It was a smile that warmed your heart, that made you willing to lay down your life for him.

He and Lord Edmund had been in France together three years ago for the trial of Joan the Maid at Rouen and the coronation of the boy King at Paris. That was in December, and the following spring they had come back and stayed for a while in the home of the newly wed Lord Edmund, where there were feasting and games, dancing and music. Where Eleanor had first met him, and fallen in love with him. Like any soldier home from France he had a will to enjoy himself and an eye for a pretty girl. Eleanor was beautiful, and he danced with her, teased her and complimented her, praised her singing and her dark eyes. And one day, as they walked in the pleasance just out of earshot

of the rest of the party, he had drawn her into the shadow
of a bower and kissed her.

Eleanor's young heart, all unguarded, had no chance.
His voice, his smile, even the brush of his sleeve against
her hand as they sat at the high table, were all that filled
her mind and heart day after day, and she knew even in
the heady excesses of her love that she was mad to let herself love him. For he was no ordinary Richard—he was
Richard Plantagenet, the Duke of York.

He was rich, powerful, a general and a statesman, the
head of his family, a Duke, and some said more royal than
the King himself, for he was descended by his mother from
the second son of Edward the Third and by his father from
the fourth son. And she was Eleanor Courteney, a penniless orphan. Sometimes she was in the depths of despair,
knowing how disparate were their positions. At other times
she was hopeful, for if he loved her, he might marry her—
there was no one to gainsay him, and he might do as he
chose.

She clung to her hope and her dreams, and to the one
tangible memento she had of him: last Christmastide he
had sent gifts to the family, and had remembered Eleanor
too. He had sent her a small leather-covered missal with
her device—a white running hare—embossed on the cover.
It was an expensive gift even from a duke, but she trea-
sured it more because he had sent it than because it was
valuable. She wore it attached to a chain that hung from
her belt, and at night it was under her pillow. She was
never without it—it was her talisman.

A noise at the door drew her back suddenly from her
reverie, and she realized that the light had almost gone and
she would not be able to finish her fine work. The next
moment the door was flung open, and her master entered,
followed by a servant carrying his chair. Lord Edmund had
two chairs, and he was justly proud of them. This one, in
red velvet with gold cords and embroidery, went everywhere with him, even to war, where it occupied pride of
place in his tent; the other, in green velvet with silver embroidery, kept its place on the dais in the hall and was used
by honored guests or, when there were none, his wife.

Eleanor and Belle had risen at his entrance, and he signed them to sit as he himself sat down and sent the servants away. Belle sat again on her stool, and at a sign from her master Eleanor left the window and took a cushion on the floor beside Belle.

"For it was really you I came to see, mistress Eleanor," Lord Edmund said. He treated her to an unaccustomed scrutiny, and was apparently satisfied at what he saw, for he smiled and said, "You have a pretty color in your cheeks today, mistress. I hope you are in good health?"

"Perfect, thank you, my lord," Eleanor said, mystified.

"That is good, for I have found you a husband, and you are soon to meet him."

Eleanor turned pale at the words, and her hand went instinctively to the fold of her surcoat, fumbling for the chain of the missal, her talisman. A husband? Who? Could it be, could it possibly be? But no, he said he had "found" a husband. He wouldn't say that about *him*. Lord Edmund looked on, smiling at her confusion, though not knowing, of course, the wild thoughts that were tumbling through her mind.

"Yes," he said, "you are surprised, and I expected it, for you have been left so long a maid you must have thought I meant to ignore my duty to provide for you." He smiled, waiting for her quick denial, but she did not speak, and he went on. "Well, you may be at ease. You are eighteen, and overdue for marriage, but I have a good match for you, and one that will see you as comfortably set up as even your parents could have wished. It is to be the son of Edward Morland."

Eleanor heard the name with a dull shock. She could not at first place the man, and she thought in vain of the various men she had heard of in her master's acquaintance. And then she remembered him. He had been once to the summer castle last year, a tall bony man with a rough northern accent. He was, she remembered in horror, a sheep farmer, one of the common people from whom the government borrowed money for various purposes. She had to speak now, and she found her voice only shakily.

"My lord, I believe I recollect the man—he was a sheep

farmer from the north—?" Her eyes pleaded to be told she was wrong, but Lord Edmund did not observe the expression.

"Aye, that's right. Edward Morland of York. He owns a great deal of land on the south side of the city of York. He is, in fact, one of the richest men in Yorkshire, and a great asset to the war party. We are glad to get him so unequivocally on our side as this suggests—"

"But, my lord, a *farmer*?"

There was a brief silence as Eleanor realized she had, in her anguish, interrupted her master, a terrible crime. His face darkened as he stared at her.

"Yes, mistress, a farmer. The only son and heir of a farmer is to be your husband. And let me remind you that while you may be related to a noble house, it is but a distant relationship, and you have no dowry—no dowry at all. The match is very fair, and if I expected any comment from you, I expected a suitable gratitude."

Eleanor's cheeks now flamed, and her head hung as she tried to fight back the tears. Gentle Belle allowed her hand to drop as if by accident to her friend's shoulder and she spoke up to draw off the attention from her.

"Of course Eleanor is grateful, my lord. I think it is just the suddenness of the news that has surprised her. When, pray, may we expect these most welcome guests?"

"They are already on the road, my dear. They should be here the day after tomorrow, in time for dinner."

"So soon? Well, that is news indeed."

"Yes, the day after tomorrow. They will stay for a few days, a week perhaps, while the betrothal takes place, and then they will take mistress Eleanor back with them."

Belle felt Eleanor stiffen and she said in a gently anxious voice, "She is to go away at the end of a week? Why, we had hoped that she might be able to be with me when my time comes to lie-in—"

"No, my dear." Lord Edmund shook his head firmly. "It's of no use. We must get her north before the bad weather, and if she doesn't go with her betrothed, it will be necessary for me to arrange an armed guard for her, and that might not be convenient."

"I am to be married, then, at York?" Eleanor found her voice, but a very small voice.

"Yes, mistress, you shall be married at your new home. Normally, of course, you would spend some months there to learn the ways of the household, but there is no mistress there to teach you, Morland's wife having died long since. So you must teach yourself as you go along." He smiled encouragingly, but Eleanor could not shift the lump of misery and shame from her heart; she could not smile. Belle, guessing a little at her feelings, tried once again to excuse her.

"My lord," she said, "will you not give mistress Eleanor leave to withdraw? I see the news has come as a shock, and perhaps she has need of time to compose herself."

"Of course, my dear. You have leave, mistress," Lord Edmund said graciously.

Eleanor curtsyed deeply, flung a look of gratitude at Belle, and hurried from the room. Once through the door she ran down the stairs, through the hall under the surprised eyes of the servants, and out into the pleasance. Here she walked up and down, wringing her hands together and turning her wretched thoughts over and over in her mind. It was borne upon her then how great was the difference between a hope, however slender, and no hope at all.

It was only a few minutes before she was found there by Gaby, her nurse, who had hurried after her as fast as her stoutness allowed when she saw Eleanor run through the hall. Gaby had been her wetnurse and had graduated from that position to that of personal maid. Eleanor's mother had died when Eleanor was an infant: Gaby was all the mother she had ever known.

As Eleanor turned toward her at the end of the walk Gaby was shocked by the distress in that loved face.

"What is it, mistress? What's happened?"

"Oh, Gaby! My lord has just told me—I am to be married!"

Gaby's breath was released in a rush. So it was no worse than that, God be thanked!

"Well, mistress," she said reasonably, drawing Eleanor

into the shelter of the bower and sitting with her on the little wooden bench, "you are eighteen years old. You should expect to be married, it is only right. Most girls are married long before this, you know."

"I know, Gaby, but you don't understand." Eleanor turned tragic eyes upon her. "They are to marry me to a farmer's son. A Yorkshire farmer!"

Gaby shook her head sadly. "You are too high, my little lady. The match is a good one—not what I would have liked for you, you being a gentleman's daughter, but a good match none the less. He is the only son, and heir to great wealth. The father is very rich and becoming quite influential in government circles. Remember, my love, you have no dowry. A man of higher standing would not take you."

"Would not?" Eleanor whispered. "He might if—if he loved me."

Gaby made a sound expressive of disgust. "Love! What has marriage to do with love? You are talking nonsense, mistress, and you know it. Once you are married, that is the time for love. You will love your husband as the Bible bids you, and be happy."

"I will not," Eleanor said in a low voice, and her eyes flashed angrily. "They may marry me to a vulgar northern barbarian, but I will never love him. I *hate* him!"

Gaby crossed herself automatically at these words, but her face darkened with shock and anger. "You wicked girl! Never let me hear you say such a thing again! Why, it is your sacred duty laid down by our blessed Lord himself that a wife should love her husband—"

"You forget yourself, mistress Gaby," Eleanor said coldly, drawing herself up. "You should not speak to your mistress in such terms."

For a moment they stared at each other, and then Gaby said quietly, "I beg your pardon, mistress. I spoke from my heart, for you know that I love you like my own child."

Eleanor stared a moment longer, and then melted suddenly and flung her arms around her kind nurse. "Oh Gaby, I'm sorry, I shouldn't have said that. You know I don't mean it—only I'm so unhappy. How could they do it to me—how could they think so little of me as to marry me to a farmer?"

"My dear mistress, your ideas are more high than just. A farmer may be a kind, godly, and educated man as well as another. Besides, there is nothing you can do about it. The choice is not for you, and you must make the best of it that you can, and make him a good wife, and learn to love him."

"Well, I will try to be a good wife," Eleanor said in a low voice, "but I can never, never love him."

"You think of that other," Gaby said, glancing round her to make sure they were not overheard. Her voice sank to a whisper, but was none the less forceful. "Put him from your mind, mistress! It was madness to think of him. You, a penniless orphan, to think of a royal duke? Madness! Do not dare to love him, mistress, or it will make you miserable and wicked. Put him from your thoughts now forever, and never speak a word of it to anyone—*anyone!*"

Eleanor looked at her sadly. She knew that here was an end to her hopes, yet she knew also that she could never forget him. She would love him still, though it would be her secret. They would and could marry her off as it pleased them, but what was in her heart was between herself and God, and they could not make her love as they willed. But to Gaby she showed the properly submissive face, a face in which she was going to have a lot of practice over the next few days.

2

Well, it was over. By ten o'clock on the day after the arrival of the Morland party, the betrothal had taken place, and Eleanor was as good as a married woman. The ceremony took place quietly and with no unseemliness, and the bridal party then repaired to the hall for the feast. Everything had been done in the grandest style: the hall itself had been made ready, with fresh rushes laid down, the hangings beaten, the tables and benches scrubbed, and the high table was laid with a beautiful damask cloth upon which were set the trenchers and goblets, the napkins and towels, the salts and breads, all in their proper order.

Lord Edmund and Belle led the way in, followed by Eleanor and her betrothed and Morland, all in their best clothes. Eleanor looked as beautiful as she ought, dressed in her best surcoat of crimson wool over a cotte of sky-blue linen. Her little waist was cinched in with a belt of gold wires set with lapis, her bride-gift from her master, and from it hung her missal, and an ivory pomander ball, Belle's bride-gift to her. On her head was a headdress *à cornes* with a veil of stiffened fine muslin: it was heavy, and difficult to balance, and it ensured that she walked with her head up, like a queen.

Her husband-to-be thought she was a queen. He had been dazzled by her from the first moment he had set eyes upon her, and the fact that she evidently thought little of him did not deter him. He realized that he *had* made a bad first impression, coming in dirty and dusty from the journey, with the added disadvantage that the puppy had bathed him all the way down in a stream of urine, which added its own particular pungency to the smell of sweat and horses. Even now, bathed and dressed in his best, he knew that he looked like a sparrow amongst jays. *His* best clothes were little fine; and his lean, gangly body was not one that best set off fine clothes. He walked beside her nervously.

As they entered the hall, Eleanor looked around her and was pleased and touched at how much effort had been made to make all fine for her feast. She glanced at the man beside her: a very young man, with mousy hair and sandy eyelashes and a gentle, shy mouth. He had reminded her at first of a sheep, for her heart had been full of another's image. She loved a square-jawed, soldierly man with a confident smile; a thickset man with the strong neck of a stallion and the broad, muscular shoulders of a swordsman. How could she find the good in a nervous boy with the mouth of a poet and the body of a dancer?

But now as their eyes met she remembered that this youth to whom she had just been bound for life had brought her a puppy, the best of the litter of his own favorite bitch, as a gift. A little gift, a silly gift beside the valuable bride-gifts that had been unloaded from the packhorse: but he had tried to please her, and so she smiled at him. It was a slight smile, but it was enough for Robert. His heart leapt, and he smiled back at her adoringly, hers from that moment for the rest of his life.

They took their places at the high table, and the rest of the household and all the servants, retainers, and tenants took their places at the long tables down the sides of the hall. A trumpet played a fanfare and all fell silent while Lord Edmund pronounced a grace in a ringing voice. Another trumpet, and the pages brought the silver bowls to the table for the guests to wash their hands, and then the butler brought up the mazer, the loving cup, for the ceremonial toasts.

"To Master Robert and Mistress Eleanor, that their union might be attended by God's blessing, that it may be long and fruitful, and rich in the knowledge of virtue and godliness," was proposed by Lord Edmund, and Eleanor dropped her eyes, the rich color rising to her cheeks. She was not used to being the center of attention. He then toasted the King, and his honored guest, master Edward Morland, and Morland replied with a toast to his hosts. And then the mazer was removed; the priceless nef, in the shape of a jeweled galleon, was placed in the center of the table, from which each man could help himself of spices; and the first course was brought on, to the sound of music.

"My Lord Edmund, you keep a good table," Morland cried, his eyes bright with appreciation. "I should think you have a good cook."

"I have, sir," Lord Edmund replied. "My uncle the Cardinal got him for me. He was cook to an alderman in London, and could not be prized away until his master died, so he combines genius with loyalty—two rare qualities, and rarer still in combination. The dishes meet with your approval?"

I should think they might, Eleanor thought scornfully. Venison frumenty, maumeny of capons, fillets in galantine, and a roast swan with all its feathers cunningly replaced to represent the living bird; and there were to be another two courses, each of at least four dishes, with subtleties in between. The approval of a barbarian farmer could not be so hard to obtain.

She turned to Robert and asked him in a sharp voice, "I

do not suppose you often have such a dinner, sir? I suppose you do not normally serve above three dishes?"

Robert blushed with shame, and answered without looking at her. "No, mistress, I'm afraid we don't. We have an indifferent cook—it is hard to come by a good one."

"That's true enough," Morland said, catching the exchange. "I have kept my eyes open, but every fair passes and leaves us still lacking."

Lord Edmund smiled lightly. "A good cook is the first essential for any household, and you have my sympathy for all the years you have suffered. But, mistress Eleanor, do not fear, I shall not send you to that same suffering. Jacques, my second cook, has agreed to go with you and serve you in your new household, so you shall eat almost as well in York as you ate in Dorset."

Eleanor was brought almost to tears by such generosity, for a man's cook was his most essential servant, the highest paid and the most highly prized member of the household. "Oh, my lord," she said, "how can I thank you enough? It is very, very kind of you."

Lord Edmund patted her hand and smiled kindly. "Did you think I'd send you away empty-handed? For all that you have no dowry, I shall see that you have full hands to come to your husband, in addition to the blessing of yourself." And he glanced at Robert, and saw quite clearly from the youth's expression that he thought Eleanor sufficient treasure in herself. However, it was not Robert he designed to please, but his father.

"I have set aside some furniture for you," he went on, watching Morland's face out of the corner of his eye, "and some bales of cloth for your wedding gown and hangings, and you shall take your maid with you, too, and a groom. It is not fitting that you should have no one to attend you on your journey."

All this was intended to impress upon Morland how important a wife he had got for his son, but it did not diminish Eleanor's pleasure one whit. She was to go north with three servants of her own, the nucleus of a personal household, and furniture and cloth of her own. This was style indeed; this was better than what she had imagined, than going north as a supplicant, having to be grateful for even her bread at the hands of a man she felt her inferior.

While she smiled her speechless thanks at her master, Morland nodded his approval and said, "That's right, my lord, that's right. My own servants are pretty rough, though it's good fighting men you need to attend you in Yorkshire and they suit me as they are. But they're not ladies' maids, I can tell you! No, they are men as *are* men. The house is none too pretty either—it has lacked a woman's insistence on finery all these years, and the maid might find it in need of fixing up. But these things can be done, they're not so difficult. And I'll give her a horse of her own when she's wed to make up for it."

Now Morland was trying to impress upon Lord Edmund that he had no need of a dowry or valuables of any kind with Eleanor; but as long as the two men vied with each other, Eleanor seemed likely to come well out of it, and she smiled her thanks at each with good grace.

At the end of the first course the bowls were brought again for hand washing, and then the first subtlety was brought in—a wonderful sugar confection in the shape of a red deer stag.

"Animals of the chase," Lord Edmund said, "since we are into the season of hunting. Do you hunt much in Yorkshire?"

"I don't myself," Morland said, "but the lad does. There's rare hunting to be had—all kind of birds, deer, hare, boar: you won't lack for hunting there."

The second course was being brought on now, roast mutton, herring pie, mortrewes, and blandissory, and the music ceased in favor of a young page reading aloud from the *Parlement of Fowles*.

Eleanor turned to Robert, feeling that an effort was due from her, and asked, for want of a subject, "What are you thinking about?"

The answer when it came was incomprehensible, for Robert spoke in his own native Yorkshire instead of in the southern speech which he had been carefully taught from childhood. Eleanor stared at him, feeling a sinking of her heart, for she knew that most people would talk like that in her new home, and she would be a stranger in a foreign land, unable even to make herself understood.

"I cannot understand you," she said. "I cannot tell your northern speech."

Robert muttered an apology, and repeated himself in his careful English. "I was wondering how you shall like Micklelith."

"What is Micklelith?"

"Where we are going. The house—it's the name of the house. The Mickle Lith is the great gate—the Great South Gate of York. Our house is in sight of it, on the great south road."

"Is it a large house?" Eleanor asked, interested in spite of herself.

"I don't know if you'd think so. It's a farmhouse, and there've been bits added on over the years, so it seems big. It's old," he apologized, "and not so fancy as this." He thought of the bare, dirty, drab old house, and wished that he could have seen it made fit for Eleanor before she entered it. "We'll do it up before the wedding, I promise thee," he added.

Eleanor nodded without enthusiasm. A farmhouse, she considered, was likely to be pretty uncomfortable, whatever was done to it. "You are near to the city, then," she asked next.

"Why, yes—so near that we go on foot to the church within the gates. And we are right on the great road, so we get all the news—almost as soon as you get it here, I should think. And we see everything that passes—all the merchants and traveling players and jugglers and healers and the fine lords and ladies—" He stopped abruptly. He had been eager to reconcile Eleanor to going away, but had forgotten in his eagerness that she was used to the company of fine lords and ladies. He saw her lip curl in disdain, and cursed himself for his clumsiness.

Eleanor turned her attention back to the main conversation, which was about the war, as was inevitable, but her mind was not on what was being said. She was thinking of fine lords and ladies, and of one fine lord in particular. She was remembering that she was going to the Duke of York's own county, moving nearer to his home, though he

spent little enough time in it. Nearer to him—yet away
from him entirely, for he would never stoop to cross the
threshold of a ramshackle farmhouse. She was moving out
of his sphere forever, and if she ever saw him again, it
would not be as before, privileged to speak to him and be
spoken to by him. If she saw him again, it would be as one
of the crowd who lined the road to watch as he passed with
his retinue, one of the crowd on whom the dust of his passing fell.

CHAPTER TWO

They started out in the gray cool dawn of the first of October. There had been a light frost and the round cobbles of the inner yard glittered with it, and the horses' breath rose like a faint smoke to the low eaves where the sparrows sat with all their feathers puffed against the chill. There was nothing of summer in that dawn, but a grim reminder that winter was approaching, and that it would find Eleanor in a far colder place.

Having heard mass and breakfasted the party set out, and quite a cavalcade it made as it trotted through the little village: children ran out into the road to watch, and even men and women appeared at the doors to see what was passing. Some of the villagers recognized Eleanor and called a blessing to her as she rode by. She waved to them, and thanked them with tears in her eyes, knowing that it was against all likelihood that she would ever see this place again. She was feasting her eyes on the sight of her long home—the tall gray mass of the castle on its high mound, the gray-and-gold houses of the village, and rounded green hills with their beards of deciduous trees all around. Corfe Castle, which they called the summer castle; from its highest tower you could see the sea. She had been happy here: she said good-bye to it in her heart, and drew her hood forward to hide her tears as she left it behind her.

The journey was long and tiring. Eleanor, dressed in her warmest clothes and a thick cloak lined with rabbit fur, rode a stout pony called Dodman—"snail"—who lived up to his name, but had been chosen as a stayer who would not fall by the wayside. The groom who had been chosen to attend her was a boy of thirteen called Job, and Gaby rode pillion behind him, for Lord Edmund was not willing to spare a horse for her. Jacques, the cook, rode his horse at all times as close to Eleanor as he could get, for he regarded Morland's men as little better than savages, and not to be trusted. A pair of mules carried Eleanor's baggage and with the five Morland men and their pack horse completed the party.

They were four days on the road, stopping each night at an inn where the accommodation was crude and dirty but the food was good. As they went further north it grew colder and the land grew wilder and more desolate. Sometimes they went for hours without seeing a single roof or any other person but themselves. They passed great tracts of forest and moor and wild land where the unwary traveler could be robbed and murdered without any hope of aid, but they were not attacked, despite the presence in their party of two women and three baggage-beasts. The Morland men all carried their arms conspicuously, and looked as if they would give a hard time to anyone foolish enough to try them, and it was enough to deter the outlaws in favor of more easy pickings.

On the fifth day, they set out from their overnight accommodation in teeming, freezing rain. The roads had been good so far after a long dry spell, but as they were now nearing York and on the great south road, which was always busy, they had not been riding above two hours when they found the going much changed for the worse. By nine o'clock they were struggling at a snail's pace through mud fetlock-deep, and at Eleanor's tentative query as to whether they might expect improvement in the road later on, Morland told her tersely that she might expect what she liked, but she would see mud up to her girth before the journey's end.

It was a bit of an exaggeration: the mud reached knee-deep consistency, and there was certainly mud *on* the girth, and on their garments in great gobbets and splashes. Poor Dodman with his short legs fared worse than the taller

horses, and at times Eleanor wondered if she was going to
have to get off and walk—or rather, wade—but his endurance saw him through. By midday they had reached the
short section of paved road that covered the last few miles
to York city itself, and the road was filled with travelers of
all description, more than Eleanor had ever seen before in
her life.

"Is it always as busy as this?" she asked in wonder.

"Nay, mistress, we dunna call this busy," Morland told
her scornfully. As they went further north, his speech had
become more careless, slipping more toward the northern
tongue. "Tha s'lt see what's laike on fair-day or market
day."

"Are we nearly there?" she asked a little farther on.

This time it was Robert who turned and answered her,
with a shy smile, "We *are* there," he said. "Look, can you
see the great gate, there, up ahead? And the walls of the
city?"

"Why yes—yes I can. So this is the city of York?"
Eleanor was pleased and excited. She had been once to the
great city of Winchester, but apart from that she had never
been in anything larger than a village, and she was all agog
at the idea of living so close. As they rode closer and she
stared ahead of her in excitement, she began to be aware of
the smell of the city, drifting down to her, and the clamor
of church bells in a wave of sound pouring over the beautiful white walls. Both made her gasp: as to the smell, she
had never come across anything like it, having lived all her
life in rich men's houses which were "sweetened" regularly.
This was the stench of an accumulation of human and animal filth collecting and rotting undisturbed in confined
spaces. As to the sound, it was a clamor of different bells
all over the city, beating their brazen tongues till the very
air seemed to rock.

"What are the bells ringing for?" she asked Robert, who
was riding beside her still.

"They ring all the time," he said. "Some tell the hour,
some call folk to meetings, some are passing bells; many of
them are obits. I should think most of the big churches
have to ring all day to get through the obits alone."

"It's a lovely sound," Eleanor said. "I think when I die I should like to know a bell will be rung for me every year."

"If you like bells, just wait till the end of the month, on Hollows' Night. Every bell of every church rings all through the night, and on All Souls Night, too. We're so close to the walls we can scarcely sleep unless the wind's away from us."

"Tell me," Eleanor said suddenly, staring ahead at the Great Gate, "what are those brownish things on poles above the gate? They look like pumpkins or giant turnips or something."

There was no immediate answer to her question, and when she turned to look at him, she saw that he regarded her with a curious expression.

"Why, don't you really know?" he said.

She shook her head. "I wouldn't ask if I did."

"They are the heads—what's left of them—of felons executed within the city. They are hanged, drawn, and quartered, and when the remains are scattered, the heads are put up there on poles until they rot off, or are carried off by kites."

"Oh," said Eleanor, and looked away. It was right and fitting that felons should suffer the penalty, but she didn't care about the idea of passing through the city gate under their blind and rotting eyes.

"You'll get used to it," Robert said, trying not to grin at her obvious discomfort.

Eleanor did not like to be thought a country bumpkin. "I care nothing about it, sir," she said tartly. "I only wondered what would happen if one fell on you as you passed through the gate."

"Well you won't need to worry about it this time—here we are home."

Home! The word sounded odd to Eleanor, who had left her home far behind her. Yet this place was to be her home for the rest of her days, and she would have been a strange person if she did not look about her with interest. A battlemented wall fronted the property on the road side, and the great iron-studded gate stood open at their approach, which had presumably been seen from afar. They rode in through the gateway and found themselves in the farmyard, where chickens scratched and pigs rooted in the mud, and Eleanor had her first sight of the house itself.

It was mainly a wooden building, with a great pointed gable facing eastward and covered balconies at first-floor level that gave access to the upstairs rooms. Behind it, and on either side, stretched other buildings that had been built on at various times, so that there was a motley collection of roofs, gables, and structures to be seen on all sides. And the whole messy collection made up Micklelith House, the name having been carved into the stone lintel over the main door. It looked what it was, in fact—a large, extended farmhouse.

Robert was watching Eleanor's face anxiously as Job, dismounting, led Dodman forward to a place dry enough for Eleanor to dismount.

"There are gardens on the south side of the house," he said, hoping to see some relaxation of the line of her mouth, "and from the west windows you can see over the moors towards the hills. All our land lies to the southwest. The land to the northwest belongs to one of the Earl of Northumberland's men, but he doesn't farm it."

Eleanor didn't care. She was exhausted, wet and cold to the bone. All she wanted was a warm fire, a meal, and a comfortable bed, and her hopes were all fixed on finding what she wanted within. Some male servants or retainers had run out as they rode into the yard, and now were conversing with Morland in harsh, loud voices in that language she did not understand. It sounded to Eleanor like the yarping and braying of beasts, not like human speech at all. She had dismounted and was standing shivering in the shelter of the balcony, waiting to be given the welcoming cup and to be escorted within, but it didn't seem to be happening that way. Her own servants—Gaby, Jacques, and Job—were huddling close to her as if for protection, Job carrying the mewling puppy which had had such a long journey away and back for so little purpose. Some men had led the horses away, and Morland himself, shouting forcefully at his men, had gone with them. Robert was staring about him as if wondering whether to follow him or not.

He knew that something was due to the guests, and especially to his betrothed, but to play the host was to draw attention to his father's omission, which didn't seem to him to be a wise thing to do. At last he decided to go and find his father and remind him as tactfully as possible, and with a muttered excuse he splashed off round the side of the house, leaving the guests where they stood.

Now Eleanor found herself in a quandary. She relieved her feelings by complaining, which got her nowhere.

"The barbarians," she said savagely, "to leave us standing here in the rain. No word of greeting, no loving cup, no one to conduct us inside. This is what we have come down to, Gaby—we have less care than the horses and dogs."

"Horses and dogs, mistress, are perhaps more valuable up here," Jacques said bitterly. He spent most of his life in the furnace atmosphere of a great lord's kitchen, and he hated cold and was particularly susceptible to it. He had been contemplating all through the journey on his chances of still being alive by next spring.

"There is no woman of the house, mistress," Gaby reminded Eleanor, and it was this that decided her. Drawing herself erect, she set her jaw against any gainsaying, and started toward the door.

"Follow me," she said to her servants, and they were only too pleased to do so. Inside the house was dark, for the shutters had been closed against the rain, and the only light came in through the smoke hole in the roof, and the small unshuttered slits high up under the gable. Eleanor found herself in the hall, which was bare, drab, and undecorated. The rushes were deep on the floor and had evidently not been changed for some time, for the debris was perfectly visible and the stench rose up to her nostrils at every step. There were no hangings on the walls, and though there had evidently been paintings on the walls at some time, they had worn and flaked away and could only be seen in patches.

Worst of all was that the fire on the raised hearth in the center of the hall had been allowed to run down, and there was nothing but a handful of embers among the wood ash to give warmth to the room. The fact that there were no dogs around it showed that they had abandoned the hall for some warmer corner of the jumble of buildings—and that was a sign like rats leaving a sinking ship.

Signaling her people to wait, Eleanor stepped gingerly across the squelching rushes toward the screen beyond which she knew must be the buttery and pantry, thinking perhaps that the house servants were in the kitchen. The gap in the screen that led out of the hall was covered with a cowhide curtain, and she had just put her head to it when a harsh voice arrested her.

"Where do you think you're going, mistress?"

She turned and saw that Morland had come in through the screen at the other end of the hall. She guessed there must be another external door through there.

"I am going, sir, to find the servants. They have let the fire go out, and we require food." Eleanor felt it necessary to sound assured and confident. She was so demoralized by cold and hunger that she was afraid she would cry, and one thing she had determined was that her father-in-law should not see that happen. "It seems, sir," she went on boldly, "that your servants have all run away."

Edward Morland stared at her as if he were not sure whether to beat her or admire her. "By God, mistress, you have a serpent's tongue in that pretty face of yours. Well, I like spirit in a ewe, for a spirited ewe brings forth strong lambs." He made a gesture towards the empty hearth. "The servants are all without. This is a busy time of year for sheepmen—they have too much to do outside to be tending fires and making meals."

"We require food," Eleanor said again. "Why was no meal waiting for us?"

"Dinner is over, mistress, and supper is at five. You will have to wait." He turned as if to leave, and then turned back again. "I will tell my cook when he comes back from the field that your man is now in charge. It is a duty he will be glad to give up. And, mark ye, I like spirit, but I will not brook insolence, so curb your unruly tongue, or I will beat you, like any beast that disobeys."

And with that he left the hall by the way he had come. Eleanor stood erect and proud, biting her lip in anger. She said nothing, but as she watched him go she thought,

"Someday I shall be mistress of this house, Edward Morland, and then we shall see who does the beating."

Gaby touched her arm anxiously, and brought Eleanor back to reality. It was good, at least, when one was downhearted, to have others depending on one. It made it easy to be brave.

"Job," she said, "do you go and see if the horses have been properly cared for. They still belong to my lord Edmund. Stay—give me the whelp, I'll look after it for now. Jacques, go you to the kitchen and see if you can find anything for us to eat—any scraps, milk, anything. Well for these northerners to wait for supper, but I need something now. If anyone tries to stop you, come straight to me. And Gaby, you come with me. We'll go up those stairs and see what there is above. It's my guess the bedchamber is above here, and perhaps there may be a solar as well."

Together the women passed through the screen at the other end of the hall and found themselves in a tiny lobby from which the stairs ran upward. There were other doors in the lobby: she guessed that one of them must lead to the cellar, but where the others led she could not tell. At the top of the stairs was a door leading on to the balcony, and a door leading into what did, in fact, turn out to be the bedchamber.

"Oh, my precious child, do they expect you to sleep here?" Gaby wondered as she looked round the dark room. Light filtered in through the cracks in the shutters, which were closed against the rain, but when Eleanor opened the shutters on the other side of the room—the balcony side—they saw a very dismal, bare room. There was no decoration of any sort on the plaster walls—not so much as a painted rose. A garderobe in the corner had no curtain to cover it. There was a large bed with woolen hangings that might once have been red but were now a blackish brown with smoke and dirt, a small truckle bed under the far window, and a crude wooden chest pushed against the wall, and that was all.

"It must be changed," Eleanor said grimly. "I can't understand it, Gaby—they surely cannot lack money. Surely Lord Edmund cannot have been deceived about their wealth? And yet, with all their gold, they are content to live like animals with never so much as a spot of color to brighten their lives."

"It is the lack of a mistress to the house," Gaby said. "Men can be strange cattle when left alone."

"I never knew any man who did not want to be as fine as a peacock if only he could afford it," Eleanor said, perplexed.

"Only when there are women around to play the peahen, mistress," Gaby said. "Depend upon it, when there is nothing but men in a house, they do not care a plucked hen what they or their house looks like."

Eleanor shook her head. "It seems strange to me, all the same. However, as soon as I am properly mistress of the house, things will be different."

The rest of that floor consisted of one long room that had been divided by screens into storerooms. Here the two women saw one or two pieces of furniture among the other stores that suggested there had once been a solar and even a guest room up here.

"I should say that this was once the great hall," Gaby said, looking at the high beamed roof that stretched the whole length of the wing. "You often see in old houses, mistress, that they had the great hall on the upper floor. I expect they turned this into chambers when they built the bigger hall down below."

Eleanor nodded, and shivered, and Gaby, noting it, was about to suggest that they go back down and try to coax some life out of the fire when they were found by Robert.

"Ah, there you are," he said nervously. He shifted from foot to foot in his embarrassment as he plucked up courage to speak to his betrothed, for he felt that she had been slighted and would be justly angry; and while he wished to apologize for the oversight, he did not know how to do it without seeming to criticize his father.

Eleanor looked at him contemptuously. What a ninny! she thought. Like an overgrown bull-calf.

"Well, sir?" she prompted him tartly.

"I have come to tell you—to ask you—" He swallowed. "I have come to make you comfortable."

"It will take more than you can do to make me comfortable," Eleanor snapped. "I cannot find any accommodation made ready for me—or do you Yorkshire men expect your women to sleep in the hall with the servants?"

Robert flushed. "I'm sorry," he said. "Instructions were left to prepare the guest chamber for you, but there was trouble with the sheep and everyone had to go out and give a hand. They're still out there now—that's where my father has gone. He sent me to—"

"To make me comfortable," Eleanor sneered.

Robert felt he was being baited. "I will do what I can," he said in mild protest.

"Well, where is this guestchamber? Perhaps my own servants can do what yours have failed to."

"This is it," Robert said, indicating the storeroom they were standing in. Eleanor looked around her. She said nothing, but her face was expressive.

Robert felt compelled to explain. "Since mother died, you see, we haven't used all the rooms. We live mostly in the hall. This was the guestchamber then, and there were others beyond there, too, but now they're all storerooms. I'm sorry that nothing is ready for you—but if I had been here—"

Gaby felt sorry for him in his obvious discomfort and said, "Never mind, sir—if you've a couple of men to shift out these stores, we'll soon have the room in order. Mistress, why don't you go down to the fire, and send me up young Job, and we'll make a start?"

"Have you men free now?" Eleanor asked Robert.

"They will be in from the fields soon. Father has directed two of them to bring up your baggage from the stables."

"That's right, sir. Now you take my mistress down to the fire before she starves of the cold, and I'll see to things. I suppose—" she said in sudden doubt, "I suppose you have got a bed for her?"

"The guest-bed is in store for you and her to use until—"

"Until?" Gaby prompted.

Robert's face was afire, "Until the wedding."

"Ah, yes," Gaby said. "Well, do you go down, mistress, and take that poor perishing puppy with you."

Eleanor smiled her thanks at Gaby and made her exit, followed by Robert, like a Queen followed by a page. But

she was a chilled and hungry Queen in mud-draggled clothing, an unhappy Queen who saw nothing in her immediate surroundings to compensate for the home she had left
behind.

2

The date for the wedding was set for just under a month's
time—the day after All Souls, it was to be, the third of
November—and that gave little enough time indeed to do
everything that Eleanor felt needed doing. The house had
to be cleaned, the bedchamber prepared with new hangings
and covers for the bed and new decorations for the walls;
the new clothes had to be made, and the bridal feast prepared. In the meantime, Eleanor had to find her way
around the house, learn the names of the inmates and some,
at least, of their language, and begin to learn the duties
that would finally be hers when she had married Robert
and become mistress of the house.

From her first day she took over the ordering of the
meals, in which Jacques helped her enormously. With his
help she made up lists of what was needed in the way of
provisions, and these were got from the city's markets.
Morland liked good food, and the improvement in the
meals brought about by the advent of Eleanor and her cook
caused a corresponding improvement in his temper, so that
he was ready to agree to almost anything Eleanor or Robert
suggested for the cleaning or decorating of the house.

Under their direction the foot-deep mulch of filthy
rushes was cleared out of the hall and fresh rushes put
down. Sweetening was generally done quarterly, but
quarter-day was only a month past, and there was more
like six months' worth of garbage there. It seemed clear to
Eleanor that no one felt responsible for ordering such
things in this household and that they were done very
much haphazardly. The trestles and benches were scrubbed
white with holystone, and all bad plaster was scraped off
the walls and replaced.

In the bedchamber, they had the walls painted with a
design of red and yellow roses and green vines. The bed-
curtains and coverlet that Eleanor had brought with her

were of crimson and yellow striped cloth lined with sarcenet, and she had also two green cushions embroidered with yellow and white daisies that she put on top of her little silver oak clothes chest to make a seat. With oiled linen stretched across the windows to let in light while keeping out the wind and rain, and a brazier of charcoals kept alight all the time, the bedchamber was soon the brightest and pleasantest room in the house. Since there was no solar, Eleanor planned to use it as a sitting room as well as a bedroom. It was the only place in the house where there was enough light to work by on those days when the weather was too bad to have the shutters open.

Planning these improvements and carrying them out meant that Eleanor and Robert were much in each other's company, and from time to time she found herself agreeably surprised by something he said or did that revealed his education or gentlemanly upbringing. When it could be arranged, he took her out on horseback to see as much of the estate as possible, and those were the occasions on which he felt the happiest. Riding Dodman, with her puppy, whom she had called Gelert, on the front of the saddle, Eleanor would follow him out into the fields or up onto the moors. The wind would bring color to her cheeks and brighten her eyes, and the fresh air acted like wine on her spirits. Robert, cantering old Sygnus slowly to match Dodman's short-legged pace, would watch her adoringly. He worshiped her, and would have given his life to please her, but pleasing her was not that easy. One moment she might be laughing with him, or even at him, talking eagerly about what could be done to make the house cheerful and bright, and the next she would withdraw to that icy distance and regard him with cold eyes that seemed almost contemptuous.

He did not know what caused those changes of mood, but that did not make him love her less. Queens and goddesses were known to be capricious. As to Eleanor, she could not so soon forget her home and the hopes she had had to give up, and any small thing was likely to remind her. Out in the fields or on the moors she was happiest and most at ease—for grass and heather in Yorkshire smelled much like grass and heather in Dorsetshire, and under the

open sky she could pretend that she was back home and all
was well.

In the evening of the third of November, Eleanor stood
trembling by the side of the handsomely decorated bed as
Gaby undressed her of her bridal finery. The room was lit
with handsome beeswax candles and scented with pot-
pourri, and between the fine sheets of the bridal bed rose-
petals had been scattered, for Gaby was determined that
everything should be as well done for her mistress as if she
had married a lord. Gaby had eaten well and drunk better
during the feast that followed the return from the church
of Holy Trinity within the gate, and her eyes were moist
and her cheeks flushed as she undressed her mistress.

"You looked like a Queen today, my little lady," Gaby
said, drawing the surcoat of russet velvet trimmed with fox
over Eleanor's head. "I always knew you'd grow up to be a
beautiful woman, but you've never looked so lovely as today. And your husband looked as fine as a man may be in
his wedding clothes. Even Jacques was saying that we need
not be ashamed of our new master, for all that we worked
for Lord Edmund."

Eleanor said nothing, letting Gaby chatter on as she took
off her cotte and her underlinen and helped her on with
her nightgown. She scarcely listened, for her mind was far
away and, though she knew that it was wicked, indescrib-
ably wicked on her wedding night, she was thinking what it
would all have been like had it been Richard she had just
married. I would not be afraid if it were he I was waiting
for, she thought. I should be so proud and happy. But tonight, in a few minutes, Robert will come through that
door and we shall be left alone together, and then all hope
will be gone. I shall belong to him for the rest of my life.

Gaby took out the pins from Eleanor's hair and let it
tumble to her shoulders and then took up the hairbrush.
"Such lovely hair you have, child, it always seems a shame
to cover it up. Well, your husband will see it in all its glory,
and he's the only man who ever will. We must hope he
appreciates it as he should. There now, smooth and glossy
as a rook's wing! I think you are ready, my precious. Shall
I call them in?"

Eleanor drew her trembling lip between her teeth and nodded, and Gaby touched her arm comfortingly. "Don't be afraid," she said. "Remember he is also young, and perhaps also nervous. You will help each other."

And Eleanor flung her arms round her impulsively and hugged her. "Oh, Gaby," she said, "what would I have done if you hadn't been here? I couldn't have borne it."

"Of course you could, silly girl! But old Gaby's here, she'll never leave you. Now then, now then—stand tall, my love, and I'll call them in."

Robert had been undressed by his groomsmen and was now led in, also clad in his nightgown, by his father, and followed by the rest of the wedding party. Ceremoniously the couple were put into bed, and, sitting up side by side, they were given the loving cup to drink from, while their father pronounced a blessing and the guests made various loud and laughing remarks, which, fortunately, Eleanor could not understand, since they were in the local dialect. Robert understood them, however, and though he grinned, his cheeks turned from red to white.

Morland, mazy with ale and wine, clapped his son on the back and jerked a thumb toward his new daughter-in-law, who sat, neither smiling nor crying, beside him.

"She looks frozen, lad," Morland said. "You'll need to thaw her a bit. Do your bit like a man." He belched softly and leaned closer. "I've bought thee a gradely ewe, and put thee to her. The rest is up to thee. Tup her right and mak her sweet, and she'll yean thee bonny lambs." He straightened up and waved the empty cup in the air. "A son! A son!" he shouted, and the guests joined in with cheers and laughter. The couple were bedded, and the curtains drawn, and the guests marched out of the chamber to resume their drinking and merry-making below.

In the bedchamber the silence that fell was oppressive. In the close and smothering darkness of the curtained bed, the young people lay side by side, not touching or speaking, but so aware of each other that they almost felt each other's breathing. Robert's mind rang with his father's words: "Tup her right and mak her sweet"; but to him she was already sweet, the finest flower of womanhood. He adored her, loved her so wildly it was like a fever in his blood, yet he felt himself unworthy. How could he even make so bold as to touch her? He who was so low and uncouth, and she who was like an angel. And yet he wanted her, so much that he trembled. The image was in his mind of her white body clothed only in that long black hair. He groaned inwardly with his private struggle.

Eleanor waited passively. There was nothing she could do to escape her fate, but she was not going to do anything that might smack of compromise. Inside she rebelled, she would not accept this clumsy farmer. He might—he must indeed—take her body, but that was all he should have, and that unwillingly, without grace, without kindness. She waited—but why did he not make a move? She knew what was to come, she knew what was to be done—why did he not begin? In the silence that prolonged itself, the tension grew, stretching their nerves taut.

"Well?" said Eleanor at last. Her voice startled them both, coming abruptly out of the darkness.

Robert cleared his throat, but he could not speak. Eleanor grew more impatient, in her misery, to have done with it.

"Well?" she said again. "Are we to be man and wife? Or don't you know how?"

It stung him. Out of his anguish over wanting her and being ashamed to touch her, he was roused by her cruel words to anger. He gritted his teeth and flung himself on top of her, knocking the breath out of her with his hard body. He tore with frantic fingers at her nightgown, sobbing for breath in his sudden passion. There was no yielding in her, no gentleness between them, and he hurt her and hurt himself, beating his body against her like a bird flinging itself against the bars of its cage.

Eleanor's eyes filled with tears of pain but she made no sound, holding her lip between her teeth and biting it as he hurt her, biting it until it bled; and then as the burning pain was at its worst he gave a strange desperate cry, and suddenly it was over. He subsided against her, falling limp as a corpse, though she could feel his heaving chest as he fought for breath. Was that all, she wondered? Surely it should not be like this? It seemed to have caused him as

much pain as it did her, and that was not how she had
been told it would be. In a moment he dragged himself off
her and flung himself to the opposite side of the bed,
where he lay facedown, his arms over his head as if he
were hiding.

Robert's mind was an agony of shame and mortification.
Wanting her and being afraid of her, loving her and being
ashamed to touch her, had unmanned him. His anger had
fired his blood for a few moments only, and taking her in
anger had given him only pain. He hid his face, he wanted
to sink down into the earth and be hidden forever from the
knowledge of his inadequacy; but as the first storm of grief
subsided he became aware that Eleanor, too, was distressed—she was crying.

"Don't cry!" he exclaimed in anguish, turning toward
her in the bed and reaching out trembling, tentative hands
to touch her. Her rigid, shaking body moved at first neither toward nor away from him, but as he stroked her hair
and then her shoulder she began to relax, and at last, em-
boldened, he took her in his arms. "Don't cry," he begged
her again. "I'm sorry, I'm sorry. It will be all right. Oh,
don't cry."

She did not speak, but he felt her grow softer in his embrace, turning toward him until her face was against his
shoulder and he could feel her tears wet on his skin. Murmuring to her, caressing her, he felt strong and capable: he
felt brave: he felt he could comfort her: he felt like a husband. "Ah, don't cry, my lamb, my little lamb," he said,
using endearments that he had not known he knew, that
had never been used to him in his motherless childhood.
"My lamb, my hinny, it's all right."

The hands were strong, were comforting. Eleanor allowed herself to be stroked, caressed into quietness. Robert
could not know she was remembering another's strong
hands, another's firm lips. In the dark it is easy to pretend.
"My lamb, my lamb," Robert murmured, and Eleanor
grew soft as a bird in his arms. In the dark he was strong,
capable and beloved; in the dark she was the wife of her
beloved.

3

By Martinmas they had been married a week and were
beginning to settle down into ordinary life. They no longer
had the bedchamber to themselves, of course: they slept in
the big curtained bed, while Morland slept on a truckle on
one side of the room and Gaby on another on the other
side. During the day the little beds were pushed underneath the big one, and the two clothes chests drawn out to
make seats. Gaby and Eleanor spent a part of every day
here doing the perennial task of spinning; the spun thread
for the household was woven by John the Weaver and his
wife Rabekyn, who lived in one of the many cottages that
huddled around the house; the cloth then came back to
Eleanor and Gaby for making-up. Rabekyn came in sometimes to help with this, too, for there were the winter
clothes for the entire household to be made.

Eleanor learned her duties one by one, spurred on by the
knowledge that her dour father-in-law would hold her responsible for anything that went wrong. He was busy at
that time with the winter kill, and the salting down of
enough meat to last them through till spring. It was Eleanor's job to make sure they did not run out of anything else.
With the help of Gaby and Jacques she made long and
frantic lists of everything they might need: almonds, rais-
ins, sugar, gentian, rhubarb, bays, silk, laces, velvet, candles, treacle, oranges, dates, spices, wine. Some things
could be got from York, others had to be ordered from
London. Each of them in turn remembered yet another
thing to be added to the list and Eleanor was always sure
that they had still forgotten something. She had never before had to do more than obey orders: now she had the
ordering, feeding, and welfare of fifty people on her hands.

In addition to the ordering of provisions, it was officially
her job to arrange the preparation, curing, and storing of
the farm produce, the meal, game, and fish; the dairy,
brewhouse, and kitchen were all under her control, and the
supply of wood for the great fires in kitchen and hall. She
was also supposed to organize the daily routine of the
household, from the tending of the fires and the prepara-

tion of the meals, to the clothing and general behavior of the inmates, and even the arrangements for their weekly bath. In this last matter she found Micklelith House very deficient: Robert had been accustomed to bathe more or less regularly, having been brought up to gentlemanly ways and being fastidious by nature. Morland bathed when he thought about it, which wasn't often; the inside servants bathed when they were told to, which was hardly ever; and the outside servants regarded bathing as a health-hazard, quite likely to be fatal.

It was hard for Eleanor, not speaking the native tongue, firstly to discover what her duties were before she was cursed for not performing them. Most of the administration had been done by Morland himself, and he, having bought his son a wife, wanted to pass all the duties on without delay. Much of the general routine was coped with piecemeal by the servants, and they of course were only too anxious to give up their responsibilities, and frequently did so before Eleanor had been able to find out what they were. When a fire went out or when milk wasn't brought up to the house or the fish wasn't caught for Friday's dinner, Morland cursed Eleanor roundly. She didn't know much Yorkshire, but what she did know was mostly unrepeatable.

Secondly, having learned what a duty was, it was hard for her to get it done, since she did not speak the same language as her servants. In this respect, though, she had help from her three friends from Dorset. Jacques, from having served in a kitchen all his life, knew a great deal about household routine; he was used to the calculation of quantities of food for large numbers of people; and being the cook, the highest servant, and having a sour temper himself, he was able to command the respect of the Yorkshire servants.

Job, being young and having a quick ear, was learning the language rapidly, and he often acted as translator to Eleanor, so much so that she soon took him from the stable duties he had been sent to perform to being her page and general factotum. And Gaby, of course, was her aid, her comfort, her support, and her firm admirer. In Gaby's eyes Eleanor could do little wrong.

But although her task was hard, Eleanor liked it. It was

a challenge, and she found it stimulating to be continually on her mettle. The worst thing about being married was her husband. While she was working, worrying, and organizing she could forget him entirely, put him out of her mind, the more thoroughly because he was almost always out of her sight. During the day he avoided her as much as possible, and Morland was agreeably surprised in his rush of energy about the farm. But in the evenings, between the hour of supper and the hour of bed, they were forced into each other's company, and it was hard for either of them to think of anything but the approaching marital struggle.

Every night, behind the drawn curtains of the bed, Robert would fling himself on her, teeth gritted in determination and anguish; Eleanor would lie rigid, enduring the pain that her own unyieldingness partly caused, and scarcely ever allowing a sound to escape her. It was, at least, a brief pain, for Robert came almost as soon as he touched her; and they would spend the rest of the night sleeping uneasily as far apart as the bed would allow. Robert, though he loved and desired her, would sooner have forgone the episode, for it gave him no pleasure, and he knew that Eleanor hated it and despised him; but it was his duty to cover her until she was pregnant. His father, he knew, would expect her to conceive at the first possible opportunity, and Robert was more afraid of his father than of Eleanor.

It was with relief, therefore, that Eleanor learned she was to have a night apart from her husband. Morland announced it on St. Martin's Eve. They had finished supper and were all gathered in the hall around the fire. Morland was engaged in mending a piece of harness while Robert read aloud one of Chaucer's racy tales. Eleanor and Gaby, sitting to the distaff side of the fire, were sewing shirts. The retainers were drinking and singing—as yet quietly— further down the hall.

As Robert came to the end of a tale, Morland signed him to stop, and said to Eleanor, "Well, mistress Eleanor, we shall be going to the Martinmas fair at Leicester tomorrow, so you may give me a list of anything you need fetching back. Robert and I will be going with a couple of men, and we'll stay in Leicester overnight, so you'll be on your own. You'll have enough men around you to keep you safe, though, so have no fear."

"I am not afraid, sir," Eleanor said with dignity. So she was to have a night of peace, without that terrible silent battle over her body! She tried to hide her pleasure. "There are certainly some things I shall wish you to get. I must have a word with Jacques."

"You don't know what you want?" Morland said sharply.

"It is rather short notice for me to have the details at my fingertips," Eleanor said sarcastically.

Robert was used to his father's secretiveness—he hadn't known until the night before that his father had found him a wife—and he was rather shocked at her answering him back. Morland merely raised an eyebrow and let it pass. He liked her spirit.

"I hope you will use the time profitably," Morland said now, "and not sit idle because your masters are not there to keep an eye on you."

"I will use the time," Eleanor said, "to organize the bathing of the female servants."

"Bathing?" Morland said explosively.

"Yes," Eleanor said, undeterred. "I discovered the bath yesterday in the logshed full of kindling. But it can easily be emptied. We'll have the kitchen fires bright and plenty of hot water, and while the men are in the hall, we'll have all the women in the kitchen and do them all." She spoke with relish. She had not enjoyed having some of the women about her. "I'll post Gaby and Job on the door to keep the men out."

Morland laughed explosively. "You'll need them on the door to keep the women in!"

"Perhaps," Eleanor said. "But the women will be easier to persuade, and the men won't be so surprised when their turn comes on Friday."

"The devil it will!" Morland said, and there was no laughter in his face now. "You've a lot of fancy ideas, mistress, but you seem to forget I'm the master of this house."

"You seem to forget I'm the mistress of it!" Eleanor

flashed back with spirit, and she received a blow on the side of the head for her pains. She cried out, and clutched her head with her hands, and Robert half rose to his feet in protest.

"Father!" he cried in horror.

"What, you too, you young cub?" Morland quelled him with a look. "I'm not averse to beating ye both, so don't forget it. Madam here seems to think she can order my servants about like a dog at the sheep. But you know what we do to sheep worriers."

Eleanor, still holding her ringing head, said through her teeth, "You are constantly telling me that running the house is my job. Well, I won't be surrounded by servants who smell like the cesspits. My own people are accustomed to bathe weekly, and it's my duty to organize bathing for all the servants."

"Eleanor, don't," Robert whispered to her anxiously, but she threw a fierce look at him.

"I will speak my mind," Eleanor said. "If I am to be blamed, then I must be able to act also."

For a moment there was a tense silence as Eleanor and her father-in-law stared at each other across the fire. Then Morland shrugged and went back to his mending.

"Ah, well," he said, "I dare say you're right. You may bath the household if it amuses you, just as I may cuff your head if it amuses me." This last was a threat, as they both knew. "It won't do them any harm. I bath myself when I have a mind," he went on.

"I hope, sir," Eleanor said severely, "that you will—"

"Silence, girl!" Morland roared. "Don't think you can organize me, unless you want to feel the palm of my hand again."

Eleanor wisely subsided, and continued with her sewing with the pleasant knowledge that she had won all she meant to win. Morland regarded her out of the corner of his eye, with the flicker of a smile at the edge of his lips that he took care no one should see; and Robert stared at his wife with open admiration for the way she had stood up to his father, whom he had never been able to cross in anything, however little.

* * *

Eleanor got all the female servants bathed, in spite of their protests, and warned the men that their turn was coming on Friday. The house was cleaner, the food was better, and she was beginning to be turned to by the servants for orders and advice. Yes, she was making her mark on Micklelith House, little by little. Morland and Robert went to the Leicester fair. They hadn't told Eleanor, but it was the great horse-fair of the north, where all the finest horseflesh of three counties was gathered for sale. When they returned to Micklelith the next day, Eleanor ran out of the house to meet them, and she found both her husband and her father-in-law smiling genially at her, while between them they held the most beautiful little white palfrey she had ever seen.

"A white mare for the white hare," Robert called to her exuberantly, remembering Eleanor's device of the white hare.

Morland nodded complacently. "I told thee I'd buy thee a horse," he said, "and not even thy master Lord Edmund could have bought thee a better than this."

Eleanor went forward, speechless with pleasure, and rubbed the creature's soft white muzzle. The mare rubbed her head against her, her dark eyes alive with intelligence. Eleanor looked up at her new masters, the two Morlands, and smiled. She had to accept that she belonged to them, now and forever; and for the first time she realized that she could belong to them for good as well as for ill. She must accept what came to her, and be thankful for the good moments, like this one.

She called the mare Lepida, the white hare.

CHAPTER THREE

After two months in which the land had been gripped by an iron cold, there intervened a spell of warm, damp weather, perfect for hunting.

"The scent will be breast high!" Robert cried exuberantly. "We shall get a fine big red stag today."

"Please God we shall," Eleanor said. "I'm so sick of salt meat. In Lord Edmund's household there was always someone out hunting to get us fresh meat."

Robert looked hurt. "I've brought you in hares enough."

Eleanor shuddered. "You know I can't eat hares. It's like—I don't know—like murder."

Robert smiled at her indulgently, and then went to fling back the shutters of the bedchamber. "Listen to the hounds singing!" he cried. "They know, all right. And there's young Job holding back Gelert. That boy will make a fine huntsman one day."

"A better huntsman than Gelert will make a chaser," Eleanor said teasingly. Robert regarded Gelert's reputation as much his concern as Lady Brach's, and would not have anything said against the young hound.

"He'll settle down when he's been out a few times. It's in his blood—he's bound to be good." He looked down again into the courtyard and stirred eagerly. "Come on, wife, aren't you ready yet?"

"Yes, I'm ready."

He turned from the window, and they regarded each other with admiration. They were dressed in matching hunting clothes: Robert in emerald green hose and a crimson tunic embroidered in white and gold, trimmed with fox; Eleanor in a surcoat of emerald velvet, fur-trimmed, over a cotte of crimson wool. Their cloaks were saffron, their hats emerald and furred; they made a brilliant couple.

As they descended the stairs to the courtyard, Eleanor was conscious of a feeling of contentment she had never hoped to feel. What Robert's lovemaking had lacked in style it had apparently made up in efficacy: Eleanor's first flux after her marriage had been due on St. Katherine's Eve, just three weeks past her wedding day, and Eleanor had made ready the bindings and prepared for this monthly nuisance, and it hadn't come.

Gaby, who knew her mistress's cycle as well as Eleanor herself, had known at once and had said special prayers that it might not turn out to be merely late. When a week had gone by, Eleanor, on Gaby's advice, had told Robert but asked him not to tell his father. Robert had been dumbstruck, excited, and terrified. He agreed to keep silence, and also desisted from then on from making his nightly assaults on Eleanor in bed. Another three weeks had confirmed what the women expected; on Christmas Eve it was formally announced that Eleanor was pregnant, and the household's excitement and pleasure added another dimension to the usual Christmas revels.

And now, in mid-January, Eleanor found herself more contented in her husband's company than she had ever thought she could be. Since he no longer attempted to make love to her, the chief cause of their unhappiness with each other was removed. Eleanor was overjoyed and a little relieved to be so quickly pregnant—Morland, typically, had taken the credit to himself by saying when he first heard the news, "I told thee I could pick a good breeding ewe." Robert was even more glad to have had his manhood so quickly and amply vindicated, but most of all it increased his already absorbing love for his wife. He was tender to her, courtly and adoring. His education had fitted him better to make idealized, courtly love to Eleanor than to make physical love to her, and now that his advances were confined to poetry, gallantries, and loving glances, Eleanor found him all she could wish as a lover.

The hard weather and the long dark evenings had thrown them on each other's company. They had played tables and cards together, and, since Christmas, chess; for Robert had bought her for her season's gift a beautiful chess-set, brought all the way from Italy to London and thence by road to York. They had also found pleasure in talking together, writing poetry together, and in singing. They both loved music, but as yet the house boasted no musical instruments. They meant to remedy that omission as soon as the better weather came. Now that Eleanor was pregnant, Morland would deny her nothing that money could buy.

Out in the courtyard the selected hunting party was waiting for them. Morland had taken advantage of the mild weather to pay some visits on business to other land-owners in the area, so Robert and Eleanor were going out alone with a small party chosen from among the younger men of the farm. Job was the first to greet Eleanor, leading up Lepida to her and holding the frantic Gelert on a leash.

"Let me help you mount, madam," Job said formally. He was now livery-clad as Eleanor's personal page, and he took his new duties and position seriously. He pulled the mounting block into place, and held gentle Lepida as firmly as if she were a knight's mount in a tourney, while helping Eleanor with his other hand. Eleanor rode cross-saddle, scorning the French fashion of sidesaddle which she felt was suitable only for ambling about a private park or paddock. Lepida was beautifully caparisoned in green cloth edged with crimson, and she was wearing the new bridle of crimson leather that was another present from her adoring Robert at Christmastide.

"Lepida looks so pretty in her new bridle," Eleanor called across to her husband, who was mounting the while on Sygnus, who, though almost as old as Robert, behaved at the chase like a two-year-old. Robert glanced across and smiled.

"She shall have some gold swags to hang from the brow-band the very next time I go into the city," he promised. "And then she shall look almost as pretty as you."

Job had arranged the folds of Eleanor's cloak and skirt and put the reins into her hands, and was now mounting his own horse, still holding the leashes of Gelert and the other lymers. The foot servants held the mastiffs, already straining against their collars in excitement, and at the upsurge of feeling the horses began to dance and throw their heads about. Gaby, who had been watching from the doorway, hurried forward.

"Oh, do be careful, mistress," she begged Eleanor. "Take care—don't do anything foolish or bold."

"Peace, Gaby, I shall be all right. It's a wonderful day! I can almost taste that roast venison now!"

Gaby crossed herself at this rash tempting of fate, and said anxiously to Robert, "Take care of her, won't you, master? You know what a wild girl she can be."

"I know, good old Gaby—don't worry. I'll look after her."

"God have you both in his keeping."

"Amen to that. Come, Ben, are you ready?" Robert called. Ben, today's huntsman and son of the man who generally hunted for Edward Morland, was mounted and was calling his harsh orders to his men. "Do well today, Ben, and you shall have as much wine as you can drown in tonight."

And then they were off, riding out of the yard into the early morning in which the sun was doing its best to struggle through the thin gray clouds.

"Just smell the air!" Robert said exuberantly to Eleanor. "You can smell the grass and the trees and the rich damp earth. It's as good as wine after being indoors for so long."

"The horses think so, too." She laughed as Lepida performed some little tittuping steps. She danced along beside big old Sygnus like a child walking with her grandfather, and Sygnus arched his neck and blew softly at the frivolous mare as if she were putting new life in him.

"He's a great hunter, is old Sygnus," Robert said proudly. "He could almost do it by himself. Ah, here's the sun at last—look how it picks out the dew on the hedges like diamonds.'

"You're a romantic!" Eleanor said. "That isn't dew, it's

rain. I never knew such a country as this for cold, rain, wind, and general unfriendly weather. And so bare!"

Robert rose to her teasing as always. "But you've only seen it in the winter," he said anxiously. "Wait until spring, and see how lovely everything is. The flowers—"

"I know, I know. I'm only teasing you," Eleanor interrupted. "All the same," she added with a hint of weariness in her voice, "I shall be mortally glad to see spring, as soon as ever God can send it here. It has seemed so cold, and such a long winter."

Robert looked at her anxiously. She's thinking about her home-country, he thought sadly. She seemed to him such a rare and precious creature that she was like some exotic bird that had been driven by accident to his home by some freak of weather, as sometimes happened to migrators from warmer countries. He could never be quite sure that he would not wake up one morning and find her gone.

They found their deer in a sparse copse of birch about half a mile from home. It was a handsome young outcast buck who regarded his enemies with more defiance than fear, his elegant head crowned with his first year's antlers. Ben "harbored" him with Lady Brach and her half-brother Fand, the pack's two finest lymers, and then moved him quietly and skillfully out of the trees.

He gave them a good chase, bounding clear ahead of them, doubling and sprinting almost like a hare. Ben managed his pack with firm, quick orders, putting on the relays of hounds, the van-chaseours, the middlers, and the parfytours, to keep him moving and tire him out without moving too far away from home. Robert and Eleanor gave keen chase, their servants sometimes having difficulty in keeping up with them. Eleanor kept an eye on Gelert, and was glad to see that after the first few minutes he settled down to hunt keenly like a seasoned dog.

Finally they drove the stag out onto the edge of the moor, and the mastiffs brought him down on the run, without his ever turning at bay. Ben arrived on the scene closely followed by the rest of them, and finished off the stag, whipped off the hounds and leashed them again, and then came up panting for his master's approval.

"Well done, Ben, well done indeed. Th'art almost as

fine a huntsman as thy father," Robert cried to him. Ben smirked in pleasure, showing himself not so dour and adult as he was pretending to be, and Eleanor laughed, and, beckoning Job to her, she caught the hide bottle from her page's belt and flung it to Ben.

"There, so that you need not wait until tonight to start drowning yourself!" she cried, and everyone laughed. Ben drank gratefully and passed back the bottle. Then with capable strokes of his sharp knife he pouched the deer and gave the offal to the hounds and then loaded the carcass onto the back of Dodman, who, being placid in the extreme, was a good choice for this sort of burden. He laid his ears back, but otherwise made no protest. Meanwhile, Eleanor and Robert were refreshing themselves on pasties and watered wine provided by Job and discussing where they should try next. The young servants sat on the ground to rest themselves, and they too chattered and laughed, in good spirits with the success of their hunt, for most of them were young and many had not been hunting before.

As they were getting ready to move off again, one of the young servants, whose job it was to lead Dodman with his gory load, turned the patient pony and led him past Eleanor, who was mounted on Lepida. He was inexperienced, and had taken Dodman's complacency for granted. Lepida, of more excitable nature, did not care for the reck of blood coming from the stag's carcass, and reared up. It was unfortunate that at the precise moment of the incident Job had just let go Lepida's head and turned to mount his own horse, and Eleanor was turning in her saddle to adjust a fold of her cloak. Lepida reared and jumped sideways, and Eleanor was flung off sideways and hit the hard ground with a thud that knocked the breath from her.

With a terrible cry Robert flung himself from his horse and in a second was kneeling beside her. She could not speak for a moment, and Robert feared the worst.

"Oh, merciful God, she's dead! Eleanor, Eleanor, how could this happen to you?" He lifted his head and glared round at the servants, his eye coming to rest on the scared boy still holding Dodman's head. "I'll have your head for this, you murdering lout! And all of you—I'll flog the skin off your backs! You, Job, for letting it happen. It was your business to hold her horse! I'll see you flogged raw for this!" His genuine rage held them all silent for a second until Ben, with a little more courage than most, spoke up in a voice tinged with relief.

"She's not dead, master—see, she moves."

"You're right! Oh, Eleanor, thank God you're not dead! Are you all right, my darling? Speak to me, please."

"I'm all right," Eleanor said, trying to sit up. He pushed her back down.

"No, don't move. Keep still for a moment. Are you hurt anywhere? Your limbs may be broken—this earth is as hard as iron."

"I'm all right, Robert," Eleanor said again, with less patience. "I was knocked breathless, that's all—"

"Oh, my God, and you're pregnant," Robert whispered, having just remembered the fact. His heart sank almost to the bottom of his stomach. She would lose the baby at the very least, if she did not lose her life. Anger rose up in him again. "If anything happens to you, I'll have their lives, every one, for letting it happen. You, Ben, take my horse and ride on ahead to prepare them. Have a bed made ready and send for the surgeon—"

"No! Stop, Ben. Stop it, Robert. I'm all right. I'm not hurt, and if you'll help me up, I'll remount and we'll continue. Do let me be—I tell you I'm all right. And don't frighten the poor servants any more—it wasn't their fault. If I'd been paying attention as I should, Lepida wouldn't have thrown me. It was the merest jump."

Bit by bit she persuaded her anxious husband that she was not likely to die if she were allowed upright. She did not know about the baby. She certainly felt all right, but she didn't know anything much about babies and could not tell if the fall were enough to hurt it. It wasn't much of a fall—Lepida was quite small, and she had landed on her side, taking the blow mostly with her arm and shoulder. It took her another ten minutes of hard talking before Robert would allow her to remount, and even then he was reluctant to carry on hunting. At last, however, she persuaded him that the only damage she had suffered was a large patch of mud on her clothes, and they hunted on, taking a small hart for their afternoon's sport.

Spirits rose again gradually, and by the time they were riding home, it was as if the accident had never been. It was beginning to grow dark as they approached the house, loaded with their spoils and thinking and talking happily of roast venison and other good things for supper, of hot baths and mulled wine and a happy evening round the fire in the great hall. The first person to meet them was Gaby, who came running out into the courtyard as soon as she heard their hooves. She had been worried all day, mostly out of sheer habit, but the first thing she saw was the mud on Eleanor's shoulder and arm, and she imagined the rest.

"You've had an accident!" she cried out, and at the same moment she staggered back as if she had received a blow, clutching her hands to her chest and collapsing onto the stone step.

The foot servants ran to her, and as soon as Job had helped her down, Eleanor was at her faithful nurse's side.

"Gaby, I'm all right, it was only a little fall. I'm not hurt," she cried. Gaby was gasping for breath.

"A pain, mistress," she whispered with difficulty. "Like an arrow in my heart."

"Don't try to speak," Eleanor said. "Take her inside and set her by the fire. Bring wine! Be still, Gaby, it's going to be all right."

Two servants carried the old woman inside to the fire and propped her on a stool, supporting her with their arms while Eleanor took the cup of wine from the boy who had brought it and held it to Gaby's lips. She drank, spluttered, and drank again, and then tried to speak.

"No, no," Eleanor said soothingly, "just rest for a moment. It's all right." She knelt in the rushes, chafing Gaby's hands and offering her wine to sip, murmuring endearments, as if their roles had been reversed. By the time Robert came in, having stayed behind to give orders for the care of the animals and the cutting and storing of the carcasses, Gaby's face had returned to its normal color, and her breathing had eased.

"I'm all right now, mistress," Gaby said as Robert appeared by Eleanor's side. "I'm sorry, master, to be such a trouble."

"Don't worry about that," Eleanor said soothingly. "How do you feel now?"

"I'm all right. This pain. I've had it before, but never this bad. Like an arrow in my chest, it stops me breathing. Then it goes. I'm an old woman, child, you have to expect some aches and pains. But how are you?"

"Oh, I'm all right," Eleanor said impatiently.

"It was the shock of seeing you . . . you've no pains anywhere?" Gaby asked, nodding significantly. Eleanor shook her head.

"No, no pains anywhere. A Courteney's as hard to kill as a Morland. Now you must go up to bed and rest."

"Yes, mistress."

"I'll help you upstairs."

"No, I'm all right, I can manage. I'm sorry to be a nuisance—"

"Go on, now, and rest."

Eleanor watched her from the room, and her face was dark with worry. Robert put his arm round her shoulders.

"She seems all right now," he said. "As she said, it was just the shock of seeing you'd had a fall."

"Hmm," Eleanor said, and then, "I don't like the way she agreed to go up and rest. Normally she'd want to fuss around me. I think she's worse than she says she is."

"Well, what can you do?" Robert asked.

"Nothing." Eleanor sighed. "Nothing, of course. That's the trouble."

"Try not to worry," Robert said. Eleanor shook off his hand impatiently and headed for the stairs.

"As if I could do anything else," she said.

2

It was a hot August day, and the heat fell around them almost like a shower of gold. Eleanor was sitting out of doors in the pleasance, which she had designed with Job's help on the sheltered side of the house. When she had arrived at Micklelith House last October it had been no more than a bare patch of ground: now, thanks mainly to Job's help, it was beginning to take shape, and was already the most pleasant place to be on a day like this.

"Just imagine how lovely this will look in a few years time," Eleanor said to Job, who was sitting on the ground at her feet trying to pick out a tune on her guitar. She was teaching him to play, feeling it would be useful to have a musical page. "When the rose has grown into a proper hedge and the arbor's finished. It amazes me how much you know about how many things, Job."

Job looked up and smiled. "Here's one thing I know nothing about, mistress," he said, gesturing with the guitar. "I can't get a tune out of this."

"But you made this bench for me, and planted all those flowers, and—oh, lots of other things. How do you know so much when you were brought up as a groom?"

"The same way as I learned to speak the outlandish language hereabouts," he replied. "I just picked it up."

"He's a quick learner, all right," Gaby said. She was seated next to Eleanor on the bench, and Eleanor cast a quick anxious glance at her. Since January Gaby seemed to have got fatter and fatter. She also had difficulty breathing, and had to move very slowly when she moved at all. Even sitting still she would sometimes get attacks of breathlessness, and her face would turn that terrible gray color and she would get stabbing pains in her heart. Eleanor worried about her constantly, but Gaby would tell her only that she was getting old, and that you had to expect some aches and pains.

But she liked it here in the pleasance. It reminded her of home, for the flowers were the same, perhaps chosen by Job for that very reason. Because of the heat the two women had left aside their headdresses and wore only light linen veils, held in place by headbands. It was a piece of pleasant informality not often to be indulged in.

"Job's quick to learn all right," Gaby was saying. "But you be warned, my lad—quick to learn good is quick to learn evil. Be on your guard against the evil one."

"Oh, don't worry, Gaby—Job's never idle," Eleanor said. "Even when I don't give him anything to do, he's out collecting gossip—aren't you, child? Tell us what you've heard today. Being the size I am, I can't get about to hear it all firsthand. What was that terrible quarrel in the kitchen this morning?"

Job laid the guitar aside and folded his arms about his updrawn legs. Next to horses, he liked gossip best. "That was Jacques, mistress, in one of his tempers. He was trying out a new sauce for your dinner tomorrow, and young Toby poked the fire and a piece of ash floated up and fell in the sauce. Jacques almost went for him with his bare hands." Job chuckled. "He was already in a bad mood, and that put him in a worse."

"Why was he in a bad mood?" Eleanor asked.

"Because of the news from France. Master was talking to a merchant this morning who'd come from France only last week."

"News about the peace conference?" Eleanor asked with interest.

"What our Lord Edmund's at the head of?" Gaby added. Her heart was still with her old master. Job nodded.

"That's right. It was not good news for Jacques. It seems as though they aren't never going to be able to make peace—not until the King comes of age, anyway."

"I don't understand why," Gaby grumbled. "These foreign wars keep menfolk away from their homes. Look at poor Lady Eleanor, with her husband in France when she's about to have another child."

"I've explained it all before," Eleanor said patiently. "They can't make peace unless they give up the claim to the throne of France, and no one can give up that claim except the king himself."

"And why should he give up France?" Gaby demanded stoutly. "King Harry was king of France, and so should his son be!"

"Spoken like an Englishwoman!" came a loud laugh from over what would one day be the rose hedge. It was Morland, riding back in from the outlying fields. Job, who had been lolling against Eleanor's legs, jumped to his feet at the sound of the voice. "We can have peace, or the throne of France, but not both, old woman. Here, boy, take my horse round to the stable and rub him down well," he said, dismounting and holding out the reins to Job. Job cast a swift glance at Eleanor before obeying, and it caused a slight frown to appear between Morland's brows. "What the devil are you looking at her for?" he shouted. "Do as you're bid!"

"Yes, Master Morland," Job said, having received Eleanor's almost imperceptible nod. His feelings about Morland were shown by the way he called him Master Morland, while he called Robert simply master. When he had led the horse out of sight Morland turned on Eleanor. "What the devil do you mean by teaching the brat to defy me?"

"Job is not a stable boy," Eleanor blazed back. "He is my page, and I will not have him used for any other tasks. There are plenty of other servants."

"Your page, is he, madam?" Morland said nastily. "Then teach him to behave as one, and not to hang about you like a lover! You let him touch you more than your own husband."

"Don't be disgusting—" Eleanor began, when old Gaby broke in.

"Now, master, my mistress shouldn't be upset so near her time. You don't want the child's temper spoilt, do you?"

Morland bit back his next remark, and breathed hard to control his temper. In a quieter voice he said, "You're right, old woman. Very well, madam, I'll say no more this time. How *is* my grandson today?"

"Quiet, sir," Eleanor said with an effort at civility. "I think it must be the heat."

"Well, well. Take care of him, mistress. Nothing must happen to that child. He will be heir to everything I have, a great estate. His will be a name that is known everywhere in the county. Take care of him, madam, I say."

Eleanor smiled to herself. She was uncomfortable, so big with child it was hard to move around and impossible to bend, and she felt the heat badly in her condition, but she was contented because this child gave her power. When she had become the mother of Morland's heir, her position would be unshakable, and then she would really begin to remold the household.

"I'll take care of him, sir," she said.

When Morland had gone the two women were silent for a while, thinking of the events to come. Then Eleanor said in a rather small voice, "I'm so glad you're with me, Gaby. I don't think I could have faced up to it without you here."

Gaby knew that by "it" she meant childbirth, and that in thinking of childbirth Eleanor was thinking of poor Belle's struggles.

"Not everyone has as hard a time of it as Lady Eleanor, my lamb. Mostly it's easier than that. But you'd have faced up to it like the brave girl you are, whether or not I'd been here. After all, you are surrounded by friends."

"Not friends," Eleanor said in a small voice. "Rabekyn and Alice and Annie are good women, but they aren't friends. There's only you."

Gaby looked troubled. "You have a loving husband, child—"

"Oh, him," Eleanor said contemptuously.

"Don't speak like that, Eleanor, you know it grieves me. You have a good husband and loyal servants and you'll soon have a string of fine sons. You won't need old Gaby."

"Why, Gaby," Eleanor said, laughing, "you talk as if you're thinking of going away."

There was a pause, and then Gaby said slowly, "Perhaps I was, mistress."

"Going away? But where?" Eleanor said in surprise. Gaby avoided her eyes, staring instead at the small bright patches of flowers Job had planted.

"This will be a lovely garden when it's finished—in a few years time, when everything is at its best. But it isn't home to me, mistress. I can't change so quickly as a young person. I was thinking that perhaps, after you've had your child and you're on your feet again, perhaps you'd send old Gaby home."

Eleanor stared at her aghast, and then with an effort she swallowed and said, "If that's what you want, Gaby—if you want to go back to Dorset, instead of staying with me—all right, I'll try to arrange it. I had thought you'd—"

"Thank you, mistress," Gaby said serenely. "You're a kind girl. And I know you can do very well without me. I'd have liked to see this garden at its best, but—"

And the two women were silent again, their thoughts very far away.

That night Eleanor woke from a nightmare to the awareness of pain. At once she cried out for Gaby, and Gaby, sleeping lightly with an ear open for that very call, was up at once.

The two men were roused and, much against their will, driven out of the room. Morland had forgotten what it was like, for it was twenty years since it had last happened in this bedchamber, and he grumbled loud and long about being sent to finish the night in the hall among the servants. Robert went quietly, looking rather green, and casting many backward looks at his wife. He felt horribly guilty that he had condemned her to this.

"Rouse up the women when you get down there," Gaby told Robert. "There is much to be done, and I am too old and too fat to do it. Now, mistress, get up out of that bed and help me."

The procedures had all been worked out in advance, and so it was with the minimum of confusion that the birth chamber was prepared. It was a hot night, and they had been sleeping with the shutters open, but these were now closed, and two braziers of hot charcoal brought up to heat the room still further, for even cool air was supposed to be fatal to newborn babies. Job was sent on horseback to summon the midwife from the city, the one that all the ladies of fashion were using at that time, and when he returned he was posted at the foot of the stairs leading up to the bedchamber to make sure no man set foot on them, for this was an exclusively female rite.

Eleanor had chosen the women who were to attend her—they were Gaby, of course, and Rabekyn, whose cheerful good humor she liked; old Alice for her seniority and experience; a younger woman, Annie; and a granddaughter of Alice's, called Anys. Anys was quick and neat in her ways, and could read and write, and Eleanor had chosen her to be nursemaid to the new baby.

By dawn the preparations were all made, and the pains were coming faster. So far, Eleanor thought, it isn't so bad—not much worse than the pains she sometimes had at the time of her monthly flux, and certainly bearable. She had been ordered by Gaby to keep walking up and down, and every time she got tired and attempted to rest Gaby would drive her on again with a verbal lashing.

"The more you walk, the easier the birth will be," she
told her. "So don't stop, my child, not for a moment."

Little Anys, her eyes round with excitement and apprehension, walked with Eleanor, her hand hovering near
Eleanor's elbow and a cloth ready to wipe the sweat from
her brow when it appeared. It was stiflingly hot in the
chamber with the door and shutters all closed and the two
braziers burning, and at times Eleanor would have given
anything for a breath of fresh, cool air; but the heat itself
gave her a feeling of security, for she knew it was right and
good, and so she bore the sweat trickling down inside her
clothes with equanimity.

Soon after dawn the midwife arrived with her assistant
and was let in, the door being locked again after her. The
midwife approved the arrangements made and inspected
and praised the birth stool and delivery stool.

"Good and roomy," she said. "I like to have enough
room to move. Now, mistress, do you lie down on the bed
and let me see how far you've got. Ah, very good, you're
coming along nicely. Your first, of course—yes, I saw the
menfolk downstairs pacing about as if it was them in labor!
When I see that I never need to ask if it's a first time.
That's the sure sign. Now, mistress, on your feet again and
walk. That's right, nurse, you did quite right to tell her so."

Eleanor walked again, amused at the expression of indignation on Gaby's face at being told by this stranger that she
had given Eleanor the right advice. Now the pains were
beginning to really grip her, and her awareness was being
narrowed down to the small world within her flanks. It was
impossible while the pains were on to think about anything
else, and difficult between the pains to think of anything
but their resumption. She began to cry out when the gnaw-
ing pains grasped her vitals, and the midwife was cheerfully encouraging.

"You're a good healthy girl, mistress, you'll make nothing of this," she prophesied. Outside the unknown day beyond the shutters broadened and grew hotter, but for
Eleanor time had ceased to move. She was locked inside an
endless world of pain, in which pain was all there had ever
been and all there ever would be. She was dimly aware of
other people moving about the stifling room, but she did

not know who they were, or what they were doing there. The pains were now continuous, and Eleanor remained still at the center of a white-hot circle of agony, suspended out of time and space forever.

At intervals she had been driven to her feet to walk up and down, supported by the two young women, and at last the midwife called to them to bring her over to the birth stool, for it was time. Eleanor's hands were placed on the arms of the chair where they at once gripped white. Anys was ordered to stand behind her and hold her shoulders back to brace them. The midwife took her position on the low stool in front of her and all was ready.

Now Eleanor heard orders being shouted at her. The pain was extreme, but it was no longer important—what was important was to rid herself of this burden. She struggled frantically, hearing the cries of "Push! Push!" in her ears, groaning and sweating with the effort. Now she knew why it was called "labor." She was frantic now to be rid of it. She braced herself and pushed until she felt her heart would burst, and there was a searing, burning shaft of pain and a sensation as of a flask being uncorked. Cries and murmurs came from the women, and the midwife's voice cut through the red mists clouding Eleanor's brain.

"Very good, child. That's the head. Rest a moment, and then we'll do the rest."

"No more," Eleanor said weakly. "No more."

"Not much longer now," the midwife promised her. "The pain's all over now. The rest won't hurt, no more pain. Now then, are you ready?"

One last heart-rending effort, and the sensation of something slithering away from her, and then a baby's cry cut through the air sharply. The women's voices rose in a combined murmur of pleasure, but Eleanor heard it only through a daze. She thought, good, the child's alive, but she had no more interest than that. She only wanted to sleep. Anys was wiping her brow, and she felt herself drifting away.

A little later she drifted back to hear the women murmuring amongst themselves and someone—she thought it was Alice—saying "Not now. Let her sleep first. Tell her later." Tell her what? she wondered, but she didn't care

enough to find out. She was helped into bed, and bound
and bandaged, and gradually the baby's cries and the
voices of the women faded, and she slept the sleep of exhaustion.

And thus it was that at half past two in the afternoon of
the 17th of August, 1435, Eleanor's first child was born. It
was not until she woke from that first sleep at about five
o'clock that they told her the bad news. The baby was large
and healthy, but it was a girl.

3

Morland had been furious, and had told Eleanor exactly
what he thought of her, leaving her in no doubt that she
had most miserably failed in her duty by bringing into the
world a useless girl instead of the desired, the promised
son. He reminded her that she had brought no dowry with
her, that her only way of repaying them for taking her at
all was to produce sons. Weak and exhausted from the ordeal, Eleanor had been unable to defend herself as she
might otherwise have done, and she cast a bitter look at her
husband who stood by, miserable and ashamed, but unable
to pluck up the courage to defend her to his father. He had
already been sworn at for pointing out that the baby was
unusually healthy, large, and comely. Robert was only too
glad that Eleanor had survived the ordeal; the fact that the
baby was alive and well was so much of an added bonus,
he scarcely cared about its sex.

In the end it was Gaby who drove the two menfolk out
of the room, saying that her mistress needed to rest and
that shouting at her would curdle her milk. Anys took the
baby away, already devoted to her new charge, and Gaby
was left alone, sitting beside Eleanor's bed and holding her
hand. Tears began to run down Eleanor's cheeks.

"My poor precious lamb, don't cry," Gaby soothed.
"Don't let him make you cry. The baby's the bonniest,
healthiest little girl I've ever seen, and you'll have plenty
more as handsome. The next will be a boy, you'll see."

"It's not that, Gaby," Eleanor cried. "It's because—he
just stood there and let him abuse me. My husband's a

mouse. *He* would have defended me." And by *he* Gaby knew Eleanor meant Richard of York.

"Do you still think of him?" she said, distressed. "Oh, my little lady!"

The tears dried on Eleanor's face, and she said in a weak, sad voice:

"I wish you weren't going, Gaby, now when I need you most."

"I'm glad I was here to see you through your first childbirth, but now that's over, you'll never need me so much again. I have to go, child. You'll be stronger without me. You're a woman now."

"Do you really *have* to go?" Eleanor asked in a low voice.

"Yes," Gaby said, and there seemed no more to say.

Three days later the child was taken to be baptized at Holy Trinity church. Eleanor went, too, carried on a litter and dressed in her very finest dress, but Gaby said the journey would be too much for her, and she stayed behind. The child was christened Anne after Robert's mother, and Morland forgot his anger enough to boast to the neighbors who had been invited to the christening about the child's health and beauty.

Afterward they returned to Micklelith House for the christening feast, but as they approached the house a servant ran out to meet them, and spoke quietly to Robert, who turned to Eleanor and took her hand.

"It's bad news," he stammered, looking ashen with worry. Eleanor gripped his hand fiercely.

"What is it? Tell me quickly!" A horrible certainty came over her. "It's Gaby, isn't it?"

Robert nodded, unable to speak.

"What happened? Where is she?" Eleanor cried, trying to struggle upright.

"Lie still, darling, you'll hurt yourself," Robert said anxiously. "I'm afraid—she had another of those attacks—the pains—"

"She's dead?" Eleanor whispered. Robert nodded. For a moment she stared at him in disbelief, and then the tears began to roll from her eyes. In her weakened state she could not restrain them. Robert tried to comfort her, but she pushed him away. "Take me to my room," she ordered. She felt that her heart was breaking.

Later she sent for Job. "Tell me about it," she said. She was sitting on her silver oak chest by the window, and beside her was the other chest where Gaby had always sat while they worked together. Job sat on the floor at her feet, for he could not take that seat.

"There's little to tell, mistress," he said. "She went out into the pleasance to sit in the sun. I helped her out there, because she was very breathless, and saw her comfortable on the bench with a bit of sewing. She said how nice it was out there—"

"What did she say exactly?" Eleanor interrupted. "I want to know."

"She said 'This is almost like home,'" Job reported. "And I said 'All you need is the sound of the sea,' and she said 'I can hear that inside my head.' And then I went away. And when I went out a while later to see if she needed anything, she was just sitting there with her hands in her lap and her head dropped forward as if she was asleep. She must have died very quietly. So I told William and he sent for the priest, and Jacques and I carried her in. It was right that we should do it, being her friends."

Eleanor nodded. She was crying again, but quietly, without violence. There was nothing to mourn deeply in that quiet end; the loss was all Eleanor's, the loss of the friend who had been as good as a mother to her. "She talked of going home, Job," Eleanor said after a while. "Do you think she knew, do you think this is what she meant?"

Job nodded. "I think so. I think she wanted you to get used to the idea of being without her. She's been ill for a long time, you know." Eleanor nodded again.

"She'll be in heaven now, with our blessed Lord. She was a good woman all her life, and He'll want her by Him."

Eleanor remembered the day they first came to Micklelith, and the sound of the churchbells pouring over the walls in a wave of sound. "I'll have an obit rung for her. She'd like that. It seems hard that she should be buried here, so far from home."

"She'll be with friends." Job comforted her. "She'd like

to be where you are, and where your family will be growing up. It will seem like home to her."

"Perhaps," Eleanor said, and she thought of the last
words Gaby had said to Job. "So now I'm all alone," she
went on. "Now I've really got to manage by myself. That's
what she said to me—I'm a woman now."

"You won't be alone, madam," Job said. "You have your
husband and your new child, and all your new family and
servants."

"And you," Eleanor said, smiling wanly at him.

"And me," Job agreed, with an indefinable expression
on his face.

"You're a great comfort to me, Job," Eleanor said.
"Fetch my guitar, and we'll go on with your lesson. It
would be nice to have you to play for me."

Over the next few days Robert did his best to help
Eleanor, knowing how much she missed Gaby, and trying
to enter into her feelings. But Eleanor treated him as dis-
tantly as ever, and turned always to Job, who was never far
from her side, for comfort and conversation. It seemed that
what Robert could not give her, her little page could.

CHAPTER FOUR

It was another hot summer.

"I'm so tired of being this size every time the hot weather comes," Eleanor grumbled, looking down with distaste at her swollen belly. "I'm too hot even to sew." She was sitting in the shade of the woven branches of the arbor. In three years the pleasance had matured into a proper garden. The rose hedge was so thick with flowers that they looked like pink snow, and the air was sweet with their scent and that of the honeysuckle and the stock. It was a pleasant place to be.

"Pity the men, madam," said Anys, who was sitting beside her on the bench, holding little Isabella on her lap. Isabella was just over a year old, and already up to as much mischief as she could pack into her waking hours. For the moment she was quiet, sucking the red bead that hung round her neck on a thong to keep off the evil eye, but soon she would start wriggling and want to be put down. She could crawl at a wonderful speed, and liked to make use of her new accomplishment.

How different was Eleanor's second baby, another Eleanor, but called Helen to distinguish her, and because of her great beauty. Helen was two, and so quiet and good that Anys worried about her and sometimes murmured that she was too good for this world. Helen was sitting on the ground at her mother's feet where she had been put, and she would stay until she was taken away. She had no curiosity about life, but she was a contented baby, and sometimes made little crooning songs to herself.

"Why pity the men?" asked the other member of the domestic party, a young girl called Ankaret who was eleven years old and had been taken in by Eleanor to learn the ways of a gentlewoman by acting as maid to her. Ankaret's parents were a rich wool-merchant of York and his wife, friends of Morland's.

"Shearing in this heat," Anys answered her shortly. "There can't be a much hotter job, or a smellier job, or a more tiring job."

"I'd sooner their job than mine," Eleanor said. "When they get too hot they can plunge into the river to cool down. And when they get too tired they can leave off and rest. But I can't. I'm stuck with this great bulge. I seem to spend all my life lying-in. And for what!"

"Oh, madam," Ankaret said in gentle protest, "you have such lovely children."

"Three girls," Eleanor said disparagingly. "One after another. My father-in-law thinks I do it on purpose to spite him. As if anyone would go through this if they didn't have to!"

"You should thank God, madam, that you have three live healthy children," Anys said piously.

"If you talk to me like that I shall box your ears," Eleanor said crossly. "I wish Job would come back—I want some music. He's been gone too long—he was only supposed to go as far as the bottom field and then straight back."

"Why don't you play for us, madam?" Anys suggested, hoping to keep Eleanor occupied. "Let Ankaret fetch your guitar—"

"Stop humoring me, girl!" snapped Eleanor. "Take Isabella for a walk round the garden—she's beginning to get bored." The baby was indeed wriggling on Anys's lap.

"I never knew such a fidget," Anys began, and then broke off. "Ah, here's Job now. At least, here's Gelert, so Job won't be far behind."

Gelert trotted into the garden and up to Eleanor and, having greeted her and washed the face of baby Helen with his tongue, he flopped down in the small patch of shade by his mistress's feet. Sure enough he was followed almost at once by Job, from whom the dog was never parted for long. Robert's first gift to Eleanor had decided for himself to whom he belonged.

"Ah, there you are," Eleanor cried gladly. "You've been far too long. That child shouldn't be kept out in the sun so long—it's bad for her." Job came into the garden with little Anne, Eleanor's firstborn, riding on his shoulder. Anne was three now, a forward and well-grown girl for her age, and a great favorite with her father. She had ash-blond hair and blue eyes and a rosy, pretty face, and even Morland had a soft spot for her, though he tried his best to conceal it lest anyone should think he had forgiven her for not being a boy. But Morland had been a sick man for some time, and often the only thing that would soothe his invalid's ill temper was for little Anne to play to him on the dulcimer and sing him a song in the Yorkshire tongue, which she had learned from the servants.

"I'm sorry if you were worried, mistress," Job said, swinging Anne down and setting her on her feet. "We went as far as the shearing pen, and watched for a while."

"You should have come straight back," Eleanor said. "Come here, my pet. Pooh! You smell of sheep! Anys, you must wash this child—I can't abide that smell in the house."

Anys and Job exchanged a glance of understanding over Eleanor's head. Her temper was often frayed in the last weeks of her pregnancies.

"Master was in the shearing pen, mistress. He wanted Mistress Anne to watch a while. He said she's a sheepman's daughter and ought to know what goes on."

"She may be a sheepman's daughter, but she's also a gentlewoman, and a gentlewoman does not get herself covered in sheep yolk."

Anne looked up at her mother's beautiful, cross face, and her own face fell. "I'm sorry, madam," she said. Eleanor glanced at the crestfallen face and relented.

"Never mind, child. Anys shall wash you when we go in. Sit on the grass now and cool off, and Job shall sing us a song. Won't you, Job?"

"Whatever my lady wants," he said with a charming

bow that was designed to cover all three women. Job was
seventeen now, and had grown into a tall, well-built and
handsome man. Working still with horses and dogs as he
did had built up his muscle, while dancing, which was one
of his duties as a page, had made him graceful and light on
his feet. His voice had broken and had settled at a pleasant
light baritone; he wore his shining coppery hair in love-
locks, and his green livery was specially chosen by Eleanor
to complement his looks. She felt he was a page she could
be proud of in any company; Anys and Ankaret and all the
young women of the household thought he was simply too
handsome and romantic to be true.

He fetched Eleanor's guitar now from the house, and on
his return settled down on the grass with his back to a tree
trunk, facing the women, and began to pick out a soothing
and pleasantly melancholy love song to sing to them—a
song that perfectly suited his voice. As soon as he began to
sing, baby Isabella wriggled down from Anys's lap and
crawled across to him and sat in front of him and began
sucking her thumb and staring up at him. Anne, too, gradually slipped from her place, leaning against her mother's
shoulder, to the grass in front of her, and thence closer and
closer to the young man singing. Anne adored Job. He was
her knight and champion, and she was as happy riding his
shoulder as riding in her father's arms or on her own pony.

No one saw Robert arrive and stand at the garden door
looking on at this scene of domestic content. Even Gelert
was too heavily asleep in the heat to hear him. It was a
pretty scene, the bright and shady garden, the handsome
young man singing, the three prettily dressed women, and
the rosy, healthy children; but something about it displeased Robert, for a frown drew down his brows, and he
almost scowled at them. The song came to an end, and
before anyone else could speak or move, Robert broke into
ironic applause.

"Very pretty," he said, striding forward into the garden.
Eleanor looked up at him and wrinkled her nose.

"Sheep," she said in disgust. "Couldn't you have washed
first?"

"At this time of year," Robert said savagely, "every man
on a sheep farm ought to smell like that."

Job knew this was aimed at him, but it was not his place to notice it, nor would it have been wise to make any comment. Eleanor answered for him. "What a terrible idea! I know shearing time is hard work, but I really don't see why you have to get covered in sheep yolk. Surely you have enough men to do the messy work for you? I should have thought you would only need to supervise."

"My father never shirked the work, and now that he's too ill to be out there—" Robert began.

"Quite," said Eleanor, "but all the same, you aren't your father. He liked getting dirty, and he would have done it even if he didn't have to. But I still don't see why you should need to get into that state."

"We're shorthanded," Robert said. "If *every* able-bodied man on the farm did his fair share—"

"Not quite *every* one, husband," Eleanor said firmly. "There are some whose own work necessitates their keeping clean. Like Jacques, for instance. You surely wouldn't want your cook out there wrestling with sheep?"

"There are others," Robert retorted, "whose job seems to be playing with children and singing songs in the garden."

"That's precisely my point," Eleanor said. "If you would only organize your men properly and stick to supervising instead of running round in the heat after sheep, you would have time to play with your children and sing songs to me in the garden."

Robert resigned at that point. It was never any good his arguing with his wife. She had cut her teeth on his father, and found Robert easy going. But it didn't make him like Job any more.

Having won her point, Eleanor was prepared to be pleasant.

"Well, now you *are* here," she said, "for goodness sake sit down and get cool. No, not *too* close; sit on the grass there, in the shade. Job, run into the house and bring the master a jug of ale—the coolest. Ask Jacques—he always keeps some in a cool place for me."

"Yes, madam," Job said, and went. Robert was a little mollified to see his hated rival so meekly fetching and carrying for him, and he sat down on the grass with better grace, prepared to be pleasant.

"Well," said Eleanor, "and how is the shearing going?"

"Considering we're short of men, very well, I'd say," Robert replied. "We should have the whole flock done by St. John's Eve, and that will give us a chance to get it packed before the brogger comes on quarter-day."

"What outlandish names you sheep farmers have for things," Eleanor said. "The brogger's the woolman, isn't he?"

"Of course," Robert said simply. He was so used to these words that he took them for granted and could not see that they were strange. "He buys up all the clip from every sheepman in the district, and takes it to Hull or to London and sells it to the staplers, who export it to the foreign weavers."

Eleanor nodded—she had heard this before—but she was thinking.

"The brogger has to make a living for himself," she said thoughtfully. "And he has to cover the cost to himself of keeping all those ponies and mules, and the wages of the drivers he hires."

"Of course," Robert said indifferently.

"So to do that, he must pay you less for the wool than he will get from the staplers. Otherwise there'd be no living in it for him."

"Of course. You have a good thinking head on your shoulders, mistress," Robert said, pleased that she was showing an interest in the farm.

"Well, then," Eleanor went on, "why don't we take our own wool to London and sell it to the staplers instead of to the brogger? Then that profit would be ours instead of his."

"Because we're sheep farmers, not wool merchants," Robert said.

"Why not change? Is there a law that says you mayn't be both?"

"No," Robert said. "There are some merchants who keep sheep themselves, but—"

"Well, if there are merchants who keep sheep, why not sheepmen who are merchants?" Eleanor said excitedly. "Surely it would mean a much greater profit?"

"Father would never agree," Robert said.

"Well, of course, working the way he worked, he

couldn't have done it anyway," Eleanor said. "He always
did everything on the farm himself, helped the men with
every job, so he wouldn't have had time to be a merchant
as well. But if you have a foreman to supervise the men,
that frees you for other things."

"Yes, I see that," Robert said, "but Father would still
never agree. For one thing, he would never trust anyone
else to do the things he does. He could hardly bear to trust
me with the farm when he had to go to see Lord Edmund,
let alone trust someone who wasn't even a member of the
family."

"But I'm not suggesting he should become a merchant—
I'm thinking of you."

"Father still owns the farm," Robert said. "And while he
owns the farm, things will be done his way. He would
never agree to what you suggest, and I advise you not to
even suggest it. You know what his temper's been like recently."

At that moment Job came back with the jug of ale and
some pewter tankards.

"Here you are, master," he said. "It's beautifully cool—
it's been on the shelf inside the well. May I pour for you?"

He spoke so deferentially that Robert was mollified, and
allowed him to pour him some ale, watching him with a
critical eye.

"You do it very well," he said grudgingly, observing the
neat way Job handled jug, cups, and towel.

"I've been well taught, master," Job said, with a small
smile in Eleanor's direction. Robert felt himself nettled
again.

"What else have you been teaching him?" he asked his
wife.

"To play and sing, and to read and write and reckon,"
Eleanor said.

"You will be a very accomplished young man, then,"
Robert said. "You are lucky that your mistress takes such
an interest in you."

"Not lucky, Robert," Eleanor laughed. "The more I
teach my servants, the better they are as servants. Job will
be more useful to you in the future career as merchant if
he can read and reckon. He is a better steward for me if he

can write. The same applies to all the servants—surely you know that?"

She was smiling at him so pleasantly that Robert felt his feathers smoothing down again. She regarded Job only as a servant and useful to her! That was good. And she was preparing the boy to be useful to him, Robert—that was better! He smiled at his wife, and thought how much better life was seeming all of a sudden. He shot a draft of cool ale down his dusty throat.

"Of course, my dear, you're right, and I agree with you about the other matter, too, the selling of the wool. But for that we must wait until I am master of the farm. Then we may do as we please. For the moment, don't mention it to my father. Some more ale, Job! And attend to the mistress's cup, too."

Job bent to his task, concealing a smile as he did so. He was very fond of the master, almost as fond as he was of the mistress, but he thought him a very transparent fellow. And the mistress certainly knew how to handle him! Robert Morland might talk about "when he was master of the farm," but Job had little doubt who would really be master.

Robert took another mouthful of ale and felt the world growing rosier by the minute. "And now, my dear," he said to Eleanor, "how have my daughters been behaving today? What have they been doing? Anne, come here to me and speak to me in French, so I may see how you are getting on."

"She has had her lessons this morning," Eleanor said, "and little Helen has learned a new song—though I'm afraid she may have forgotten it by now. Have you, poppet?" She lifted up the dark-haired child onto her lap and Helen shyly shook her head, but did not take her thumb from her mouth.

"And the baby has pulled the head off a great number of flowers," Anys added, "and has played with a bee without getting herself stung. She has a remarkable way with animals."

"That's true, sir," Ankaret said. "She rides on Gelert just like a horse."

And while Anne talked to her father in French and was praised for her scholarship, Isabella was given a ride around

the garden on Gelert by Job while the women looked on,
laughing, and in the end even Helen took her thumb from
her mouth and chuckled, too. Somehow, it seemed, Robert
had had his thunder stolen again.

2

The child was due on the 21st of August, and so on the day
after little Anne's third birthday Eleanor took her women
and retired to the birth chamber, while the menfolk were
confined to the lower regions of the house. For some time
now Edward Morland had not, in any case, been sleeping
in the bedchamber, but had had his truckle bed moved into
the stewards' room on the ground floor. In this way he
could retire to bed whenever he felt he needed to, without
anyone else knowing about it. Also he had been suffering
pain for some months and to sleep alone meant that if the
pain made him wakeful he could light a candle. William,
the butler, slept in the hall nearby, and he had not needed
a hint from Robert to keep an ear open for his master.
Often when Morland had a bad night, William would appear at the bedchamber door with a cup of hot wine, into
which he or Jacques sometimes slipped a dose of poppy.

It was unwillingly that Morland gave up any of his tasks
to Robert, but as he grew less able to cope, Robert grew
more able in proportion. Morland rode out to the fields
every day—he could no longer walk far without tiring himself—holding himself rigidly upright on his horse, to supervise the work. His temper was worse when the pain was
worse, and the men were forbearing with him, for, harsh as
he had been, they all loved him for a fair and generous
master. When the pain was too bad for him to go out, he
would fret and fume indoors, and send messengers every
half hour to find out what everyone was doing.

On those days Robert would see to everything but pretend to consult his father as often as he could make time.
Job would find himself accidentally in the vicinity with a
piece of gossip, or the latest news gathered from a horseman passing on the Great South Road; and Anys would see
to it that Isabella escaped her and crawled into the stewards' room, or that little Anne clamored to be allowed to

recite her latest lesson to Grandpapa. All these arrangements had to be made without any suggestion to Morland himself that he was being pandered to or pitied, or he would have been furious.

Even Eleanor, though she could not bring herself to love the old man, found great sympathy in her heart for him. It was plain that he was sick unto death, and was only surviving by the sheer strength of his will: he was a walking skeleton, his skin had an unhealthy gray-blue tinge, and his hair had turned quite white in a matter of weeks. It was generally thought that he was suffering from the mouths that ate you away from inside, and there was no cure for that.

On the day that Eleanor took to her bed, Morland took to his, and stayed there. His bed in the stewards' room was drawn up against the window that looked out onto the courtyard, and propped up by bolsters he could see out and watch the to-ing and fro-ing that went on all day long, but his interest was listless and irritable. He seemed to be listening for something, or so Robert thought when he went in to give him a progress report one morning.

"—and I've put the hundred ewes into Moor field for the time being while Ben and Elyng mend the gaps in the hurdles round the pastures. Father, are you listening?"

"Yes, yes," said Morland irritably, his eyes fixed on the window. One thin hand caressed the head of his old hound, Duras, who sat beside the bed with his head on the counterpane and his soulful eyes fixed on his master's face. "I hear you. What else have you to say?"

Robert racked his brains. "Jacques is broiling a pair of pigeons in milk for your dinner—"

"Not food!" Morland snapped. "Haven't you got anything more interesting to talk about? Job has a readier tongue than you for news—perhaps I should send for him."

Robert flushed dully at this, but tried not to feel hurt, because of his father's illness. Morland's eye took on a wicked gleam at the sight of Robert's discomfort—at least there was one pleasure in life he could still indulge himself in. He cocked his head suddenly and listened, and then relaxed, seeming not to have heard what he wanted.

"Where is everyone else?" he asked. "Where are the children?"

"The children are in the garden with Ankaret. Perhaps that's the noise you heard—she hasn't the knack of keeping them all quiet together—"

"I heard no noise," Morland said flatly.

"I thought—"

"Where is Anys? I thought she was the nursery maid?"

"She's with Eleanor, of course," Robert said. Morland nodded.

"Of course. And how is Madam?"

"No news," Robert said. "I haven't heard from them to-day, but they would have told us if she had started labor."

"A lot of damned fuss," Morland grumbled to himself. "I don't remember Anne retiring to her chamber a week before she had Edward or you."

"It isn't a week, Father," Robert said tentatively. "It's only three days. Some ladies retire weeks beforehand."

"Don't lecture me on the ways of fashionable women," Morland snapped. "I may be only a sheep farmer, but I know a damned sight more about people of fashion than you do. I've been to stay with them often enough—Lord Edmund, my Lord of Bedford—God rest his soul. Duke Humphrey, the Duke of York. Aye, I know them, and they know me. Edward Morland? they'd say if you asked them. Edward Morland? Aye I know him, they'd say."

Robert nodded encouragingly, but did not speak. His father, he could see, was talking for his own comfort, not requiring an answer.

"And the King," Morland went on, "we all rubbed shoulders with the King when we went to France. King Harry, we called him. We were his men, body and soul—he knew how to make men love him. A great king, a great soldier, but he knew us all by name, just as if there was only a handful of us. Us and him, that's how it felt. And we beat the French, though they had ten times as many men in the field as we did."

Robert had heard these tales before, not only from his father but from every veteran of the French wars who had survived—it was a time they could never forget, and never cease regretting. The "Good Old Days," they would say.

"And I met the Queen once, not in France, but afterward, in England. Queen Kate—Kate of Valois. Oh, she was bonny, the bonniest girl I've ever seen, and she *was* no more than a girl, too. She spoke only a few words of English, and I spoke no French, so I don't know what she was saying, but she had a voice you could listen to all day. Like a bird, she was." And his face darkened then with recollection. "But she was bad all through, for all her prettiness, rotten through like all the French. Remember that, Robert, that the Devil can come in pretty disguises to fool a man. Keep a watch for him. Well, she's dead now, Queen Kate. Died in a convent, where, God grant, they managed to save her soul, the wicked wanton creature."

Robert remembered how upset his father had been when the news came last year of the death of the former queen in Bermondsey Abbey, where she had been sent by the government to end her days; and how even more upset he had been the year before when the scandal had broken, that since the death of her lord the king she had been living in sin with one of her servants, a Welshman, Owen Tidr, and had borne him three bastard sons. It had seemed to Morland a fall from grace in one he had admired so much, a fall the more shocking because of that very admiration.

"Women are the Devil's tools," Morland said. "The Devil uses 'em, as he used Queen Kate, for all her beauty, and those sons she bore are the Devil's children. You've got to beat the Devil out of 'em!" He slammed his fist into the palm of his hand. "Like Madam up above—she's too much pride. Beat it out of her, son. Three daughters! Three daughters!" He suddenly shouted, directing his fury upwards at the ceiling as if he hoped Eleanor might hear him. "What use is that?"

Robert was gathering his wits to try to find something soothing to say, but he was saved the trouble. At that moment William came hurrying in to say:

"Master, it's happened! The mistress is in labor!"

Robert jumped up, the excitement not diminished for him, though it was the fourth time in three years. "God protect her and help her through it!" he cried.

"Amen to that, Master Robert," William added heartfeltly. He had lost his own wife in childbirth, and the child as well.

"God send her a son," Morland said wearily, closing his eyes. "That's more to the point."

"You're looking tired, master," William said anxiously. "Shall I bring you something?"

"No, no. Just let me rest. Go away now, Robert. I want to rest." The eyes flew open again. "But let me be told at once the moment it's over. I want to know immediately what Madam has."

"Of course, Father. You'll be the first to be told."

"Very well. Now go."

That was nine o'clock. It was a short labor. Just before noon Robert came again to his father's room, his face red and his hands shaking with excitement.

"Father—!"

"I heard the baby cry. What is it?" Morland asked eagerly.

"A son! My lady hath a son!"

"Is the child well? Is all well?" Morland struggled up onto his elbow in his anxiety. Robert came forward to him, his face one huge grin of delight.

"A perfect child," he said, "small, but perfect and healthy, lusty even. And Eleanor is well too—a quick and easy labor—she says she is hardly tired!"

Morland brushed that aside, Eleanor concerned him not at all. "A son at last," he whispered, and his face was transfixed with an almost holy joy. "Thank our Lord in heaven for His infinite bounty. And for His grace in letting me live to see it."

And he slumped back onto his pillows, drained of all energy. His hand rested limply on his dog's loving head, his eyes fixed on the ceiling, but his grim old face never ceased to smile.

"Father, will you take your dinner now?" Robert remembered to ask, for Morland had refused meat and drink while Eleanor was in labor. But Morland waved Robert away with a weak gesture.

"Send William," he whispered. "And bring me the child."

As soon as the child had been washed and bound, Robert, surrounded by the anxious women, carried him down on a cushion to Morland's room. William, his face grave and sorrowful, was with his master, propping him up against his shoulder; the dog Duras had been sent to lie down out of the way in a corner, but his eyes were fixed on his master, and he whined softly in his nose at every sound or movement.

"Here is the child, Father," Robert said, his voice bursting with pride. "A beautiful, lusty child."

"Give him to me," Morland said weakly. The child was laid on the bed with him, and Morland peered into the small wrinkled face, seeking some assurance—only he knew what. The baby's eyes were tightly closed, its lips moved softly as if it were mouthing a prayer. Small and helpless it was, and Morland, as he lifted it up, was suddenly tender, as he had never been since his own childhood.

"A son. The heir to all I have. He shall be called Edward," he decreed. He laid his thin, shaking hand on the child's sleeping head. "A father's blessing on this child. God keep him safe from all harm, and let him grow to strong and pious manhood. He is born a gentleman, and he is a Morland. In him rests the honor and the future of the family."

"Amen," said those gathered around. And then Anys hurried forward to take the baby from him. She had seen the look of unutterable weariness cross the old man's face, as if he had keyed himself up for some tremendous effort that he could no longer sustain.

"My baby, my little baby," she murmured as she lifted the child out of the old man's arms. Morland's eyes followed the white bundle from the room, and then closed.

"Leave me now," he whispered, and quietly they filed out as William carefully lowered his master to his pillows, and Duras came back, unbidden, from his corner to push his nose into Morland's limp hand.

Shortly afterward the pain returned so badly that William gave him another poppy draft without even asking Robert. Morland slept then, woke in the afternoon and slept again. At sunset the dog Duras suddenly flung back his head and howled, and all the dogs in the hall joined in in an eerie chorus that chilled the blood and made the hair stand on end. William called Robert, who in turn called the priest, who was on hand to give the last rites; and before the last of the light had faded from the August sky, Edward Morland was dead. He was fifty-two years old.

Duras would not leave his master's side, even in death. The old dog died during the night, and was buried with his master in the family plot, within sight of Micklelith House.

3

The ceremonies and celebrations that would normally have been held to mark so important an occasion as the birth and christening of the Morland heir had to be curtailed because the household was in mourning for the elder Morland. Eleanor privately thought it was just like the old man to die when he did, just when it was most awkward for everyone; but she cried all the same at the funeral, for he was a Christian soul and her father-in-law. But as soon as Morland was buried, she turned her mind to the future and the plans she had been storing up for the time when she would no longer be restrained by the master of Micklelith. She anticipated no trouble from her husband: he had always been ready to please her, and now that she was the mother of his son, he would have gone to any lengths to satisfy her slightest whim.

Eleanor adored her son, and planned a great future for him. Like old Morland, she wanted him to be a gentleman in everything, and this necessitated a gentleman's household.

"The trouble is," she said to Robert one evening as they sat around the fire in the great hall, "that this house is simply not a gentleman's house. It's a farmhouse with improvements. Still, we must do what we can with it until better comes along."

"What had you in mind?" Robert asked, half amused at her air of determination.

"Well, first of all the children must have their own establishment. They can't sleep in the bedchamber with us anymore—they must have their own suite of rooms."

"My dear wife, they are not the children of a lord," Robert began in mild protest. Children slept in the bedchamber with their parents until nine or ten years old among folk of his class; then the boys slept in the hall with the retainers and the girls continued to sleep with the parents until they were married or otherwise sent from home. Only the children of great houses had their own rooms.

"They are the children of a gentleman," Eleanor interrupted him fiercely. "And who knows what Edward might be one day. Do you want him to look back on his childhood with pride or shame?"

"He shall not be ashamed of anything," Robert said, and Eleanor took his words for capitulation.

"Very well, then. The old hall upstairs is already divided into rooms. They can be cleared out and used as sleeping chamber, study, and nursery for the children. And we must have more servants. I wish Anys to be promoted to the children's governess until Edward is old enough to need a governor. We'll need at least two nursery maids."

"No doubt you have someone in mind," Robert said sarcastically. Eleanor ignored the sarcasm.

"Anys has two cousins who are good, quiet girls; Mary and Jane are their names—they are grandchildren of Alice's, of course, and they're eleven and twelve years old. Anys can have the teaching of them—she knows my ways by now."

"And what about Ankaret? What's to become of her?" Robert asked.

"She is to be my attendant. I must have proper waiting women who are gently born, now—Edward's mother must not be attended by farmhands' daughters."

"Well, if you please," said Robert. "If you take in maids like Ankaret, it can only increase our sphere of influence, and we shall need all the friends we can get if I am to merchant my own wool."

Eleanor looked up at that, and clasped her hands together in delight.

"Robert, you have decided? You intend to do what we discussed?"

"It will need much thought and planning. We have too few dependable men on the farm who are book-learned, and if we leave stewards in charge they must be at least able to read and write. And we need to increase our wool production if the venture is to be profitable. The more wool we handle, the better the profit."

"Of course." Eleanor nodded. "But what had you in mind?"

"We must get more land, buy more sheep. Father has gold in plenty hidden away, and the best use we can make of it is to expand our estate. There are lots of farms vacant in the county, acres of land that no one has claimed since the Black Death killed off the owners. We must look into them and see if we can make a claim to any of them—that's the best way."

"And if we can't?" Eleanor asked. Robert grinned sheepishly.

"We claim them anyway. Chances are no one will contest it, and if they do—we have gold, and we have friends. I must write to Lord Edmund and ask him for his patronage. Seeing I married his ward—" He smiled at Eleanor.

"That much at least I brought you," she said, pleased.

"That was why you were chosen," Robert replied simply.

The letter was duly written and sent, telling Lord Edmund of the birth of Edward and the death of Morland, assuring him of Robert's continuing service and loyalty, and begging Lord Edmund would extend his good-lordship to the new generation of the Morland family.

It was toward the end of November that the reply came: a letter speaking of good will toward Robert and Eleanor and all the children, offering congratulations and commiserations at once, and accompanied by Christening gifts for small Edward. The finest was a silver goblet with a gold stem, engraved all around with a hunting scene in which three gentlemen on horseback and their hounds and servants pursued a white hare—a compliment to Edward's mother. Another gift was a scarlet parrot in a cage, to amuse the children, and two beautiful ivory ornaments in the shape of roses for the browband of a bridle—these Robert gave to little Anne, who now had a pony of her own and rode almost as well as her mother.

The letter concluded by giving some items of news about the situation in France, where the great Earl of Warwick had been given command, and made mention of something that particularly interested Eleanor:

> Our friend Richard Plantagenet, Duke of York, has at last celebrated his marriage to his cousin Cecily Neville. At twenty-seven it is none too early, but I understand he had been betrothed to the maid almost since birth, so perhaps he felt there was no hurry.

Robert read on through the last formalities, but Eleanor had ceased to hear. Her hands were resting in her lap, and one of them sought and found the missal, which still hung from her ceinture, hidden in a fold of her black mourning eyes as vividly as if she had only a moment before seen him gown. So he had married! His face came back before her in the flesh: and Cecily Neville, who was reputed to be one of the loveliest women in the country, had married that jewel of manhood, to whom she had been betrothed since birth. Well, at least that accounted for his long bachelorhood. She might hold that balm to her heart, that even had he wanted to marry her, he could not have, being already betrothed.

Robert put down the letter and looked toward her for her comments, but she could not speak of it. She must hide her feeling from him at all costs—looking around wildly she saw Job watching her, and read sympathy in his eyes, though his face was impassive.

"Some music," she called, with an effort to be gay. "Job, some music—a song, at once. Let us be gay. We have good reason."

And Job, thinking quickly, stood up and began straightaway on an unaccompanied song that most of the servants knew, knowing that they would join in as soon as he established the tune; and while he sang he clicked his fingers to one of the boys and sent him for Eleanor's guitar, which he then handed to her with a bow, never faltering in his singing. It gave her something to occupy her hands and an excuse to hide her face; and in a moment she had recovered herself, and could appear as gay as Robert would expect her to be, after receiving such a promising letter.

CHAPTER FIVE

Robert returned from York one November day in 1441 in high good humor. He flung the reins of his horse to the nearest boy and strode into the house, yelling for his wife. He had changed a lot in the years since his father had died and he had become lord of Micklelith House: he had filled out, broadened, and taken on weight and muscle; his air had more authority—his walk, his bearing, and his voice were all more confident and masterful. He was now, indeed, a man worth looking at, and women in the town often did cast him admiring looks as he rode or walked by in his bright, rich clothes—for Robert had discovered in himself a hitherto unsuspected love of finery.

Job met him in the hall—now a handsome man of twenty-one, dressed in his steward's livery—and stopped him in mid-shout.

"The mistress is in the steward's room, sir."

"Oh? What's she doing there?" Robert wanted to know. There had always been a slight uneasiness between them, born of Robert's unspoken jealousy of the younger man.

"She's going through the accounts with the bailiff, sir. I think he's got himself into a muddle again."

"I see—oh, Job," Robert remembered as he was about to turn away, "there's a package in my saddle-bag—I forgot to take it out. Have it brought to me straight away, will you."

Job bowed and turned away, and Robert went through

the screen doors and into the steward's room. Eleanor was sitting at the table with the accounts and tallies while Reynold, the estate bailiff, stood behind her looking puzzled and apprehensive. Reynold was a good man, capable and well liked by the men, over whom he held very effective command. He knew a great deal about sheep, and even more about wool, but though he was book-learned, he was a poor hand at accounts, and although Robert did not know it, it was generally Eleanor who did that part of Reynold's job for him.

Eleanor looked up as her husband came in, and at the sight of his expression she smiled.

"All's well?" she suggested. Robert lifted her hand and kissed it gently.

"All's well, my lady," he said, thinking how beautiful she looked in her new winter gown of violet wool, trimmed and lined with the fleece of black lambs. "The hearing was quite straightforward, and we should get judgment by next month. And then—the Manor of Twelvetrees will be ours."

"It had better be," Eleanor laughed, "since we've a hundred ewes grazing on it already."

"Why not? It's as good as ours now! And I was thinking as I rode home that we should move into the house straight away. It's a far better house, bigger for one thing, and warmer for another. Sometimes I think I shall perish in this drafty pigeon-basket of a house. Well, Reynold, how are things?" Robert added, remembering they were not alone.

"Very well, master," Reynold said apprehensively.

"What are you troubling the mistress for now?"

"The tallies, master," Reynold began, but Eleanor waved him to silence with her hand.

"I'm helping him and he's teaching me," she said quickly. "I want to know the whole business, from breeding the ewes to collecting the money."

"There's no need for you to worry about the business," Robert said, "especially in your condition." For Eleanor was only a month off her sixth lying-in.

"The more I know, the better wife I'll be to you, Robert," Eleanor said, knowing well how to please her lord and master, and then added frankly, "besides, I never could bear to be idle, and I can't move around too much at the moment. Well, Reynold, I think we must stop now. You may go—perhaps I shall find time to carry on tomorrow."

"Yes, mistress. Thank you, master," Reynold bowed his way out. Robert regarded his wife with a quizzical smile.

"Job tells me he was in a muddle over the accounts."

"Job talks too much," Eleanor smiled, and then shrugged. "He's a good bailiff, and he's honest. It would be a shame to come down too heavily on him because he can't cope with the accounts. Why not let Job take over that part of the job from him?"

Robert frowned slightly. "That's the bailiff's job, and Reynold's the bailiff. Job has enough to do."

"He could manage," Eleanor said, but without emphasis. She didn't want to start a squabble over her steward. "But in any case, I don't mind helping him. And talking of the servants, I wanted to speak to you about Edward."

"What about Edward?" Robert said. His son was the apple of his eye.

"Oh, don't worry—he hasn't done anything he shouldn't. In fact, I worry sometimes because he's so quiet. A child should be obedient, but I like to see a bit of spirit, too."

"Like Isabella?" Robert said dryly. Isabella at four and a half led the household a merry dance trying to keep up with her perilous exploits. Only a week ago she had escaped the vigilant eye of Anys, the governess, and gone missing for half a day. With the house in uproar and most of the servants out looking for her, she had eventually been brought in by Ben, who had rescued her from a tree, where she had climbed to escape an irate ram. She had been trying to ride on its back, and it had at last turned on her and held her at bay. She had been soundly whipped for that episode, but it wouldn't do any good. Next week she'd be up to some other mischief.

"Not quite like Isabella," Eleanor said. She got heavily to her feet, and Gelert, who was lying beside her chair, stood up and pushed his nose under her hand. Taking Robert's arm, she strolled with him out into the sheltered garden. "But Edward is three, now, nearly three and a half. He's out of his petticoats and into his man's clothing. It's time he left petticoat government too."

"Anys can manage him, can't she?" Robert asked. Eleanor tapped his arm in annoyance.

"Of course she can. He's such a quiet, obedient child, I believe he'd look after himself. But that isn't the point. He ought to have a proper tutor, a gentleman to teach him to be a gentleman. Edward needs a governor—and he can share one with Rob."

"Rob's only two," Robert pointed out. The youngest of the family had had his second birthday only last month.

"I know," said Eleanor, "but he's a more spirited boy than Edward. I think Anys would be glad to pass him over and just look after the girls and the new baby."

"Very well, my dear," Robert said. "I shall ask around tomorrow after church and see if anyone can recommend a suitable person. If Edward is timid, it may hearten him to have the guidance of a man."

"My thoughts exactly," Eleanor began, and then broke off as Job came out into the garden. "Yes, Job?"

"I've brought a package for the master, madam," Job said, handing the cloth-wrapped bundle to Robert.

"Ah, yes—it's a present I brought for you, my dear, and left in my saddle-bag by mistake. Here—take it, with my love."

Eleanor received it with a smile, which, to Job, looked more like a smile of amusement than one of great pleasure. Robert showered her with gifts, hardly ever returning from any trip, however short, without presents for Eleanor and sometimes for the children as well. It seemed he did everything he could to win her heart, and always without success. Eleanor treated him with respect and sometimes with the same sort of brisk affection she showed to the children and her favorite servants, but nothing more.

Robert wanted her to melt, to smile on him as a lover, to respond in their marriage bed to his advances with more than just tolerance. He had loved her obsessively since the first time he saw her; his desire for her when they were alone, despite seven years of marriage, was overwhelming; but physically she merely accepted his attentions as the necessary preliminary to pregnancy; and in every other way she seemed only a little less than indifferent to him. She unwrapped the cloth now from a handsome leather collar, set with gold and enamel ornaments, and there seemed to appear that faint gleam of amusement accompanying her thanks.

"How kind, Robert—it's beautiful. Thank you so much," she said, and kissed her husband's cheek formally.

"I thought old Gelert's collar was looking shabby," Robert said shyly, feeling compelled, as always, to explain himself.

"Shall I put it on for you, madam?" Job asked.

"Yes, do," Eleanor said, handing it to him carelessly. Her eyes met Job's, and there was a slight expression of disapproval in the latter's. As if to compensate for his mistress, Job turned the collar over in his hands and said:

"It's a beautiful piece of work, master—the colors and the craft of it!" He reached out a hand for the dog. "Come here, Gelert, good fellow." Gelert sat before Job and rested a paw on the man's bent knee, his tail thrashing the ground as Job unbuckled his old collar and fitted the new one. "There, now, don't you look a fine old dog, eh?"

"That will do, Job. You can go," Eleanor said sharply. Job smiled and turned away, and Robert called after him, "Thank you, Job," with only a slight wistfulness. It was hard that his greatest champion was the one man he didn't really like.

"Now," Eleanor said, "before my women come and find me, tell me what you were saying about Twelvetrees."

Robert's face brightened at once. "Ah, yes—I was saying that I think we ought to move in right away—tomorrow, in fact. Yes, I know it's not easy for you in your condition," he went on, as Eleanor glanced significantly down at herself, "but the servants could manage everything very well—there'd be no need for you to do more than supervise from a chair. And, you see, if we don't move now, you'll be lying in next month, and then it will be Christmas, and what with one thing and another we'll be stuck here for the coldest months, instead of having the comfort of the better house. Twelvetrees has horn panes in all the windows," he added temptingly. "Just think of that."

Eleanor thought of it. One of the worst annoyances

about Micklelith House was that to get any light you had
to open the shutters, and with the shutters open there was
nothing to keep out the icy wind, the rain, or even the
snow. You had to choose between the light and the
weather—and sometimes you had to choose light.

"I'd like to move," Eleanor said, "but aren't we a little
ahead of the law? The judgment hasn't been given yet."

"A matter of time only," Robert assured her. "It's bound
to be for us."

"But what about the rival claim? What was the man's
name?"

"Jessop? Oh, that's only a formality. John Jessop hasn't a
claim in the world to that land. He owns Coney Farm on
Twelvetrees's northern boundary. He wants to spread
southward, just as we want to spread westward. But he's no
right to the land. He bases his claim on the fact that his
grandfather once slept there for the night on his way
home."

Eleanor laughed. "And is our claim so good?"

"It's better than that." Robert smiled. "At least we can
trace bloodlines to the last owner but one. And if we do
move in, it will strengthen our claim—there'll be all the
more reason to find for us if we present them with a fait
accompli."

"Well, I've no objection to moving out of this house,"
Eleanor said, looking back at the building. "But how will
we manage it?"

"No problem," Robert said. "There's nothing much
doing with the sheep at this time of year. Most of the farmhands can come down and help. We could move everything
in three days."

"First," Eleanor said firmly, "the new house will have to
be swept and cleaned."

"Four days, then. We will be there by next Sabbath.
And—but here come your women, unless I'm mistaken."

Ankaret and the new girl, Beatrice, came running out
into the garden, their young voices preceding them. On
seeing the master and mistress they dropped a low curtsy.

"Job told us you'd finished with Reynold, madam," Ankaret said. "Would it please you to come and see the children before supper?"

Eleanor and Robert exchanged a glance, before Eleanor replied, "We'll both come. Beatrice, run on ahead and tell Mistress Anys so that she shan't be taken by surprise." The little girl bobbed and ran, and the other three followed at a more dignified pace.

Twelvetrees was a fourteenth-century modernization of a twelfth-century house. It was built largely of stone, and had a fortified wall round three sides, and a moat across the fourth side that faced a stretch of marshy land running down to the river. The farm buildings were separate and built round their own yard next to the main house. The courtyard of the house was laid out as a formal garden, though it had gone to the wild through its lack of occupation and there were signs that there had once been pleasure gardens laid out on the east side of the house.

The furniture was moved to the new house on oxcarts and sleds and positioned by the servants under Eleanor's direction. Jacques was delighted with his new kitchen, a huge octagonal room at the end of the hall with three fires and four ovens, and a separate room in one of the angles for his own private quarters. While the other servants were laboring away with the furnishings, Jacques and his boys were scrubbing and cleaning the kitchen and starting great fires in all the fireplaces and ovens that would not be put out except to sweep the chimneys once a year.

And, as Robert had promised, by the following Sabbath they were settled in the new house and resuming their routines. The servants who had lived in the hall at Micklelith House had made the transfer to Twelvetrees's servants hall, while the servants and estate employees who had lived in the small village of cottages that clustered round the old house stayed put and came up to Twelvetrees when they were wanted—people like Elyng, the carpenter; Ben, the huntsman; John, the weaver; John, the shepherd; Reynold; and the packer, Master Clement. And their duties lay mostly on the estate and not at the house. The children, who had run wild for four days, were very loath to settle down to their routine again, and Eleanor mentioned again to Robert the urgency of getting a governor for Edward and little Rob.

"And another thing," she said to her husband on the eve

of that first sabbath in Twelvetrees, "we'll have to get a chaplain for the household, now that we've moved further from the city. It will be too far to walk, especially with the children, in bad weather."

"I'll see about that, too," Robert promised. "But we'll have to manage tomorrow. It's Martinmas, and we can't stay away."

"I didn't intend to stay away," Eleanor said sharply.

It was quite a procession that set off the next morning for mass, walking over the fields toward the white walls of the city. First there was Eleanor, riding Lepida and carrying her missal embossed with her device of the white hare. Beside her walked Robert, attended by his two pages—Owen, his cupbearer, and Hal, his sewer—and on the other side of her Ankaret and Beatrice stepped along demurely. After church they had leave to visit their parents in the city, returning before dark in the afternoon.

Behind came Job leading Edward by the hand, and Anys carrying Rob, and behind them Mary and Jane attending the three girls—six-year-old Anne, five-year-old Helen, and little Isabella. And bringing up the rear were William, the butler, and Arnold—Alice's son—who was the pantler. The rest of the servants would go to the evening mass. As Eleanor said, they would have to get a chaplain—this was too inconvenient.

But apart from their Sabbath duty, going to church was for them the main social event of the week. When the service was over, the congregation came out into the churchyard and met their friends, gossiped, exchanged news and views, and arranged their future meetings at each other's houses. Eleanor was in her element here: in her fine clothes, with her beautiful children and well-trained servants around her, she was a focus of attention and envy; and, moreover, thanks to Job's remarkable skills, she generally had the news ahead of any of her neighbors and so was able to tell it to them before they could tell it to her.

She had had some remarkable "scoops" in her time—like last year, when she had been first with the news of the recapture of Harfleur by the English army under Lord Edmund Beaufort. Lord Edmund had been invested with the order of the Garter for that piece of work, and Eleanor and

Robert had had the treble pleasure of being first with the
news, of having good news to tell, and of being under the
patronage of the lord in question. And earlier this year
there had been the scandal of the trial for witchcraft of the
wife of the Good Duke Humphrey of Gloucester.

Duke Humphrey's wife, Eleanor, had been found guilty
and imprisoned for life, and inevitably much of the shame
had rubbed off on the Duke himself. The common people
sympathized with him, as they always would, but the
Duke's position had been damaged, and this gave virtual
supremacy to the Beaufort party, which again was good
news for Eleanor and Robert; for the higher their patron
went, the higher they stood in their own society.

But there was no great news to be exchanged today, only
domestic matters to attend to. Eleanor talked to the respec-
tive parents of Ankaret and Beatrice and discussed the
girls' behavior and progress, and mentioned to the rector
their need for a resident clerk, while Robert asked among
their most influential friends if any of them could recommend a suitable gentleman to take the position of governor
to Edward and any further male Morland children. When
they joined forces again for the walk home, Robert had
good news.

"I have heard of a man who might be suitable to look
after Edward," he told Eleanor as they left the churchyard.
"It was Master Shawe who told me—"

"Master Shawe?" Eleanor asked. "Do I know him?"

"He owns a large estate on the other side of York—
beyond Walmgate—a sheep farmer like me. A gentleman,
of course. The poor man has recently lost his wife in childbirth. They weren't long married—this child was their
first, to make it worse for him, and it's a girl."

Eleanor nodded in sympathy, but prompted him, "And
who does he recommend? Who is the man he mentioned?"

"Peace, wife, I'll tell you in my own way," Robert protested gently. "Now, then—Master Shawe had not long
been master of the estate—not above a year—and he kept
on his own tutor, who had taught him as a boy, to be tutor
to his own sons. Now, of course, he has been left with no
wife and only one daughter, and so he looks to find a good

place for the tutor, who only reminds him of his dashed hopes."

"But he will marry again," suggested Eleanor. "He may have sons yet."

"He's certainly young enough—but he adored his wife, and says he won't marry again. Of course he may change his mind in a year or two, but for the moment he's quite determined."

"And this tutor's a gentleman?"

"Oh, quite. If you'd met Master Shawe, you'd see he is advertisement enough for the tutor. But I've arranged for Master Jenney to ride over and see us tomorrow, so we can form our own opinion then."

"That's his name, is it—Master Jenney?"

"William Jenney, aye. Well, we shall see him tomorrow, and if we like him we must invite Master Shawe to dinner to settle the matter. I'd have liked to ask him before, but with his father dying and then his wife—"

They had turned by this time off the main road and onto the narrow track that led to Twelvetrees, entering a small copse that shaded the track near its beginning. Robert's words were broken off in mid-sentence as, from behind the trees on both sides of the path, there sprang men wielding knives. The women screamed at the sudden attack, and Lepida reared and leapt sideways, almost throwing Eleanor from the saddle.

"Thieves! Robbers!" she yelled, trying to control Lepida and ride her at the attackers. There were four of them, and they flung themselves at Robert, who drew his own knife and backed away before them. The women scattered to the side of the track, dragging the children against them, while Job thrust little Edward out of the way and ran to Robert's aid, followed by Arnold and old William.

Possibly the men had not expected to be faced with four opponents, even though one of them was an old man; or possibly they had not intended to do more than give the Morlands a scare; but as soon as the servants came to Robert's aid, the attackers fell back. Their leader shouted:

"P'raps this'll teach thee not to meddle in Jessop's business!" And with a last slash at Robert he fled, closely followed by the other three.

Robert's knife fell to the ground and he clutched at his left arm, grimacing with pain. Job went to pursue the attackers through the trees, but Eleanor shouted to him,

"No, Job, let them go! See to your master!" Then she wheeled the still-prancing Lepida to face the women and said, "Mary, Jane, stop squealing. No one's touched you. Anys, can't you stop Rob yelling like that? Now, girls, now Anne, Helen, stop crying. Look, Isabella's not crying—"

"I'm not crying either, Mother," Edward called up to her. Eleanor considered him with slight surprise.

"No, you're not, my son. That's very brave."

"I saw Job wasn't afraid, so I wouldn't be afraid," Edward said. Better not say that to your father, Eleanor thought, but she said, "Well, now, suppose you comfort Mary and Jane and the girls, like a man, while I see to Papa." She turned Lepida again, and rode to the other group. Robert had taken off his doublet and Job was bandaging his upper arm with his handkerchief.

"How are you? Are you all right?" Eleanor asked Robert. He looked up at her grimly.

"It's nothing, my dear, only a slight cut. Thank God it was not worse. And that they confined their attack to me. But are you all right?"

"Don't worry about *me,*" Eleanor said. "I was only startled. I'm getting used to violent shocks during my pregnancies. But who were they—why did they do it? Were they out to rob us?"

"I think not, madam," Job said, tying the knot and stepping back. "There, sir, that should stop the bleeding."

"Thanks, Job," Robert said gruffly. "I think I have to thank you for more than that. I think perhaps I owe you my life."

"No, sir—I don't think they meant to kill you. If they did—there were four of them, and they had the advantage of surprise."

"But *why* did they do it?" Eleanor insisted. Robert looked up at her.

"You heard what they said. They are Jessop's men, warning us off Twelvetrees so that he can claim it. Unless we withdraw our claim, he hasn't a chance—so he's trying to frighten us. No doubt the next time he'll tell them to do a little more damage."

"Don't talk about it now," Eleanor said quietly, glancing over her shoulder. "You'll frighten the women. Wait until we get home." She made to dismount. "You'd better have Lepida."

"No, no, I'll walk. I can't expect you to walk in your condition."

"There's nothing wrong with me. Come, take the horse—you look pale."

"You've lost some blood, sir." Job put in his word. "I think you had better ride."

But Robert would not be persuaded, and so with Eleanor riding they made their way slowly to Twelvetrees. After dinner, Robert and Eleanor withdrew to the solar, and called Job and William to them to hear the discussion.

"Now tell me," Eleanor said while they were waiting for the two servants, "what do you mean—the next time? Do you think they'll try it again?"

"Certainly they will, unless we give up Twelvetrees."

"And we're not going to do that," Eleanor said.

"I'm glad you feel that way. But remember, you'll be in danger too, and the children, and everyone in our household."

"But that's intolerable! We must do something!"

"I intend to—ah, here's Job and William. Come in. Now, you know what happened today."

"Yes, sir," said Job. "And they'll try again, as sure as eggs are eggs."

"That's why I've got to get help," Robert said.

"Help? From whom?" Eleanor asked, but she had already guessed the answer.

"From Lord Edmund. I must ride fast, tell him the story, get a letter from him to the judge directing which way the hearing must go. With that sort of backing, Jessop won't dare try anything. And if necessary, Lord Edmund can give me armed men to back up my claim."

"When will you go?" Eleanor asked. "Tomorrow?"

"No, I must leave now, at once."

"But—"

"I can be ten miles on my way by dark. And the quicker I get back, the better. I don't think Jessop will try anything immediately, and I want to be back here before he attacks again."

"Very well," Eleanor said. "I agree, you must go. But who will you take with you? You can't ride alone."

"I'll get Ben—he's good with his knife, and a quick thinker—"

"And Job—he must go with you," said Eleanor.

"No, madam—" Job began, and Robert broke in with: "But you'll need him—you mustn't be left alone."

"I shan't be alone. I have a house full of servants," Eleanor said. And to Job: "Your place is with the master—he needs you. And you can add your weight to the argument, should Lord Edmund be reluctant to do all we ask. No more talk now—I could not rest easy at night if Job was not with you, Robert."

Job bent his head in submission, and Robert kissed Eleanor's hand, all his emotion in that gesture.

"Now," Eleanor said briskly, "we must prepare. Job, you had better go and get the horses ready. William, it will save time if you send one of the boys ahead to find Ben and bid him get ready. Then you can help me prepare food and drink and blankets for the travelers. Come now, there is no time to be lost."

It had been necessary to be brave, but when her menfolk had gone, Eleanor could not help a chill of fear passing over her. They could hardly do the journey there and back in under ten days at this time of year. And then, allowing a day for the granting of their request and the preparations for the journey back, it would be eleven days at least before she saw them again; and what might not happen in that time?

She was not alone, of course—she had William and Arnold and Jacques and the pages and kitchen boys, as well as the women and children. But William was old, Arnold elderly, and Jacques—she did not suppose Jacques would be much of a hand at fighting. All the real fighting men were back at Micklelith House. If Jessop were to attack in force . . .

And yet she could not believe that he would attack *her*. It would be a foolhardy thing to do, a thing bound to bring the wrath of the county down on his head. But if he did, it would be cold comfort to Eleanor to know her death would be avenged. It was a subdued and nervous household that went about its business over the next few days.

But as the days passed and nothing happened, they began to relax. Eleanor was making preparations for her approaching lying-in, which was about three weeks away. It would be her sixth lying-in, and so far she had produced five live children—three girls and two boys—all of which had survived. It was a very good record. She had already amply repaid her father-in-law's generosity in taking her without a dowry. She had done well—better than Richard of York's wife, Cecily Neville. The girl was so beautiful, she was called the Rose of Raby!

Eleanor had heard the news from time to time, brought to her often privately by Job, whose wish in life was to give her everything she wanted. Richard's first child had been a girl, born the year after his marriage. Eleanor was struck forcibly by the coincidence that his first child should be a girl, should be born in August, and should be named by him Anne! There had been no child the second year—last year—and this year Duchess Cecily had produced a boy in February, at Hatfield, and had lost him only weeks later.

It was a small, private triumph for Eleanor; she locked that sort of unworthiness deep inside her and admitted it to no one; scarcely even to herself, for how could she rejoice in something that must have brought pain to Richard? She could at least more openly rejoice in the news that came in May that he had been reappointed to his position in France and had left for Rouen to take command of his army. He had had immediate success in relieving the besieged Pontoise; and his wife had joined him at Rouen, and was pregnant again. Eleanor had not seen him since her marriage, but she carried his image inside her, immutable, and to it she could still say in her private moments, *You should have married me, Richard*.

The week passed quietly enough, and Friday came, and Jacques prepared fish for the dinner of the masterless household; and the short winter afternoon passed, and at four it began to get dark, and the members of the household began to drift into the great hall for supper and the long evening before the fire. And then suddenly the peace was rudely shattered. The dogs, lying around the central hearth, jumped up and began barking, and Robert's page, Owen, raced into the hall, breathless and white, shouting:

"Bar the doors! Bar the doors! Men coming, armed men!" No one present was quick-thinking enough to take up his meaning. He skidded to a halt and stared around desperately for Eleanor. "Where's the mistress?" he gasped. "Call the mistress! Shut the doors and put the bars on, quick, oh, quick!"

"Here, I'm here—what is it? Owen, what's happened?" Eleanor came down the stairs as quickly as her bulk permitted, taking in the scene even before Owen had managed to gasp out his warning again.

"Arnold—Hal—run out quickly and bar the outer gates," she ordered. "How many, Owen? We may be able to hold them outside—the outer gates are strong."

But it was already too late. Even as Arnold and Hal ran to the door there was the sound of shouting and horses' hooves in the yard, and two women who had been outside ran into the hall screaming. Eleanor and Owen both reacted at the same instant. They flung themselves across the hall, clapped the doors to and between them heaved the bars across, even while Eleanor was shouting to the other servants to secure the other house doors and windows. Instantly there was a thunderous hail of blows on the main door, so heavy that Eleanor, still leaning against the central bar, could feel it shake. Servants were running to and fro, lifting shutters onto those windows that could be covered from the inside—Eleanor could not tell if they were all present, but if any were left outside, they would have to find somewhere to hide.

The dogs were barking clamorously, the children were crying, the maids asking questions and shrieking at each other across the din. Jacques came in from the kitchen to demand an explanation and to shout at his boys when they did the same. Never before had Eleanor so much missed Job with his cool mind and authority. Everyone was appealing to her now that the doors were shut. The children ran to her for comfort, the servants for orders, reassurance, information. She dealt with them as best she could: she picked up baby Rob and sent the other children to Anys, posted servants at each door, gathered the women around the fire and tried to quiet them, tried to find out what weapons they had, if any, among them. The blows on the door ceased for a moment, making it easier to talk, but making Eleanor wonder what was coming next.

What did come next was an attack at the small corner door. At the first blow Hal, who had been posted there, yelled for help. A quick inspection told Eleanor that this door might, unlike the main door, collapse under the strain, and she ordered a trestle to be dragged up and wedged against it with any heavy weights they could find. There was a nerve-racking ten minutes during which it seemed that they might batter their way in through that door, but at last the action ceased as abruptly as it had begun and silence fell again.

Tension inside the hall built up. A child whimpered and was hastily silenced by one of the women as every soul strained to hear what was going on outside: the silence was more menacing than the noise. Gelert, who had run to hide in a dark corner at the first attack, crept out now and slunk up to Eleanor, pushing his cold nose into her hand, making her jump. She fondled his head absently, and her fingers touched the handsome decorated collar that had been Robert's present only two weeks ago.

Outside a horse whinnied, and there was the sound of hooves again. For a moment hope sprang up—could it be help arriving? But sense soon said that the hooves were going away, though the voices remained.

"They're leading the horses away," Owen said. He whispered, as if they were hiding from their enemy, and he was afraid of giving away the hiding place.

"What are they going to do?" Mary asked, and there was incipient panic in her voice. Gelert whined, and Eleanor hushed him, folding her hand around his muzzle to stop him from barking. Now the voices outside had stopped, too. Nerves were stretched to breaking point in that silence. Eleanor wanted to scream. . . .

And then with a tremendous crash the horn panes of the courtyard windows were broken in with staves, and through the apertures were flung burning rags, half a dozen of them. Wherever they dropped, they fell on rushes, which flared up with eager, licking flames. Dogs and women ran shrieking here and there. Eleanor shouted, directing those of the servants who weren't panicking to beat the fires out. Jacques brought a bucket of water from the kitchen, but there was not water enough in the house—the well was out in the courtyard. The hall filled with smoke, and Eleanor knew she was beaten.

"Open the door, Owen," she cried. "We'll have to get out. Anys, keep the children together. I have Rob. Mary, Jane, stay with Anys. Open the door, Owen!—William, help him!"

The doors gave with a crash and a clatter, and as the smoke rolled out into the torchlit courtyard, men forced their way past the servants struggling to get out, and began to attack the heaps of burning rushes. Of course, Eleanor thought bitterly, they don't want the house to burn down either. There were a few skirmishes, but on the whole the Morland servants only wanted to get out of the smoke-filled room. Outside there were men with dark, cruel faces and bright knives.

"Out you go, woman," they shouted as Eleanor stopped to stare at them. "Get out—all of you—get out, or it'll be the worse for you."

"It will be the worse for you when the men get back," Eleanor shouted defiance. "Don't think you can get away with this! I'll remember your faces."

"Get you gone, woman, before I lose my temper and hit you," one man shouted, and he thrust his flaming torch toward her, making her jump back and shield her face from the heat. Owen plucked at her arm anxiously.

"Come, mistress, please come away," he cried. The servants had run out into the darkness, chased out, some of them, by the knives of the torchbearers. Only Anys and the children were near her, and Owen. She led them out of the courtyard, and as the doors were clamped shut behind them, the darkness fell over them like a pall.

There was no gleam of light anywhere—moon and stars

were hidden behind a thick pall of cloud. It began to rain, and Eleanor was aware suddenly that it was cold. In the hall it had been stiflingly hot, and they had left it so quickly they had not had time to gather up any belongings, not even their cloaks. They were turned out with nothing but the clothes they stood up in.

"What will we do, mistress?" Anys asked her. Helen began to cry, and Anys shook her quite roughly and said, "Hush now. I've no time for your crying."

"Shall we go home, Mother?" little Edward asked. Eleanor looked down at him, at the white blur that was his face in the darkness.

"Home?" she said vaguely, and then she realized what he meant. "To Micklelith—of course. Yes, my dear, we shall go home. Keep together, now, Edward, take my hand. Anys, keep hold of the girls. Isabella, hold Anys's hand, and don't you let go of it for any reason—do you understand me?"

"Yes, Mother."

They waited and called in the darkness for the rest of the servants, but no one appeared. Some of them had fled from the back door of the hall; others had scattered in their panic and were probably already on their way to Micklelith. When it seemed sure everyone had gone, Eleanor started her little group in the direction of the old house, and shelter.

It was a long walk in the cold and rain. Owen soon had to carry Rob for Eleanor, and when Edward grew too tired to walk further, he gave Rob to Anys and took Edward on his back. The three little girls stumbled on bravely, helped by Mary, Jane, and Eleanor, but the way was rough and they were cold and hungry; they couldn't help crying. Eleanor could not cheer them much. She had a dreadful pain in her back, which she was trying to ignore, and she was worried about what the intruders would do to the house, where the other servants were, and what had happened to Gelert. She had expected him to join her and he hadn't—she hoped he wasn't hurt.

And then, somehow, they lost their way. It was easy enough to do. None of them knew the way very well, and in the pitch-dark and the rain things look different. They wandered around apparently aimlessly for some time. Eleanor could be no help now, for the pain was increasing, and she knew that it was the child on its way. They must find shelter before long, or she and the baby would die. Dazed, she stumbled along, clutching Isabella's hand and no longer sure who was helping whom.

"A light—mistress, a light!" Owen cried suddenly, and Eleanor felt a surge of relief.

"Where? I don't see it?"

"There, there look!"

"Yes, a light—it must be Micklelith. Come on, we'll be home soon!"

"Come on, children. Mistress, let me help you."

New life came to their exhausted limbs. Mary and Jane helped Eleanor, one either side, leaving the children to cling to Anys's skirt for support, and they staggered down the slope of the last few yards, crying out to those within for help. The light they had seen was the cottage of John the shepherd, who lived in the most outlying of the houses that clustered around Micklelith.

The door was open, and John and his wife, Tib, were in the doorway, anxious and frightened. Others of the servants had already come past with the news, but the mistress and the children had been wandering in the dark for several hours, and many had feared they had somehow perished.

Shyly Tib pushed forward a stool and begged Eleanor to sit.

"Only a moment, mistress," she assured her, "just to rest yourself. The others are making the hall ready for you. When you've rested a minute we'll help you up to the house."

Eleanor groaned and shook her head. She knew she could go no further.

"No, good Tib, I'll have to stay here. I'm sorry it should be so, but my time has come."

"Oh, mercy on us!" Tib cried, her hand flying to her mouth; but she had had six children herself, and she knew what must be done. "Now, then, John," she said to her husband, "you must take yourself off, for we'll need our bedchamber for the poor mistress right away. You and little Owen take the children up to the House, and tell them what's come of the mistress, and send some of the women to help."

"I'll stay and help, too," Anys said. "Mary, Jane, you go with the children."

"See they're dried properly and made warm," Eleanor gasped through her increasing pains. She met Anys's eyes. "Hurry."

"They'll see to it all right, mistress," Anys said reassuringly, and hustled them out while Tib helped Eleanor into the inner chamber of the tiny cottage.

The child was born half an hour later. It was a boy, and Eleanor called him Thomas.

Lord Edmund granted Robert's request without demur, and when he and Job arrived home a week later, it was bearing a letter to the judge in the case, directing him as to the verdict he must reach, and accompanied by half a dozen men-at-arms with which to intimidate Jessop. It was fortunate that the party called at Micklelith House on their way up to Twelvetrees, or the outcome might not have been so favorable, for eight men are easily put down when they ride into what they think is their own haven.

As it was, servants running out to meet the party soon told what news there was to be told, and Robert and Job quickly dismounted and ran into the old house, where the family was living on borrowed sticks of furniture and nursing a fine crop of colds and chills among them. Rushing to the bedchamber, Robert found his wife huddled over two charcoal braziers trying to rid herself of a chill that had got into her bones that she didn't seem to be able to shake off. On her lap was the skinny, mewling new boy-child; her red eyes and black clothes were for baby Rob, who had been burnt up by a fever in the lungs as a piece of straw is consumed by fire.

So it was with a more righteous cause that the Morland party set off to recapture Twelvetrees, inspired by a manly grief rather than a worldly ambition. It wasn't much of a fight: six men-at-arms and a dozen servants bearing scythes and staffs, backed up by Lord Edmund Beaufort's letter of support, was too formidable a force for Jessop and his men to resist. A few bloody noses and broken heads, and it was all over, and Twelvetrees belonged to the Morlands again. By the Sabbath the household had moved back in, and all was as it was again.

Eleanor brooded a little over the loss of her chubby baby Rob, whom she had loved better than meek Edward; but she had her new child to brood over, and, weakened by her chill, she was less active for the first weeks of Thomas's life and spent a lot of time nursing and playing with him, developing in the process an affection for him that she had not felt for any of her other children.

The loss of his brother had done something for Edward, too. Though he could not change his quiet, serious nature, he grew more bold and forthcoming, and adopted a protective attitude toward his sisters, who before were only kept from bullying him by the firmness of their governess. The acquisition of Master Jenney as his governor increased his status among the children, both his sisters and the children of the servants; he began to acquire a little of that air that befitted the eventual lord of all he surveyed; and as he became more like her ideal of a firstborn son, Eleanor found she could like him more.

Gelert was never found again. He was not in the house when Robert reoccupied it, and it had to be assumed that he had fled out into the fields when the doors were opened. Job was upset by the loss of him, and for some weeks spent his spare time riding about the countryside calling him and asking every passerby if they had seen him. But no word ever came back of him, and Job gave up the search and mourned him as dead. But Eleanor told him it was much more likely that someone had taken him in, if not for the sake of his fine physique, then for his richly ornamented collar.

"He would have found his way home," Job insisted, but Eleanor shook her head.

"Not he—he would have stayed as long as they fed him and were kind to him. He never had any loyalty, that dog."

Robert did his best to console Eleanor for a loss she did not feel. He promised her the pick of the next litter, and Eleanor thanked him, and smiled that faintly amused smile.

CHAPTER SIX

Eleanor was giving her three daughters a needlework lesson. Each was engaged on a piece of work suitable to her skill, and Eleanor, in the intervals of her own work, went from one to another, criticizing, helping, and praising, while her lady's maid read aloud to them all from the autobiography of Margery Kempe. The maid was a twelve-year-old girl named Lucy; this was 1447, and both Ankaret and Beatrice had long since married and gone away.

They were sitting in the solar of Twelvetrees House, and Anne, as befitted her most difficult piece of embroidery, was sitting in the south window seat where she could get the best light. She was almost twelve, and since at twelve a girl could well be sent away to another household, or even married, she had to count as almost adult. She was a womanly girl, small but well grown, with the beginnings of a nicely rounded figure; a fair, rose face; and gray-green eyes that just now were rather serious as she frowned over the difficulties of the wall hanging she was embroidering. Under her linen veil her hair was golden and curling: she was a pretty, maidenly child, and well aware of the importance of her position as the eldest of the family. When there were no adults present, she felt it was upon her to keep the rest of the children in order, and this sense of responsibility showed in her grave deportment.

On a stool at her side was Helen, only a few weeks off her eleventh birthday, and already taller than both her sisters. Helen was the acknowledged beauty of the family, slender and lovely, with Eleanor's dark hair and blue eyes, a wonderfully pale skin, and her father's sensitive features. She was working on an embroidered cushion, but her needle moved slowly, and she spent at least as much time stroking the folds of her dress and rearranging the fall of her veil as in working. Eleanor found something vapid and spiritless in Helen. She was an obedient child, but she seemed to care for nothing but her own appearance. She followed Anne's lead in everything, adopted her opinions, used her expressions, and Eleanor could only be glad that she had chosen anyone as firmly orthodox as Anne to copy.

On a cushion on the other side of the circle, and as near to Eleanor's stool as Eleanor could persuade her to sit, was Isabella, who would be ten in May and who was already a problem to Eleanor. Isabella was no beauty—she had mousy hair and pale eyes and a bony freckled face. Her body was thin and gawky, and she was always untidy and almost always dirty. She hated sewing and spinning and playing the dulcimer and reading and writing and in fact almost any of the things she had to do. Whenever she could, which was pretty often, she escaped from these hated tasks and slipped out of the house, and spent the day on the hills with the shepherds, or paddling in the stream catching minnows with the farmhands' children, or rabbiting in the woods with the dogs.

She wouldn't have been so much of a problem if she had been born a boy: she would have made quite a creditable boy. She could ride any horse, handle hawk and hound, hunt and fish and shear a sheep. On Sundays when the menfolk had all to attend archery practice by law, Isabella could hit the bull three times out of four, if she was lent a bow, and she could throw a spear farther than any of the boys of her own age. She was bold and fearless, inquisitive and adventurous; she loved to run and romp all day and come home covered in mud with her hair a tangled bird's nest down her back. The only girlish thing she liked to do was to dance, for then she could let herself go and frolic.

Eleanor almost despaired of her. How was she ever to get this child of hers married? Who would take her as she was? Robert laughed, and said leave her be, she'll change when she's older, but Eleanor would only shake her head and wonder. Even now, when her proximity to her mother made thought of escape impossible, she was wriggling uncomfortably on her cushion and struggling ineptly with the simplest piece of plain sewing that Anne could have done better when she was only five.

"Isabella, sit up straight, and stop fidgeting!" Eleanor ordered her sharply. "What, have you knotted your thread again? Really child! I don't know how you manage it—here, let me have it."

Isabella yielded up the hated sewing gratefully, and while her mother tried to unknot the thread she got up and wandered over to the window listlessly. Then all at once her face brightened and her bearing changed.

"Oh, look! Here's Job coming back!" she cried.

"Where?" Anne asked, craning forward to the window, and her solemn little face lit in a rare smile. "Ah, he sees me!"

"It was me he smiled at," Isabella said indignantly. "Mother, can I go down and meet him?"

"Certainly not!" Eleanor said indignantly. "Sit down at once, Isabella, and take back your work. Anne, get on—I'm surprised at you. And Lucy, there's no need for you to stop working." The children subsided, abashed, and Isabella returned to her cushion and took her rather grubby piece of work back with a sullen expression.

"He might have a letter from Papa," she said, unable to restrain herself.

"Silence," Eleanor said. "Lucy, continue to read. I am going to leave you girls for a few moments—Anne, I expect you all to continue to work as if I were still here."

"Yes, Mother," Anne said, and gave Isabella a ferocious frown of warning as soon as her mother's back was turned.

In the hall Eleanor and Job met with smiles on both sides.

"Well?" Eleanor asked him. "I can see it's news from your face."

"A letter from the master," Job told her, "and a piece of gossip you'll like."

Eleanor laughed gaily, seeming in that moment no older

than when she first came to Yorkshire thirteen years ago. "All the gossip has been bad news for I don't know how long. The news from France—all bad. The news from court—all bad. What is it this time?"

"Another juicy bit about our sovereign lady," Job confided gleefully.

"Ah! Then we must retire to the garden—come. Bring the letter, too, and I will read it there. Well, now," she said when they reached the quiet of the box walk, "what has she done now?"

The lady they were talking of was the Queen of England, Henry's young bride Margaret of Anjou. She had brought nothing but scandal from the beginning. The Earl of Suffolk had gone to France to negotiate with the French king, Charles, for a wife for King Henry, and the wily Charles had duped Suffolk into accepting, instead of one of the French royal family, the penniless daughter of the Duke of Anjou. A truce with France had been signed, and secret concessions were made by Suffolk, that the English would surrender certain territories, including Maine and Anjou, to the French. It had been a high price to pay for a pauper bride.

The Duke of York had been furious over the way the matter was handled, and said so, and it was the beginning of a rift between him and the Beaufort party that was never to be healed. Queen Margaret, once firmly crowned, had settled down to make herself felt, and soon had the King eating out of her hand. She persuaded him to give up Maine to the French, and had Suffolk on her side, against a stout opposition headed by good Duke Humphrey. She worked behind the scenes to scotch the marriage plans of the Duke of York for his eldest son, Edward, and the princess Madeleine of Valois, and kept Richard and Edmund Beaufort contending for the position of Lieutenant of France so that they shouldn't join forces, which would be a danger for her.

Then in February of this year there had been the worst thing of all. Parliament had met at Bury St. Edmunds, and when Duke Humphrey arrived, the Queen had him arrested by a large force of soldiers she had brought with her for that purpose. He was to be impeached for treason, and was taken to a house in the town and imprisoned there, and from that prison he never emerged. What happened no one would ever know, but five days later the good Duke was dead, and there was scarcely a soul in the kingdom who did not believe the Queen had had him murdered.

She had appointed York, who was of Duke Humphrey's party, Lieutenant of France to quell the public uproar, but less than a month later she had canceled the appointment on hearing of the death of Cardinal Beaufort. This was because the death of the cardinal left Lord Edmund Beaufort head of his family and heir apparent to the throne—far too important a person to alienate by giving the coveted appointment to the Duke of York. Ever since Queen Margaret came on the scene, politics had been in uproar, and even the members of the Council themselves hardly knew from day to day what was going to happen next.

"What has she done now?" asked Eleanor.

"You remember that Cardinal Beaufort left all his money to the King in his will?" Job asked.

"Yes," said Eleanor. "And the King refused it on the grounds that it wasn't fair to the rest of the relatives."

"That's right. Well, the Queen isn't troubled by any such qualms. She's seized the lot!"

"But she can't!" Eleanor said, aghast.

"Who's to stop her?" Job said simply. "Only the King can gainsay her, and he does anything she asks."

Eleanor considered. "But surely that will annoy Lord Edmund—I thought she wanted him on her side?"

"She has to have him on her side—as heir to the throne, unless she produces a son, which looks unlikely. But she has other ways. She'll make him Lieutenant of France and head of the Council, and that will be enough to make him forget his uncle's money."

"Is that certain?" Eleanor asked.

"Oh, it's only a rumor at present, but it will happen all the same." He regarded his mistress slyly. "What it is to have divided loyalties, eh?"

Eleanor flushed. "My loyalties are not divided, and you had better remember your place if you want to keep it."

Job said nothing, but he continued to smile. He knew that Eleanor could not do without him now. He also knew

that since the disagreement between Lord Edmund and Richard of York had placed them on opposite sides, Eleanor
had struggled hard with her own feelings. Of course she
and Robert owed everything to Lord Edmund. She had
been his ward, had grown up with Belle, his wife, had been
married by him to her present advantage, and had received
his patronage as a married woman. Now that he was heir
apparent, the Morland's social position went up in line with
the rise in his own status. By his good offices Robert had
been made a master stapler, one of the company granted
exclusive rights to export wool from England, a position of
immense power and prestige, and one that brought enormous increase of wealth to the Morland family.

Of course her loyalty had to lie with Lord Edmund, now
more than ever. Yet it seemed that Richard had been
wronged; that he had been slighted and passed over; command had been given in France over his head, and he had
been recalled from a successful campaign so that a political
appointment might be made. The Council had refused to
pay him the £20,000 it owed him, and then had ennobled
Suffolk for the part he played in the disgraceful marriage
of the King and the ignominious truce with Charles. It was
hard not to feel sympathy for Richard; it was hard to be
wholeheartedly on the side of Lord Edmund's party.

To hide her face now, Eleanor opened and read the letter from her husband, at present in Calais at the master
stapler's headquarters. It was a short letter.

"The master is coming home next month," she said to
Job when she had finished it. "He says things are getting
restless over there again, and that war seems likely. The
French king wants to know why we haven't surrendered
Maine yet, and is going to resort to arms to get it."

"Pray God he does. War would be better than this disgraceful truce," Job said.

"I expect Lord Edmund would think so, too, only I suppose he'll have to take the side of that scheming baggage if
she makes him head of the Council."

Job laughed and touched Eleanor's cheek with his fore-
finger. "So fierce, my lady! But that 'scheming baggage' is
the wife of our sovereign lord the King—"

"For the moment," Eleanor said. She looked up into Job's face, a firm, handsome face, seeing the sunlight shining through his auburn hair and turning it to burnished gold. It suddenly occurred to her to wonder why Job had never married: he certainly could have had his pick, attractive man that he was.

"Will you ever marry, Job?" she asked him. "We all thought at one time you'd marry Anys—you seemed fond of each other."

"I am fond of her," Job said, "but—"

"Don't you *want* to be married?" Eleanor insisted. Job's eyes were looking straight into hers as he answered:

"I am a man as other men are, lady. But sometimes a man gives his whole faith to one thing, and it leaves no room for anything else."

"What did you give your faith to?" Eleanor asked, but she already knew. She was finding it unaccountably hard to breathe, as though there were a tight band around her chest.

"Lord Edmund gave me to you, and bid me serve you," Job said gently. "And I do—with all my heart."

For a long moment they looked at each other, their eyes saying things that were not possible in speech; and then Eleanor turned away abruptly, her cheeks poppy-red and her heart pounding with a strange kind of happiness.

"I had better read their father's letter to the children," she said, almost at random. It was as good an excuse to move as any. "Job, do you go in and bid Master Jenney to bring the boys to the solar to hear it." And she lifted her skirts and ran indoors like a young girl.

Master Jenney—a fair-haired, soldierly man whom Eleanor had liked and trusted at first sight—came at once at her bidding. There were three boys in his charge now: Edward, tall and dignified at nine years old; Eleanor's favorite, Thomas, a handsome six-year-old who already knew how to use his charm to get his own way; and her youngest child, Harry, who at three-and-a-half was just out of petticoats. The boys all bowed to their mother as Master Jenney had taught them, but as soon as they straightened up, Thomas ran to her and kissed her, and claimed for himself the best place at her knee as the children gathered around her to hear their father's letter.

She was just about to begin when a commotion downstairs made her pause and listen, and signal to Job to go and see what it was. Moments later he was back, accompanied by a dusty, breathless shepherd boy, who seemed terrified to find himself in the presence of the mistress and all her family.

"Speak up, boy," Eleanor encouraged him, not unkindly. "What's wrong? You look as if you've been running."

The child gulped once or twice and then stammered. " 'Tis thieves, mistress—my lady—raiders, a gang of 'em. Driving off the ewes, mistress, off the hundred acres. They caught our two shepherds, but they didn't see me—I was up a tree. So I took John's pony and come here."

"How many?" Job snapped.

"Too many to fight, sir," the boy told him. "We was only three—John and Hughie and me. We couldn't have fought 'em—they was armed. And driving off our best ewes, mistress—sir."

Eleanor thought quickly. "You did right to come, boy. Go and wait in the yard with your pony, to show us the way. How many of the raiders are there—can you count?"

The boy shook his head. "I can tally, mistress, come harboring-time, but not count numbers. But there was—" He screwed up his face in the effort to work it out, and then held out his hands. "As many as my fingers, I think, my lady."

"Very well. Go now and wait. Job—" As the boy went out she turned instantly to her steward. "Ten of them, if the boy is right, and armed. Jessop's men perhaps?"

"Maybe. Someone who knows the master is away, anyway."

"If they think they will have an easy time because the master is away, they have reckoned without the mistress. How many men have we here?"

"We can muster about eight, I suppose," he said. "And horses."

"Right—get them in the yard, mounted, armed with anything they can find. Then ride as fast as you can to Micklelith and get as many men as possible and bring them up

to Hundred Acre field. If we're gone from there I'll leave
someone to bring you on."

"We? Mistress, you can't mean to go?"

"I *am* going," Eleanor said grimly. "Those are my ewes,
and my men. I'll not give them up so easily. Hurry now—
don't waste time in arguing."

Job knew when to take orders—it was one of his fine
points. He nodded and ran from the room, and Eleanor
jumped up and snapped her fingers to Lucy.

"Fetch my cloak, child. I'll take the Italian dagger the
master brought me home last time, too. Master Jenney, I
leave you and Anys in charge here—take care of the children—"

"Mother!" This was Edward, coming forward urgently,
his eyes on her face. "Let me come, too."

"No, Edward—it's too dangerous," Eleanor said instantly.

"Mother, *please*." Edward's whole heart was in his face.
"I'm nine now. With Father away I have to take care of
you. Please, Mother."

This child of hers was trembling on the brink of manhood, and all his pride hung on her decision. Eleanor's eyes
met those of Master Jenney over the boy's head, and then
looking back to Edward she knew she must not shame him
in front of his family and his tutor.

"Yes, of course you're right," she said. "Very well, Edward. Run on ahead and get Hawk ready for yourself, and
Lepida for me. And put on your cloak!"

A holy joy dawned in the child's face and he bowed to
her and then ran. Hawk was his father's horse—Edward
understood the implications.

Five minutes later Eleanor was riding Lepida hell for
leather across her fields, Edward beside her on Hawk, and
seven men and boys behind her well mounted, following
the shepherd boy on his little hairy shepherd pony.
Hundred Acres was the most outlying of their fields, the
kind of place sheep raiders would choose to strike, even
without the temptation of the best ewes in the country. It
was on the footslopes of the hills, fine sheep-land, dry and
well grassed, but far from Twelvetrees and farther from
Micklelith. Eleanor had not much hope of her reinforc-

ments reaching her before she came up on the thieves. She must trust to surprise and righteous anger, and hope that the boy had over- rather than under-estimated the numbers. He probably had no clear idea of numbers, since he said he could only count by tally—that was the way the shepherds told their sheep. The sheep would be driven through a bottleneck past the tallyman, who would recite his tally rhyme, one word for every sheep that ran past him. Each time he finished the rhyme he would make a mark on the stick he held, and these notched "tallies" would later be translated into numbers by the baily or steward. A person who could only count that way would be unlikely to have any clear idea of a number of men running around among a flock of sheep.

When they neared Hundred Acres Eleanor led her group round the sheltered side of a small copse of birch and furze that flanked the field; and pausing in its shade, Eleanor saw the raiders. They had gathered the sheep together and were driving them through the gate at the far side. There were in fact eleven of them, but two of those were occupied with holding the prisoners, and only two were mounted.

"Right," Eleanor said quietly to her men. "We'll go straight at them—yelling. We may frighten them off. If not, we'll have to fight. Don't let them pull you off your horses—that's your advantage. Edward, and you, boy, go straight past them and try to turn the sheep back. I don't want them scattered all over Yorkshire. Right? Everybody ready? Then—charge!"

They broke from the trees with a yell that made the horses rear and prance, and galloped down on the startled raiders. It was a broad field, and by the time Eleanor's band came upon them, the thieves had had time to realize what was happening. They didn't run—they turned and drew their knives, and the two holding John and Hughie realized their handicap and knocked their prisoners down so that they could join the battle.

The Morland men were mostly armed with clubs and sticks, and as they reached the thieves, they swung them lustily as the thieves tried to duck under the blows and get in close with their knives. Edward and the shepherd boy galloped past round the flank of the flock and turned them at the gare. Some dozen or two were already through the gap and scattered, but the main body of the flock milled around, bleating in terror and handicapping the thieves on foot more than the rescuers on horseback, as Eleanor had calculated.

Eleanor rode straight at the nearer of the mounted men. He was trying to drive the flock on while the footmen held off the Morland party, but as Eleanor reached him he swung his horse round on its hocks to face her. Eleanor caught a glimpse of his rough, grimy face as she stabbed at him in passing. She felt the blade catch in something, almost being wrenched from her hand as Lepida carried her past. She reined the mare in savagely and turned her, rearing, to the attack again. The man was ready for her before she had properly gathered herself, and she felt his blade in her arm—a strange cold burning, but with no pain to it.

Instantly all her fear left her, and she was filled with a flood of hot anger. She heard herself yelling, and saw the man's face freeze with surprise as her knife blade went into his throat. Lepida was screaming with fear, her breast locked against that of the man's struggling horse. She tried to rear as Eleanor wrenched her knife from the raider's throat and his blood gushed out over her head and neck, and as Eleanor wrenched her back she went up on her hind legs and struck out wildly, catching the raider's horse a blow on the shoulder that sent it leaping away with its dead burden.

Eleanor whirled Lepida around, controlling her with one hand. Some of her men were dismounted, struggling hand to hand with the raiders, and there were more loose horses than one. Edward, having turned the sheep as he was bid, was riding into the battle, hitting out at groups of struggling men with his stick. Of the shepherd boy Eleanor could see nothing. She rode at a struggling pair where her man was getting the worst of it, forcing the maddened Lepida forward, and when the raider saw the blood-spattered horse and its fierce rider he relinquished his hold on the Morland man's throat and tried to back off. Eleanor drove her knife into his shoulder, feeling it grate on bone before it was torn from her hand by the force of the blow. The man reeled backward, clutching at the hilt of the knife that projected from his cloak.

And then without knowing how it happened, Eleanor found herself dragged from the saddle. She clutched despairingly at Lepida's mane, felt the mare surge away from under her, and hit the ground amid the milling of feet and cloven hooves. The next few moments were all confusion as she was trodden on by struggling men and battered by the sharp little feet of the panicking ewes. Something hit her forehead, and she felt herself dizzying, heard the shouts and bleats whirling around her, booming and fading.

And then she was being lifted up by strong arms, a hand was smoothing her face, a voice was calling her through the ringing in her head. She opened her eyes, to find herself staring into Job's face.

"You got here," she said weakly.

"It's all over. We have them. You should have let me come with you," he said reproachfully. "Anyone could have fetched the men from Micklelith."

Eleanor shook her head, and then wished she hadn't. "You were the best. No one else had the authority."

"What happened to you? You've a cut on your forehead and—what's this? Blood on your arm? Lepida's soaked in it."

"Not all mine," she said faintly. "I killed one. I'm all right. Are we—?"

"Minor wounds. A few broken heads. But Hughie's dead. One of their lot knifed him."

Eleanor's eyes closed. "Poor Hughie," she whispered. He had been a good man. They flew open again as she remembered. "Edward?"

"He's all right," Job reassured her. "Not a scratch. He's thrilled to bits with himself because he knocked down a raider. And Isabella's all right, too."

"Isabella?" Eleanor struggled to get up. "What do you mean, Isabella's all right?"

"Oh, didn't you know about her? No, rest a while, don't try to get up."

"I'm all right—help me stand up. I'm all right, I tell you. What's this about Isabella?"

Job smiled a little grimly. "She didn't like being left behind with the women and children," he said. "So she slipped out while Anys's back was turned, grabbed herself a horse, and followed you. When I got here she was belaboring one of their number with half a fence-post. He had a knife in his shoulder so he wasn't giving much trouble. I don't know if she was responsible for the knife as well."

Isabella was unrepentant. "Why should I have to stay behind just because I'm a girl?" She faced her mother defiantly. "I'm older than Edward, and I can ride better than him."

"You stay behind because I say so," Eleanor said angrily. "That's enough."

"Father would have let me go."

"Father wouldn't," Eleanor said.

"I wanted him to be proud of me." Isabella turned her appeal to Job. "I wanted to save his sheep."

"Your father wouldn't be proud of your disobedience to your mother," Job said gently. "He wouldn't expect you to go out fighting sheep-stealers, but he would expect you to do as your mother bids you."

Isabella looked unconvinced. "You would have let me come. Mother's always telling me not to do things."

Job had difficulty hiding his amusement, but he managed a fairly stern face. "I certainly wouldn't have let you come. I don't like to hear you talking like that. I think you should apologize to your mother."

Isabella, still rebellious, looked disappointed that her hero Job should suddenly and unaccountably side with the enemy; but under his steady gaze her eyes at last fell shamefacedly and she curtsied to her mother and muttered an apology. Eleanor accepted it without further comment, but she had been a little disturbed to see how much Isabella admired Job, and how much she disliked her mother. She was going to be a difficult child, Eleanor thought with a sigh.

* * *

Eleanor's knife wound, though deep, was clean, and healed quickly, as did most of the wounds taken that day in a good cause. One of the men, Foley, had a nasty wound in the breast, which turned bad and carried him off in a fever three days later, but, with Hughie, he was the only casualty. It made, at least, a good tale to tell Robert when he returned, laden with presents, from Calais. He was proud of his wife, and prouder still of his son and heir, whose part in the adventure he never tired of hearing about; and though he tended to make light of Isabella's mad exploit, he chastised her severely for disobedience, which did not make her love her mother any better or her father any less.

One lasting consequence came of the raid: it spurred Robert on to begin building the new house he had been thinking of for two years.

"It isn't right that you should have to send so far for help if I'm away," he said to Eleanor. "This place is too small. We need one central place where we can have all the servants and retainers together. We'll build a new house halfway between here and Micklelith."

"A new house," Eleanor breathed, delighted at the idea. Robert nodded.

"A big house, the biggest anywhere around, fitted for us and our family—one where our new rich friends wouldn't be ashamed to visit us. Our patron is the heir to the throne of England—we shouldn't be living in a place that's little better than a farmhouse."

"Can it be a modern place, with real glass windows?" Eleanor asked excitedly.

"We'll build it of these Flemish bricks you see so much of down south. In some parts all the new houses are made of it—and rare pretty it looks, too. And we'll have chimneys in all the rooms for the fires, to conduct the smoke away—"

"Chimneys!" Eleanor laughed. "I don't know what the old folk will say! They say that the smoke is good for you, keeps your lungs strong."

"And we'll have the bedchamber and solar walls paneled with wood," Robert went on, ignoring this, "and we'll be as sung as a cow in a barn."

"And gardens laid out as you never saw," Eleanor added.

"And we'll be the finest people in Yorkshire—"

"In England—"

"And our son and our son's sons will live there forever." They gazed at each other in a rare moment of shared pleasure, and then Robert took her hand. "Oh, Eleanor, my dear wife," he said. "My father's dreams are coming real. If he were here now, he would be so happy and proud. As I am. I could never have hoped for a better wife. You make me so happy."

Eleanor gazed around her, past her husband to the rest of the household grouped around the smoldering log fire on its raised dais in the center of the great hall: she looked at her seven healthy, handsome children; her well-trained, much-valued house servants; the lusty, loyal retainers; and she saw that she had come a long way from that half-terrified, half-defiant green girl who had first come to Micklelith all those years ago. So much had happened, and yet she felt that they were only at the beginning of their story. She felt that a new chapter was about to begin.

CHAPTER SEVEN

The month was May, the loveliest month of the year, when the shallow and unsubstantial beauty of spring is deepening into the full richness of summer's verdure; when everything is bursting with life and vigor, and in the long golden days anything seems possible. Eleanor was infected with the gaiety of the "merry month," which started with the glorious madness of May Day's vernal celebrations. On May Day morning, before dawn, the young people had gone out to bring in the May, the garlands of wild flowers and sweet green boughs that were to decorate the house and form the bower for the May queen.

The tables and trestles had been carried out into the open air, and dinner taken there, the whole household together with their guests, Master Shawe and his little daughter, Cecily, and their servants. Then there had been a Robin Hood pageant, with Helen playing Maid Marian in a rather simpering manner, and a magnificent performance of the wicked sheriff by Job. Anne had been crowned as the May queen, and had sat in her bower while the children danced round the maypole, and then there had been morris dancing and sword dancing, the boys spurred on to higher leaps and wilder shouts by the ale that flowed like water. It had been a marvelous day, marred only slightly by the absence of Robert, who was spending more and more time away from the farm on business.

When he came back, a few days later, Eleanor had determined that he should have some pleasure, since he had missed the May Day frolic, and so she persuaded him to slip away with her after dinner, sneak their horses out of the stable, and ride over to see the new house. It was a wonderful golden afternoon, when the light lay soft and thick on the fields like butter, and only the lightest of breezes stirred the grass and the thick new leaves on the trees. It was a holiday, so there was no one about. From a long way away they could hear the peaceful bleating of the sheep and the tinkling of the bellwether's chimes; from a hedge a blackbird fountained out his spray of shining notes, and far above them the larks made love to the blue sky.

"It's so good to be home," Robert said happily as they walked their horses through the lush fields. "The one penalty of riches and status is that they take me away from home too much. Especially at times like this."

"I've been lonely, too," Eleanor said, discovering it only then.

"You have the family and all the household around you," Robert said. "How can you be lonely?" He meant it simply. He could never believe that he meant anything to her.

"I've missed you," Eleanor admitted. "I've had no one to talk to in the evenings."

They rode on in silence, strangely shy with each other for two people who had been married almost fifteen years. They came through a break in the copse, and there was the new house before them, its rosy brick glowing pleasantly in the afternoon sun.

"It *is* a lovely house," Eleanor said. "It's almost finished now—it should be ready by next winter if all goes as planned."

"It's a handsome house," Robert said. "Those tall chimneys, and the great windows with the colored glass—"

"Imagine it when the moat's been dug and filled with water, and the gardens laid out on the south side," Eleanor put in, "and the great trees—the beech and oak—"

"The trees won't be at their best for a hundred years at least," Robert pointed out. "We shan't see them."

"Our children's children may. It's a grand house, on a grand scale. We mustn't be niggardly with time any more

than with money or with space." They looked at it happily
for a moment, and then Eleanor said, "Let's go in."

Robert looked slightly surprised, and then he smiled.
"All right. We'll look round. It will be the only time we'll
ever be alone there."

They left their horses in the inner courtyard and walked
together through the airy, empty rooms. The hall had great
soaring hammer beams, and its tall stone-mullioned oriel
windows, set into the thickness of the walls, were roofed
with delicate fan-vaulting. The sun flowed in through the
colored glass of the windows to leave jewel-bright pools on
the floor, as if rubies and sapphires and emeralds had
somehow been melted there.

They went upstairs through the silent house to the solar.
It was not near completion—the window was a hole in the
wall, letting in the balmy May air, and the walls were bare
brick, awaiting their paneling. Eleanor walked across the
broad, fair boards to the window and looked out over the
burgeoning countryside.

"The view is wonderful," she said. "It's going to be a
lovely room, winter or summer."

"I can't even think of winter on a day like this," Robert
said, walking over to join her. "The air smells like wine—I
feel almost drunk with it." Eleanor turned to smile at him.
"How beautiful you are," he said softly. "Like a rose."

"My lord is learning to say pretty things like a courtier,"
Eleanor said gently.

"Not like a courtier," Robert said. "I really mean everything I say. I know I've never been more than half a man
to you—" Eleanor lifted her hand in protest to stop him,
and he caught it and kissed it. They stared at each other,
feeling a strange sympathy flowing between them. It was
true what Robert had said. His love for her had always
unmanned him, and he had never been much of a lover to
her. All sexual commerce between them had ceased after
the conception of their last child, Harry, almost seven years
ago. Since then Robert had been away so much, and when
at home the old trouble had prevented him from daring to
attempt to make love to her.

"It's true," he said now, holding her hand in both his.

"But you know that it isn't because I don't love you—it's because I've always loved you too much."

"Robert—" Eleanor began, but she did not know what she wanted to say.

"But seeing you here now fires my blood. You are more beautiful than when I first saw you. You are as beautiful as May."

He drew her against him and kissed her tenderly, while the soft breeze fluttered around them, kissing their skin like the touch of a butterfly's wing. Privacy was almost an unknown commodity in their world, and it acted on them like a draft of wine. Tenderness gave way in his kisses before passion, and soon his strong fingers were pulling at the fastenings of her gown. His surcoat and her gown made a bed for them on the floor; Robert pressed her down gently while his fingers caressed her throat and breast, sending moth-wings of sensation fluttering through her body.

Eleanor had never known sensation like this. The deep springs of passion in her nature had never been touched before; she was in her heart still a virgin, but now as he kissed and caressed her she began to yield, the barriers began to break down and let through a flood of sweet, mad passion that threatened to overwhelm her. There was no difficulty this time; Robert was master of the situation, Eleanor was yielding and clinging, their minds flowed in sympathy and their movements harmonized, as they moved together cleanly, like swimmers in a current, coming together to that place where they had never before been able to meet.

And afterward he wiped the good sweat from her brow, and she smiled a little, peacefully.

"I love you so much," he said.

"I never knew before," Eleanor said, "what it could be."

And the deep silence of the summer afternoon poured in around them and held them in their dream like the nautilus locked in the heart of the crystal.

The child conceived of that strange, dreamlike episode was born in the February of 1450. It was a boy, and he was named John. He was born into a country that was seething with unrest. The war was going badly, despite the excellent soldiering of Lord Edmund Beaufort—now Duke of Somerset. The Council had deprived itself of the services of the other great soldier of the day, the Duke of York. He had been given the appointment of Lord Lieutenant of Ireland, which was tantamount to banishment. Richard resisted taking up his appointment as long as possible, but, once having gone to Ireland, typically he made the best of it, established peace, and made himself a lot of friends.

That same February the Council at last managed to detach the unpopular Suffolk, the Queen's creature, from his royal mistress, and indict him. Lord Edmund was unwilling actually to execute him, and so in April he was exiled forever; but the people were not content with that, and the ship bearing him away was intercepted, he was roughly beheaded on deck, and his body unceremoniously thrown out on Dover Sands. At the Queen's request, King Henry ordered the body to be recovered and decently buried, and that caused more dissent.

It was an expensive thing to wage war, especially an unsuccessful war, and the Council had to raise the money by taxes. In June of that year the most heavily taxed class, the gentry, rebelled, and under the leadership of one Jack Cade marched on London to protest the extortion they had suffered at the hands of the government's agents. The rebellion was put down quite easily, but there was a lot of talk that it had been promoted by the Duke of York, especially since Cade himself demanded that the Duke of York be given back his rightful place on the Council.

And hardly had the home counties settled down again after that, when the Duke himself came back from Ireland, raised an army in the Marches, and took himself to London. Lord Edmund Beaufort, who was conducting the war in France at the time, was hastily called home to deal with this new threat, and so the two men who had once been friends met again in hostility.

Robert, who had been in London at the time, described it afterward to Eleanor. Whether or not Richard Plantagenet had meant any serious threat was the one thing that they argued about.

"You could see he meant no evil," Eleanor claimed

hotly. "The very first thing he did was to swear allegiance to the King."

"He didn't mean it—it was simply a show, meant to disarm any opposition," Robert argued.

"He did mean it. You don't know him—he would never swear anything he didn't mean. And he's loyal to the crown. It's the first thing a soldier learns—loyalty to the King."

"Then why did he bring an army with him?" Robert said. "That doesn't look like a peaceful, loyal man simply coming to say hello to the King."

"He needed the army because of his enemies. They'd have stopped him coming at all if they could. Particularly the Queen. Look what happened to Duke Humphrey."

"It's never been proved that he was murdered," Robert protested. "He may simply have died of natural causes."

"Very conveniently," Eleanor sneered. "And suppose the Duke of York had just conveniently died between Wales and London?"

"A bodyguard would have done. He didn't need a whole army. He must have meant to take over."

"If he'd meant to, he would have done it. No one could have stopped him. But what did he do? Swear allegiance to the King."

"And demand to be recognized as heir to the throne instead of Lord Edmund."

"As is his right. By right of blood, the true blood. He is heir by rightful line, descended from the second son of King Edward, while the King is only from the third son, and a usurper."

"Since when has blood been the deciding factor?" Robert said quickly. "There's no hard and fast rule as to who should succeed. It's the strongest that wins, and if the king is weak, as the last king Richard was—"

"And as our present King is," Eleanor said triumphantly. Robert stared at her, backed into a corner by his own argument. "You see? Either way, he should be the heir."

"Well, I'm for our own Lord Edmund, whatever you say," Robert said firmly. "We owe him our faith, and he's the heir to the present king and of the line that's been in

power for the past fifty years, however it got there in the
first place. Lord Edmund's as strong as your Lord Richard,
and he'll make a good king."

"But his line's illegitimate. He *can't* reign. The Duke of
York is the only *legitimate* heir."

The argument went on unproductively, for they could
not meet on this ground. Eleanor was for the bloodlines,
the legitimate heir who could trace himself clearly back to
the king without taint of illegitimacy. Robert was more
simply for the status quo and for the man to whom he
owed his prosperity; but they wrangled on the whole good-
naturedly, feeling no threat in the air, and aware that nothing they could do would alter anything anyway.

It was in that August that the new house was finally finished. It had taken longer than first expected because Robert and Eleanor had thought of several improvements they
wanted made, but now it was as near perfect as anything
on earth could be. As Isabella said, "Even the stables are
like palaces." The final touch was the white stone panel set
into the rosy brick above the great door on which was
carved the Morland device of a sprig of heather and Elean-
or's white running hare; and above it the date, 1450, and
below it *Deo Gratias*, thanks be to God. It gave that final
touch of elegance.

The house, with its stained glass windows, moat, and tall
chimneys, was unlike anything within a day's riding and
was a talking point in the district as enduring as the
French war. They called it Morland Place, for this was to
be the home and foundation of the dynasty they hoped they
had begun. They moved into it on Lammas, and the blessing of the house was the first official action of the young
clerk who was to be their household chaplain. Green
boughs were hung everywhere, and a table was set with
food and drink for everyone who arrived to welcome them
to their new home—which was pretty nearly everyone
within ten miles who had enough legs to carry them.

A fortnight later it was Anne's fifteenth birthday, and
on the eve of this great occasion Eleanor took the girl into
the solar to speak to her alone. Eleanor surveyed her eldest
daughter with satisfaction.

"You are looking very well, my dear child," she said, unconsciously echoing her guardian's words to her on a similar occasion. "You have a fine color in your cheeks. And tomorrow you will be fifteen years old."

"Yes," said Anne, smiling and unsuspecting. "I only wish my father would be here for it."

"Do you know where your father has gone?" Eleanor asked. Anne shook her head. Her father was away so often it never occurred to her to wonder where he was. "It is on your account he has gone this time, child," Eleanor said. Anne's cheeks took on an even more rosy color as she began to have an inkling as to what was coming.

"On my account, madam?"

"Yes. He has gone to arrange for your betrothal. Fifteen is a great age for a girl to be unmarried. I would have liked to marry you last year, but your father wished to keep you at home." Eleanor's voice was disapproving. A lord's or a gentleman's daughters left home very young. It was not a gentlemanly sentiment to want to keep your daughter at home until she was fifteen, and Eleanor felt that was Robert's bad blood coming out.

"You were not married until you were eighteen, madam," Anne pointed out. "You told me so yourself."

"I was not boasting when I told you that. It was hard for my master to find a match for me because I had no dowry. You, Anne, have a large dowry, and your father will have no difficulty in arranging the match we want."

"May I know who it is?" Anne asked in a small voice. Eleanor walked up and down the room, her silken skirts rustling against the floorboards.

"It is a very good match for you," she said. "When my brother died, my father's estate passed to my cousin, but it was much encumbered. The estate has since been cleared, and is now a very valuable property, a large area of good farmland in Dorset, and three houses. He has five hundred sheep." Eleanor paused for Anne's comment on this wealth, but her eyes were fixed on the floor and she said nothing. "Your husband is to be my cousin's son and heir, John Courteney."

Anne looked up at this point. Her eyes were bright with tears, but she had control of herself still. "John Courteney," she whispered, as if trying the name on her tongue. Eleanor's expression softened into a smile and impulsively she took her daughter's hands.

"You shall have my name, my dear—you shall be Anne Courteney, Mistress Anne Courteney. And it will bring the land back into my family—all the land that would have been mine if I had been a boy. Think of that!"

"It is so far away," Anne said in a small voice. Eleanor squeezed the hand she held.

"You will not mind that. You are a sensible girl—the only one of my daughters, I sometimes think, who has any sense at all," she added grimly. "You always knew that you would have to go away some time."

"I didn't know it would be so far."

Eleanor ignored this. "You will be going back to my home. You'll love Dorset—it's a warmer, greener land than this. And the sea is everywhere. That's what I miss most, the sound of the sea." She turned her eyes to the window and gazed out unseeingly. "You will go home to my country just as I came north all those years ago. You'll be happy there."

Anne looked into her mother's face searchingly. "Were you unhappy when you came here, Mother?" Eleanor smiled, aware that she had given too much away.

"Of course I was homesick at first—that's to be expected. But I had never expected to be married, and I had been at home a good deal longer than you. You will soon forget your home here. Once you are mistress of your own house, you will find everything else fades away."

"But you still miss your home?" Anne persisted anxiously.

"This is my home, child," Eleanor said, smiling into those worried gray-green eyes, that fair rosy face always a little too solemn. She stroked the rounded cheek. "A woman's home is wherever her master takes her. Your cousin John is a fine young man, a little older than you, but that's as it should be."

"Is he handsome?"

Eleanor did not know. "Yes," she said. Anne appeared to consider this.

"When am I to go?" she asked a little more cheerfully.

"I cannot tell exactly until your father returns. I should have thought next month, perhaps. The betrothal will take place here, and then you will go to live with your father-in-law for a few months until the marriage."

"I see. And you are glad about it?"

"I shall be happy to see you well placed. We must see about finding good matches for your sisters as soon as possible—I hope they may be as advantageous."

"So I have a few weeks left?"

"Enjoy them, my child, and then look forward to your new life with your husband. Do your duty by him, and you will be happy."

"Yes, madam. May I go now?"

Anne was very quiet for the rest of the day, which was only to be expected. That evening when they were all gathered in the hall Anne asked Job to play a game of chess with her, and withdrew a little way with him to get the quiet necessary for the game. Glancing across a little while later Eleanor saw the game suspended and the two of them deep in a very serious conversation, Anne asking questions and Job expounding answers. When the children had all withdrawn to bed, Eleanor called Job over and asked him what they had been talking about.

"Anne was telling me about her betrothal," he said.

"I thought she might be—but what was she asking you?"

Job smiled. "She wanted to know how her mother took it when a similar fate befell her."

"Not so similar," Eleanor objected. "I was older and had less to look forward to. At least she will speak the same language as her household. Oh, Job, do you remember those days when you had to translate my orders for me?"

"I remember. I told Anne about them, to show her how hard it had been for you and how much easier it would be for her, but she didn't seem impressed."

"Why not?"

"Modesty forbids me to repeat her answer."

"Modesty? What do you mean? What did she say? I demand you tell me."

Job gave a mock reluctant sigh. "If you order me, how

can I refuse? When I told her the hardships you had borne so nobly, she said, 'It can't have been so hard for mother. She had you, Job.' "

Eleanor laughed and dismissed him. It was only afterwards in the quiet of the night that she recalled Anne's expression as she faced him across the chess table and wondered if he might have been serious.

The betrothal took place on the thirtieth of August in the small but beautiful chapel on the east side of the house. Anne was dressed in white brocade and primrose silk with a simple veil of lawn over her golden hair, and as she took her vows beside her husband-to-be, she seemed suddenly content, and smiled up at him with trust. He was a fine young man, as Eleanor had said, tall and broad-shouldered with the Dorset auburn hair and blue eyes and more freckles even than Isabella, which gave his face a merry look, even when he was solemn. The young people seemed to take to each other at once, for there was good sense on both sides, and they may well have each privately decided to make the best of things.

As she knelt with her family around her, Eleanor's mind wandered a little from her devotions. Anne was well settled, and they had already heard of a possible match for Helen, a widower of twenty-three, a spice merchant who lived in the city and who would be able to keep Helen in the luxuries she liked. Lovely, Helen looked as she knelt in her new silk gown, her face set in serious mold as she thought it should be on that occasion: pretty, silly Helen would make light of leaving home, would revel in the new clothes and the ceremonies and of being the center of attention. She played to an audience all the time, and would as gladly play the part of devoted wife as any other.

Isabella was a different kettle of fish. Before the ceremony, when the girls had come up to kiss Anne and wish her well, Isabella had squeezed her sister and said:

"I'm glad it's you and not me, Anne. I don't want ever to get married. I want to stay here on the farm and help Father with the sheep, and go hawking with Job."

With a large enough dowry Isabella would be no more difficult to get rid of than her sisters, but she wouldn't like it one bit. She was at the end of the row of benches now, as near as possible to Job, who was across the aisle on the servants' side. She looked for once almost pretty, having been forcibly cleaned and tidied and put into her new gown and forbidden to stir out of the house before the ceremony by Anys; but even as Eleanor looked, Isabella caught Job's eye across the aisle and winked at him and gestured with her head toward the altar as if the betrothal were a tremendous joke. Eleanor was glad to see Job shake his head reprovingly and look away.

Between Helen and Eleanor sat the boys: Edward, just twelve years old and beginning to fill out a little into his manly shape; then Harry, a month off seven years old; and beside his mother, Thomas, nearly nine and as beautiful and charming a boy as you would find anywhere—his mother's firm favorite. The baby John was in Anys's arms in the row behind. The boys would be no problem—under Master Jenney's care they were brought up to be manly, learned, and obedient. She had given Robert four sons—she had done her duty, and could only hope that Anne would do hers as well.

On the second of September the party set out for Dorset, and there were farewells both happy and tearful in the courtyard of Morland Place. Anne curtsied to her mother and father, and Robert touched her cheek and said:

"Be a good girl, my darling. It isn't farewell for us—I'll see you from time to time when I come down to Dorset."

"Yes, Father. I'm glad of that—it doesn't make me feel so much as if I've been cast off."

"Do your duty, Anne, and God will bless you," Robert said. Anne hugged her brothers and sisters and promised to write to Helen, who was weeping openly.

"I don't know what I shall do without you, Anne," she said. "I wish I could come with you."

"You'll be going to a place of your own soon," Anne said comfortingly, but she would not be consoled. Isabella was more sanguine.

"I hope you have lots of horses," she said. "Mother says there's good hunting in Dorset. Perhaps I'll ride down to see you one day."

"Not until you're grown up," Anne said, horrified at the

thought of her wild sister stealing off one morning and attempting to ride alone across the length of England. It was just the sort of thing Isabella might try. "Do remember you're a woman now."

Isabella made a face. "Father says I should have been a boy. I'm not going to be a woman until I absolutely have to."

Anne kissed the baby and gave Anys a convulsive hug to thank her for all the good care she had taken of her over the years.

"You'll be a credit to me, darling," Anys whispered through her tears.

"I'll try, Anys. I'll write to you," Anne promised, and turned hastily away before she broke down too. The horses were ready, and Anne was to ride pillion behind a servant of her new family. Job was holding the horse, and was ready with the mounting block and his outstretched hand. As she placed her small white hand in his strong brown one, Anne looked up into his face searchingly, and he smiled reassuringly at her, a smile which she could only return wistfully.

"Remember what I told you," Job said. Anne nodded.

"I'll try. Will I ever see you again, Job?"

"No," he said. "But it doesn't matter."

Anne's lip trembled. "I'll try and remember that, too," she said bravely. Job swung her up onto the pillion. "Goodbye," she said.

"God bless you," he said, and turned away.

The Courteney party clattered out of the yard on the first leg of their long journey south, and the Morlands waved them out of sight, and then scattered about their business. Anys and Master Jenney gathered up the children and began shooing them in the direction of their studies, and as Helen wiped the tears from her eyes, Isabella said to her scornfully:

"I don't know why you're crying. You aren't the one to have to go away."

"I shall miss her. And she'll miss me," Helen said, sniffing. Isabella snorted.

"That's not why she was crying," she said scornfully.

"She was crying because she's in love with Job. Silly creature. Job's fun—all this love is just nonsense. I'll never fall in love, you can bet your life."

"Enough of that talk, Isabella," Anys said sternly, hearing only the last part. "When you are married you'll love your husband, as any good woman does. And that will be right."

She hustled the children indoors, and as she went on ahead Isabella whispered incorrigibly to Helen.

"There's another one in love with Job. How he does get about, to be sure!"

"Hush, 'Bella, or I'll tell Mother," Helen retorted righteously. Isabella stuck out her tongue and ran on up the stairs, her skirts flying.

CHAPTER EIGHT

Morland Place was a ferment of activity: servants were sweeping floors, laying fresh rushes, scrubbing benches and trestles, washing windows, beating and freshening hangings; in the kitchen Jacques and his assistants and boys were already sweating over a menu larger than any of them had seen before, devising new dishes and planning subtleties; upstairs the family was looking over its clothes, deciding on new outfits, planning entertainments. A guest chamber was being prepared with the best the house could provide in the way of furniture, counterpanes, hangings, cushions, and other necessaries of genteel life. A great day was approaching: Morland Place was expecting a visit from Richard Plantagenet, otherwise his grace the Duke of York, Earl of March, Earl of Rutland, Earl of Ulster, Earl of Cambridge, Lord of Clare, Trim, Connaught, and Ossory.

Eleanor and Robert were delighted at the prospect, not only because of the high honor of entertaining such a noble person, but because only a few months before such a visit would have been impossible. In the February of that year, 1452, the Duke of York had simultaneously declared his allegiance to King Henry and his enmity for Edmund Beaufort, and had raised an army and marched on London. With him had gone two of Eleanor's Courteney cousins—the Earl of Devon, and in that Earl's train John Courteney, the husband of Anne.

It had been a painful episode for the Morlands to witness. Anne was at home nursing her firstborn son, who was then only a few weeks old; her husband's allegiance was to the Earl of Devon, whose loyalty was with the Duke of York, who was marching against Robert's friend and patron. Eleanor could not help siding with the York-Courteney cause, especially now that Lord Edmund was so closely allied with the Queen, whom Eleanor hated. It split the family quite effectively down the middle.

In the summer the French war had continued its disastrous course and the last of England's possessions was finally lost with the fall of Bordeaux. Now all England had of her French lands was Calais, and the people were naturally angry, and resentful that all the heavy taxes they had paid had achieved so little. The Queen had therefore decided to take the King on a progress through the land to try to quieten the populace, and they set off in October.

At that time the Duke of York was at home in Fotheringay, where his Duchess had just laid in of her eleventh child, a puny boy-child they called Richard after his father. Of the other ten children, six had survived infancy: the two elder girls, Anne and Elizabeth, were residing with noble families for their education; the two elder boys, Edward and Edmund, had their own establishment at Ludlow in the Marches; and only the two youngest, Margaret and George, were at home in Fotheringay.

The Duke had been in virtual arrest since his abortive attempt of February at regaining his position on the Council, but the King liked and trusted Richard, and took a notion to visit him at home while on his progress north. A happy reconciliation was the result: Richard swore his faith to the King, and the King proclaimed his love for Richard, and in the face of so public a declaration the Queen and Lord Edmund could only make gracious noises.

The royal household then went on to York, and the Duke and his Duchess were to attend the King there, and to stay a night in Morland Place as a sign of good faith and a compliment to Lord Edmund. Robert felt that compliment very keenly. He was one of the richest men in Yorkshire, a master stapler and the protégé of the heir apparent to the throne; but the visit proved that he was of high enough standing for his friendship to have political significance. It was more than he had ever hoped for—his father would have been happy!

As for Eleanor, when she heard the news she trembled so much that she had to find an excuse to leave the room and seek the privacy of the garden. Richard Plantagenet, under her roof! She would see him again for the first time in twenty years, see in the flesh the man whose image was never far from her mind, whose life and career she had followed with close and painful attention from a distance she never thought to see reduced again. She sat down in a bower and put her hands over her face and tried to tell herself that she was behaving ridiculously, but all she could think was, "I shall see him again! I shall speak to him again!"—a litany of insane joy.

She was still in the same position when Job found her. "Mistress!" he called to her, but she did not remove her hands from her face or answer him. He knelt down in front of her and took hold of her wrists to try to pull her hands away.

"Go away," she said, her voice muffled.

"Mistress, listen to me," Job began.

"You don't understand," Eleanor said.

"I do. Mistress—Eleanor, listen." His voice was low, urgent. "You know my loyalty to you. Lord Edmund sent me with you when I was no more than a child. You know that I love you—I would give my life for you." Eleanor slowly lowered her hands from her face and stared at him, seeing some of her anguish mirrored in his eyes. "I tell you, you must not let it show. Whatever is in your heart, lock it up there, never let anyone know what you feel—*especially not him.*"

Eleanor did not need to ask which him was referred to. Job saw her understanding and acquiescence in her face. "You know that I'm right. It could destroy you, and everything you have. Go in now, behave normally in front of the master. He does not yet suspect. You *must.*"

"Yes," she whispered. "You're right."

He released her wrists and got to his feet, standing back from her respectfully as if he had simply knelt to serve her at the table. Eleanor stood up, smoothed her skirts, feeling almost without knowing it the familiar heavy jerk as her missal fell to the length of its chain attached to her ceinture. She turned to go, and then looked back at her steward, her loyal friend.

"Job—I'm sorry," she said. It was painful to say, as painful for him to hear. His mouth made a wry attempt at a smile.

"It doesn't matter," he said, much as he had said to Anne on the day she went away. "When you give your faith, you give it forever."

"Yes," said Eleanor. "I understand." And she held her head high, and went in.

It was easier after that to hide her feelings. She flung herself wholeheartedly into the preparations, and allowed only her natural joy to appear. The Duke and Duchess were to come to dinner and stay for the night, traveling on the next morning. Some of their retinue would be housed in Morland Place, along with the Morlands' own servants, but a large part of it could not possibly have been fitted in, and it was lucky therefore that Micklelith and Twelvetrees were both near enough for the Duke's retainers to be sheltered for the night. Guests had to be invited for the dinner—just one or two, of sufficient importance for the Duke not to feel insulted or bored. Helen and her husband would be there—she had been married last year to the spice-merchant, John Butler, and Eleanor could only hope that they would be sufficiently in awe of the occasion not to open their mouths, for she had no very great opinion of either.

The day had come. Jacques had surpassed himself and produced a banquet fit for a king at least, and Eleanor was sitting at the high table hardly able to taste a single one of those wonderful dishes, because beside her was the man who turned her bones to water and made her feel as helpless and silly as a child. She had stood trembling like a green girl in the courtyard of her house as he rode in at the head of his train, wondering what he would think of her after all this time. A moment before, she had felt she looked beautiful in her new gown: a surcoat of kingfisher-blue velvet, with ermine, over a cotte of gold brocade. The

surcoat had great hanging sleeves lined with white silk brocaded with gold; her headdress of white and gold bore a
long veil of gauze under a frontpiece of stiffened muslin
that framed her face and drew attention to her broad forehead and large eyes.

But as soon as the horses turned in at the gate, her assurance leaked out of her like water from a sieve, and only
the knowledge that Job was standing right behind her
stopped her sagging at the knees with this foolish weakness.
And he had arrived, jumped from his horse, exchanged
greetings. She had heard his voice again, looked into his
face, given and received the customary kisses of welcome.
And he was not changed, not a bit. Oh, of course he was
older—there were more lines on his face, lines of authority
and of sadness as well as the lines of good humor and
laughter. And his hair was turning gray—the sight touched
Eleanor unbearably, though she did not know why. But the
essential man was the same. He was the same stocky,
broad-shouldered, soldierly man that he had been, with the
same frank, open face, and the eyes that seemed to look
past your face into your soul. He greeted Eleanor with a
smile and a kiss, and said:

"Why, mistress Morland, you are as lovely as I remember," and she was his, in her heart, forever.

And now at dinner Eleanor was glad that he was seated
beside her and his Duchess beside Robert, for she did not
think she could have found anything to say to her. In the
first moment of seeing them together Eleanor had seen that
he really loved his wife, that woman who had been called
in her youth The Rose of Raby, and who was still possessed
of a golden beauty that made any young woman beside her
pale into insignificance. But seated beside him and at a
distance from either her husband or his wife, Eleanor could
enjoy for a little while his undivided attention. Her nervousness and shyness had disappeared almost at once, melt-
ing like snow before the warmth of his frank, good-
humored enjoyment of the situation. He praised the food,
the entertainment, and the house, and then turned the conversation to her.

"You're looking well," he said. "In truth, you've not
changed at all from the way I remember you—but I dare-

say you don't remember dancing with me at Corfe, do you? It was a long time ago."

"I remember perfectly, my lord," Eleanor said. "And you haven't changed either."

He laughed. "Why, mistress, that's nothing but the barest flattery! Shame on you, talking like a courtier!"

"No, no, I assure you," Eleanor said, straight-faced. "And I have kept as one of my greatest treasures the gift you gave me the following Christmas, which I dare swear *you* have forgotten." And she drew up from her skirts the missal. As his eyes fell on it she saw he *had* forgotten and there was no reason why he should not have. He took it in his hand, smoothing the leather with his fingers in a way that would have told even a complete stranger that he loved books, despite his calling as a soldier.

"I am truly flattered that you have kept such a small gift all this time. You must have had a kind opinion of me."

"Always, my lord," Eleanor said firmly.

"In spite of—" He cast his eyes around the room, indicating all she must have received at the hands of her former guardian.

"I owe a great deal of loyalty to Lord Edmund," Eleanor said quietly. "But I honor justice more. And I am, after all, a Courteney."

Richard's eyes flickered to see that they were not overheard, and he said in a low voice, "So you are. And cousin to my lord of Devon, as I recall. Well, mistress *Courteney*"—he emphasized it with wry humor—"I owe much thanks to that family. I know how to appreciate loyalty."

"You can count on my family, too, my lord, most truly," Eleanor began earnestly, but a slight shake of his head warned her to desist as one of the pages came up to offer them the washing bowls and towels at the end of the course.

At the end of dinner there was dancing, and Eleanor was glad that etiquette demanded that Robert lead out the beautiful Duchess Cecily while Richard ask Eleanor to step out with him. Other couples then formed up behind them, and under the cover of the music and general conversation it was possible to talk again. It was Richard who revived the subject that interested them both.

"You speak of loyalty," he began. "It must have been hard for you to have your loyalty to your patron so tested."

He was sounding her out, Eleanor thought. "As I said, my lord, I honor justice, and justice was not done. You were wronged—"

"Do you know how wronged?" Richard asked her, low and urgent. "Did you know that a certain person tried on two occasions to have me killed?"

"You mean—*the Queen*?" Eleanor whispered, horrified.

"On my way to Ireland and on my way back. Secret agents were sent out, to intercept me. I was not intended to reach the King's ear, nor the Council's table, again."

"And did Lord Edmund know about this?"

"Assuredly. That is why—"

"You took the army to London?"

He nodded. "He has pursued a bad policy in France, and lined his pockets at the people's expense. And *she* is intent on killing me, though why she hates me, I don't know."

"I think I know," Eleanor said. It was necessary for her to say as incriminating a thing as he had, so that he might know he could trust her. "She is afraid of the blood of kings. The true blood."

She looked into his face, trying to imprint on it all her love and loyalty, trying to make him know her. His eyes looked into her soul, it seemed, and read what was there.

"If it should come to war," he said at length, "could we count on you?" He glanced sideways at the couple at the head of the dance. "On him?"

"My lord, I do not rule him, but I can influence him. If I cannot persuade him to fight for you, at least he will not fight against you."

He nodded and then quickly changed the subject, smiling a quite different smile. "Is that your daughter in the scarlet dress? I thought so—she's the image of you."

"She's called Eleanor, too, but we call her Helen, because of her beauty." Eleanor went along with him, knowing he was a skilled campaigner.

"And I must dance with your other daughter—Isabella, isn't it? She looks like a young lady of spirit."

"She would be honored if you would, my lord. She admires nothing more than a soldier."

Richard led Isabella, red as a poppy at the honor, out for the next dance, while Eleanor took the floor with a gentleman of Richard's household. She watched them in pleased amusement, seeing how kindly he drew the awkward girl out, and seeing how, as the dance progressed, Isabella gradually found her tongue and began to chatter freely. Toward the end of the dance Eleanor and her partner were standing beside Richard and Isabella, and Eleanor could hear the latter's healthy young voice saying:

"Oh, of course I was betrothed last year when I was fourteen, but when Father got the new manor out by Bishopthorpe, Mother canceled it because she said he wasn't good enough for me."

"And did you mind?" Richard asked, his firm lips hardly twitching, though his eyes danced with amusement.

"No, I was glad," Isabella averred stoutly. "He was such a milksop. I don't want to be married at all—I hope I never marry—but if I do, I hope at least that he'll be someone who can ride and hunt and fight. Someone jolly like that."

"So you'd like to be a soldier's wife?"

"If I've got to be anyone's—I shouldn't mind someone like you."

Richard laughed at that, and catching Eleanor's eye he said:

"No, don't scold her. There's nothing of the courtier in your daughter, at any rate, and that's a refreshing change." He bowed to his partner. "Mistress Isabella, I thank you sincerely for the compliment." And that effectively silenced her.

Eleanor could not sleep. The night was clear, and there was a brilliant hunter's moon whose blue-white light was filtering in through a gap in the bed-curtains and shining in her eyes. Robert was asleep, well asleep with the combination of good food and good wine and much dancing, but Eleanor was wide awake with the knowledge that He was under her roof, asleep only feet away from her in the guestchamber.

Tomorrow he would leave with his wife and his retinue and his servants and his baggage, and for all she knew she might never see him again. To sleep would be to waste these precious hours of his nearness. The house was silent and still, every creature but herself sleeping soundly. Carefully she sat up, slid her legs over the edge of the bed, and slipped out through the curtains. If anyone woke, she was simply going to the garderobe. The moon's light flooded in like molten silver, picking out the quiet humps of the other sleepers. She crossed the room quietly and went out into the passage and walked the few steps to the door of the guestchamber.

There she stopped. Impossible to go in! She put her hands against the broad, smooth oak of the door, and then rested her forehead on it, and thought of him and how hopeless it was. And as she turned away from the door, it opened, and he came out.

"I thought I heard something," he whispered. "I sleep lightly these days. It seems you couldn't sleep either?"

She looked up at him, and there was no need for her to tell him what she wanted, for it was written on her face. He hesitated only a moment, and then took the step toward her; one hard soldier's hand held her by the waist, feeling the softness of her flesh through her thin nightgown; the other passed around her body, fingers splayed against her back, and drew her against him as he bent his head to kiss her. His mouth came down on hers, his tongue was in her mouth; skilled love-maker that he was, her response surprised him. Her hands came up to rest on either side of his face as she kissed him; he felt the heat of her body and her hard nipples pressing against him through the fine linen.

After a moment he lifted his head and gazed down into her eyes.

"I didn't know it was like this for you," he said softly.

"Always," she said. "Since that night when you danced with me, and you kissed me in the garden—since then." She stroked his face, hardly knowing what she was doing.

"Oh, my dear," he said sadly. "You know that even then I was bethrothed to Cecily."

"I know that now."

"You know that I love her."

"I know. And I'm glad for you. But it doesn't make any difference to me. I've always loved you."

For answer he kissed her again, holding her close and stroking her long dark hair, and then he put her back a little and looked at her. "You're very beautiful," he said. "I've never seen you with your hair loose before. I'd like to make love to you, but there's nowhere we can go. Not with a house full of servants." He continued to stroke her hair, and she gazed up at him, mesmerized by his presence and her love. The moon, moving around, was leaving them in darkness. He would leave her soon, because there was nothing else to be done.

"Kiss me again," she whispered; and when, reluctantly, their lips parted, she said, "You can trust me, you know, in spite of this. I will do all I can to help you, and your family, always. Do you know this?"

"I know. I trust you. I understand what you want to say."

"Do you think it will come to war?" It did not seem strange to be saying these things while their hands still avidly caressed each other's bodies.

"She means to kill me. God knows I never wanted it to come to this, but I mean to live, and if that means taking the throne—I'll do it. It has been her doing, if we are enemies. I'll keep the peace while I can, but if she forces me to it, I will have to kill her to live."

"You are the rightful king," Eleanor said. "I will support you. Does your wife—?"

"Cecily will stand shoulder to shoulder with me through anything God sends. She is the best wife a soldier could have." He spoke with simple sincerity. There was no deviousness in him—he was a simple man, an honest man, a soldier.

"I will stand by her and your children as by you," Eleanor said. He kissed her brow one last time, and then stood back from her. It was dark now in the passage and they could not see each other's faces. From the door of his room he said:

"I hope we meet again, but if we don't—I shan't forget you, or your promise. God bless you, Eleanor Courteney."

"God keep you, my lord," she whispered.

2

The Morland family was attending the Easter Sunday service at the Minster in the city, as usual. As they stepped out of the great east door into the bright spring sunshine, Isabella lifted her head with a sense of regained freedom and breathed in deeply, catching the smell of grass and flowers even through the normal stench of a city. She had been sorely troubled during the service by a young man sitting on the benches across the aisle from her, who had continually grinned and winked and pulled faces at her, so that she had a hard job to stop herself from laughing. She glanced around her now and was not surprised to see him quite near her, still smiling at her. She frowned, and he slipped through the crowds to her side.

"What do you want?" she said crossly. "What did you mean by making faces at me?"

"I wanted to make you laugh," he said openly. He was a little older than Isabella, she guessed, perhaps eighteen or nineteen. He was not a handsome youth, but he had a pleasant, good-humored face, and his clothes were those of a rich man's son. "You looked like a merry maiden—you looked as though you wanted to laugh—so I thought I'd oblige."

"Laugh—in church?" Isabella said disapprovingly.

"Why not? Today one ought to be happy—it's the day Our Lord rose from the dead. He'd want us to laugh and be happy."

Isabella considered this and found it reasonable. She glanced over her shoulder to where her parents were talking with neighbors a little way off.

"My mother mustn't see us talking," she said, edging him a little farther away.

"Why? Are you troth-plighted to someone?"

"No, not now. But she'd be angry if she saw me talking to a stranger. She's pregnant, and that always makes her temper worse."

"Well, I'll introduce myself, then I won't be a stranger, will I? My name's Luke."

"Mine's Isabella."

"I know who you are—your father's Master Morland, who entertained the Duke of York last November."

"That's right," Isabella said, and added proudly, "I danced with him. He's nice."

"Do you like dancing?"

"Very much. Do you?"

"Of course. I say, will you dance with me on May Day?"

"How can I?" Isabella said scornfully. "We have our own celebrations up at the house. I dare say you'll be in the city somewhere."

"I'll come to your celebrations," he said. Isabella gasped at his daring, and instinctively lowered her voice.

"How? How could you do it? You'll be seen."

"I could slip away from here easily enough. My tutor doesn't keep much of an eye on me now. And when I get to your place—there must be dozens of young people there, mustn't there? I'll dress up as a servant or a yeoman or something."

"People come in from the villages to us—and there're all the farm people and their children," Isabella said, liking his plan. "But suppose you get caught?"

"I'll get a beating, I suppose," he said carelessly, "but I won't get caught. Look for me, then, Mistress Isabella. And don't dance with any more lords or I'll be jealous."

And then he was gone, slipping through the crowds like an eel. Isabella was not left to wonder about his abrupt departure, for the next moment she heard her mother's voice behind her.

"Isabella—what are you doing, girl? We are ready to leave now. What were you staring at?"

"Nothing, Mother," Isabella said sullenly. Eleanor sighed. She really found this daughter of hers very trying. And as Isabella had said, she was pregnant again, and this time she was not feeling too well. She was tired and pale and irritable.

"The sooner we get you married, the better," Eleanor said. Isabella didn't answer. She was thinking of the merry-faced lad who would dare a beating to come and dance with her. If she could marry him, life might not be so dull.

* * *

May Day was as glorious a day as it ought to be. Job brought Eleanor a cup of ale as she sat watching the dancing, too heavy to be able to join in.

"Smile, mistress," he said. "Today's a day to be merry."

"I don't feel very merry, Job." Eleanor sighed. "I feel rather ill. And you've heard the bad news from Norwich?"

"About the Queen being pregnant? I was going to tell you."

"Robert told me. It's dreadful, isn't it?"

"I thought it was rather good news myself. It ought to mean the end of the rivalry between our two illustrious patrons, at least."

"You don't understand," Eleanor said impatiently. "She'll be even more anxious to kill him once she has a child to defend. She thinks he wants her throne. And with the King wandering in his mind, there'll be no one to stop her. Lord Edmund hates him just as much now."

Job leaned forward, his eyes twinkling. "Some say that Lord Edmund is the father."

"Job, I'm ashamed of you, repeating that sort of thing— and to the mistress," Robert said, coming up on them at that moment.

"Sorry, master. I was trying to cheer her up."

"I don't think there's anything in that to cheer her," Robert said.

"I wouldn't be surprised if it were true," Eleanor said irritably. "He's in her pocket often enough. I wouldn't be surprised if—"

"Eleanor, let's not talk about it now," Robert said warningly. They looked at each other tensely for a moment. The quarrel between them over Lord Edmund and the Duke of York had worsened in the past months: though nothing was said, Robert somehow knew how she felt about Richard, and she knew he knew. When they quarreled, the unspoken knowledge was always underneath.

"No, you're right," she said. "We should enjoy ourselves today. Let's watch the dancing. What on earth is Isabella doing? She keeps wandering around the dancers, but she never dances herself."

But even as they watched, a young man in leather jerkin

and green hose came up to her, bowed, and led her into the thick of the dancing.

"I thought you weren't going to come," Isabella said breathlessly, holding his hand tightly as if afraid he might escape.

"I had to wait until my tutor was well settled with his jug of ale," Luke said. His eyes were dancing with merriment. "And then I had to get my horse out of the stables. There was only one old groom left on duty, so I took him up a flagon of ale, and he blessed my kind heart and quite soon I could have taken every horse out under his nose and he wouldn't have noticed."

Isabella laughed gleefully.

"You look very pretty when you laugh," Luke said, and Isabella flushed and felt the stirrings of a new emotion that confused her, and she cast about for a new topic of conversation.

"I have a horse of my own, too," she said. "Do you like hunting?"

"Yes—do you?" She nodded. "What's your horse like?"

"Would you like to see him? Come on then—"

It was easy enough with all that crowd to slip away and make their way to the stables. The dogs barked, and then seeing who it was left off and went back to their basking in the sunshine. Isabella's bay gelding came forward to sniff at her hands and nuzzle her.

"His name's Lyard," she said. "Isn't he beautiful?" She looked up and saw that Luke was not looking at the horse but at her. "Why do you look at me like that?" she asked uncomfortably.

"Don't you know?" he asked, stepping nearer.

"I—" she began. And then in a panic: "Someone's coming!"

"Meet me tomorrow," he said quickly. "It's a holiday. Can you get out on Lyard? We'll go for a ride."

"I don't know. I think so."

"Do you know Deadman's Copse? Meet me on the south side as early tomorrow morning as you can, I'll wait for you. I'll be there at dawn."

Excitement ran through Isabella's veins. She threw back her head. "I'll get out somehow. Now go—quickly!"

Luke delayed only long enough to kiss her hand, and with a cheerful grin he was gone, vaulting over the gate and haring across the in-paddock; just in time as Job came into the yard from the other end.

"Ah, Isabella," he said, just as if he hadn't known she was there.

"Hello, Job," she said nervously. She smiled. "Did you want me?"

"You aren't dancing," he said.

"I just came to see if Lyard was all right," she said with an unnatural laugh.

"Who was that with you?" Job asked carelessly.

"With me? Why should you think there was someone with me?"

"I heard you talking," Job said.

"I was talking to the horse," Isabella said, thinking quickly. She met Job's eyes defiantly, and after a moment he shrugged and turned away, looking as though she had disappointed him. "Your mother's looking for you, wondering why you aren't with the others," he said. "That's all."

Isabella could not bear that he should think badly of her. "Oh, Job—!" she called. He waited. She could not think of anything to say. "All right, I'll come," she said sulkily, and followed him back toward the noise and music.

She could not think of any way in which she could legitimately absent herself the next day, so she simply crept downstairs as early as she could, before the household was awake, saddled Lyard herself, and rode out. She knew there would be trouble when she got back, but she decided she didn't care. She wanted to see Luke again.

It was that gray time before dawn, when everything is still and tender and dew-damp, waiting for the sun to bring back the color to the world. Birds sang remotely through the slight mist, and the only other sound was the swishing of Lyard's hooves through the grass, leaving a dark trail through the dew-silver, and the ringing of his shoe as it struck a stone. As they went up the slope toward Deadman's Copse, the sun began to edge up over the horizon, a great flat gold coin in the haze, and its first rays touched a gray horse standing quietly among the silver birch boles at the edge of the wood.

Lyard whickered through his nose, and Isabella pushed him into a canter as her heart beat faster with excitement.

"You made it, then," Luke said as she pulled up beside him. "You're a wonderful girl—there's no one like you for daring."

She smiled. "I don't care what happens. Let's just have a wonderful ride. Come on—I'll race you to the end of the wood!" And she swung Lyard round and put him straight from stand to a gallop.

"Hey—that's cheating!" Luke called, and plunged off in pursuit.

For a couple of hours they rode together through the May morning, just waking into its full beauty, absorbed with each other, aware that their time was limited, and enjoying each other the more intensely for that.

"You ride better than any girl I've ever seen. Better than most men, too," Luke said.

"My father taught me," she said. "And I used to go hunting with Job."

"Who's Job?" he asked with quick jealousy.

"My mother's steward," she said, affecting not to notice. "He's been with her ever since she first married. He's practically one of the family. You'd like him."

"I don't know that I would," Luke growled.

They were silent then, riding back toward the copse, knowing that they must return to the alien world.

"I wish I could just see you when I wanted to, instead of having to be so secret," Luke said discontentedly.

"If only our parents visited each other—" Isabella said. "I've just realized, I don't even know your other name. Who is your father?"

"Cannyng's my name. My father's master vintner. We live in Petergate."

"Oh, my sister lives there—perhaps you know her—she married John Butler—"

"The spice merchant? Yes, I know them. Father's quite friendly with Master Butler. So that's your sister—she's very pretty, isn't she?"

"Yes."

They were silent, both thinking how this acquaintance could help them.

"Perhaps if Helen asked me to visit her——?" Isabella said tentatively.

"I don't know. It might help," Luke said. He thought for a moment, and then began, rather more shyly than was his usual manner, "Isabella, if our parents would let us—would you—would you like to be married to me?"

"I think so," she said shyly. "I think—it might be fun."

Their eyes met, and then they looked away again.

"But they won't agree," he said bitterly. "My father would be quite pleased, I dare say, but I wouldn't be grand enough for yours. *My* father doesn't entertain lords."

Isabella wanted to say something to comfort him, but she knew he was right, and there was nothing they could do.

"Perhaps," she said, "perhaps if no one else comes for me—Mother might be glad of you. She's always saying she'll never get a match for me. I'm nearly sixteen." It was a great age to be still a maid. "My birthday's in three weeks."

"I'm eighteen," Luke said.

"But it doesn't matter for boys."

They had reached the point where they met, and knew that the time had come to part. Luke reached across and took her hand.

"Isabella, I must see you again. I can't ask you to risk getting out like this again. But if I come at night, could you get out of the house and meet me—say in the garden?"

"When?" she said, breathless with excitement.

"I don't know when I can get away. But I could throw a stone at your window to wake you up."

"I'll hang something white—a ribbon or something—so you know which one it is. It's on the south side of the house."

They made their plans excitedly, knowing, but not caring, about the possible consequences.

"I'll come one night soon, then. Think about me sometimes, won't you. I'll think about you. And—Isabella—don't let them betroth you to anyone else, will you?"

She looked at him helplessly, knowing that that was a thing beyond her competence.

"No," she said at last. "I won't let them."

* * *

It was three days later when Isabella, lying wakeful in the room she shared with Anys and the baby, the two nursery maids, and the three daughters of gentle folk who served her mother, heard the clatter of gravel on the window. It sounded terribly loud in the silence of the night, but none of her companions stirred. She slipped out of bed and hurried over to the window and pushed it open. She had tied a piece of white veiling to the outside of the casement so that it hung down the wall conspicuously, and she pulled it in now as she leaned out. Below in the dark she could just make out the white blur of a face. She waved her hand, saw him wave in reply, and, catching up her cloak from the clothes-chest, she crept out of the room and ran silently downstairs.

"The dogs didn't make a noise," she said when they met.

"I'm good with dogs," he said. "They like the smell of me, I suppose. Did you get into trouble the other day?"

She nodded. "But not badly. I thought I'd get a beating at least, but Mother went on and on at me, about unlady-like behavior, but she didn't suspect I'd gone to meet anyone. She thought I'd just gone off on my own. I used to do it a lot when I was younger, you see. So she sent me to my room without any food and kept me locked in all day."

"I'm glad you weren't beaten. I kept thinking about that and cursing myself for letting you risk it."

"I'd risk that much for you."

"I know. I think you're wonderful."

"But what about you? Did you get into trouble?"

"Oh, not me!" he said. "No one knows where I am most of the time. Oh, Isabella—we've got to do something."

"But what can we do?" she said.

"We could try talking to our parents."

"Impossible. As soon as they knew about us, we'd never be able to meet anymore. They'd watch us like hawks."

"They might agree to let us be betrothed."

"They wouldn't. I know they wouldn't," Isabella said desperately. "They'll marry me off to some rich man, and I shall *die*, I know I shall!"

He took both her hands, and pulled her toward him a

little. "Isabella, look at me." His voice was very serious, and she lifted her head and looked steadily into his eyes. "There is one way—but you would have to trust me."

"What do you mean?"

"If we were to make our vows to each other—"

"But they wouldn't pay any heed to that," she said.

"They would if—if you could go to them and say we were as man and wife to each other. They couldn't marry you to anyone else then."

"I—understand you," Isabella said slowly. Her mouth was dry. If they were to commit the married act, the church would count that as a contract. And of course, there would be the possibility of a child as well, to take into account. But—

"You said you wanted to marry me," he urged her. "Why not this way? Does it matter if it's sooner rather than later?"

She looked at him steadily, and his shining eyes did not falter.

"Then we would be together always. I would stay with you. No one could part us then. Do you trust me?"

"Yes," she said, and then, in a low voice, "I love you." She put her hands up to his shoulders, and he took her in his arms and kissed her. They sought the shelter of the box-walk, and there Luke threw his cloak down on the grass and gently pushed Isabella down on to it. As he stooped toward her she held him off a moment, apprehensively. He understood her mute plea.

"I'll be careful," he said. "I won't hurt you, my hinny."

"Have you done this before?" she asked.

He smiled his charming, wicked smile. "Now what do you think?"

Later—a hundred years later it seemed, they parted by the side door of the house.

"I'll tell them when I can. I'll have to choose the right moment," she said. She clung to him, and he kissed her hair and cheeks and hands.

"Do it soon," he said. "I want to be with you all the time."

The passion had been woken in Isabella's wild nature, and she returned his kisses with fervor.

"I must go in, now," she said reluctantly.

"I'll come again tomorrow night—will you come out to me?"

"Yes. Oh, yes. And I'll tell them as soon as I can. You do love me, don't you?"

"You know I do. I'll never leave you, Isabella. I'll be with you all your life."

The time did not seem right. Her mother was ill with her pregnancy, and that made her fretful and irritable. Her father was worried about her mother and about other things—things to do with the government, and to do with business, two classifications in which Isabella had no interest. Each night she met her lover in the garden, and each day she failed to find the courage to speak to her parents. It went on for a week—it could hardly have gone on much longer without their being found out. She left Luke to hurry in one night when they had stayed out almost until dawn, unable to bear to part with each other, and, secure in her week's safe conduct, she ran heedlessly into the dark passage and ran hard into someone who was standing inside the door.

She gave a shriek, muffled by her hands, which flew up to her mouth, and her heart gave a terrible lurch before she saw that it was Job.

"Oh, how you startled me!" she cried, relief flooding through her.

"Where have you been?" he asked her sternly.

"Just to get a breath of air," she lied gaily. "If it's any business of yours."

"A good lungful you must have had by now," Job said. "You've been out all night."

"Nonsense," she said sharply, trying to pass him. "I've only just gone out. Let me by, please."

"Don't you think you'd better tell me who he is?"

"I don't know what you're talking about. Let me by, please."

Job stood aside and let her pass, his face grim. Isabella hated lying to him, but she was too afraid to do otherwise. She tried to look haughty as she passed him, but succeeded only in looking guilty.

"Just as you please, mistress," he said quietly. "But you're going to need my help, I think."

She turned back and stared at him, hardly daring to hope he would be on her side.

Before she could say a word he had caught her by the arms and was shaking her with rough tenderness. "You young fool," he said. "How long did you think it would go on unnoticed?"

"Does Mother know?" Isabella gasped, her heart in her mouth.

"Not yet. Who is he?"

"Luke—Luke Cannyng. He's the son of the Master Vintner. They live in Petergate. Helen's husband knows them." She looked defiantly into Job's uncompromising face. "I love him. We want to be married."

"You know there's no chance of that," Job said.

"No, you don't understand. We *must* marry—"

"How far has this gone?" Job asked, suddenly catching her drift.

Isabella gulped. "We—we are as—as husband and wife."

Job groaned. "Dear God above, Isabella, what have you done?" He thought for a moment. "You'll have to tell them, you know. Did you think they would agree if you did this thing?"

She nodded.

"Is that what he told you?"

She nodded again.

"You are a fool, Isabella. That's the oldest trick in the book."

"No, no, you don't understand! He loves me! We love each other—we want to be married!"

"Well, I hope for your sake he does. It doesn't work, you know—it can be hushed up just like anything else. You know your betrothal was put aside, and that is supposed to be as binding as marriage."

Isabella stared at him, her eyes filling with tears.

He roughed her hair kindly. "But in your case—it might just work. It wouldn't be too bad a match, and your mother might just be glad to get you off her hands. His father won't object, I suppose."

"Oh, Job, will you tell them? Please—you can make Mother do anything," Isabella pleaded.

"You flatter me, child." He laughed rather grimly. "But I'll try for you. It would come better from me. Now go up to your room, and for heaven's sake do your best to please your mother today. Behave like a lady—don't make things harder for yourself."

"Thank you. Thank you, Job." Isabella stood on tiptoe to kiss his cheek, and ran off up to her room with a lighter step.

CHAPTER NINE

"No. No, *no, no!*" Eleanor said angrily, walking about the room. "I won't be blackmailed by my own daughter! I don't care what you say, Job."

Job stood by the window of the solar, enjoying the view while Eleanor let off steam. He knew that with Robert on his side she would be easier to win over. He hadn't told Robert the full story—just that Isabella had fallen in love. Robert was a romantic. His own marriage had been a love-match from his point of view, and since the boy in question was not totally unacceptable, and since he didn't need at that time to marry Isabella for advantage, he was inclined to want to see her happy.

Eleanor was another matter, though.

"I have plans for that child," she was saying. "All her life she's done just what she wants to do, without any thought for her parents or her family. She's a bad, selfish girl, but she's not going to get away with this. She'll marry who I say she'll marry, and that's that."

"And if she proves with child?" Job suggested.

"Damn her! And damn you, Job. You're on her side—I know it. She's always been your favorite, though I can't tell why."

"I'm on your side, first and foremost," he said soothingly. "You know that. Sit down and listen."

"Oh, I know your honey tongue of old . . ." Eleanor said, but she sat down all the same, placing her hands over her swollen belly, and looked up at him. "Job, I feel so ill and tired. Why does this child have to torment me now of all times."

"She's in love—and when a person's in love, they don't think of the consequences. You should know that," he said meaningly.

She winced. "Don't."

"Eleanor, here's a chance to get the girl off your hands. The match isn't a bad one. The boy's a good lad on the whole."

"A vintner!" Eleanor said scathingly.

"Your ideas are very high since you played host to a duke," Job said severely. "You won't get a lord for her, you know."

"I can do better than a vintner's son!" she spat.

"Can you? Can you now she's no longer virgin?"

"That can be hushed up. We'll keep her locked up until we've proved if she's with child. No one knows but you and me."

"You'd save yourself a lot of heartache if you accept a *fait accompli*," Job said. He came and knelt in front of her. "It's for your sake I say this. You shouldn't be worrying about this sort of thing. Let the girl marry him. What does it matter. You don't need her marriage—you have land and gold enough."

Eleanor stirred irritably. "I can't bear to be got the better of."

"Pride. That's a sin, you know. You have more common sense than pride, mistress. Come, what do you say?"

Eleanor hesitated, and then tapped his cheek affectionately. "You know how to get round me. Did she put you up to it? No, don't answer. I don't want to know. You're right—it isn't worth the worry. If Robert thinks the match is all right, let him go and see this—wine merchant." A sudden thought struck her. "You didn't tell Robert about the—*fait accompli*, did you?"

"No. No one but you."

"Good. No one must know that part of it. You may tell mistress Isabella that she may have her tavern boy if she wants. But for God's sake make sure she doesn't tell anyone else how she did it—especially not her father."

Job stood up and bowed. "You have made the right decision, I'm sure," he said, and went away with a small private smile that he would not have cared to explain.

Master Cannyng was delighted with his son's good fortune, and agreed to a contract at once. It was decided there was nothing to wait for, and an early wedding was planned, to take place in June, but at the beginning of that month Eleanor was brought to bed before her time of a daughter, who lived only two days, and the wedding had to be postponed.

In July came the news that the King had been struck down by a strange madness that rendered him deaf and dumb and apparently oblivious to his surroundings. The Queen wept and clung to his hand, but he merely turned his head away. He did not recognize her. He was locked away behind a strange barrier of the mind. At first she and her party tried to keep the news from the Duke of York, but it leaked out and eventually she had to call a Council and let him take his place at the head of it.

"Don't you think it's time to change our allegiance?" Eleanor asked Robert when they heard this news. "You see that our patron has acted ill. With Lord Richard at the head of the Council, Lord Edmund will be impeached, perhaps executed."

"I'll wait until it happens," Robert said. "I don't want it said that I'm a turncoat."

"You don't have to give loyalty to a man who doesn't deserve it," she said sharply.

"There's wrong on both sides, I am sure. We'll see what York does. He may turn out to be as rapacious as the others."

Eleanor's health continued poor, and the wedding was put off until October. Meanwhile, Isabella was sent to stay with Helen and her husband so that she could meet her betrothed under proper chaperonage. She was blissfully happy, and with this new radiance looked almost pretty, so that Eleanor admitted grudgingly that she might make a fairly presentable bride, and ordered her wedding clothes with the beginnings of enthusiasm.

The wedding was to be on the sixteenth of October, and

on the thirteenth Isabella came home from Helen's to prepare for it. Her mother met her almost kindly, and as they went through the preparations together, something almost like affection seemed to exist tenuously between them. Then on the fifteenth, a carrier passing the gates told the news that the Queen had been delivered of a healthy baby boy, who was to be named Edward—a king's name, a direct reference to Edward III, from whose blood all the contenders to the throne claimed descent.

Eleanor was cast into despair. "It's the worst thing that could have happened," she cried. "If she had died, or the child had died—even if it had been a girl! But she will fight to keep her brat upon the throne, and we shall never have an end of the wars, or of this cursed usurping line! Suppose the King should die now—and who knows what turn his illness might take?—we should have another child-king, and twenty more years of faction and unrest."

Even Robert was shaken. "I had not thought of that. Perhaps it would be best if Lord Richard were to take over. As protector, perhaps, at first . . ."

But Eleanor interrupted him. "She will kill him. As protector he could not survive a year. She will have him murdered for her child's sake. She is like a ravening she-wolf, she has no idea how civilized people behave."

Eleanor was for putting off the wedding. "How can we make merry at such a time?" she said. But Robert and Job together presuaded her not to do anything so extreme.

"People would laugh and say we gave ourselves airs. We are ordinary folk. It's nothing to us if the Queen has a son. You can't cancel the wedding for a thing like that."

Isabella was on tenterhooks for two hours while they talked, and afterward, even though her relief should have made her sing, she could only glare sullenly at her mother.

"She'll spoil it for me if she can," she muttered to Job, and was soundly rated by him.

The day dawned fair, a crisp autumn day, with a fine rime of frost on the fallen leaves. The household arose early and took mass together, and then Isabella went up to dress. Jacques was already in the kitchen cooking the bridal feast;

the servants were decorating the great hall with the red and bronze flowers of autumn, and with boughs of golden leaves and crimson creeper.

Anys helped Isabella dress, but first she plucked her eyebrows and forehead, soothing the red skin with witch-hazel afterward, and hid the worst of her freckles with a whitening cream. She touched Isabella's sandy lashes with black, and squeezed a drop of belladonna into each eye to make the whites whiter, and the pupils blacker.

"A little red on your lips, my child," Anys said, "and then we shall see how you look with your headdress on." She fitted the heavy pearl-trimmed construction over Isabella's mousy hair, and arranged the veil, and then turned her to see herself in the disc of polished silver that she held up. "There. What do you think of the bride?"

Isabella stared at her reflection. Shyly she said, "Is that really me? I look so different. Almost—pretty."

"You look beautiful, just as you should. Every girl looks beautiful on her wedding day."

"I'm so happy, Anys—can you tell? Maybe that's why I look pretty. I never thought I could be happy to be married."

"Getting married is the beginning of your problems," Anys said, not unkindly.

"It will be the end of mine," Isabella prophesied, and Anys crossed herself, just in case. "We shall have such fun. He's going to give me a kestrel for my bride-gift, and the very first thing we're going to do is go out hawking on the moors."

"The idea," Anys said, scandalized. "A hawk for a bride-gift! It's not lucky."

"I don't believe in that sort of thing," Isabella said boldly.

"Well, you won't have much time for hawking when you start having children. Like the mistress—five children in four years she had. You can't go hunting and hawking with a full belly."

"Was that why you didn't get married, Anys?" Isabella asked innocently. "Because you didn't want to have children?"

"None of that talk, now, miss," Anys said briskly. "You

come here and let me see to your dress. When a woman marries, she has children, that's her duty."

"Helen hasn't, and she's been married two years."

"She'll have them when God sends them. Now hush! You should be getting yourself into a proper reverent frame of mind to be going to church, not prattling on about things that aren't your concern."

Isabella took the rebuke, and hugged Anys. "Th'art a dear old thing," she whispered.

And Anys said, "Go on with you," but a tear glistened in her eye all the same.

At nine the Morland party reached the door of the church of the Holy Trinity, and discovered to their surprise that the Cannyng party was not there. Eleanor's brows drew together at the insult, but there was nothing to do but wait. At half after nine there was still no sign of the groom and his family.

"This is too much," Eleanor said angrily, but in a low voice, to Robert. "This is what comes of having to do with such people."

Isabella was looking fearful, but defiant. "He'll be here soon. He wouldn't be late without a good reason," she said to Anys.

"Of course, my child," Anys said absently.

"You don't sound as if you think so," Isabella said quickly. "What is it? What do you fear? That someone will stop him coming?"

"No, no, of course not. Calm yourself. Don't let people see you are upset. Look calm and happy. People are watching."

"Yes, yes, you're right. I mustn't be afraid." She heard Luke's voice inside her head—I'll never leave you, he had said. No one would be able to stop him coming.

Robert meanwhile had spoken quietly to one of his pages, who slipped off up Micklegate toward Petergate, but he could not have crossed above half the distance when one of the Cannyng servants came running into the churchyard, pale, red-eyed, and distraught.

"Master Morland—Mistress—" he panted.

"What is it?" Robert seized him by the arm to stop him from falling. He was an elderly man, probably a scrivener

or clerk in Cannyng's service. His haunted eyes stared up at
Morland and his lips moved wordlessly, unable for the moment to speak. Morland signed Eleanor to keep back and
spoke firmly and quietly to the man. "Calm yourself, my
man. Tell us what's happened."

"It's the young master, sir," the old man said at length,
and tears began to roll freely from his eyes. "As he was
coming out of the house, sir, to come to the church—all in
his wedding clothes—" He caught sight of Isabella, and the
tears rolled faster as he instinctively addressed himself to
her. "The wind slammed the house door behind him—and
one of the pantiles fell from the roof. The vibration—it
must have been loose. . . ."

Robert stared, aghast. Those pantiles were made of solid
stone, about two feet square and three or four inches thick.
It took two men to lift one.

"It hit him?" he whispered.

The old man nodded, speechless.

"Dead?"

"Dead, sir," he said, but he looked at Isabella as he said
it.

Her face went white and her hands flew to her throat as
if she were choking. She stared unbelievingly at the messenger, unable to take it in, and then helplessly from one
face to another as if someone might tell her it was not so.

"My child—" Anys put an arm round her, but she shook
it off. She made a little moaning noise in her throat, and
then her eyes sought her mother's face.

"*You,*" she choked. "*You* did this! You couldn't bear me
to be happy—*you* had him killed!"

"Isabella—you don't know what you're saying," Eleanor
said aghast. She stepped forward, holding out her hand.

"No, don't touch me!" Isabella screamed, jumping backward. "I know it's true. It couldn't have happened, just like
that. You never wanted me to marry him from the beginning! But why did you have to do this? Oh, why?" And
then she began to cry, a terrible, tearing sound that seemed
to be wrenched out of her very heart. "Luke!" she cried
out, and she turned this way and that as if seeking somewhere to run. Anys tried to take hold of her, but she thrust

her away, sobbing in a terrible unhinged way, so that they feared for her reason. Her mother, her father, her sister, all tried to comfort her, but as they touched her she began to scream, seeing them all her enemies, and at last she ran to Job, buried her face in his chest, and allowed him to coax her gently away.

Job shook his head as Robert and Eleanor would have come too. "Let me take care of her," he said. "I'll take her home. You follow when you're ready." He stroked Isabella's hair—her headdress had fallen in her struggles. "Poor child," he said. "Poor young man." He lifted the weeping girl onto his horse, mounted behind her, and rode slowly out through the Mickle Lith and under the dying trees toward home.

It was a sad winter for them. At first they were afraid that Isabella would lose her wits altogether, for her grief was so extreme that she would cry and cry until she was sick, scream until she lost her voice. She would not eat, and could not sleep, and became in a week a pitiful, haunted skeleton. She persisted in the notion that her mother had arranged to have her betrothed killed, in spite of all Job or Anys could say to the contrary. Even after her fits of hysteria had ceased and she began to creep up the long slope toward recovery, she was silent and brooding, and avoided her mother as much as possible, glaring at her darkly when they happened to be in the same room together.

In November Lord Edmund was impeached by the Council and sent to the Tower, and it seemed that his patronage was no longer a thing of advantage to the Morlands. Robert was still unwilling to abandon the man to whom he owed so much, but there seemed little doubt that he was guilty of the things whereof he was accused, and if he regained his freedom it would only be by the intervention of the Queen. Robert reluctantly agreed that he would not support the Beaufort party with money or men from that time, but he would not yet agree to support the York party, and quarreled bitterly with Eleanor when she suggested it.

They had a very quiet Christmas, with no guests other

than Helen and her husband and Master Shawe and his daughter, Cecily, a solemn child of twelve. Helen had changed little since her marriage. She was happy with her husband, who was proud of her beauty and kept her dressed in the latest of style, but their lack of children was beginning to worry them both, and she, too, was pale and drawn, though beside her younger sister she looked as blooming as a rose. Isabella was no more a child. All her spirit and boldness was gone. She started nervously at any sudden noise, was irritable with the children, and scarcely ever spoke, brooding darkly over her lost love and her fancied wrongs. The only person with whom she would talk at all was Job, and he did his best to coax-her out of her darkness, without success.

With the coming of spring things seemed a little better. Eleanor conceived again, and with a resurgence of spirit and energy not uncommon in the early months of pregnancy, she attempted to persuade her husband to begin to divert their fortunes out of wool and into cloth.

"That's where the money will be made in the future," she said. "The great days of the woolman are over. There's too much competition, and now that we've lost France we can't hope to control the prices as we used to."

Robert wouldn't hear of it. "There will never be an end to the days of the wool man," he scoffed. "Everybody wants wool, and there is no finer wool than English wool. Everyone knows that."

"Of course everyone wants wool—but what do they want it for? Why, to make cloth!" Eleanor retorted. "They buy our wool cheap, make it into cloth, and sell it dear."

"Our wool isn't cheap," Robert growled. "We see to that."

"Oh, yes, my lord Stapler, I know that—but still they make a profit, a large profit. Look what we have to pay for a length of fine Lincoln or Kersey! Don't you see, it's just another step in the same direction as we have already taken? We turned to selling our own wool so that we could take that profit instead of the brogger and the merchant. Why shouldn't we make our own cloth from our own wool and take the colothier's profit?"

But Robert could not be convinced. He was settled in his ways now. He enjoyed his position as a merchant, he didn't want to start all over again at the bottom as a clothier. "You'll be asking me to steal other men's jobs," he said. "What's to come of the country if we don't stick to our trades? No, no, wife. I'm a woolman, and a woolman I'll stay." He patted her hand affectionately. "You're always full of these mad ideas. Always after something new."

"And you're like those old men who tut-tutted when we had chimneys built in our new house, and said we'd die without the fire-smoke to breathe," Eleanor said, but she smiled as she said it. She did not expect to win the war in the first battle.

In April, the Duke of York was appointed Protector, to act for the King until he regained his sanity, if he ever did. Eleanor's fears for his life were not realized. His first action was to call together all the nobles of the land and make them swear allegiance to the infant Prince Edward, and perhaps that was enough temporarily to keep the Queen from his throat. He restored order to the turbulent kingdom, put down trouble, and dispensed justice with an impartial hand. The good times seemed to be beginning at last, and the unhappy country settled down under his firm hand just as Ireland had. Perhaps, thought Eleanor, his time there had not been wasted.

Robert had now to agree that the best thing that had happened to the country was this good duke, and that he was the only hope for England's peace, and he finally settled himself on York's side by sending a letter of support and offering money to York's government should it be needed. A kind letter came back from the Duke, thanking them for their offers of assistance, which he would keep in mind. It brought back to Eleanor's mind the image of his face that moonlit night when he had kissed her and she had sworn faith with him.

In the autumn Eleanor had to bid a sad good-bye to her much loved son Thomas, who at thirteen was being sent to Trinity Hall in Cambridge to read law. It had been her idea in the first place, though Robert had heartily approved. "We could do with someone in the family who

knows the law," he had said. But it was one thing to make
plans, and another to part with the handsome and charming boy who had cheered her through her sad times.

"Don't worry, Mother," he said on the eve of his departure, "I'll come home for holidays when I can."

"When you can," Eleanor said sadly. "Well, dear child,
don't worry about money. If money is all you need to get
you home, only let me know and I will send what you need
at once."

"Study hard, child, and obey your tutor in all things,"
Robert advised him.

"And don't take to drinking wine like some of the boys I
hear of," Eleanor added sharply. "Ale is all you need at
your age."

Thomas grinned. "Yes, Mother, I'll remember. I'll come
home to you as good and honest a lad as I went."

Eleanor pinched his cheek. "You're a saucy boy," she
said. "Write to me when you can. You know I'll pray for
you every night."

The following morning, before dawn, he was on his way,
riding with a group of travelers who were going the same
way and had agreed to take charge of him. He would study
at Cambridge for four years, and then go on to one of the
Inns of Court in London, so it was likely that, except for
brief visits during the vacation, she would not see her son
again until he was a grown man.

Whether it was partly her sorrow in losing him could not
be told, but on the day he went away she began to feel ill,
and less than a week later she was brought to bed of a
daughter, who died almost immediately.

The long, harsh winter set in again. At Christmas the
King recovered his wits quite suddenly and unexpectedly,
and the triumphant Queen dismissed Lord Richard and released Edmund Beaufort from the Tower. Richard hastened north in terror of his life to raise support for himself.
All the old troubles were beginning again, it seemed: the
Queen would try to kill him, and he would try to defend
himself, and the country would be torn apart between the
two of them in this battle for survival.

It gave the Morlands their first taste of fighting. The
Queen had persuaded the King that Richard was his en-

emy, and he determined to get to the King to tell him otherwise, but there was no way he could do that without an army. He gathered his forces in the north, and Robert provided twenty men and his own sword toward that force. Richard and his army marched south; the King, Beaufort, and his army marched north; and they met at St. Albans. It wasn't much of a battle—in an hour it was all over and Richard's side was victorious—but for such a minor struggle it took a toll of a great many of the country's most important men, including Lord Edmund, who was killed in the first minutes of fighting.

The poor quaking King waited for Richard to kill him, as his wife had led him to believe he intended, and was astonished and happy when, instead, the Duke knelt before him and swore his allegiance to him. Robert described the touching scene to Eleanor when he came home, after the York army had escorted the King back to London.

"But it won't do any good," he said gloomily. "The King does whatever the Queen wants, and believes anything she tells him. The Queen is Lord Richard's enemy, but he can't strike at the Queen without seeming to strike at the King. And if he waits for her to strike first, he's likely to find himself imprisoned or dead."

"That woman—how I hate her!" Eleanor said, clenching her fists. "There'll be no peace in this country while she lives. If I were a man, I'd kill her myself."

"Then I must be glad you're a woman, because if you did that you'd certainly suffer a most horrible death," Robert said. "But it's a dilemma, all right. I don't know what he can do, except pray."

"I never stop," said Eleanor, "but it doesn't seem to help."

CHAPTER TEN

Eleanor and Robert, followed by a maid and a page, were riding home through the city after a visit to a prospective husband for Isabella. Isabella was now twenty-one, and almost beyond marriageable age, but still Eleanor's ideas for a husband for her were higher than Robert's, and they were wrangling peaceably over the latest candidate as they rode along. Around them the narrow, overhung streets of the city teemed with life. Stalls displayed every variety of wares, and more were piled around the doors of the shops, making the narrow streets narrower, and drawing crowds of loiterers who fingered the goods and argued over the price with the stall-holders. At the stalls of the butchers and fishmongers there were growing heaps of blood and bones and entrails around which cur-dogs crept, looking for a chance to dash in; the vegetable stalls were a prey to stray goats and pigs.

Automatically the Morlands edged their horses around the worst of the filth. The sides of the roads were thick with refuse at which swine rooted, and the heaps of animal and human manure which were meant to be swept into the channel in the center of the street often didn't reach it. A dead dog had been lying for three days outside a house on the corner of Nessgate, because there was a quarrel going on at the time over which of two householders had the responsibility of removing it. A group of young boys ran past

pursuing a goose with sticks, making the horses flirt their
heels nervously, and ran straight into a procession crossing
toward the Thursday Market, of an accused whore in her
striped hood who was to be pilloried.

They crossed the Ouse Bridge and saw the great barges
going down loaded with wool and cloth—some of it their
own—on its way to the Low Countries. The barges coming
up were unloading at the King's Staith their freight of
spices, wines, tapestries, stockfish, woad, pitch. The human
and animal din beat on their ears, and overall there was the
eternal ringing of the church bells: in the city one had to
shout to be heard.

"He's no better than a yeoman farmer," Eleanor was
saying. "I'd sooner send her to a nunnery than marry her to
him."

"It may come to that," Robert said. "At least as a nun
she'd be respectable, and provided for, for the rest of her
life. With a large enough donation she could live like a
lady."

Eleanor shook her head impatiently. "There's no profit
in that. No, no, we'll find something for her. After all,
she's looking better these days. That perpetually mournful
expression seems to do something for her."

"Poor child," Robert sighed. "She might welcome a life
of retreat. She never stops thinking about that poor lad,
you know."

"I know," Eleanor said briskly, "but she'd soon forget
him if she had a husband and children of her own to worry
about. We should have married her off before now—it was
a mistake to give her so long to get over it. It's become a
habit with her."

Robert smiled at her. "My dear wife! Always seeking an
active solution to every problem. You could never bear to
sit still and await events, could you?"

"I'd sooner do something than nothing," she said. "But
I've had enough experience of awaiting events." She placed
one hand over the bulge of her belly. "Thirteen times."

"You're feeling well?" Robert asked her anxiously.

She nodded. "By God's will, we shall be all right this
time." Her last four pregnancies had ended sadly: three

children who died within days, and the last time a stillbirth. They smiled at each other affectionately. They had changed little over the years in appearance, growing only a little grayer and a little more lined. Robert had grown stouter recently, while Eleanor had become, if possible, more slender than before. But they had come to know and love each other better as the years passed, and the troubles that had attended the early years of their marriage were behind them now.

"You've been a wonderful wife to me," Robert said now. "You are an example to all womanhood. And if little Cecily makes our Edward as good a wife as you've been to me, he'll be the happiest man alive."

Eleanor made a wry face. "You speak too kindly of me, Robert. And as to Cecily—I should have had her years ago to make any impression on her. A few months before the wedding aren't going to be enough."

Little Cecily Shawe had been betrothed to their son Edward for two years, and the wedding had been set for May. As was usual, Cecily had been residing with the Morlands for some weeks to learn the ways of the household, but as she was now seventeen, she was rather old for learning new tricks.

"But you find her tractable enough, don't you?" Robert asked. "She seems a quiet, obedient sort of child to me."

Eleanor looked at him shrewdly. "I know—you think I'm too severe with her, don't you?"

"I never said—"

"You didn't have to say. I've seen the way you look at me. But she'll learn quicker if she's afraid to do wrong. There's nothing like fear for spurring a person on. I remember my own experiences with your father when I first came here."

"All the same, my dear—"

"All the same, dear husband, I must confess that I like the girl very much. There's a deal of good behind that pretty face. I sometimes find it hard to be strict with her."

"You're growing mellow with age," Robert suggested.

"Perhaps. Perhaps. But she reminds me of myself at that age, and it troubles me."

Robert laughed. "You've come a long way since then. Do you realize that it's twenty-four years come autumn since we were wed?"

"Is it? Yes, of course it must be. So much has happened, hasn't it, Robert?"

They rode on in silence for a while, thinking over the years that had gone by. They passed under the Mickle Lith, and were saluted by the sergeants on duty, who knew them by sight now, as did most of the city's officers. They pushed through the mill of beggars who waited outside the gates, hoping for a chance to slip past the sentries into the city, threw a coin to the hermit in his hut, and turned their horses off onto the road to Morland Place.

"One of the best things about the wedding," Eleanor said cheerfully as they urged their horses into a trot, "is that we'll have Thomas home for a while. How I long to see that boy!"

"Not such a boy now," Robert reminded her.

Robert was right. The "boy" was very much a man: a very handsome man, too, with Eleanor's thick dark hair and bright blue eyes, and a smile so ravishing he could scarcely fail to get his own way in everything he attempted. He had grown tall, but, unlike his brother Edward, he had filled out and developed a powerful pair of shoulders to balance his height, while poor Edward looked like a maypole, straight and thin all the way up.

Thomas sat at Eleanor's right hand, eating and drinking and laughing and talking with enormous vitality, while Eleanor scarcely touched a thing, so fascinated was she with watching him. It seemed to her amazing that this huge and dazzling creature could have been the fruit of her womb. She felt shy, almost girlish before him.

"I must say it was good of you to prepare such a welcome home for me," he said, waving his knife in the air to indicate the dinner, the entertainments, and the general company. "And to go to the trouble of providing me with a beautiful new sister—"

He grinned sideways at Cecily, who was sitting on his other side, and she blushed and looked down at her plate.

Edward, who was so painfully earnest and rather plodding beside his brother, said, "It wasn't done for your benefit, Thomas."

"Come, now, Edward, don't be modest! Don't try to hide your own kind heart. I know you were thinking only of me when you agreed to marry this little daisy—for daisy she is, with her golden petals and her cheeks touched with pink! She almost makes up for the loss of my own sisters. How are they, Mother? How are Anne and Helen?"

"Both well," Eleanor said, glad that he had turned his teasing gaze away from Cecily and Edward before the latter's jealousy began to stir. "Anne has had another boy— they've called him Robert after your father."

"Compliment indeed!" Thomas said. "I must see if I can't get down to Dorset one of these days and see my nephews and nieces. And what of Helen?"

"Just the same," Eleanor said. Poor Helen had still not conceived by her husband, and it looked as though she never would. A husband might put aside a barren wife, but John Butler seemed genuinely fond of Helen, and had not even hinted at such a course. "She compensates by having pets. She has a monkey now—I can't say I like it much. It has some nasty habits."

"Monkeys are very fashionable," Thomas said. "I must see what I can bring her next time. Dear old Helen. Do you remember that parrot, Edward, that the girls had when we were children? Poor thing—I think it couldn't stand the cold. They are supposed to live for hundreds of years. Of course, our teasing it might have shortened its life. I believe you used to give it a sad life, didn't you, Edward, before I came on the scene to keep you in order?"

Even Edward laughed at the idea of Thomas keeping anyone in order. Harry, at the other end of the table, was gaping in his effort to hear what this dazzling brother had to say.

"Lord Edmund gave that to your sisters," Eleanor reminded him.

"God rest his soul," Thomas said, crossing himself. "The Beaufort cause goes on, though, Mother, with the Queen's aid." He nodded significantly. "You heard about Lord Edmund's niece?"

"That piece of news doesn't seem to have filtered this far. What of her?"

"Only that she was married to Edmund Tidr, the bastard half brother of our sovereign lord the King."

Eleanor heard the news with her usual fury against the Queen, and she did not speak for fear of saying something improper in front of the children. Edmund Tidr was one of the sons that were born to Harry the Fifth's queen Katharine as a result of her affair with her wardrobe-man, Owen Tidr, and everything about that affair made Eleanor's true-bred blood boil.

"Oddly enough," Thomas went on, "it only lasted a matter of weeks. The Tidr wasn't yet thirty, and the maid wasn't thirteen, but in a few weeks he was dead and she was quick. She had a son last year." The bright eyes met Eleanor's, and then passed on to Robert's. "They call him Henry, and if anyone thinks that isn't significant, they must be very simple. The Queen knows what she's doing."

"It will confuse the issue," Robert said, shaking his head. "Besides, she's of no importance—Lord Edmund Beaufort had other sons."

"She seeks to consolidate the royal party," Eleanor said. "The King was always too easy on his bastard half-kin. No good ever comes of encouraging vice."

"That ought to be true," Thomas said, "but I'm afraid, Mother, that experience says otherwise."

"What are things like now, Thomas?" Robert asked, to avoid an argument. "You are nearer the center of things than we are."

"Pretty bad," he said. "Feeling swings one way and then the other. We all thought the Queen was done for last year when she organized that French raid on Sandwich—but she got out of it. She made Exeter her scapegoat, and made a big pretense of making friends with my lord Warwick and the Duke of York. The King made them all shake hands and go to mass together during the January Council meeting—"

"We heard about that," Robert said.

"They had a procession through the streets, we heard, two by two, the Queen and Lord Richard leading the way hand in hand," Edward added.

"That's right. But no one believed in it, except, possibly, the King. The people love him, you know. Whatever happens, it's the Queen they blame."

"That she-wolf!" Eleanor exploded, unable to prevent herself.

Thomas smiled and patted his mother's hand. "You're a bit of a wild animal yourself, aren't you, Mother? I'd give a lot to see a meeting between the two of you on neutral ground with no armed men to call on. I'll bet you'd have her hair off her head."

"Hush, boy, don't put ideas into the children's heads," Eleanor said with a laugh.

"No one in this household loves the Queen," Robert said quietly.

"None but her own creatures love her," Thomas said. "She thought to buy public opinion by giving my lord of Warwick the Channel command, but though he's doing great things up and down the coast, it's him they credit and not her. The people hate her. And she's deep in debt—she owes her household their wages for almost two years back, and she owes thousands in household bills. If it weren't that people love the King so, I dare say she wouldn't be able to get the shopkeepers to supply her."

Robert nodded. "I'd heard something of that. The garrison at Calais hasn't been paid either. There was a lot of unrest when I was over there for the last meeting of the Staplers. They were saying then that if the garrison didn't get its pay, we'd have to pay them ourselves or have a rising on our hands."

"But why doesn't Lord Richard *do* something?" Harry demanded fiercely. "The people love *him*. Why doesn't he get an army together and—and—"

"And what?" Thomas asked. "Take the King prisoner? He can't remove the Queen without removing the King, too."

"It's what I'd do," Eleanor said. "An enforced protectorship."

Thomas shook his head. "I think it will have to be all or nothing in the end. But the trouble is he's too honorable. He swore faith to the King as a soldier, and he won't break that faith. She'll force him to it in the end, but I'm afraid if he doesn't act wholeheartedly, she'll win—and kill him."

Robert looked from one to another of his sons, and thought how strange it was that they were all so wholeheartedly for the Duke's party. Lord Edmund, it seemed, was not only dead, but forgotten. There was Thomas, worried about his statecraft, Harry itching to take sword to his enemies, even quiet Edward nodding agreement and looking as though he'd take up arms if he were asked. Only little John, sitting at the far end of the table with Isabella, was indifferent. He was in a world of his own, a world of dreams that he inhabited more than the real world. Robert wondered if he would become a priest or a monk.

And Isabella, almost ignoring her young brother on his first visit home for four years, paying no attention to the conversation—she was in another world too. That world had only two inhabitants. Robert had always felt kindly toward his wayward daughter, but he feared her mind would never mend, and that in the end a nunnery would be the best place for her. She was full of dark, brooding fancies. She still hardly ever spoke to her mother; still believed, though she no longer spoke about it, that Eleanor had had Luke Cannyng killed on that fateful morning. Her reason impaired as it was, perhaps they were not doing the right thing to try to marry her off.

But a silence had fallen over the high table, and he felt it was time to break into it.

"Well, now, let us not think about dark things. This should be a happy time. Let's not forget we are all here together to celebrate the marriage of our dear son, Edward, and our dear daughter, Cecily. We should be making merry," Robert said, smiling across at his eldest son, and receiving a shy response from pretty Cecily.

Thomas took up the cue promptly. "Of course—long life to them! I for one intend to have as merry a time as possible while I'm here. They keep us so close in the college we hardly dare sneeze without express permission."

"A good thing, too," Eleanor said with mock severity. "I dare say you get away with enough even so."

"Oh, don't worry, Mother. My tutor at Cambridge is ev-

ery bit as strict as our good Master Jenney. Does he make
you speak nothing but Latin during school hours, John, as
he did us?"

"Do you have to speak Latin in your college?" Harry
asked.

"Like priests," Thomas said with a wink. "Which is what
my tutor wants us all to be."

"Don't you let him persuade you." Eleanor rose to the
bait as Thomas knew she would. "We have a better use for
you than that—oh, saving your presence, Master James,"
she added hastily, remembering a little too late that the
chaplain was sitting beside Isabella. Everyone laughed, and
the conversation turned to other things.

"Shall we get in some hawking while I'm here, brother
Edward?" Thomas asked.

2

Everyone said afterward that it was the best wedding in
human memory. It was an occasion of ribbons and flowers
and banners and trumpeters; of singing and dancing and
feasting and drinking. Cecily rode to the church on Elean-
or's good old mare, Lepida, whose milk-white coat had
turned snow-white now with age, but who stepped out
proudly under her caparison of crimson and primrose-
yellow silk and ribbons. Six children, chosen for their
beauty, danced ahead of her and strewed the way with
flowers, and Thomas and Harry both acted as her groomsmen, whose traditional function it was to see that she got to
church safely and was not snatched away *en route* by ri-
vals.

Edward was pale with nervousness, but he acted his part
with great dignity, though he could not match the high-
spirited merriment of his brothers. His crimson surcoat was
well padded about the shoulders and arms, and cinched in
tightly at the waist, and so did his height justice—he
looked a fine figure of a man. His hose were of sky-blue
silk, his shoes of gold brocade with the fashionable long
points, his great crested hat of crimson brocaded with gold:
from head to toe he looked a gentleman of fashion, and

Eleanor was pleased and proud that there was nothing of the country farmer about him.

After the service, the bride and groom rode back to Morland Place in a noisy procession of family, friends, and retainers, preceded by two liveried trumpeters and followed by a group of minstrels and a choir of twenty boys from the city, who were being paid a shilling each as well as everything they could eat and drink at the feast. All the neighbors had been invited, and every person of any importance in York, as well as all their servants and retainers, who now numbered around two hundred.

The great hall had been decorated with flowers and green boughs and bunches of ribbons, and over the dais was a wooden shield painted with the adopted Morland device of a white hare leaping over a sprig of heather, and Cecily's device of a coppice—"shaw" was the local word for a small wood. The guests of honor were greeted and escorted to their seats by a pageant of dryads—again in Cecily's honor—from among whom one was chosen as the woodland Queen and crowned by the lord Pan.

The loving cup was passed, and the feast began—a magnificent progression of dishes, ten in the first course, eight in the second, and six in the third. There were chickens, pheasants, capons, pigeons, lambs, sucking pigs, rabbits (no hare—Eleanor never would countenance hare upon her table), and swans; pastries, doucettes, melanges, maumenies and frumenties and galantines; great whorls and cartwheels of bread; gallons of ale and tuns of wine. The first subtlety was of dryads, fauns, and lord Pan; the second, to strike a less pagan note, was of the infant St. John, whose day was not far off; the third, a great favorite, St. George, whose day was not far past. As each dish was finished, its remains were carried to a central table set with flowers, and when the feast was over, all the broken meats were carried out to an accompaniment of fanfares—which had been sounded also before each course—and distributed to the poor outside the gates. There was a large crowd there of people who had come, some from miles away, carrying baskets and bundles for this very purpose.

The feasting over, there was an interval of singing from the choir and entertainments from a group of tumblers

hired for the occasion. They juggled with colored balls and
with each other, walked on their hands and turned somer-
saults; and when one of the men had finished swallowing
the swords, one of the women walked on her points. Then,
when the great feast had been sufficiently digested, the
minstrels struck up, and there was dancing. It went on far
into the night. There were too many people for all to be
housed within, and many danced outside in the courtyard
and on the lawns, lit with flaring torches and flickering
lamps. Wine and ale flowed; many a couple of young people slipped off into the darkness, and probably many another wedding was planned or even made necessary. Master Shawe, who had wept openly through the wedding
ceremony at the thought of losing his lovely daughter,
danced all night with Isabella, talking to her mournfully
about his dead wife, and eventually fell asleep on the
rushes with his hand curled about a wine-cup and a peaceful smile on his face.

Eleanor danced with Robert and with Thomas for pleasure, and most of the leading men of society for duty.
Thomas, when he wasn't with his mother or whispering impossible things to the prettiest girl in the room, was dancing
with Cecily, whom he continued to call "daisy," saying that
that should have been her device, and not a wood, even of
the slenderest silver birches. Edward watched him with res-
ignation and looked forward to the time when he would
have his wife to himself. Master Jenney surprised everyone
by tripping a stately measure with Anys and apparently
pleasing her enough to make her cheeks turn poppy-red.
Job danced impartially with Eleanor's maids and was much
sought after by the young women from the estate and the
nearby villages, and Master Shawe, who had fallen asleep
in the arms of Bacchus after dancing with Isabella, later
went with her to make sure that all was well in the stables
and the mews and that the animals weren't frightened by
the noise and lights.

The merrymaking went on for a long time after the
young couple were bedded—a much more dignified ceremony than the one Eleanor remembered with some
shame—and it was almost dawn when the last of the guests
were seen on their way and the torches put out.

"A wonderful wedding, Mother." Thomas yawned. "I shall remember it with great pleasure when I'm back in my dungeon at Cambridge. I can honestly say I've never had a better time."

"I hope you didn't say anything serious to any of those girls you danced with tonight," Eleanor said pleasantly. "Some of them were looking at you with very warm expressions."

"Oh, I don't think I swore to marry more than five or six of them," he said airily. "But in any case, you needn't worry about your plans for me. When the time comes I'll be a good boy and do what I'm told."

"You sly puss." Eleanor laughed, patting his cheek. "You dare to make fun of me?"

"Never, Mother!" Thomas opened his eyes very wide. "Besides, of all the girls in the hall tonight, the two most beautiful were already married. One was that little daisy who'd just married my brother."

"And the other?" Eleanor demanded.

"She married my father long ago," Thomas said. "And now I must go to my bed, or I shan't be fit to tease Edward tomorrow." He knelt to his mother. "Good night, Mother. Bless me."

Eleanor placed her hand on his shining hair. "Good night, my darling boy. God bless you," she said, and there were tears of love in her eyes as she watched him go.

Robert found her there a moment later.

"We missed our usual walk," he said. They had taken recently to walking together for an hour at dusk, sometimes to discuss important things, sometimes just to enjoy the quiet and each other's company. "Would you care to walk with me now and watch the sun rise—or are you too tired?"

"I'm tired, but not sleepy," Eleanor said. "I think I'd like to walk—the air will smell wonderful. Listen—the birds are singing already."

Robert fetched her cloak and they slipped out of a side door, crossed the moat, and walked along the side of it across the lawns. The air was cool and gray and hazy with the milky before-dawn light. The birds were singing their crazy dawn chorus from every tree and bush and rooftop, and the dewy world smelled of grass and the good earth and trees and flowers and fresh, verdant life. Eleanor felt, despite her tiredness, a surge of vigor running through her veins, and as if in answer the child in her belly stirred and kicked. She put her hands over it and laughed.

"Another son, my lord, if I'm not mistaken."

Robert looked up at her, pleased and interested. "Can you feel him? Dear God, what a strange thing it must be to be a woman!"

"I often think that about men." Eleanor laughed. "This one's a lusty one, all right. We shall come safe to harbor this time."

Robert took her hand and kissed it, and continued to hold it as they walked along.

"Not cold, are you?" he asked.

She shook her head. "They will be happy together," she said after a moment, "—Edward and his Daisy. She's a good girl, and he's a good man, too—slow, but dependable."

"A change for you to be talking of them being happy," Robert teased her. "What boots it them be happy, so long as they are good?"

"How can you separate the two?" Eleanor said. "When I was unhappiest, it was because I was doing wrong. Gaby was right," she added cryptically.

"My dear, when have you ever been wrong?" Robert asked.

Eleanor shook her head. "You think too much of me. I am as faulty as any creature. More than many, I suppose. More than Edward's Daisy, I warrant you." She paused. "There's the sun—look! It's going to be a beautiful day. I love May of all months—so green and lovely, so peaceful, but so full of life and vigor. I feel as though I should live forever."

Robert glanced at her, seeing her shining eyes fixed on the gold rim of the sun as it lifted over the trees, seeing the flush of healthy blood in her smooth cheek, her lips parted with pleasure, the shadow of her dark hair, almost untouched with gray, under her simple veil, for she had taken off her elaborate headdress. She was forty-two, but she had lost none of her beauty. She was like a magical creature to him. Hares are often thought to be witches or fairies in disguise; the white hare was a white witch, perhaps, and would never grow old.

And even as he thought that, her mind had already traveled on with more vigor and force than his. Her next words were far from his romantic musings.

"They'll have a great estate to inherit—and it will be even greater if we put our fortunes into cloth instead of wool. Just think, Robert—"

"No," he said firmly. "I don't want to think of that now. I don't know if I ever want to think of it. But certainly not now. Let's just walk, dearest wife, and be at peace. Don't start another argument at this of all times."

Eleanor stared at him in surprise for a moment, and then shrugged, and then smiled. She pressed the hand that held hers. "Very well," she said compliantly, and then spoiled the effect by adding, "there's plenty of time to change your mind."

Incorrigible, he thought. But I love her.

CHAPTER ELEVEN

Just before dusk Robert arrived back at Morland Place. He had been, with Reynold the bailiff and Clement the packer, to look over the Shawe estate.

"There is a lot that could be improved upon," he told Eleanor in answer to her inquiry. "I think Master Shawe has been finding things a little too much for him recently. His packer is an out-and-out thief. I'm sending Clement over there tomorrow to take over until we can find someone else."

Eleanor nodded her approval. "I think you're right about him finding things too much for him. He needed a son to take over and back him up. That was why he kept Cecily at home for so long, I think—just to comfort him."

"Strange how some people go that way," Robert mused. "He was young enough to marry again when his wife died. He could have taken a young wife and got him ten sons by now, but somehow he just never let her go in his heart."

Eleanor tossed her head scornfully. "If he had done his duty he would have married again. He thought of himself more than of his duty."

"Lucky for us that he did," Robert remarked mildly. "If he'd had sons, Cecily would not have had the estate. I think we might do worse than to send young Harry over there with Clement. Let him try his hand at running the estate. It will take the strain off Master Shawe and be good training for the boy. Clement will see he doesn't go too far wrong."

"A good idea, husband," Eleanor said, crossing to where he sat to kiss his forehead approvingly. As her lips touched his brow, she frowned and straightened abruptly. "Your forehead is burning hot," she said. "Have you a fever? Are you ill, Robert? You look very tired."

"I feel tired," he admitted unwillingly, "and my head is aching. Perhaps I've been riding too hard."

But Eleanor placed her hand across his brow and shook her head. "I think perhaps you had better not take a walk with me this evening, but go to your bed and rest. You certainly feel very hot to me."

Robert caught her wrist and kept her hand where it was. "Ah, that feels good," he said, smiling up at her. "Your hand is so cool. I almost think you could charm away my headache with your touch alone."

"Nevertheless, I think you should go to your bed, and I'll make you up a draft and bring it to you."

Robert made a face. "I know your black drafts," he said.

Eleanor laughed. "Just like a child!" she said. "But even if you screw up your face, you shall take it, to please me. Come now, you know I should be humored, being so near my time."

"To please you, then," Robert said, pushing himself to his feet wearily. He was secretly pleased to be bullied by Eleanor into going to bed, for he felt worse than he would admit to, and he thought it would be pleasant to rest between cool linen sheets and have the women running about taking care of him—even if it did mean one of Eleanor's bitter herbal drinks.

His pages helped him upstairs and undressed him, and a little later Eleanor brought him the draft in a beech bowl.

"What's in it?" Robert asked suspiciously, looking at the greenish liquid from which there rose a sour smell.

"Never mind what's in it," Eleanor chided him. "Just drink it."

He tasted and made a face.

"Don't sip at it like a green maid, drink it off."

"Not until you tell me what's in it," he said stubbornly, childlike.

Eleanor sighed impatiently. "Green rue and rosemary for the headache, belladonna for the fever, and mandrake to make you sleep."

"Oh," said Robert. He had never troubled to learn about herbs—Eleanor and Job between them had laid out the herb garden and tended it—although many gentlemen of fashion liked to discuss herbs and medicines and swap recipes for sovereign cures. He drank off the draft quickly and made an involuntary sound of disgust as the bitter taste gripped the sides of his tongue.

"Good," Eleanor said with approval, taking back the bowl. She passed it to her maid in exchange for a cup from which a wisp of steam arose. "And now, to take the taste away, a caudle."

"Ah, that's better," Robert said, taking the cup in both hands and sniffing. "And what's—"

"Milk and honey and cinnamon and nutmeg and white of egg," Eleanor said quickly. "And when you've drunk it, you should lie back and rest. Would you like me to read to you?"

"No, no, my hinny, you shouldn't tire yourself," Robert said. "My page shall sit with me for a while. I feel as if I might sleep a little."

Half an hour later the draft had done its work and Robert was sleeping. Eleanor touched his brow and thought he felt cooler and decided that it was simply too much exertion in the heat of the day that had brought on the headache. Robert slept quietly right through the night, but the next day when Eleanor woke she found him drenched in sweat, and obviously still slightly feverish, and her heart sank.

"I shall call for the doctor to see you," she said.

"No, no, dearest, I must get up. There is much to be seen to," Robert said anxiously.

Eleanor pushed him back gently onto the pillows. "There are plenty of others who can see to the estate. That's what you pay them for. You must lie abed and wait until the doctor has seen you. You know you mustn't worry me in my condition."

Using that excuse again she got him to consent to stay

abed, but very unwillingly. As she left the bedchamber she found Job, like the good servant he was, just outside where he was wanted.

"Is the master ill, madam?" he asked.

Eleanor shrugged slightly. "I don't know, Job. He seems a little feverish, and I've made him promise to stay where he is until I've seen the doctor about him. It may be riding about in the hot sun that's brought it on. At any rate the rest will do him good."

"Best send Owen for the doctor, madam," Job suggested. "He's the quickest-witted, and if the doctor isn't at his house—"

"Yes, of course," Eleanor said. If the doctor wasn't at his house, Owen would go and look for him, whereas a stupider page might just come back and report failure. "Job, when you've sent Owen, I think it would be a good idea to go in and see the master and let him know that everything about the estate is being taken care of. That way he won't worry so much."

"Yes, mistress," Job said, smiling over this gentle deception. "I'll ask Reynold what was to be done today, and make all the arrangements."

"Good," Eleanor said, and rested her hand a moment affectionately on Job's shoulder before hurrying off to see to her household.

Dr. Brackenbury came just before dinner time, riding in on his fine chestnut horse, which was as much a part of his professional accoutrements as his gold-knobbed stick. A patient would sooner get better if he trusted in his doctor, and he would sooner trust in his doctor if his doctor were obviously a wealthy and successful man. Dr. Brackenbury's black robes were of the finest cloth, and trimmed with rich fur, and he wore a broad gold chain around his neck about which he was suitably mysterious. Some said it was a gift from the great Earl of Warwick himself, presented to Dr. Brackenbury after he cured him of an ague. The beautiful chestnut gelding was also supposed to be a gift from a grateful patient, but Dr. Brackenbury in his modesty would never talk about it.

But despite his air of fashion and supposed wealthy patrons, the doctor did not subscribe to any new wonder-cures or fashionable treatments, but contented himself with the well-tried herbal remedies, charms, and simples, in which he had great faith. In this he was like Eleanor, and it was partly because of this attitude that she called on him—for she would never have much respect for someone who disagreed with her on a subject she felt she knew a lot about. He was also kindly and gentle in his manner, which was useful when Eleanor called on him to attend and dose sick servants, who tended to panic badly when faced with any kind of illness.

On this occasion the doctor chatted genially with Robert while he examined him: he felt his face, handled his limbs, looked into his mouth and eyes, sniffed at him, and stood for a while with his eyes shut, sucking the gold head of his doctor's cane as if awaiting inspiration. Then he opened his eyes, smiled at Robert, and bid him good morning. Outside the bedchamber he spoke to Eleanor, with Job and Anys to give her courage.

"A little fever, I think, mistress," he said gently, nodding and smiling as if to rob his words of their menace. "I cannot tell at this stage of what sort. It may be a marsh fever. Has he been near any swampy ground recently?"

Eleanor shook her head doubtfully. "I don't think so. Unless you count our evening walks by the river. It's damp there, but not really swampy."

"I shouldn't think that would matter," the doctor said. "However, we shall tell better in a day or so. It may pass off quite quickly. In the meantime—shut the windows up tight and keep a good fire in the room, day and night. And the herbs you have been administering—quite satisfactory, but with the addition of camomile and fennel. And I will have my apothecary to send round an electuary of my own recipe, and a henbane draft to make him sleep. I will call again tomorrow, mistress. God keep you."

"And you, Master Brackenbury," Eleanor said. "Job, when you have seen the doctor safe on his way, come to me in the herb garden. I shall need your help. Anys, you had better see about the fire, and tell Jacques to make up another cordial. I must go and see Master Jenney and see the children are kept away."

"Yes, mistress. But, mistress, shouldn't you be resting. In your condition—" But Anys's gentle plea was hardly heard and certainly not regarded. Eleanor could never bear to do nothing when there was anything at all that needed doing.

On the second day Robert's temperature was higher, and he did not even speak about getting up. The doctor called again, and bled him with leeches, saying the blood was overheated. Robert seemed to feel relief at once, but the relief lasted only a very short time. That night he tossed and turned and muttered in his fitful sleep. Eleanor slept on a mattress beside the bed so that he could thrash about without danger to the child she was carrying.

On the third day, Robert's fever was higher again, and he was intermittently delirious, sometimes raving and flinging himself from side to side in the bed, sometimes shivering and sweating both at once, sometimes lying still, his eyes staring sightlessly at the canopy of the bed, his face flushed, murmuring and moaning quietly. When his senses returned he would watch Eleanor as she moved about the room or sat beside him, trying to smile with lips cracked by the fever, not talking, but crying softly if she left the room for any reason.

Dr. Brackenbury did not smile at all as he spoke to Eleanor. The expression of his eyes was kindly, but grave.

"It may be one of two things, madam," he told her. "It may be marsh fever, in which case we may hope for a good recovery as soon as the fever breaks. But it may be smoke-fever, or tuphos-fever as we call it, and if that is the case the situation is more grave. There can be grave complications, internal complications, with that kind of fever."

"And how will you know which sort it is?" Eleanor asked, dry-mouthed.

"With tuphos-fever there are always spots, red spots on the chest and abdomen," the doctor said simply.

"But there are no such spots," Eleanor said, looking up eagerly.

"They do not always appear at once. We must wait, and hope."

"Is there nothing more we can do? No remedy you know of?" Eleanor's eyes searched his face pleadingly.

"Well," he said doubtfully.

"Anything at all," Eleanor said. "You know that we are a wealthy family. Whatever can be got for gold, we will get it."

"Madam, there is a substance, distilled from the bark of certain trees, a febrifuge said to be of sovereign power."

"Well, then," Eleanor said, starting to her feet.

"The doctor held up a restraining hand. "I do not have any of this substance. The trees do not grow in this country. The liquid is rare, and can be got only at great trouble and expense. It is brought, I am told, from China."

That was the other end of the world, as far as the stars. Eleanor sank back down, turning her hands against each other anxiously.

"It could never be got from so far in time," she said.

"It can be got," the doctor said, "and generally the great households can obtain it. If they had ordered any of it for a previous occasion and still had a little left—your patron, I believe, a great man—wealthy—a large household—" He gave a discreet cough, hoping he had said enough.

Eleanor's eyes glowed suddenly with renewed hope.

"Write down the name of this substance for me, Doctor. I will write at once. Owen, fetch me paper and pen, and then go and saddle your master's horse. You shall take the letter for me. Her grace is at Fotheringay with the children, I believe. Job! Job! Ah, there you are! Tell off two armed men, see them mounted on good horses. They are to go with Owen—I'll explain everything later. Hurry now. Doctor, thank you for your help. If this can save my husband, if it can be got from my lady, I will reward you a thousandfold. God bless you, for you are a wise man."

The doctor bowed. "I will call again tomorrow, madam. And be of good heart. It may yet turn out to be only marsh fever. God be with you."

After the flurry of activity that saw Owen and two armed men off on their urgent mission, bearing a letter of impassioned plea from Eleanor and a saddlebag of gold that necessitated the armed guard, a quietness fell on the house, for there was nothing else to do but wait. Eleanor and Anys sat with Robert, sharing the task between them, for he was not comfortable without one or the other of them by him. Job saw to the running of the house. Isabella was sent off to stay with her sister Helen, and Harry and John were taken by Master Jenney to stay with Master Shawe for the time being, to get them out of the house. Master James came into the bedchamber to say the morning and evening prayers with the sick man and his watchers, but though Eleanor would have liked the chaplain there more often, she found that his presence disturbed Robert, and so kept him away.

On the morning of the fourth day when the doctor came to examine Robert, Robert was in a kind of stupor, lying still, his eyes half closed, apparently neither seeing nor hearing, unaware of his surroundings or of anything that went on. Dr. Brackenbury seemed depressed by that quietness, and having bent low over his patient he called Eleanor to him with the gravest of expressions.

"Look," he said.

Eleanor looked, and her heart seemed to jump up into her throat and choke her. The doctor had unlaced the neck of Robert's bed-gown, and the white chest he had exposed was disfigured with small red spots.

"Sweet Jesu," Eleanor whispered. "Is it—?"

"I fear so," Dr. Brackenbury said gravely. "There can be no doubt now. The stupor, the spots—I'm afraid there is no doubt."

Eleanor could not speak for a moment. Reaching behind her for support she found and grasped Anys's work-roughed hand. "What will happen?" she asked.

"If no complications develop, and if the fever breaks soon, there is a chance. The disease is very weakening to those who survive it. He might be an invalid for a very long time."

"And if not?"

"Madam, it would be wrong of me to give you false hope. If complications develop, and perhaps even if they do not, he may die. There is nothing we can do but pray to our Lord God to have mercy on us, and to spare His servant, if it is His will."

"But—the medicine—I sent for—the one you told me about—if it should come?" Eleanor whispered.

"Even then—the medicine is a febrifuge, it brings down the fever. If the fever is brought down before the patient is too much weakened by the disease, he has a better chance. That's all. There is no cure for the tuphos-fever."

Eleanor stared at him white-faced for a moment, and then sank to the floor in a faint. Anys cried out and dropped to her knees beside her, and then quickly called out for her maids.

"She is under great strain," Dr. Brackenbury said. "She should not, so near her time, be subjected to such strain. See if you can keep her from the sick room, get her to rest, nurse your master yourself."

"I'll try," said Anys, "but my mistress is strong-willed, and it is her husband—"

"I know, child, I know. But try."

"I'll get Job to speak to her. He can sometimes persuade her," Anys murmured, more to herself than to the doctor. With the help of the maids she saw her mistress to another room, and then went back to take her place by the master's bed.

Nothing even that Job could say would keep Eleanor away from the sickroom. She felt that the child would take care of itself—her place was with Robert. She had always been the stronger member of the partnership, and had always undervalued Robert's quiet virtues. In the beginning of their marriage she had despised him for his weakness, his inability to face up to his father, and, though only obliquely, his difficulties over the marital act. She had developed a habit of thinking little of him, and had scarcely realized that her own attitude was changing, until she had been faced by the doctor with the realization that she might be about to lose him. Then she saw vividly what her life would be like without him; then she saw how much he meant to her, her quiet, kindly, loving husband.

He had always loved her, always thought her right whatever she did. She felt horribly guilty that she had never given him his due as her husband, had never in her secret heart given herself to him, although he could not know about this. She longed to confess to him, to break down and pour out to him the story of her secret guilt, to hear him say he understood and forgave her. That was impossible, of course—she could not have that comfort. But she would nurse him with all the skill and patience at her command, sparing herself nothing, nurse him if it cost her her life and that of the child. Only thus could she appease her sense of guilt and remorse.

So she sat with him day after day. It was tedious, heart-breaking work. Most of the time he lay in a stupor, neither stirring nor speaking, and there was nothing to do for him but to mop the sweat from him, and, with the help of Anys and the maids, change his linen from time to time, and try to spoon into him the herbal medicines that seemed to have no effect on this horrible disease that gripped him in its deadly maw. At other times he would shiver violently and at others again would thresh his limbs freely and shout and mutter in delirium.

The flesh seemed to melt from his bones, leaving him a gray skeleton covered tautly with skin, skin mottled with the horrible red spots, some of which began to suppurate. His lips were cracked and white with the fever, his tongue swollen in his mouth. And the room stank from the accumulation of foul airs, the smoke and herbs and sweat and the sweetish-bad smell of fever, but the doctor forbade the least breath of fresh air in the room—it would be instantly fatal, he said.

Job persuaded Eleanor to leave Robert to take her meals, and then she would sometimes sit in the herb garden for a little while, glad to get away from the stifling stink of the bedchamber and to breathe the delicately aromatic scent of the plants and shrubs and feel the cooling breeze on her face. Job would sometimes try to delay her there by talking to her, but she had no interest in anything but Robert, and would scarcely notice that he was speaking. She was in a kind of daze of tiredness and anxiety and remorse; she hardly felt anything anymore.

Then in the afternoon of the seventh day, before they looked to see them, Owen and his two attendants rode in on foundered, lathered horses. The men were gray with dust and fatigue, having ridden to Fotheringay and back without staying even a night there. Their eyes were red-rimmed and the horses were sagging at the knee with effort, but Owen held in his hand a small vial of the precious bark-juice, and in his breast a letter from the Duchess Cecily.

"Thank God, thank God," Eleanor cried when her fingers curled round the vial. The exhausted men lolled on benches in the shade of the stable-block, too done up even to seek their quarters. That they had ridden so hard was a testimony to their love for their master, but Eleanor could not stay to thank them nor read the letter from her benefactress—she was running as fast as her bulk allowed her into the house and up the stairs to the room where Anys kept watch with fading hope over her master's coma.

"It's come, Anys—it's here!" Eleanor cried, holding out her hand with the vial.

Anys jumped up, her hand going to her throat, her eyes fixed on that small object on which all their hopes hung. Eleanor's hands trembled so much she could not even unstop the vial, and she had in the end to pass it to Anys and sink weakly on a stool, her hands wound together and her eyes on her husband's face. Anys added the few drops to a little milk as they had been instructed by the doctor, in case the medicine could be procured, and then lifted Robert's head from the pillow and tipped the draft into his mouth. For a second nothing happened, and then he choked and swallowed convulsively, and a little milk ran out of the corners of his mouth.

"We have to repeat the dose every four hours," Anys said.

"Yes," said Eleanor. Their eyes met, and then they looked away again, ashamed of the mingled hope and fear they read in each other's faces.

The long evening passed and the long night began. They administered another draft every four hours to the unconscious man, hardly knowing what they expected to happen, or even if any of the precious liquid was going down his throat. The candles burned low, and then guttered and went out. The fire smoldered into glowing ashes, and the two women dozed, one on each side of the bed. Around them the house was as silent as a tomb, and outside the closed window the night was black and soundless, too. It was as if the end of the world had come, and there were nothing after it.

Eleanor woke from a fitful doze to this unearthly silence, and found the room full of a gray light, the pearly light that comes before dawn, before the birds waken and begin their morning chorus. It must be time to give the bark essence again, she thought, and with an effort stood up and moved stiffly across to the bed. She felt unreal, as if she, too, were in a fever: a numbness combined of exhaustion and strained emotions. She was stiff and a little cold, and she saw that the fire had almost gone out. That was bad—she must call for a boy and get some kindling to it quickly, before the last glowing jewels went out.

But then she saw her husband's face, and she stopped, all other thoughts drained away. He was dead. His face was calm and quiet, with an unearthly peace that left her in no doubt that he was dead, even before she realized that she could no longer hear his hoarse, labored breathing in the silence. The unreality extended around her as she stared down at that peaceful face, and she felt nothing, nothing at all, no grief, no surprise, nothing. She thought only, "Now it doesn't matter about the fire."

Outside the first blackbird threw a few tentative notes into the air, where they shimmered like dew, and then began his song in earnest. It didn't matter now about keeping the window shut, Eleanor thought. Suddenly she was seized with the longing to breathe clean air again, and she went to the window and opened the casement wide, letting the clean, soft, scented air of dawn steal into the room. Eleanor closed her eyes and breathed in deeply. How strange that this stuff that was like wine to her as she dragged it deep into her lungs should be so dangerous to invalids! And then she heard Anys give a little cry.

"Mistress! Look!"

Eleanor turned. Anys had waked and gone to look at her master, and found him sleeping naturally, his breathing quiet, his skin cool and damp. And then the breath of fresh air had stolen across him, and he had awaked. Robert's eyes were open; he looked at Anys and then at Eleanor with recognition. He tried to smile with his poor parched lips.

"Eleanor," he whispered.

"Oh, my darling," she whispered in reply, "you're well again."

"The—air—smells good," he said with difficulty. He tried to raise a hand toward his wife. "Eleanor—"

Eleanor ran across the room and took his hand in hers, and then sank to her knees beside the bed, cradling the hand to her cheek and weeping and smiling at the same time.

"Oh Robert, oh, Robert, I thought you were dead," she cried foolishly. "Anys, run and wake the house—call Job— tell them all—" And then she could speak no longer for tears.

It was a strange, wonderful day, like a feast-day. The news flew around the house as if on wings—the master was recovered—and everywhere the servants sang amid their tasks and smiled at each other as they passed. Eleanor sat with Robert the whole day, just as she had while he was unconscious, but now it was no vigil—it was a time of purest joy, and she sat beside him, with his hand in hers, often silent, sometimes talking, but always with a heart full to bursting with happiness that he had been spared her.

Robert was very weak, and sometimes he dozed off into a deep, quiet sleep for an hour or two, but when he woke he smiled gladly at Eleanor, and they talked together as if they had been apart for a year.

"When I thought you had died," Eleanor said at one time, "I felt as if I had died, too—everything inside me was black and empty."

"I didn't know you loved me so much," Robert said, and because he was weak his eyes filled with grateful tears. "Anys says you've never left my side. Oh, my hinny bird, you've done so much for me."

"No, Robert," Eleanor began, ashamed.

He stopped her with a glance. "I'll make it up to you," he promised. "I know I've never been more than half a man to you—well, only the once"—Eleanor blushed red at the memory, but her heart scalded her with shame that he should feel he had let her down—"but it was not because I didn't love you. It was because I love you too much. Since the first moment I saw you, I've loved you with all my heart and soul."

"Robert, don't—" Eleanor cried softly. "I'm so glad you love me, but—" Impossible to go on. "When you're well again, we'll be happy, really happy this time. God is good, He has given us another chance."

Robert did not fully understand her, but he was too weak and tired to wonder much. He wandered now to his inner thoughts.

"While I was ill, you know," he said, "I thought a lot about things. I felt as if I was locked inside myself, unable to speak or move, but otherwise quite rational, normal. I kept thinking about our lives together, and the way things have happened to us. And particularly about Lord Edmund, and all we owed him."

Eleanor saw the sadness in his face, and half guessed what was coming.

"And do you know what I kept thinking?" Robert went on. "I kept thinking of him dying, Eleanor, dying betrayed. I fought against him in the battle in which he died. I betrayed him—"

"No," Eleanor cried out. "That's not so. You didn't betray him—he betrayed you. There is no faith owed to a bad man. He turned bad, Robert, so you gave your faith to another."

Robert shook his head tiredly. "I wish I could believe that—it would be comfortable. But I can't. All I know is, a man is nothing without his honor, without that faith he makes to his master, to serve him to the end. It isn't for the servant to question the master's acts."

"How can you say so?" Eleanor asked urgently. "What else does our conscience do but force us to question every act? If we give our faith blindly—"

"Yes, blindly. It isn't for us to judge—that's for God. And if you once give your faith—" He paused, coughing, and then resumed more quietly, "—once given, you have not that faith to give again. I was Lord Edmund's man. I still am. And I betrayed him."

Eleanor said nothing, but she began to weep silently. She knew in her heart that he was right, for she had given her faith to Lord Richard, and she knew that whatever he did, she would never be able to withdraw it. Yet she had forced Robert to do just that, rationalizing the move to him, because she wanted her whole family to serve the lord she had chosen. She had forced Robert to betray his master. And yet Robert did not blame her—gentle husband, he took the blame to himself. Helplessly, she wept, and Job coming into the room called her maids and bid them take her to the guest chamber and make her lie down.

"You must rest, mistress, or you will make yourself ill. You are worn out. Go and sleep now. The master will sleep too, and I will give orders for you to be called when he wakes. Now, does that satisfy you?"

Eleanor did not argue. She was in truth exhausted, and when she reached the guest chamber, she did not even have the strength to stand up while her maids undressed her: she sank as she was on to the bed, and was asleep as soon as her head touched the pillow.

She slept right through the night, and, since Job had given orders behind her back that she was not to be woken, no one disturbed her. When she did wake it was broad morning, the birds were singing, and the world was fresh and bright with the dew beginning to rise in the hot sun. Anys came in to her.

"Good morning, madam. You have slept well, I see. You look much better."

"How—"

"The master slept, too, and he's awake now and hungry. Food is being sent up to him. There is hot water—will you bathe, madam? You will feel fresher. And then breakfast?"

"Yes, Anys. That sounds wonderful. I feel so much better today, I feel as if I should live forever. Yes, I will bathe. Let me get these clothes off—I must stink like a beggar, for I'm sure I haven't been out of them for a week."

While Eleanor was bathing and dressing, Robert was eating ravenously, with Job supporting him and spooning gruel into him.

"Slops," Robert said disgustedly between mouthfuls. "I'm hungry enough to eat a whole ox, and you give me slops!"

"Dr. Brackenbury says you shouldn't have solid foods at first," Job said imperturbably.

"Nonsense," Robert said. "How can I get my strength back on slops? Are you trying to kill me? I want meat and bread, not this foul sheep-dip."

"It's very strengthening gruel," Job said, suspending operations to look sternly at his master, "and what Dr. Brackenbury says is law as far as the mistress goes."

Robert accepted another spoonful, grumbling. "A man should know what his own stomach needs."

Eleanor sat with him again all morning. Their hands were interwoven, and they talked together as if they would never tire. She was shocked by how thin and gray and old he looked, and could hardly believe that he was alive at all, except that he spoke so cheerfully. His spirit was strong, though his body was weak, and it was that which led to tragedy.

It happened that Eleanor had left his bedside to go and see the children and tell them the good news. Job and Anys and Owen were all busy about the house, and Robert's young page was attending him.

Robert bid the boy fetch him food, a cold fowl, and some bread and a cup of wine; and the boy went down to the kitchen and found not Jacques, but only some of the kitchen boys who didn't know any better. He made his request, the boys gave him what he asked for, and he bore the loaded tray back to his master.

"That's more like it," Robert said eagerly. "Help me to sit up, boy, and then cut up that chicken. Oh, don't bother about ceremony. Just hack it into four—I'm too hungry to wait."

He made a good meal, and the boy took away the tray before anyone else knew of the event. Robert felt better, and told himself he had been right, that he knew best after all. But as the afternoon wore on he began to feel pains in his stomach, and then began to vomit. Eleanor sent for the doctor at once, and did not flinch at holding the basin for Robert. She was terrified by the turn of events, but Robert, ashamed now at having defied the doctor, did not mention his secret meal and so she had no idea what was happening.

By the time the doctor arrived Robert was writhing with pain and voiding blood from both ends. Dr. Brackenbury's face darkened with anger and apprehension.

"What has been happening here?" he asked. "He has been eating solid food, the which I specifically warned against."

"I gave him none, Doctor—gruel and milk was all I gave him," Eleanor cried out, frightened.

"He has had some all the same. I suggest you question your servants. The food has damaged him inside."

"Is it bad?" Eleanor was white with fear.

"Madam, I cannot conceal from you that it is very bad." He paused for a moment, and then went on very quietly, "I think you should have a priest on hand."

Eleanor gave an unearthly cry and rushed back to the bedside, grasping Robert's hand and pulling it to her as if she might drag him back out of the danger that threatened him. But Robert was writhing and groaning and did not know she was there.

It was two hours after noon when Robert began to feel the pains, and three hours after noon when the doctor came. At half past three he suffered a series of convulsions, causing his eyes to roll upward in his head, the whites glaring past his drawn-back eyelids in a horrible caricature of life. At a quarter before four, he was dead.

Eleanor at first wanted to kill with her own hands the servant boy who had brought the food, and then wanted to have him charged with murder, but Job dissuaded her, pointing out that the boy had simply obeyed an order he was bound by his service to obey; so she merely dismissed him and warned him that if he ever came to York again she would have his head.

Robert was buried with great splendor in the crypt under the chapel at Morland Place, and there were hundreds of mourners at the feast afterward, a feast that surpsssed even Edward's wedding feast for size and extravagance. Two brass and marble memorials were set up, one in Holy Trinity church within the city and one in the chapel at home, showing Robert dressed as a master stapler and inscribed "In God is Death at End."

Eleanor's deep grief had to be kept for those times when she was alone, for now she had the estate to run as well as the house; she was master now as well as mistress. And she had to prepare her black mourning clothes, and get ready to lie in with the child which was due at the end of the month or the beginning of September: the child Robert would never see, and the last child she would ever bear.

BOOK TWO

THE
WHITE
ROSE

CHAPTER TWELVE

The baby was born on the first of September and was a boy. Eleanor called him Richard, in honor of the family's patron, and asked Lord Richard to be the child's sponsor, and to her delight the Duke wrote a very kind letter agreeing to be the sponsor and sending a handsome set of silver spoons as a christening gift. A proxy stood for the Duke at the christening, sent from Fotheringay for the purpose, and Eleanor was pleased at this evidence of Lord Richard's care. It seemed appropriate on another level that the child should be called Richard, for Duchess Cecily's last child had been called Richard, too; and Eleanor remembered that the Yorks' first child had been a girl and called Anne, just as her own had, and that their firstborn son had been called Edward, again as her own had. Calling her last child Richard seemed to round off a sort of pattern, gave a rightness to the matter.

Christmas that year was a time of mixed sadness and joy. Sadness, of course, because it was their first Christmas without Robert. Eleanor's grief was locked inside her, and she would never speak of it to anyone, but it was impossible for those close to her not to know that she felt badly. Isabella, who had always loved her father best, brooded more darkly than ever, and only Harry and John were cheerful. There was added sadness in the death of Cecily's father, Master Shawe on the eighteenth of December; and in a smaller but still poignant way in the discovery of

Eleanor's mare, Lepida, lying dead in the home paddock, her coat no less white than the snow. The mare was twenty-eight years old, but had seemed fit for many more years, and her death was a shock to Eleanor.

But there was joy in the news that Cecily was pregnant and hoped to bear the heir to the Morland dynasty in July 1459; in the robust good health of baby Richard; and in the news that the Duke of York was to pay the Morlands a brief visit in January when he would be passing through. Another small but satisfying matter was the news that Robert's application for a coat of arms had at last been granted, and the coat was described as "argent, a white hare courant, proper, on a fess noir." Eleanor was delighted, and hastened to order livery for the servants, only regretting it could not be ready in time for Lord Richard's visit.

The Duke of York left home after the services on Plough Monday and was at Morland Place on the Tuesday. He and Eleanor greeted each other warmly, and looked each other over with a keen eye; probably both saw changes in the other. To Eleanor's partial eye, Lord Richard was looking older, and tired, but his charm was as potent as ever, and she still thought him the handsomest man she had ever seen. He had come bearing gifts for all the family, among which was a purple cloak for Eleanor, lined with black fox fur brought all the way from the Baltic, a gift so rich it almost made her cry; and a silver cup for the baby.

"My godson and namesake—how is he? Am I not to see him?"

"But of course, your Grace." Eleanor changed easily from tears to laughter. "The difficulty has been in keeping his governess from bringing him to meet you on the road halfway to Fotheringay."

Anys brought forward the baby in his white robes, and Richard inspected him with a serious and experienced eye.

"A fine, healthy baby, madam, stout of limb and bright of eye," Lord Richard pronounced. "And I should know— seen enough of 'em in my time. Let me hold him, nurse. Come, you don't need to worry," as Anys hesitated, "I've never dropped one yet." The baby went to him willingly enough, and was soon gurgling with laughter and waving his fists around. One of them caught Lord Richard a blow on the chin that he pretended was so painful he handed the baby back to his nurse.

"I see he's challenging me already," Lord Richard said, rubbing his chin ruefully. "I daren't think what will happen when he's full-grown. I think he'll be another giant like my own Edward. Do you realize, Eleanor, that boy's over six feet tall, and only seventeen. I don't think he's done growing yet." Talking cheerfully, they went inside to the great hall where the feast and entertainment were ready.

"How is my lady your wife, and the other children?" Eleanor asked politely.

"Well, I thank God, though I'm afraid the youngest are suffering from the lack of a father's presence at home. George and Margaret are like wild animals, for all Cecily can do, though little Richard is studious enough." He sighed, but his eyes were merry. "He takes after me, poor child. The others are all as golden and lovely as their mother, but Richard is little and dark and serious like me."

"I have to thank your lady for the great kindness she showed me when my husband was ill, in sending the medicine and such a kind letter," Eleanor said.

Lord Richard laid a hand over hers, which was resting on his arm as he escorted her up to the dais where the high table was set.

"I'm so sorry that it had not better effect," he said. "Though we cannot argue with God's will, it is often hard to bear such a loss cheerfully." Eleanor smiled a little and lowered her eyes to hide the tears which sprang unbidden.

"Tell me," Lord Richard went on when they were seated, "how are you managing? I must say that everything seems very orderly."

"It is easier than we expected it to be," Eleanor told him. "The estate servants are all very good, and I have an excellent steward and a trustworthy bailiff. I always had a strong interest in running the estate, so I was able to help my son Edward to take over the reins. But he's very capable. His father gave him a good grounding, and he's quick to learn and slow to forget."

Richard looked along the table at Edward, sitting with his wife. "He is married since I last heard from you?"

"Yes, last summer to Cecily Shawe."

"She's as pretty and blooming a girl as I ever saw."

"My son Thomas nicknamed her Daisy, and the name sticks to her. It suits her, I think. She is with child now, God be thanked."

Richard's eyes twinkled. "So, Mistress Courteney, you are to be a grandmother now?"

"Actually this will make the third time," Eleanor replied, "as our Anne already has two sons. But, my lord, how are your affairs? We have had no news since the winter began."

Lord Richard shook his head. "The news is all bad. The Queen is implacable, and determined to destroy us. Sooner or later it will have to come to arms. The King loves and trusts me, but he is entirely the Queen's creature and does whatever she bids him. I will buy time while I can, but in the end—I cannot allow her to destroy my family. In the end I must fight."

"When—if it comes to that," Eleanor said, low and intensely, "call on me. I will send as many men as I can—I can promise you twenty, maybe more—and all the gold I have in my possession. Whatever lies in my power, I will do, my lord."

"Thank you," he said simply.

Later, when they were all retiring to bed and Eleanor and Lord Richard were walking up the stairs together with their servants a little way behind, he said, "I have to thank you, Eleanor, for your hospitality, and for all your kindness."

"The honor was mine, my lord," Eleanor said, "and the kindness all yours."

They reached the dividing of the passage and stopped. Richard took her hand and kissed it, a courtly gesture the more touching on that soldierly man.

"Dark times are ahead," he said. "I shall need the help of every friend. It is good to know there is a friend at your back when you are facing your enemies."

"I would to God I were a man and could fight with you," Eleanor said fervently. "But I will send you men, and pray for all of you."

"I shan't forget. God knows when we shall meet again. If anything should happen to me—"

"Your son, Edward." Eleanor understood him. "I would make the same faith to him."

"God bless you for that. There is treachery everywhere, but I know that you and your family will hold true."

Eleanor thought of Robert then, and how he had been forced to betray his own lord. "We will hold true," she said.

They parted then and went to their chambers. He would be gone before dawn the next day, there would be no more time for speech. Eleanor lay in her bed, a lonely bed now, though Anys shared it with her, and her thoughts tumbled around in her head like stones in a whirlpool. She heard his words again and again: *Dark times are ahead* and *God knows when we shall meet again*; she remembered Robert saying, *A man is nothing without his honor* and *You have not that faith to give again.* Lord Edmund had died betrayed. Betrayal, the bitterest of blows. And Eleanor, what was she?

The house was quiet, every soul was abed. Eleanor rose and put on her cloak over her nightgown and stole softly out of the chamber and along the passage to pause before the door of the chamber wherein he lay. There was a double-edged blade in her heart, of love and honor; for a long time she stared at the door, her hand still by her side, and as if the door were made of glass she thought she could see inside, see him lying wakeful in his bed. God knows when we shall meet again. He was a soldier whose life was one long series of partings. And she was a widow. Robert was dead now, and the older faith was strong upon her. Her hand lifted to the door-latch, but before she could touch it the door opened silently. Their eyes met.

"I knew you would come," she said.

2

In the summer of 1459 Thomas came home, having finished his University course, and intent on having a short rest before going to London to enter the Temple to continue his study of Law. He found things much changed since his visit the summer before for Edward's marriage. The first surprise was to see the upper servants in livery, a smart russet livery with the black-and-white coat of arms on the back and the Morland badge of the hare and heather on the breast. Now Edward and the rest of them were gentlemen in name as well as in fact. It pleased Thomas, though he made mock of it aloud.

It shocked him to see his mother in black, for she had always been fond of bright colors, vivid jewel hues of red and green and blue and amber; but he decided that she looked well in it, for it showed up the bright blue of her eyes and the creamy pallor of her skin. She didn't smile as often as before, he noticed, but on the other hand she was full of energy, directing matters with a firm hand, often to poor Edward's frustration, and still finding time to break a fiery red colt to saddle to replace dear old Lepida.

"He's to be called Lepidus, of course," Eleanor told him when he had admired the half-wild creature and shaken his head over the possibility of his mother breaking all her bones before she ever broke the colt.

And of course there were the two new babies in the nursery—his brother Richard, who at ten months was already walking and talking like a two-year-old, and his nephew, Edward, and Daisy's new son. This baby was given the dynastic name of Edward, but was already called Ned to distinguish him. He was a rather puny baby, and his parents worried over him as much as they doted on him.

"He looks worried," Thomas announced at last after leaning over the cot and subjecting the baby to a prolonged scrutiny. "I think it must be the weight of all that responsibility on his head."

"What responsibility?" asked Isabella. Her tone was defensive, for she had greatly taken to the two babies, and since she had a propensity for loving underdogs she favored her nephew over her brother.

"Why, all this wealth he's going to inherit one day," Thomas said, waving a hand to indicate the house and all the Morland estates. "Lord of the six manors; master stapler; gentleman of coat-armor. Who knows, but by the time he inherits there may be an earldom added to it. No wonder he looks thoughtful."

Daisy laughed merrily and put her arm around Isabella, with whom she had struck up quite a friendship. "I think he's teasing, Isabella. But even if he's serious, Little Ned will be up to it. He isn't worried—he'll be the greatest gentleman that ever lived, without any trouble at all."

"And marry a princess no doubt," Thomas finished for her. "Well, that's his future assured. I understand Mother is for changing from the wool trade to the cloth trade, so I dare say he'll end up richer than my lord of Salisbury himself."

"She couldn't wait for Father to die so that she could carry out her plans," Isabella said, suddenly vicious. "It was only him that was holding her back. I wouldn't be surprised—"

"Isabella!" Daisy cried warningly. "Have a care what you are saying."

"Oh, 'Bella, you aren't still clinging to that old resentment, are you?" Thomas sighed. He took his sister's hand and led her to the window of the nursery. Outside it was a blowy, sunny day, with white clouds chasing across the great windy bowl of the sky. "Look at the world," he told her. "It's wonderful—far too wonderful to spend your life locked up in bitterness and hatred. What has our mother ever done to deserve it?"

"You don't know—you just don't know. You've been away for years. You were never here to see how she crossed him and belittled everything he did. She drove him to his grave in the end. Maybe even helped him there, for all anyone knows."

"Isabella, you are not to say such things!" Daisy cried, shocked.

"Why not? She never punished the boy who took him the food, did she? She took care to hustle him out of the house so that no one could question him. She didn't even give him a beating, though he had killed his own master."

Thomas cocked an inquiring eye at his sister-in-law, who shook her head to him and then spoke firmly to Isabella.

"That's all nonsense, and you know it. Your father adored her, and his death was a terrible accident, no one's fault. Your mother grieved for him bitterly. I think you should go to Master James and ask for a penance for your wicked thoughts."

"I'm surprised you stand up for her," Isabella said angrily. "You've seen how she behaves to Edward—she treats him just like she did Father, never lets him have a say in anything that goes on, even though he's head of the family now."

Daisy opened her mouth to retort, but Thomas stepped in firmly. "Now, now, girls, that's enough. Let's not spend the day quarreling. Come, 'Bella, why don't you take me round the stables and introduce me to the new colts? And I'm sure you must have some newcomers in your mews that you'd like to show off to me? Come, come, it's too fine a day to be indoors."

He jollied her along, and the temptation of showing him her animals and her hawks was too much for her, for she was as fond of hunting and hawking as ever, perhaps more so now that she had little else to occupy her. But it left Thomas worried about her, for she seemed unbalanced on the subject of their mother, seeming never to have got over the suspicion that Eleanor had caused her fiancé's death. He spoke to his mother privately about her later that day.

"What's to become of Isabella, Mother?" he asked.

Eleanor sighed and laid down her work. "She's a problem, I admit," Eleanor said. "Robert was for sending her to a nunnery, you know, to see her well settled."

"Perhaps that would be the best thing?" Thomas prompted.

Eleanor shook her head. "I still intend to see her married. She's twenty-two, I know, but with a good dowry she isn't too old yet, and I need an alliance with the clothing trade. I intend to find some rich clothier for her, perhaps a widower with no children would be best. I can't spare her to the church."

"What a wicked old pagan you are, Mother," Thomas joked.

Eleanor laughed. "Besides, she wouldn't be happy in a nunnery. She loves nothing now but hunting and hawking, and riding out on the moors. What would she do mewed up in a convent for life? It would be cruelty. No, no, it wouldn't do."

"You really care for her," Thomas observed.

Eleanor looked surprised. "Of course. Have you been believing her tales about how I killed her fiancé? Shame on you, Thomas, you should know better. Of course I want her to be happy—if possible, if it doesn't interfere with duty."

Thomas nodded. "Talking of duty—" he said.

"What news?" Eleanor asked quickly. "You have been nearer the heart of things than I." Thomas was as fervent a Yorkist as Eleanor herself, which was hardly surprising since he had been her favorite since babyhood and had been brought up under her influence.

"Trouble is brewing. You know that our Lord Richard took his family to Ludlow? His elder two boys are already there, of course."

"I heard they had left Fotheringay, but no more than that. What is happening?"

"The Queen is gathering an army, and this time she means to finish him off. He didn't trust the fortifications of Fotheringay, so he packed up and entrenched himself at Ludlow where he could defend himself better. Now the news is that the Queen is gathering an army at Coventry, and I doubt not there will be a call to arms at Ludlow, too."

Eleanor started up. "Is this really the time? Is it to come to war at last?"

"It seems so."

"Then we must send men! I promised him. He said he would send word, but—pray it is not too late."

"It is not too late. Calm yourself, Mother. This is only the beginning. He will send word when he wants you, never fear."

"All the same we must be ready. There will be much to do—clothes, arms, food. The men must be told off. We must be ready to march when the call comes."

"We?" Thomas asked, laughing despite the tension of the moment. "Mother, I believe for two pins you'd go yourself!"

"If I had not the misfortune to be born a woman," Eleanor said grimly, "I would be there now, with my sword in my hand."

"Thank God you are a woman," Thomas said. "We couldn't do without you. But, Mother, you shall be there, in proxy. When the call comes, *I* shall go!"

Eleanor stared for a moment, and then embraced him hard.

"My son, my true son," she cried. Then she straightened, and looked businesslike. "Come, we must plan what is to be done."

The call came in August, brought by a messenger on horseback who also gave them the news that the Earl of Salisbury had already marched with his large force of York-shiremen and had had a skirmish with the Queen's forces that had cost the royal army dear. This meant that they were committed. Salisbury's son, Warwick, was bringing over the Calais garrison men, and the Duke of York had sent Eleanor a terse note bidding her "send all you can."

"We were expecting this," Eleanor told the messenger. "We shall be ready in the morning. Will you stay and rest yourself?"

"Thank you, madam," the messenger said, looking not a little relieved. "I'll ride with your men in the morning and show them the way." He was glad not to have to ride back alone—the Midlands were in ferment.

That evening the family gathered in the solar for some private moments together on the eve of the departure, and Eleanor discovered a little more about her family's feelings than she had previously cared to know. Firstly, she was approached by young Harry, who divided his week now between his lessons at Morland Place and his work on the Shawe Estate. Harry had been talking to Thomas, who was his great hero, and was desperately keen to go to Ludlow too.

"But you're only fifteen," Eleanor said, taken aback. "You are still in the schoolroom."

"But, Mother, I'm sixteen next month, I'm a man. And Edward can't go—he has to stay and take care of everything—so it has to be me. That messenger says there are boys of twelve in the army—*boys!* Someone has to carry the Morland name—Thomas can't go alone. What if he should fall?"

Eleanor shuddered and crossed herself. "Don't!" she said sharply. She had not even considered the possibility of death. "You're too young, Harry. You will be of more help if you finish your studies and practice your sword work. Now hush, not another word. Here come the others."

Harry subsided, not in the least convinced, and determined to continue the struggle at the first opportunity. Eleanor rose to greet Helen and John Butler, who had ridden over for the evening. John was to march with the Morland contingent in the morning and Helen was to stay at Morland Place until he returned. She was inclined to be tearful, but proud that John was going with his body servant and a boy to bear arms for York. Being a city dweller, she naturally heard more pro-Yorkist talk than did anyone at Morland Place, and to her it was unquestionably right.

Isabella, however, was inclined to be scornful.

"It's a lot of hothead nonsense," she said privately to Helen.

"If you were a boy, you wouldn't say that," Helen retorted with some percipience. "You'd be bursting to ride with them, too. It's just sour grapes." Since Daisy had joined the family and struck up such a friendship with Isabella, the sisters had cooled toward each other, and it was mainly her desire to disagree with Helen that made Isabella speak against the cause.

"Our father wouldn't have gone," she said now.

Helen looked superior. "That's where you're wrong. Our father fought at St. Albans, though you seem conveniently to have forgotten it."

"It was against his will," Isabella said stubbornly. "He regretted it afterward. If he were alive now, he wouldn't go to Ludlow."

"You can't say that," Daisy interrupted. "He fought for York, whatever he felt about it."

"You didn't hear what he said on his deathbed," Isabella snapped.

"Nor did you," Daisy said warningly.

"But I heard all the same. Everyone knows—" A hand dropped on her shoulder and she stopped abruptly.

"I should hold my tongue if I were you, 'Bella," Thomas said. "Our mother may hear you."

"Hear what?" Eleanor asked, catching his words across a sudden lull in the conversation.

"Isabella was saying she'd ride tomorrow disguised as a boy if she thought she could get away with it," Thomas said to protect her, raising a laugh at the memory of Isabella's girlhood pranks.

But Isabella did not want to be saved. Defiantly she said, "I said nothing of the sort. I said I think the cause is a lot of nonsense."

"No one has asked for your opinion, Isabella," Eleanor said coldly.

"All the same, Mother . . ." Edward said uneasily.

Eleanor tried to stop him, sensing disagreement in his voice. "You can't go, Edward. You're needed here."

"Am I?" he said wryly. "Well, whether or not, do you realize what it is you're doing? Taking up arms against the King! If the Queen should win—"

"The Queen is no Queen, but wife to a King who is no King," Eleanor said angrily. "And she will *not* win."

"Mother, our sovereign lord, King Henry, sixth of that name, was crowned and anointed, and whether or not we feel he should have been, armed defiance to him is treason. If the Queen wins, we could be attainted. We would lose everything, perhaps even our lives."

"*His* forebears didn't think of that when they stole the crown from the rightful king. Now the rightful king is going to take it back. York will win, right will win, because God is on our side."

"It's still treason," Edward argued patiently. "And King Henry was the son of the former king—that's his right to the throne—"

"Right? He has no *right* to the throne that was stolen by

his grandfather, and restoring it to its rightful lord is not treason. In the morning, the Morland men will march for Ludlow, and at the head will march my two sons." She put her arms round Thomas and Harry, and the latter smirked, gratified that pride had made her give him what he wanted, "to show that this house is for York, whatever comes."

"Well said, Mother," Thomas cried, clapping his hands and relieving the tension with laughter. "Come, now, Edward, caution has had its say, and we've all listened politely, but now you can let it rest and tell the truth, how you're green with envy at the thought of Harry and me rushing off to war."

Edward gave way with good grace. "Daisy wouldn't hear of it," he said mock-ruefully. "Brother John will have to do the honors for the married men."

And from then on, the conversation waxed cheerful and thence even boastful, concerning what everyone would do in the face of the enemy. The men talked, and the women watched, Eleanor proudly, Isabella sullenly, Daisy and Helen apprehensively.

When they were retiring to bed Anys came to Eleanor to ask a favor. A nephew of hers, a lad of fourteen, was anxious to be able to join the expedition, and Anys begged that he might be allowed to go along as body servant to Thomas and Harry.

"Does his Mother wish it?" Eleanor asked.

Anys made a funny face. "I don't suppose any mother really wants her child to go into battle, but to tell the truth Colin's rather too much for her to handle alone, though he's a good boy, and since his father's going along—"

"Very well," Eleanor said. "He shall go."

It was strange, having such power, she thought as she went to her bedchamber; she may have decided between life and death for the child.

The men were to start out at dawn. As soon as three o'clock struck, mass was said in the chapel and a special intention said for the men marching to Ludlow. Having taken the Blessed Sacrament the men went to say good-bye to their wives and families and then formed up in the courtyard before the house. The whole household was out to say good-bye to them. Eleanor, who knew every one of the men personally, passed among them with a word for each and her blessing with it, and the men bowed their heads to her; they were going as much for her as for York, for they adored her as if she were a queen. There were twenty-five men gathered there, twenty-two of them in the Morland livery, their russet cloaks making a warm patch in the predawn grayness, the black-and-white Morland badge standing out clearly on their backs. The other three were John Butler's man and boy, and young Colin, who was to march at the head of the column, carrying the standard.

And now the three members of the family had mounted, and were restraining their horses while the women arranged the folds of their cloaks over the horses' backs— John Butler, solid and pleasant, a kind man; Harry, barely more than a child, his face flushed with excitement; and Thomas, tall and handsome and debonair, a soldier to carry everyone's heart along with him. Eleanor said good-bye to each of them, bidding John take care, and Harry do what his brother told him, but when she got to Thomas she could not speak. She held his hand and stared up at him, and it was he who found his tongue. He smiled down at her, his ravishingly charming smile.

"Well, Mother," he said. "Wish me luck, and bid me farewell with a smile. I want to remember how beautiful you are. Beautiful as a star. That's how I always think of you away from home." Eleanor's lips parted, and tears sprang to her eyes. "Oh, yes," he went on, "I know you're always worried about what I'm doing down in Cambridge, always afraid that I'll come back to you with a wife in tow. But don't worry—you're my one true love. It's you I think of. That's better! Now you're laughing!"

"Oh, my dear son," Eleanor said. She pressed his hand. "When you see my lord of York, tell him—tell him—well, here you are with twenty-five men. And the gold—you have it safe? Well, then. God bless you, my son. My heart goes with you."

"I won't leave his side, Mother," he said seriously. "I'm his man now."

Eleanor drew back, and for a moment everyone was

hushed as Master James spoke the blessing over them all. And then with a shout that seemed to lift the sky, the column was on the move, with a tramp of feet and the jingling of horses' harness, out of the yard and on to the road. The family drew together to watch as the men marched away: at the head the three young men on their fine horses, their cloaks bright as birds' plumage spread over the horses' glossy rumps; then the swinging column of men in their tawny cloaks; and between them the child proudly bearing the standard with the Morland badge of the white running hare—Eleanor's own badge. They were going to war, to do battle, and it was possible that some of them would not march home again, but Eleanor shut her mind to that part of it.

Eleanor turned to go in as the column was lost to sight, and Job was standing at her shoulder. Their eyes met in perfect understanding.

"Thomas goes for me," Eleanor said, and her tone begged to be reassured that it was right.

"He understands. And the master understood, too. A man has to keep faith."

"As you have done." Eleanor smiled, and, placing her hand upon his shoulder, she walked into the house.

There was no battle. All through September forces gathered, York's men at Ludlow, the Queen's at Coventry, until finally at the begining of October the latter host began to march westward. When the royal force reached Worcester, Lord Richard sent a petition to the King protesting his loyalty and desire for peace, for still he did not wish to take arms against his king. But the Queen sent back only a promise of pardon for any who would desert the Yorkist cause, and marched on, reaching Ludlow on the twelfth, and camping a mile from the castle.

The royal army was about twice the size of the Duke's; that and the strain of the long waiting, and the knowledge of the Queen's offer of pardon, broke the nerve of the besieged forces, and in the night, the Calais garrison—the only seasoned fighters in the York army—scrambled over the walls and fled to the King. It was a bitter blow— betrayal is always bitter—and after a hurried meeting between the generals, it was decided that flight was the only possible course for the remaining forces.

Lord Richard with his elder sons, Edward of March and Edmund of Rutland, and Warwick and Salisbury fled on horseback, taking only a small escort with them. The Duchess Cecily and the two small children, George and Richard, must be left to the mercy of the King, and the rest of the army must slip away under cover of darkness and go home to await the call to arms which would come again soon. It was a nightmarish scene, everyone moving in haste by flickering torchlight that threw great shadows on the walls and ceilings of the old castle, yet scarcely a sound to be heard except the occasional ring of an iron horsehoe on stone or a nervous whinney as the horses caught the tension in the air.

The Morland party had formed up ready to leave, and John and Harry were holding the horses, waiting for Thomas to join them so that they could start while the darkness held. They waited in silence in the chill blackness of the night for what seemed like hours, and then suddenly Thomas was with them, looming up out of the darkness, looking pale and suddenly older in the sparse torchlight.

"I'm not coming with you," he said abruptly. "I promised our Mother that I would not leave my lord, and I am going with him. Give me my horse, we must leave at once."

A second's silence, and then Harry's voice. "I'm coming too."

"No."

"I must, Thomas. Where you go, I go. Mother would want that."

"Very well, then. We must go at once. John, you must get the men home again safely. I know you can do it." The men clasped hands, Thomas looking down into his brother-in-law's trusty face. "Give Mother our love. Tell her we must fly now to gather our forces. We will come back, soon."

"Do you know where you are going?" John asked.

"I think to Ireland. My lord is well loved there. Now we must go. Good-bye. God bless you."

The two young men swung to the saddle and were gone, leaving John Butler to march the men home again. As he turned to give the order to march he found little Colin weeping openly.

"Come now, don't be afraid," he chided the boy gently. "We'll get home safely."

"Oh, sir, it isn't that," the child blubbered. "I'm not afraid. But I should have gone with them. I was their body servant. Now I'm shamed for ever."

John clapped his hand on the thin shoulder. "No shame to you, boy. You have no horse, you couldn't have gone with them. There's no shame." The boy lifted his face, hope dawning through the tears. "*They* know that. Come now, lift the banner and let's march out of here like men."

He mounted his horse, and with Colin holding the banner proudly aloft, they started on their long journey home, to bring the sad news to Morland Place.

CHAPTER THIRTEEN

It was not until February, four weary months after John Butler brought the Morland army home, that Eleanor had word of her sons. Before that, rumor and official proclamation had told her much of the story. It was known that the Yorkist lords split up shortly after leaving Ludlow, and that Richard of York had taken a boat to Ireland accompanied by his son Rutland, while Warwick, Salisbury and Edward of March had fled to Devonshire and thence by boat to Calais. The Duchess and the children were taken prisoner by the royal army and the King had put them in gentlemanly confinement with the Duchess's own sister, my lady of Buckingham.

In January, the news came that the Parliament called in December had attainted the five lords and many of their chief followers, and that their lands were forfeit. Eleanor in desperation wrote to her daughter, Anne, for news of the boys, but received no reply. Then, in February, a letter came through hidden in a bale of fleece from Calais, one of the last consignments to get through before the King put a ban on trade with Calais. It was from Harry.

The letter told of the flight and how the fugitives split up.

I would have stayed with Thomas, but my lord would only take six men with him. He took Thomas because he

*had promised to stay by him, but I had to go with my lord
of March. . . .*

Richard had kept Thomas by him! that was wonderful,
that was as it should be. The letter went on to say that they
were engaged in gathering money and support in Calais.

*The master staplers help us, and I borrow on our name
and our father's popularity. I cannot say anything about
our plans in case this letter may be intercepted.*

But despite Harry's reticence, the whole country knew
that the lords of Calais and my lord of York would make a
landing that summer; and all but the court party and the
diehard Lancastrian lords welcomed the idea. The King
and Queen were unpopular, their taxes high and their government inept, and the people looked to Richard of York to
make all wrongs right when he came. Something was
needed to keep the hearts of the people up. It was the
worst summer in living memory: it rained nonstop, flooding low-lying areas, rotting the crops as they lay in the
ground, and bringing the threat of famine. Roads were
washed away or buried beneath fathoms of mud; floods
washed away houses and bridges, killing hundreds and iso-
lating whole areas; and the warm, wet conditions brought
on a plague of insects.

And through the rain the Calais lords came, landing at
Sandwich on the twenty-sixth of June and marching unop-
posed to London, which welcomed them with open arms.
The Queen and the Court were at Coventry, the King and
the royal army a little further south at Northampton, and
here on the tenth of July the two forces met. The battle
was brief and bloody, and was all over in an hour. The
King was captured in his tent and taken, shaking with
fright, to London and housed in the Tower; and the Queen,
as soon as she heard the news of the defeat, fled with her
son to Wales. Eleanor, when she heard the news,
groaned—it was the Queen they wanted prisoner, not the
King!

In September a letter came through from Harry.

* * *

News has come that my lord of York has landed at Chester and my lady Duchess has gone off to meet him there in her chariot, looking like a queen, for it is all of blue velvet and drawn by eight great horses. And Thomas is with my lord, I am assured, so rest easy, Mother. As soon as he gets to London we shall call a Parliament and I believe my lord will be made Lord Protector, because the King is not fit to rule. The King is treated with all kindness, and truly I believe that he would give up the crown tomorrow if he were asked, for without the Queen to urge him on he likes nothing better than to read and attend his devotions all day.

And, Mother, I must tell you about my lord of March. His device is the sun-in-splendor, and it suits him, for he is as tall and broad as our Thomas, but fair, golden haired and fair-skinned and ruddy, and as handsome as a god. There is no woman but will come at the crook of his finger, though he, like everyone here, is too busy for much merrymaking. But my lord of March still finds time every day to visit his young brothers and sister in their lodgings and inquire after their health and progress. I go with him most days, and it is wonderful to see how kindly he talks to them, and how they adore him, particularly his brother Richard, who, I am sure, firmly believes my lord of March was sent from Heaven.

In November Eleanor received something that cheered her more than anything other than a sight of her sons could have done—a letter from Thomas. It was brief, but acquainted her with the main news.

When we arrived in London on the tenth of October the Londoners greeted my lord like a king, and indeed when we rode into Westminster to greet the lords, assembled in the painted chamber, my lord strode up to the throne and proclaimed he had come to claim it as his hereditary right. My heart rose, Mother, and threatened to choke me, and my eyes filled with tears, he looked so kingly, so upright and brave. But the lords had not his courage and feared to depose King Henry, and after much talk came to an agree-

ment: that my lord should be Lord Protector during the King's lifetime, and reign after King Henry's death. The Queen's son is therefore disinherited; and many say that she had not the son by the King, and so this is just.

But, Mother, the Queen is still at large and gathering an army, as you must know, so we must march out and deal with her. The Morland men are needed, and my lord bids me ask you to send how ever many you can. Prepare at once and send them to meet us at Northampton, where we expect to be on the day after St. Nicholas Day.

As soon as she had finished reading the letter, Eleanor called out for Job, and when he came running she told him the news and bid him order the men to arms again.

"This time they will deal with the Queen once and for all, and we shall have peace at last," she said. "Go and give the orders. And send word to John Butler to come at once; he's needed."

Thomas and Harry were together again. When they met, clasping arms, on that wonderful day when the Duke of York marched like a king into London, they had much to tell each other about the days in Ireland and Calais, which seemed to have numbered three thousand rather than three hundred. As soon as it was possible to gain the Duke's ear, Harry applied for and was granted permission to transfer back from my lord of March's lines to my lord of York's, and then the brothers could be together all the time.

Thomas was in need of his brother's support, for, despite the cheerful tone of his letter to his mother, he was aware of a sense of impending doom. The lords, even York's own son, Edward of March, had not endorsed his outright claim to the throne. During those days in Ireland, Richard of York had turned the terrible dilemma over and over in his mind. The Queen was his enemy, not the King—he wanted to be loyal to the King. But the Queen could not be removed unless the King were also. He had decided at last that the only solution was kingship, and he had claimed it, and it had been denied him. The lords had thrown him straight back on to the horns of the dilemma. True, he had power, but not power enough. The Queen could still gather support, and there was little that York could do to stop that.

Thomas felt the frustration of the great-hearted soldier who was no politician; he felt also that somehow fortune had passed them by, that dark clouds were looming. He stayed close to his master during those days, and was glad of the relief that the more sanguine Harry's spirits gave him. Harry, being younger and more sheltered—he had never been away from home before—was less aware of the problems that faced them, more cheerful and more certain of success. With the legendary Richard of York—a figure as illustrious as Theseus himself—and the bright new sun of March to lead them, how could they fail? At night the brothers slept under the one cloak, and it was Harry who flung a protective arm over his older brother.

It was not all gloom, of course. There was time for drinking and merrymaking and lovemaking. Thomas had always been popular with women, having some of his master's own charisma and a great deal more of good looks. Harry now found he could ride along on his brother's wake, and many a night found them taking a girl in under their cloaks to keep out the winter cold. All London was grateful to the Yorkists for taking over the corrupt government—what better way to show gratitude than to lend the young men their daughters?

Because the talks with the lords dragged on so, it was not until the ninth of December that the army in fact left London, so the Morland men had been in Northampton a week before the meeting took place. By that time March's men had split off and were heading for Wales; the Earl of Warwick had remained behind to keep London; and my lord of York with young Rutland and his uncle Salisbury were taking the army to meet the Queen. The Morland badge was hoisted on the right wing of the army, and Harry marched with his own men and John Butler like a young captain. Thomas stayed no more than a horse's length from his lord under the York badge of the falcon and the fetterlock. That stocky, soldierly figure, as dear to Thomas now as his own mother, seemed to have a nimbus of strange light around it, like the shining rim around the edge of a dark cloud. Thomas could not leave him for a minute.

Through the desolate winter countryside they marched, scouts bringing them news of the Queen's forces moving southward to meet them. Wherever they went, the people came out to meet them, to call blessings on their heads, to beg them get rid of Margaret and her corrupt favorites. The Queen's army was moving like a host of locusts, devouring and destroying everything in its path. The folk of the midlands and the south were anxious that the Duke of York should stop them before they came any further.

By the twenty-first of December they had reached Yorkshire, and the scouts brought word that the Queen's host was only ten miles off, in Pontefract. Richard's own castle of Sandal was close by, and he led his army there and settled them in, and sent men under flag of parley to speak to the Queen's generals. Thomas brought the news of the meeting back to the Morland contingent.

"It's a truce for the Christmas season," he announced gloomily as he appeared in the doorway. The Morland men had secured a small storeroom off the main hall for themselves, and were holed in comfortably, playing dice and cards to while away the time. A cheer went up at his words.

"That's good news," Harry said. "We should be able to make ourselves comfortable here. We might even be able to slip out and pay a visit home—it isn't above a day's ride. Why, Thomas, you don't look happy."

"I'm not," he said briefly.

"Not happy with the truce?" John Butler asked. "Surely you don't want to be fighting over Christmas?"

"It's the waiting," Thomas explained. "I'd sooner be getting on with it. I have the feeling that the longer we wait, the stronger she's getting, like an evil humor. I feel her swelling up like a snake. I can't get rid of this feeling of dread."

"Nerves," Harry said wisely. "A soldier's life is long periods of waiting and short periods of activity."

"He speaks out of the depth of experience," John Butler laughed. "Let my lord of York tell him that. How does he bear the delay?"

"It was his idea," Thomas said. "He's too good, that's the trouble. He and King Henry are alike in that way—that's why the King loves him so much. Neither of *them* would fight during the Holy Season. But he's so innocent in his heart, he isn't up to all *her* villainy. He's a soldier, not a politician." The others listened sympathetically to him. There was not a man there who wouldn't lay down his life instantly for his master, and not a man who didn't feel him to be right.

"Well, there's nothing for it but to make ourselves as comfortable as possible, since we must wait," Thomas concluded.

"True enough. What is it my lord says? Any fool can be *un*comfortable?" Harry chimed in.

"And if you want something to do," John added, "you can always go out with the foragers."

"First party tomorrow," Harry said.

Thomas grinned suddenly and shook his head. "That sort of duty's for you people. I'm one of my lord's special bodyguard. Any time you want to find me, look for my lord."

And he gave them a jaunty wave and strode away, every inch the gallant young captain.

That was how it happened that on that afternoon, a week before the end of the period of truce, Thomas was in the small room with the generals and their chief captains. York, Rutland, and Salisbury were sitting round a bare table with the captains discussing tactics, old campaigns, women, and other soldierly subjects by the fading afternoon light. Thomas and one or two other young men were lolling against the walls looking on, part and not part of the scene. A foraging party was out, but pickings were getting thin, and everyone was getting restless for the move.

Rutland was flipping a knife over and over into the table, watching it quiver by its point. My lord of York was as still as only a soldier can be, leaning back in his chair, his broad strong hand resting lightly on the table, his bright blue eyes, whose gaze no liar or miscreant could ever meet, looking steadily from one speaker to the next. Salisbury was speaking at that moment.

"Apart from anything else, it's getting difficult to keep the men occupied. Even with foraging parties going out daily, there are fights and scuffles all the time. Luckily we've very little to drink here, or there'd be more trouble."

"We'd better organize some games," Richard said. "We've another week to go—it wouldn't hurt to have some arms practice too. What I suggest is this. . . ."

But no one ever heard what he was going to suggest. At that moment one of the lookouts rushed in, closely followed by a disheveled scout.

"Sir! My lord! The foraging parties are coming back—" the lookout began. But the scout shouted over him, "The Queen's coming! My lord, the Queen's army's outside, and they've surrounded the foragers. There's thousands of them, and armed to the teeth!"

Rutland leaped to his feet. "They've broken the truce!" he shouted.

York's face darkened with rage. "Scum," he said. "They've broken faith. They're forsworn. The devil spawn—" His hand was on his sword hilt, and he was already heading for the door. To think was to act. He was so outraged at this breaking of truce that he could not contain himself. "We'll teach them to respect their oaths—in the Holy Season too. There's no place for them on this earth. Come on! We'll shew them what true soldiers are!"

He was running down the steps, and they were following him, grabbing up a helmet here and a shield there, and all those they passed fell in behind them. They ran out into the courtyard, seizing horses where they could, yelling vengeance and bloodthirsty oaths. Their blood was up, they were determined on rescue and revenge; the gates were flung back and they galloped out onto the plain. Thomas was at his lord's shoulder, and like him, he was itching for a fight, pent up with the long wait, shocked at the enemy's perfidy. But he was his mother's son, and her cold voice of reason made him glance back over his shoulder as he urged his horse on. And he saw how few they were, how very few. Ahead of them, the foragers had managed, though surprised, to form up, and were holding off the enemy gallantly; but at every moment they grew fewer. Behind them, the general alarm was sounding. Had they waited for the full force to form up before sallying out, the foragers would have perished, every one.

They were riding to the rescue, but the enemy was nearer than the rest of their own men; and spurring the horse on, yelling with the hot-blooded fury of the moment like his lord, Thomas knew a pain of despair in his heart. The sheer impetus of their arrival drove the enemy back on itself, and the beleaguered foragers gave up a great cheer of joy and fought the more furiously, falling into formation with the rescue force. And then the two lines met, and there was no order or sense to be seen anywhere.

Thomas reined his frantic horse with his shield hand while he slashed and struck, parried and stabbed, with his sword. Time seemed suspended, and the din rose to a pitch where it could no longer be heard. He seemed to be moving in a world of silence where there was nothing but the next snarling furious face popping up on one side or the other, the next reaching sword to duck, the next body to run through. Stab, and jerk the sword out, feeling the pull of the body it was sheathed in. Out of the corner of his eye he could see his lord's broad back, and beyond, the flutter of red that was Salisbury's cloak.

Then the red disappeared. Thomas's head jerked up, and in that instant his horse shrieked and went down on its knees, run through the chest. Thomas was flung off forward, managing by a violent twist to remain on his feet to meet the next man's thrust. The horse's thrashing hind legs gave him respite. He had time for one glance around, time to see his lord ahead, still mounted, engaging two men on his right side; time to see the other man coming up on his left with a javelin ready.

"No!" Thomas cried out, leaping forward. The cry and the leap were one, one movement, one second's space, and half a second too late. The javelin drove deep into Richard's side even as Thomas's sword smashed off the foot soldier's head. Richard toppled sideways like a tree, his horse leaped forward, freed of his weight, and Thomas gave a great cry of despair that in his fevered imagination seemed echoed by the earth itself. The fighting was thickest here. As he reached his fallen lord there were six, seven blades biting into him, and a deep burning inside him that told him he was struck. He struggled, but his body was no longer his, and sank away under him, the damp earth coming up to meet him.

Darkness flowed over him. There was a smell of blood in his nostrils, and feet were trampling him as the struggling men swayed back and forth like eddying water above him. He was at the bottom of the stream. His hand moved convulsively and touched hair. It was his lord. Feebly he stroked his lord's head as if he were a woman, and he thought, I didn't leave him, Mother. He began to smile. His body was full of holes, and the darkness flowed into him.

The morning of the second of January. The family and all the household was gathered in the great hall, waiting in silence for news, huddled together, it seemed, for comfort. Rumors they had heard. It was said that the battle, through treachery, had gone to the Queen. Eleanor shivered. Treachery! It seemed the very air they breathed. It was said that York's army was scattered, that the Queen was coming to York to reform before marching on London.

But it was only rumor, she told herself, gripping her hands together. It was no more than rumor. Wait for the true word, wait for news. What of the boys and John? They must come soon. They would tell her. Wait. Hope. Do not believe. They had not gone to bed. The servants kept the fire up in the hall, but had no spirit for anything else. The night seemed endless. It was midwinter, sunrise would not be until seven or after.

And then, while it was still dark, the sound of horses' hooves in the yard, and footsteps running, and one of the Micklelith servants ran in. Even in the poor light it could be seen his face was white.

"Mistress," he cried breathlessly—he was trembling—"Master Butler and the men are at Micklelith. They say the Queen is coming. They are in flight and hiding."

Eleanor was on her feet. "My sons?"

"They are not there. Only Master Butler and twelve others."

"Where are they? Where are my sons?" Eleanor seized him by the shoulders and in her anxiety was almost throttling him. Edward touched her hand, made her desist, and spoke more gently to the frightened servant.

"Speak, tell what you know. Do you know where my brothers are?"

"No, sir. I didn't wait to hear the story. Master Butler sent me to tell you they were at Micklelith. But they say the battle is lost and all the army scattered, and the Queen is coming."

Tears of fear were forming in his eyes and it was clear he was only just able to remain standing. Edward signaled a page to take him away.

"I'd better go and find out what's happening," he said. "Job, come with me."

"Me, too, Edward," little John cried out.

Edward put a hand on his shoulder. "No, John, someone's got to look after the women and children."

"Sir, I'd better not leave the mistress," Job murmured to Edward, but before he could answer Eleanor had said:

"Anys, fetch my cloak. I must go and find out what's happened." Edward did not even try to argue with her, knowing in advance that it was useless; so it was the three of them who set off a moment later, spurring their horses through the first gray light over the snowy fields to Micklelith.

John met them at the door of the old hall. He was tired and red-eyed, but unwounded.

"In God's name, tell me what's happened," Eleanor cried as soon as she saw him. Wearily, he told the story of the enemy's treachery. "God damn her black soul," Eleanor cried. "But what of Thomas and Harry?"

"Harry was with me," he said. "We didn't know anything about it until the general alarm sounded. Thomas was with the generals, and when they dashed out he was with them. They didn't have a chance, such a tiny force against so many, but they fought so bravely they pushed the enemy back for a moment. My lord was in the thick of it, and Thomas with him. We saw my lord fall. Thomas killed the man who struck the blow, but there were six of them to every one of ours."

Eleanor was deadly still. "Thomas was killed?" she asked in no more than a whisper. John Butler bowed his head, and an unearthly cry seemed wrenched from Eleanor's lips.

"Sweet, merciful Jesu!" A silence. Then, with difficulty:
"And Lord Richard, too?"

"They fell on the same spot. My lord of Rutland was
killed, too, and my lord of Salisbury was captured, but they
beheaded him the next day. The rest of the army scattered.
Some went home. Harry went with the rest to join with my
lord of March. He took some of our men. I would have
gone with him, but he said we must go home, the Queen's
army is a rabble and we must be here to defend the houses
if they come."

"Then Harry is safe?" Edward asked tremblingly.

"Not a scratch on him. A good part of the army escaped
and went with him and the other captains. With March's
army and Warwick's men, they'll give the Queen something to think about when she moves southward. But for
the present—they say she's coming to York to re-form.
And—" He paused, reluctant to continue.

Eleanor's face was awash with tears, but her voice was
defiant as she said, "His son must carry on now. Young
Edward. He's a good boy, isn't he?"

"One of the best," John said. "A soldier like his father—"

"Oh, God!" Eleanor put her hands over her face, weeping helplessly. Edward put his arm round her shoulder, and
his face was wet, too. "Richard dead. Thomas dead. I
didn't think, when they marched away—so proud, so
brave. I didn't know I'd never see him again. To die so!
Oh, treachery! Oh, sweet Jesu, to die thus, at that woman's
hand. He should have been king. Oh, Thomas, Thomas,
my son, my son."

John Butler was weeping openly, and he bowed his head
so that his next words were muffled. "He died like a soldier, fighting bravely, the best way a man can die. He
never left his lord's side, and he killed the man who killed
his lord. God will receive him with joy, for his is a brave
and true soul."

It was comfort to the mind to know that, but there was no
comfort for the heart, and worse was yet to come. The
Queen's army gathered at York, pillaging, burning, and
raping as they went. The Morland estates suffered only

minor damage, for they were too well defended by armed men for the rabble soldiers to bother with when there were easier pickings; but barns were burned and winter stock slaughtered, and in other places whole villages were wiped out and mass murder performed.

On the first day when Eleanor had come to York she had shuddered at the sight of the heads of miscreants displayed on pikes on Mickle Lith Bar, within sight of Micklelith House itself. She little thought then what horror was in store for her, for when French Margaret and her captains arrived at York she ordered the heads of her slain enemies to be impaled there—the heads of young Rutland, and Salisbury, and Richard of York.

Eleanor thought that she would go mad with grief, to see the bloody severed head of the man she had loved hung there, obscenely blackening; those noble, kingly brows encircled with a mocking crown of paper and straw; those firm lips that had smiled and kissed her crusted with black blood; to stay there until those eyes, once so blue and full of laughter, were pecked out by crows. Such a kindly, just, honorable man, a man to whom trust was more important than power and love more important than riches, to suffer so, like the meanest and blackest criminal. To have lived to see the day was to have lived too long.

"But he will be avenged," Eleanor cried. "His sons—and mine—will see him avenged."

CHAPTER FOURTEEN

As the rabble army of the Queen plundered its way southward, the remnants of Lord Richard's army worked their way westward to find Edward of March. It was bitter weather, one of the coldest winters in memory following on the wettest summer, and progress was slow, and it was not to be wondered that many slipped away to their homes under cover of the blizzards. Harry did better than many, for he was still mounted, and his horse, bred at Morland Place and hand-reared, was strong and surefooted; but his heart was heavy with grief over Thomas's death, and like every man there he was bitterly demoralized by the death of the three generals.

They discovered the March army in Shrewsbury, sheltering from a blizzard, and were welcomed with joy muted by sympathy, for the news had run ahead of them in the manner of bad news. Tall Edward, the Sun in Splendor itself, warmed their hearts with his manly sorrow for his kin and his brave determination to defeat the Queen and her mercenaries.

"But for the moment," he said, "we must hope that my cousin Warwick can hold them off from London, for there is an army of Welshmen under my lords Pembroke and Wiltshire that needs our attention first. They are heading westward, and we must march south and intercept them."

"That won't take much doing, sir," shouted out one old

veteran. "Them short-legged Welshmen don't march very fast."

"We've got a longer March with us than they've got ahead of them," shouted another, punning on their leader's name. Golden Edward laughed with the men, and ordered them all to eat and rest and take care of the Wakefield survivors.

"We start out tomorrow at dawn, lads. You'll need all the sleep you can get."

But with all he had to do, Edward did not omit to have a few words with the survivors, and even found time to welcome Harry back to his lines and express sympathy over the loss of Thomas. "I have lost a brother, too," he said. It was always Edward's way to find time for the small, important things.

It was wild country, matched only by the wild weather, and the going was very, very hard. It was not until Candlemas Eve that they came upon the Welshmen, at a place called Mortimer's Cross, not far from Ludlow Castle, where Edward of March had spent his childhood; but once they found them, the Yorkists made short work of them. Among the men captured was Owen Tidr, the adventurous Welsh dancing master who had climbed so high by seducing Henry the Fifth's widow, Katherine de Valois, and fathering three bastards on her (one of whom had married Lord Edmund Beaufort's niece, Margaret, to Eleanor's great disgust).

Owen was tried and condemned to death, but he had ridden so far on the tide of fortune that he still could not believe that his gypsy luck had at last deserted him. It was not until he was actually kneeling for the ax that he understood it, and then, as if stunned, he cried out, "The block, now, for the head that used to lie in Kate's lap?"

Even after his death, his proverbial attraction for women did not fail, and a woman of the village took down his head from the market cross where it was displayed, and washed its face and combed its hair. Harry and the ten men he had brought with him from York had their first taste of real fighting and came out of it well, with some minor wounds and a great deal of experience. "The white hare is blood-stained now," Harry said afterward, "but she knows how to fight."

Having cleared up at Mortimer's Cross they began to move south and west toward London, and in the third week of February they were met by Warwick and the remnants of his army with the terrible news that the Queen had defeated them at St. Albans, recaptured King Henry, and was even now marching on London.

"My mother? My brothers?" Edward wanted to know at once, for Duchess Cecily and the two small boys were in lodgings in London; but Warwick shook his head—he didn't know. Edward bit his lip, and his cousin patted his shoulder.

"Don't worry too much," he comforted him. "I'd back your mother against anyone for resource and courage. She'll get them away all right."

"I can't afford to lose any more family," Edward said bleakly, and turned away.

News filtered through to them from London, first that the Queen's army was sacking the suburbs and that panic reigned supreme in the city. Fugitives from St. Albans who had sought shelter in the city began to drift back to join their ranks, and at last came a servant with the falcon badge still discernible on his tattered jerkin with the news that Her Grace had dispatched the children to the safety of Burgundy by ship, but was staying in London herself to try to organize the citizens into defending themselves.

"What did I tell you," Warwick cried with glee. "I told you your mother could cope. If anyone can persuade the Londoners to hold out, it's her. London's always been for York anyway. Now we've a fighting chance!"

They had. London did resist, closing its doors to Queen Margaret's hosts, and ten days after their defeat at St. Albans the two York armies marched into London to wild cheering. To Harry, it was like reliving a dream. Everything that had happened last October seemed to be happening again, except that it was Lord Edward and not Lord Richard who was received with such joy. And this time, when Edward claimed the throne as the true heir of York, there was no opposition. The lesson had been learned: on the fourth day of March, Edward was proclaimed King of England.

Harry managed to get a brief letter off to Eleanor by a merchant traveling that way. In it he told briefly of the events leading up to the entry into London, and reassured his mother that they were all unharmed.

I wish you could have been here to see our King enter the city, Mother. But you shall see him soon, and me, too, I pray God, for we are to go north after Queen Margaret's hosts, and when we have crushed them, we shall be free to go home again, and there will be peace.

Thus it was with hearts full of hope that Harry and the Morland men marched with the army out of London's gates on the twelfth of March, led by golden King Edward, the handsomest man in Christendom, and the Earl of Warwick, the greatest of all the lords of the land.

The ex-Queen and her army fled fast, and it was not until they reached Towton, only about fifteen miles from York city itself, that Edward's army could come close enough to force them to turn at bay. Harry was pleased rather than otherwise. "Not so far to go home afterward," he told his men.

It was the twenty-ninth of March. "Palm Sunday," said someone.

"We'll be home for Easter," Harry said. "King Henry won't fight today, not on a holy day."

"The Queen will, though, mark my words. And our Edward won't be caught by the same trick his father was. It'll be today, never you worry."

They looked up at the sky. It was dark, lowering, iron-gray. The air was like a whetted knife. "Looks like snow," someone suggested tentatively. "It's almost as dark as night."

A messenger approached them. "This is it, lads," he said cheerfully. "Form up. You know your positions."

"Where's the enemy?"

"You'll find out soon enough. On a small field over yonder, between the road and the stream. Hurry now."

"At least fighting'll keep us warm," said one of the men as they got to their feet. "I haven't felt my feet in days."

"Never mind," said Harry. "Fix your heart on home. Why, if we were on top of a hill now, I dare swear we could see Morland Place from here."

The men gave a cheer at that, and grasping their weapons they took their places.

The Queen's army outnumbered them nearly two to one, as they realized as soon as it came into view. Standing, waiting for the order to charge, Harry noted, with his new soldier's sense, that they had the advantage of position, too, a slight slope in their favor, and the stream, called the Cock Beck, protecting their flank. The iron sky seemed to draw down closer, as if it were crouching over them menacingly, and Harry thought more cheerfully, We have right on our side. If that's an omen, it's an omen for them. And there's our omen, he thought suddenly as he caught sight of King Edward riding to his place. On his silk surcoat his badge of the sun in splendor shone suddenly bright in the gloom, as if the real sun had come out for a moment. Dark clouds for them, Harry thought, but sunshine for us. God is on our side. And forgetting the cold pain in the half-healed sword-cut on his arm, he smiled, gripped his sword more firmly, and waited for the signal.

At first it seemed that they might lose. After the shrinking-back of the enemy from the first charge, the struggle seemed to be going their way, and their superior numbers seemed likely to tell against King Edward's men at last. The White Hare was in the thick of it on the right wing. Men were falling all around, and Harry's wound had been reopened and deepened by a sword-gash. If he had known more about fighting, he would have known that it was the most common place for a horseman to be wounded, that and the unprotected thigh.

Almost they began to fall back. Almost they began to fear defeat. And then the miracle happened; the sign they had wanted that God was on their side. The dark, threatening heavens opened in fluttering white snowflakes, spinning down, a few at first, and then thicker and thicker, and at the same time a wind got up that blew more and more fiercely across that small plain, blowing the snow

straight into the faces of the Lancastrians, blinding them.
Their arms grew feebler, they began to fall back. With
fierce cries the Yorkists pressed forward.

Harry was fighting alone now, the vagaries of battle
having separated him from the other remaining Morland
men. His sword was red to the hilt, his hand and arm were
slippery with blood, the ground under the horse's hooves
was churning mud and blood where the snow had no
chance to settle. It was turning into a rout, the Lancastrians being slaughtered on all sides like cattle at the autumn
kill. The Cock Beck, which had been one of their advan-
tages, now turned enemy too—they were being forced back
first to its banks, then into its waters. It was icy cold, and
swift-running. Many were swept off their feet and
drowned, while others fought up to their knees in water
until they were hacked down and their blood mingled with
the running flood.

Harry's horse was killed under him, but he got to his
feet and fought on, shoulder to shoulder now with strange
men, men he had never seen before. A strange badge, a
silver lion, on a man's surcoat; he was shouting "Norfolk!
Norfolk!" The reinforcements had come then—they could
not lose now. The host in front of him was thinner than the
host behind. Harry rested his aching sword-arm for a second to glance around to try to take in the state of the battle. Far off he saw men fleeing, pursued by York soldiers.
It was over then! They had won!

And in that moment when his attention was turned there
was a cry from just by him. He jerked his head around, saw
for a moment a snarling bearded face above a red dragon
badge, and then the shortened spear was thrust home in his
neck. He felt the tip of it grind against his collarbone, but he
felt no pain, only great surprise. He wanted to cry out, but
his throat was cut; he could make no sound but an
unearthly gurgling. The snarling face was gone, passing on
to more killing. Harry sank to his knees, his hands snatch-
ing at the wound, the bright blood pumping out between his
numb fingers. He couldn't catch his breath, for his nose,
mouth, and lungs were full of his own blood, and his last
thoughts were, I'm drowning, as he pitched forward on his
face by the water's edge.

* * *

It was the bloodiest battle of all time. The killing went on after dark, after the enemy had scattered and fled, the wild Yorkist soldiers hunting the fugitives like blood-crazed hounds, giving tongue as they ran and slaughtering them when they caught them. Wearily the generals and their captains tried to call the men off. The battle was won, though the Queen had managed to save her skin again, and had collected the King and their son from York, where they were hiding, and was even now heading hotfoot for Scotland and safety.

The killing went on all the way to York itself, despite anything Edward could do to have it stopped. From Towton field to the white walls of York, the snow was red and trampled with blood, the blood ran in rivulets through the ruts and furrows of the roads, and bodies lay everywhere, the dark bread of battle. At Morland Place the news of the battle arrived before it was even over, the news of the great York victory.

"Thank God!" Eleanor cried. "Now we have only to wait for our men to come home." And she called all the family and the household to the chapel, and Master James said a special mass of thanksgiving for the victory. The news that Margaret had escaped again cast a momentary shadow. "I would that that woman were dead. While she lives, she is trouble, she is death in this land."

All through the night the dogs bayed madly, for the smell of blood was in the air, and in the darkness tattered, fleeing figures flitted past within smelling distance, trailing blood behind them, seeking to escape to a more kindly place. Eleanor kept vigil in the chapel with her faithful servants around her. Edward and Isabella kept vigil in the bedchamber with Daisy, for she was pregnant and near her time, and they were afraid that the disturbance and fear would bring the child early. John, Richard, and Ned were in the nursery with Anys and Master Jenney, trying to sleep, but clutching each other under the bedclothes at every dreadful and inexplicable noise that rent the darkness outside.

A red sun arose at last, pouring its rosy light over the gory snow, and shortly after dawn two men limped into the courtyard of Morland Place. Their clothes were soaked with blood, some of which was their own. Their eyes were red-rimmed, their faces gray with exhaustion, their black-crusted arms hanging limply by their sides, unable to lift in salute as they came to a halt. There was a swirl of greeting, of cries of welcome and sympathy, and they were drawn inside to the fire in the great hall, and food and hot water rushed to them. They were not more than lightly wounded, more tired than hurt. The family, hearing the outcry, came running from their various occupations to see the home-coming.

"Where are the others?" Eleanor asked at once. The weary men looked at each other in brief anxiety. "Where are the rest?" she urged again.

"There are no others. We are the only two," one replied at last.

"The fighting was heavy," the other explained with an effort. It all seemed so long ago, and so irrelevant. It was hard to have to go over it now, for this tall, angry woman. "Most of them were killed in the first engagement. We were outnumbered."

"Outnumbered, you see." The other took up the struggle. "Until the snow started. Dick and me and one other, we got separated. Then this other one—Jack—he got it. Then there was only Dick and me." His head drooped with the effort. Eleanor tried to understand.

"But Harry? My son, Harry?" Her voice was pleading, but she already knew. Dick shook his head, once each way.

"We looked for the bodies, afterward, when it was all over, before we come away. We found some of 'em. You never seen so many bodies. Master Harry was down by the stream. We pulled him back out the water, but we couldn't bring any of them away with us. We hadn't got no horse nor anything."

He lifted his head then, and saw with a stirring of admiration how the mistress took it, straightening up proudly as if she wouldn't show she had taken a blow. But her face was older. It was terrible bad, losing Master Thomas and Master Harry, but when one was as tired as he was, one could only long for sleep. Before he had even finished thinking it, his eyes had shut. Mal, beside him, was already asleep.

"Let them be taken care of," Eleanor said, steadying her voice. "Edward, we must get the bodies back before the scavengers get to the field. I've heard stories of how sometimes they disfigure the bodies so they can't be recognized. Best go armed in case of any trouble. You'll need a cart, perhaps two. Be sure to bring them all back. Take Owen with you, and some strong men, and take linen to cover the bodies with. Alice, Ann, fetch linen from the chest at once and take it out into the yard for the men. Hurry, now, don't stand there weeping. Job, order up horses. Why is everybody standing still? There's much to be done—hurry!"

"Mother," Edward began, stunned at the speed of events, but at that moment there was a cry from above, and running footsteps, and Lys, Daisy's maid, came in, with her coif slipping off with her haste.

"Madam, Madam, my lady's begun. The baby's coming," she cried.

Edward started and made to turn back, but Eleanor caught him firmly by the arm and turned him toward the door. "I'll look after Daisy. You are needed elsewhere. Go now, fetch home your brother and the other men. Death has its rights as well as birth."

Daisy's baby was born two hours before noon, a girl, and was named Cecily after her mother. It was not until after dark that Edward and Owen and the other men arrived back with their cartload of sorrow, for it had been hard to find the bodies among so many, and the roads were so bad that the journey back had taken longer than it should. All evening the women laid out the bodies, washing and combing their hair, smoothing their limbs and wrapping them in fresh linen, and then placing them in the chapel among the candles and incense for the vigil. Eleanor knelt beside her son, wondering at how fresh and pure his face looked, not disfigured by death, for the cold water of the stream had washed away his blood and his skin was as white and flawless as alabaster.

"He looks like a statue of himself," she thought, and it put the thought into her mind that there should be a statue of him and Thomas, here in the chapel perhaps, a memorial to her two sons, dead in battle. She did not know where Thomas lay; the dead at Wakefield had been tumbled into some common, unmarked grave; but Harry should have a fine burial, and it should be Thomas's too.

"He was so young," she said aloud.

"Aye, madam, but a fine soldier." A voice came from close by her. She turned her head to see Dick there, bathed and rested and fed, but still looking more haggard in life than Harry did in death. "He fought like a tiger, madam, to the end, and then—it must've been a quick death," he said apologetically, afraid of upsetting where he meant to comfort. But Eleanor nodded, accepting the comfort.

"They were both fine young men. Thank God their deaths weren't in vain." She caressed the ivory cheek with one finger, and it was taut and cold, not like living flesh. He is gone from me, she thought, gone forever now.

"I remember," Dick said softly, "just before—before the battle, he said—he said we'd be home for Easter."

Home for good.

On Easter Saturday the King—as they must now learn to call Edward of March—returned from his fruitless pursuit of Henry and Margaret and entered York to the mad clamor of church bells and the braying of trumpets. The first thing he did, even before he took any sustenance, was to have the wizened heads of his father, brother, and uncle removed from Mickle Lith Bar and placed with due reverence in a coffin. The coffin was set in the nearby Church of the Holy Trinity, and plans were made for reuniting the heads with bodies in a proper burial at Pontefract, the nearest of the York castles.

On Easter Sunday the King went to celebrate Easter with great pomp at the minster, and all the Morland family were there with the exception of Daisy, who was still in childbed, and her new baby. Even little Richard, at two and a half, and Ned, who was not yet two, were there, dressed in their infant petticoats and awed into unexpected silence by the splendor of the occasion, the solemnity of the mass, and the presence of the new king.

King Edward looked magnificent—six feet three-and-a-half inches tall, broad-shouldered, lean-flanked, and handsome, his glittering golden hair combed smooth beneath his jeweled cap, his bright blue eyes flashing in a way that was less reminiscent of his stocky, brisk father than of his exquisite laughing mother. Eleanor felt a joy and a wonder at him, the son of *her* Richard, but perversely she felt a loss also, because he was so like his mother, so little like his father. Richard should have been King; Edward was King for him, but Edward was not like Richard.

Afterward, there was a triumphal procession through the streets, and Edward rode slowly, waving and laughing, and girls threw flowers down under his horse's hooves—oh, yes, old folk threw flowers, too, but especially girls threw flowers. He was to bring an age of peace, he was to unite the country under his single rule, he was to administer law and order and oust corruption and evil practices; but above all, he was young and handsome, so handsome. He *looked* like a king, and that was as important to the common people as anything he was likely to do.

On Easter Monday, there was a great feast given in the Guildhall, and all the notable people of York and the surrounding district were invited to be the King's guests. Edward and Eleanor were invited.

"It's such an honor," Daisy trilled from her bed, where she was nursing baby Cecily, in whom experienced baby handlers already saw signs of indisputable beauty. "It's so wonderful. I'm delighted that you should be going. You must be sure to tell me everything about it when you come back. Try to remember what everyone is wearing—it's no good asking Edward, he doesn't know one headdress from another."

Eleanor nodded, but with the curious perversity of mind that had dogged her yesterday, she could not be excited. "An honor, you think? Well, perhaps. But he's going to need money, that young man, and we're rich."

"Oh, Mother, what a thing to say! It isn't that at all, I'm sure of it. Why he's only just finished fighting his battles; he won't be thinking about money yet."

"If he's going to be a great king, he'll be thinking of money," Eleanor said. "You can't run the country without money, and Henry of Lancaster ran up enormous debts—or rather the Frenchwoman did, in his name."

"Nevertheless," Daisy said, "I won't let you rob the occasion of its greatness. It *is* an honor, whichever way you choose, and even if you won't accept it for yourself and Edward, you should accept it for poor Thomas and Harry."

Daisy saw tears in her mother-in-law's eyes, and knew her barb had gone home.

"Yes, you're right, of course," Eleanor said.

"Besides," Daisy went on, stroking her new baby's head, "don't you remember what Harry said about him in his letter from London, how he found time in the middle of all his business to go and see his little brothers? I honor him for that, and I think he must be a kind, good man."

"Yes, yes you're right, of course," Eleanor said. "I do honor him. He is a fine man and will be a great king."

"Then let us consider what you will wear," Daisy said, pleased at having settled the matter. The women discussed velvets and brocades and feathers and jewels, and Eleanor closed her mind to that small voice that still said in her heart, *He is not his father*.

It was as grand a feast as could be contrived in such a short time, and thirty cooks had labored all through the night to prepare the food, while many more men worked on the great hall, to sweeten it, scrub benches, beat hangings, and set up candles and torches. Edward and Eleanor rode into the city as soon as the gates were open and took mass at the minster, and then rode back to the Guildhall with their servants—two maids and two pages—walking in front.

Lepidus was so striking a horse, one of the best animals in the country, that he would have attracted all eyes at any time, but today he was especially striking, his bridle chiming with small silver bells and his crown-piece topped by nodding crimson plumes, his saddle-cloth crimson velvet with black silk tassels. Eleanor and Edward were sumptuously dressed too—as Eleanor said, if you were going to be asked for a loan, you might as well make the best of it.

Eleanor's cotte was of black silk, brocaded with gold, her surcoat of black velvet, its great hanging sleeves lined with ermine. Her headdress was of black velvet trimmed with a double row of pearls, simple but rich, from which hung a six-foot veil of the finest gauze.

Around her throat she wore a priceless string of black pearls, brought from the other end of the earth by an adventurous merchant and bought for her by Robert at a cost he would never reveal to her. Her waist, still tiny despite much childbearing, was cinched up by a ceinture of gold set with pearls and lapis-blue enamel, and from it, on gold chains, hung an ivory cross and the missal given her by Lord Richard. Her cloak was that purple one, lined with fox fur, that was also a present from the new King's father.

Edward's surcoat was also of black velvet, trimmed with ermine, much padded, and cinched up tightly at the waist with a gold belt and falling to the knee. Below, his hose were of lapis-blue silk, and his shoes ended in fashionable three-inch points, which made it rather difficult to mount and dismount. The two pages were in livery, sporting the black-and-white arms of the Morland family on their russet cloaks, and the badge of the white hare on their breasts. The maids were simply and modestly dressed in fine black wool and white linen, their heads demurely wimpled. Everything was of the best—they looked what they were, a wealthy and fashionable turnout.

At the Guildhall their horses were taken and they were shown to their places, which were at the second table, placing them below only the nobles and the top dignitaries of the town. This was honor indeed, for they were near enough to the new King and his companions to hear, occasionally, what was being said. The feast proceeded with dish after dish and subtlety after subtlety, while musical entertainment was provided by ten minstrels and a choir of fourteen boys. And when all the eating was done, the guests were invited to come up one by one and be presented to the King.

When Eleanor found herself before young Edward and had risen from her deep curtsy to meet his eyes, she found herself trembling. Why, her thoughts ran unbidden, this is a king! His golden good looks had not been exaggerated by report—rather the opposite: he was more handsome than any words could convey. But more than that, it was a living, warm, vibrant, intelligent face! The blue eyes looked deeply into hers, as if he wanted to know what she was like; there was a powerful sexual attraction about him that made his blue gaze seem more like his mother's than his father's, and yet there was something of Richard there, something in the frank, candid look that made you want to trust, and to obey.

And he held his hand out to her to raise her, and kept hold of her hand after she had risen.

"I know a great deal about you by repute, madam," he said pleasantly. "I know that you were a friend of my father's, and that when he asked you for help you did not fail him. And I know you as the mother of two of our most gallant soldiers, who gave their lives in battle for the House of York. What I had not been told was that you were an outstanding beauty." His eyes crinkled when he smiled, and his teeth were white. Eleanor smiled in response before she knew she had done so. So that was how he did it, she thought, recalling stories about his popularity with the women. Then he grew serious.

"We both know what it is to lose someone we love dearly," he said. "You have my very deepest sympathy, and you have my thanks for those two fine young men. Their lives were not wasted."

Eleanor bowed her head in acknowledgment, and then said, "Your Grace, I once promised your father that if anything happened to him, I would keep faith with you. I offer the same service to you that I offered to him."

"I accept it, and right thankfully. God bless you."

She curtsyed and moved away, and was aware of a sensation like breathlessness, the sensation she had after taking the Blessed Sacrament at mass. Yes, it was commitment. She had committed herself, in that moment, without effort, to his service. Well, in a sense it had already been done, for it was a part of that faith she had made with Richard, and it was a reassertion rather than a new vow. Loyalty to Richard meant loyalty to Edward; but it was interesting to ponder, if Edward had not been Edward, would she have done it so easily?

CHAPTER FIFTEEN

In 1463 Isabella was twenty-six and still unmarried. It was ten years now since the tragic death of Luke Cannyng, ten years in which she had never so much as been betrothed, and she had come to believe that she had achieved the impossible, to remain unmarried and still live at home. Her love for the merry, fresh-faced lad who had awakened her passion remained unchanged; and at one time, in the worst of her giref, she would have welcomed a decision to send her to a nunnery; but as the years passed she found it more and more difficult to bring his face to mind. She found that there were still pleasures in life—she enjoyed fine food, and dancing, she loved riding on the moors and hawking.

Her animosity to her mother had dimmed, though not died completely, but she found she enjoyed other people's company. She loved particularly to ride out with Job, or to hawk with Edward and young John. On the whole she liked men's company better than women's, but since Daisy had come, she had found a female friend in her, and the babies had struck a chord in her, too. She was Ned and Richard's favorite playmate, and baby Cecily loved to trot along behind her clutching at her skirt. There was something nice about babies—they were more like animals than people, somehow helpless and trusting and trustworthy. They did not hide their feelings and plot against you like adults.

So she would not like to go to a nunnery now. On the other hand she would not like to be married, for the thought of going away with a stranger and doing with him what she once did so gloriously happily with Luke appalled her. Also, though babies were nice to play with, having them seemed to be a terrible ordeal; and Daisy had just recently gone through a terrible childbirth only to have the baby, a boy, die a week later. All that pain and effort for nothing seemed poor sport to her.

Her mother still talked about marrying Isabella off, and, when Father had died, Isabella thought it would really happen. But then there had been the political troubles, the wars, and the boys dying in battle that had kept her mother's mind off such domestic trivia as marriages; and since then Mother had been occupied in business matters, for the new King was borrowing very heavily, from Eleanor as a friend and from Edward as a master stapler, and so Eleanor had to make the estates produce as much as possible.

She had fifty people working for her now, spinning and weaving cloth, and she was at the moment trying to buy her own fulling-mill so that she would be independent of other clothiers.

"What she wants in the end," Job explained to Isabella one day when they were riding back from the moors with some game for the pot, "is to do the whole process herself, from breeding the sheep to selling the cloth. At the moment she has to pay to get the lengths of cloth processed—that's fulling, dying, stretching, teasing, shearing, and baling. That cuts down the profits."

"She thinks of nothing but money these days," Isabella said carelessly.

"The King borrows heavily," Job said. "The money has to come from somewhere. And don't forget, if there was no money, you couldn't have these fine horses and the best hawks and hounds—to say nothing of the clothes you wear and the food you eat. You should be grateful that you are a rich young woman, and not abuse your mother in that irreverent way."

"Oh, Job, you are so proper." Isabella sighed. "I think

you must be getting old. It's all right," she said hastily, "I'm only teasing you. You know I respect your judgment in every way, and you're quite right about Mother. Now, then! Am I forgiven?"

Job shook his head. "You are too ready with that tongue of yours, Isabella. Too ready with your tongue and not ready enough with your heart."

"Well, I can't see why Mother has to give all that money to the King," she said resentfully, for she hated to be criticized by Job.

"Because," Job said slowly and sternly, "in the first place, the King is engaged in establishing peace in this land for all of us, and keeping off the marauding Scots, who would otherwise probably overrun us and burn our houses. And in the second place, because she promised the King's father that she would help him, and she will not break her promise."

"Oh, yes, Lord Richard," Isabella mused. "He was nice—do you remember him dancing with me? Job, is it true that he was Mother's lover?"

"Certainly not!" Job said quickly. "You shouldn't listen to servants' gossip."

"But how do you *know*?" Isabella persisted. "The King is certainly very friendly with her, in a special kind of way. Like inviting her to Lord Richard's month's mind last January. And look at the way she raved about the King's little brother—Richard, I mean—saying he was the only one of the family like his father."

They were riding into the courtyard now, and a servant was running forward to take their horses. Discretion was needed.

"I don't know anything about it," Job said firmly. "But I sincerely doubt it. One person running out in the middle of the night to make assignations is enough."

"By which you mean I'm to hold my tongue if I want you to hold yours?" Isabella said. "That's mean, Job. No, it's all right"—to the servant—"I'll take him. I want to see him properly bedded down. Come, Job, you're not too grand to see to your own horse, are you?"

They walked together through the yard to the stable,

leading their horses behind them. Isabella's was a young colt, Lyard the Second, her first bay, Lyard, having died two years ago. She had broken him herself, much as Eleanor had broken Lepidus. It was the one thing they had in common, Isabella thought. Job asked her derisively where she thought she got her love of horses from, if not from her mother.

"Job," she asked him now, "why didn't you get married? Won't you ever?" She had asked him that before, on other occasions, without getting an answer—Job was always very close about his private affairs. "You're not so old—not above forty."

"I'm forty-two, mistress, as you well know," Job said, fixing her with a firm eye. "And as you also well know, because I've said so to you before, I cannot marry because I am in service to your mother."

"But you could marry without interfering with that. Suppose you married Anys? I'm sure she'd marry you."

"I don't want to marry Anys, and she doesn't want to marry me," Job said.

Isabella looked about her to make sure they were not overheard, and then spoke again, but this time with her eyes anywhere but on Job's face, her cheeks reddening with embarrassment, "Well, you could marry me," she said. There was a silence and when at last she looked up, she caught on Job's face an indefinable expression that was like tenderness, or perhaps pity, before it resumed its normal inscrutability. "Wouldn't you like to?" she asked pitifully.

"Mistress—" he began, helpless.

Isabella went on quickly, "You see—I've always liked you, and I've always been your favorite—you know I have! And, oh, Job, I'm so afraid Mother's going to send me away. She's been talking recently about getting me a husband. Well, if she does, it'll be some terrible old man, a stranger, and I'll be forced to marry him. And if she can't find anyone to take me, I'll be sent to a convent. I'm twenty-six," she finished pathetically.

"It might not be so bad in a convent," Job suggested gently. "You'd live like a lady—your mother wouldn't let you want for money."

"But I don't want to go away from here. This is my home. I don't want to be shut up forever, and never ride or hunt or hawk or feel the fresh air on my face! Oh, Job, you like me, I know you do. We could have fun together. Couldn't you love me, even a little bit?" And in her desperation, dropping her colt's reins she flung herself into his arms, pressing herself against him avidly.

Job's eyes filled with tears and he put his arms around her as if to protect her. She turned her face up to him, offering her lips, and he kissed her gently before he put her away from him. The kiss was what convinced her. It was a kiss such as her father used to give her.

"I understand," she said bitterly. "I'm sorry if I embarrassed you."

"Dear Isabella—"he began. "You know that I love you very much, but—"

"But as a father. It's my mother you love, isn't it? No, don't bother to say anything. I ought to have guessed before now. You love her and look upon us as your children." A thought struck her, and she said it before Job could stop her.

"Or perhaps we *are* your children? Jesu, I never thought of that before. Was that why you were so sure she was not Lord Richard's lover—because she was yours?"

"Isabella, you are not to say such things! Put it out of your mind at once, and ask God to forgive you for your impure thoughts! I love your mother very dearly, and in a way I can't really explain to you. I've been with her since we were both little more than children. It's true I don't feel toward her as I expect a servant to feel toward his mistress, but the feeling isn't such as you've suspected. And besides, even if I did feel that sort of love, do you suppose I'd wrong your father in his own house, when he was my master, and a good master to me?"

Isabella looked ashamed. "I'm sorry, Job," she said. "I didn't mean it—it just slipped out. It's just because I'm so worried."

"I understand," he said more gently. "But, child, if your mother does find a match for you, can't you be content with that? At least then you'll have plenty of money for the rest of your life, and you'll have your own house and servants and be able to go hunting, and visiting, and all the other things you like."

Isabella caught up Lyard's reins and turned away sadly. "You don't understand," she said. "You can't understand. You're a man. Being married means having babies." And she led Lyard into his stall without another word.

The April Parliament that year concerned itself very much with the cloth trade, and Eleanor's satisfied expression when she heard about the new laws passed suggested that she might have had something to do with it. The new laws banned import of foreign cloths, laid down standards that lengths of cloth had to meet, and determined that payment for wool and cloth had to be made in money or bullion. These rules protected the English cloth market both from foreign competition and from cheapskates within the country. It also passed a law that workers in the cloth trade must be paid in cash and not in kind, and laid down both minimum and maximum wages for workers, which tended to stabilize the labor market.

Eleanor meanwhile was searching for a suitable fulling-mill and had discovered only one that was suitable with regard to size and position. It was built across a stream that ran fast all year round, and was about four miles from Morland Place; there were good flat fields around it, very suitable for setting up tenters and trestles for performing the other necessary processes of cloth making.

The owner of the mill was one Ezra Brazen, a cloth merchant from York who had little interest in the manufacturing side of the business, but owned the fulling-mill and two flour mills more or less as a sideline. He was around fifty, a widower with no children, and was known to be a sharp man where business was concerned, and it was said that he gained possession of the three mills through practices that were only just honest. He lived alone in a large house in Coney Street with three servants, had his meals sent in from the inn next door, where he also kept his horses, and dressed, as befitted a cloth merchant, richly and fashionably.

As was customary, Eleanor opened negotiations by meeting him in the churchyard after morning mass one day, and invited him to dinner at Morland Place a week later. No one was very taken with him, for, despite his fine clothes, he was unprepossessing in appearance, with lank, graying hair, a lined, rather crafty-looking face, and bad teeth. He was small and thin in stature, but had a wiry strength that became obvious when he controlled the fidgetings of his big horse. Isabella thought he laid on the whip rather too much. Daisy disliked his table manners, which were careless, and Edward thought he didn't show enough respect to the Morland family, who after all had a coat of arms and were personal friends of the King.

None of these thoughts were voiced at the time, however, for it was assumed that after negotiations he would agree to a price for his mill with Eleanor, and that would be that. The family behaved politely to him at dinner, listened when he spoke, and held their tongues when they disagreed with his opinions. After dinner Eleanor suggested a turn around the flower garden, which meant that she was going to discuss business, and when everyone else had pleasantly declined to take the air, Eleanor departed with him accompanied only by her two maids.

They walked about the garden for a couple of hours, and then Ezra Brazen declined to stay for supper, said he must be getting home, as he had business to attend to, and was seen on his way by Edward and Eleanor. They watched him whip his horse, call his dog, and ride away, and then turned to go in to supper.

"I suppose you had to agree a pretty stiff price with him," Edward said casually. "They say he's a hard man for a bargain."

Eleanor was thoughtful. She glanced up at her son as if she had hardly heard him. "Oh—he wouldn't sell," she said absently.

Edward raised his eyebrows.

"*Wouldn't?* You mean he wanted more than you were prepared to offer."

"No, not really. Well, in a way, I suppose. He doesn't want to sell, he wants a kind of partnership."

Edward stopped and caught his mother's arm. "Mother, what are you talking about? Tell me plainly what you've agreed with him."

"Don't bully me," Eleanor said crossly.

"I'm not bullying you. The business is my concern as well, you know, though a stranger could be forgiven for thinking I have no interest in it. What have you agreed to?"

"I haven't agreed to anything," Eleanor said, hedging.

"Then what are you thinking of agreeing on?"

She sighed. "He wants to marry Isabella."

There was a brief silence. "Marry Isabella? What on earth for?"

"I suppose he's taken a fancy to her. Besides, it will bring him into the family, and that can't be anything but good for his trade, with our connections. He's extremely rich, and he has no children. If she had any children by him, they'd inherit everything; and if she didn't, she'd inherit everything. There'd have to be a dowry, of course, but that shouldn't be too much, considering the trade benefit she'd be bringing with her—"

"Mother!" Edward stopped her in mid-flow. "You talk as if you're considering this idea."

"Well, of course I'm considering it," Eleanor said, surprised. "Why not?"

"What for?"

"We get free use of the fulling-mill, plus freedom to develop the rest of the land it stands on. He markets our cloth for us on commission, instead of our having to sell it to a merchant for him to make a profit. And when he dies—and he's not very young—it all comes to us. Now do you see?"

"But, Mother—marrying Isabella! Surely there's some other way to deal with him than this?"

"Of course there isn't. And besides, what's so wrong with marrying Isabella to him? She has to be settled some time, and there may not be another offer for her. She's twenty-six. She may not be able to have children. I'm only surprised he wants her."

"But he's—he's not of our kind. He's a common man. He eats like a pig, and—"

"He's rich, he dresses well, he keeps servants, he has a fine house, and his manners, if they are a little rough, are far better than your own grandfather's were; and if I could put up with them, you can put up with Ezra Brazen's."

"Then you're set on this?" Edward asked quietly.

"I am. So there's no more to be said. Let us go in to supper."

"When are you going to tell Isabella?"

"In my own good time."

"I think she ought to be told at once. After all, it concerns her most."

"It concerns her not at all. Look what happened when she was allowed to choose her husband. A marriage is for the parents to decide—she must do as she's told," Eleanor said sharply, and ended the conversation by walking on ahead of him. Edward followed, a troubled expression on his face.

When the family was seated and Job had supervised the pouring of the wine and ale, the subject that came naturally to everyone's tongue was that of the dinner guest.

"Wasn't he a horrid little man?" Daisy said cheerfully. "I couldn't bear the way he picked his teeth with his knife-point."

"You're too particular." Eleanor rebuked her coldly. Daisy looked slightly surprised, for normally Eleanor was very strict about table manners; but Isabella, who had not noticed the interplay of expressions, took up the thread.

"What I didn't like was the way he whipped his horse. He may be a good horseman, but he laid it on too hard. And did you notice the way his dog cringed? I'm sure he beats it too."

Edward was looking at Eleanor with a "You see?" expression. Eleanor drummed her fingers on the table in annoyance.

"That's enough, Isabella. No one is interested in your opinion."

"Well all I said was—"

"Be silent!"

"But Daisy said—"

"Be silent!"

"Mother?" Edward began.

Job, on his way past the table, stopped and looked quizzically at his mistress. Eleanor met his eyes coolly, and spoke to the company in general. "Since you are all determined to discuss our guest in this ill-mannered way, I had better tell you that Master Brazen has asked to marry Isabella."

There was a shocked silence, and Isabella turned chalk-white.

Then Daisy said tentatively, "You refused him, I expect, didn't you, Mother?"

Eleanor turned cold eyes on her. "I neither refused nor accepted." Isabella drew breath again. "But I intend to accept him, provided we can agree on terms."

"Mother, no! You can't!" Daisy cried. "Such a horrid, common little man, to marry Isabella Morland, one of the richest girls—"

"You forget," Eleanor said quietly, "that she isn't a girl any longer. The match is good. He is very rich, and has no children. Isabella, or her children, if God sends her any, will inherit everything he has."

Isabella's fork had fallen from her hand, and she was staring wordlessly at her mother, her eyes like holes cut in a sheet of paper. But at the word *children* she started up with a strange cry like a wounded deer, and rushed from the room, knocking over her cup in her hasty flight and spilling its contents over the white nap in a dark stain like blood.

As the talk went on through the evening, one by one the family was won round to the idea. Daisy had to admit that it was a fair match as far as worldly status went, and that it would be better for Isabella than a convent. Edward supposed grudgingly that a man couldn't help his looks, and that his manners weren't so very much worse than those of some of the city notables of their acquaintance. Thirteen-year-old John couldn't see what the fuss was about, and only added that he thought it would be fun to live in the city where everything was going on, instead of miles out on a private estate.

But it was Job who alone entered into Isabella's feelings, for he alone spent much time with her and he alone was in her confidence. He spoke to Eleanor privately the next day before the rest of the house was astir, as she was returning from her private devotions in the chapel, where it was her habit to kneel for half an hour every morning to pray for the souls of her husband and sons. A fine marble memorial now stood just inside the door, a likeness of a young soldier. It was dedicated to both young men, giving their dates and names, but the face was Thomas's face.

As soon as she saw him, Eleanor knew that Job had come to plead. She folded her lips tightly.

"Madam—"

"No, Job. I know what you are going to say, but this time you may as well save your breath. You persuaded me once before against my judgment, but this time I'm adamant."

"She doesn't want to marry him, mistress," Job began.

Eleanor exclaimed crossly. "What? What does what she wants have to do with it? She will do as she's told, and that will be enough for her. She's always had too much of her own way. Her father spoiled her, and you've persuaded me to be more lenient with her than I would otherwise have been. What is it about Madam Isabella that makes everyone run round in circles trying to please her? She's always been a selfish, disobedient child, and there's no reason that I can see why the whole house should be organized for her pleasure."

"It isn't that—"

"Then what is it?"

"She has spoken to me—"

"I guessed she had."

"She would be so unhappy—"

"Nonsense. Look, Job, my dear friend, you know that the alternative would be to send her to a convent. She would be more unhappy there. No, this time I'm determined—it may be the last chance to settle her happily."

Job's eyes were eloquent, but he said nothing.

Eleanor placed her hand over his, and said, "What is it? What is there about Isabella that makes you speak to me like this. She's always been your favorite, hasn't she?"

Job saw a last possibility to save Isabella, and though he trembled for the consequences, he swallowed hard and said, "Yes, madam, she has. So much a favorite that—I wonder if you would consider allowing me to speak for her hand?"

"You?" Eleanor did not seem to comprehend.

"Yes, madam. I've never spoken of it before now, but if you would consent for me to marry her, I—"

"Has she put you up to this?" Eleanor asked sharply.

"I swear she doesn't know I am speaking to you now."

Eleanor withdrew her hand as if she had been stung. "You are serious about this?"

"Most serious," he said.

Her eyes narrowed, her expression grew cold. "Then you must be mad! Marry Isabella? You are my servant—*my servant*—and don't you ever forget it. Never speak to me of this again."

And with that she swept away without another glance in his direction, and Job remained, shaking a little, knowing that he had seriously offended her, and perhaps lost her trust forever. Sadly he went to Isabella, and told her what had happened.

"I can never speak of it again to her," he said. "There is nothing more I can do for you. I may even have damaged your case."

"You are not to blame," Isabella said, her eyes wide and tragic. Then they narrowed in anger, and she looked just then amazingly like her mother. "But I will not do it. You may tell her that if she asks you—say what she will, I *will not marry him!*"

Eleanor tried reasoning with her first.

"It's for your own good," she said. "It will give you an establishment of your own, provide for you. It's the only alternative to a convent."

Then, "He's an old man, he may not live long. In any case, he's bound to give you more of your own way than you have here. And when he dies, you will inherit his wealth."

Then, "You'll be living within a stone's throw from Helen and John. You'll be able to visit them, go about the town with Helen, be a lady of fashion."

And finally, "It's no good arguing, Isabella. You will marry him, and that's all there is to it. You're a wicked, unfilial girl, a disgrace to your family, and a thorn in our dear Lord's crown, but you will marry him."

"You can't force me to," Isabella said at last. "You can't carry me bodily to church. You can't *make* me say I'll take him when I get there. And if I don't say I'll take him, it isn't legal."

"That's true," Eleanor said thoughtfully. "Come with me, child."

They were in the solar, and as Isabella followed her mother out of the room, she asked, "Where are we going?"

"You'll see," Eleanor said pleasantly.

Isabella felt a stirring of apprehension. "What are you going to do?"

Eleanor did not answer. She led her daughter down passages to the part of the house where the chamber was divided into storerooms. She looked into one and then another, and finally stood back from the door of one and bid Isabella go inside.

"What is it?" she asked as she went in. The storeroom was empty except for an ancient wooden chest in which some spare horse rugs were kept, and unlit except for a tiny casement high up in the wall which gave a view of some chimney stacks and a small patch of sky.

"I can't make you marry Ezra Brazen, it's true," Eleanor said, still pleasantly as she searched along the bunch of keys that hung from her waist, "but I can make you want to. I'm going to lock you in now, and you shall stay here in this room just as you are until you agree to marry him."

"No! You can't!" Isabella cried, flinging herself forward, but Eleanor stepped back quickly and shut the door, locking it while she held it shut with her other hand. Isabella beat madly on the panels.

"Let me out! Let me out! You can't keep me here!"

"I can, and I will," Eleanor said, and left her. She went downstairs and explained what she was doing to Edward.

"But, Mother," he said, "isn't it a bit harsh on poor 'Bella?"

"Poor 'Bella is a headstrong, willful girl, and if I'd had the handling of her without interference from the beginning, this wouldn't be necessary. But as it is—she's going to marry Ezra Brazen, and that's all there is to it. Luckily

the weather's warm, so she won't perish up there. And
there are some horse blankets in that chest she can sleep
on. She can't get out of the window, it's too small. No,
she'll soon come round, when she finds she's missing her
riding and her fine food. I think just to make sure it
doesn't drag on, I'll starve her a little."

"Mother!"

"Tush, boy, it won't hurt her. I'll give her bread and
water to keep her alive, and she'll soon miss all those rich
sauces she's so fond of. That will bring her to her senses,
make her realize that once she's married she'll be able to
eat what she likes."

For a week Isabella stayed in the storeroom, with nothing but a jug of water and a little bread each day to eat.
Sometimes she raged and screamed and beat at the door.
Sometimes she paced up and down weeping and wailing.
But mostly she just sat on the chest and brooded, her face
dark and stubborn. Everyone in the house went about his
business with an acute awareness of the prisoner upstairs,
but no one dared interfere or even try to smuggle extra
food up to her. Eleanor was still angry with Job, and she
was so determined about this that no one else dared cross
her.

At the end of two weeks, Isabella was pale and thin and
red-eyed, but still stubborn.

"I don't care if I die up here," she said. "I'd sooner die
than have to marry that man."

Ezra Brazen came to see Eleanor again, and she agreed
terms with him, but said she could not yet name a wedding
date. Brazen suspected something odd and tried giving her
an ultimatum, but Eleanor dismissed him coolly.

"If I honor you by allowing you to marry my daughter,
you must be patient until I tell you the date. I shall not
keep you waiting long."

She was thoughtful when Brazen had gone, and then finally she called her maid to her. "Go to Master Jenney,"
she told her, "and ask him for his ferrule. Then bring it to
me in the solar."

When the maid brought it, she dismissed her and walked
down the passage to the storeroom, and stopped at the

door. She stared unhappily at the ferrule, with which the tutor had occasionally punished Thomas or Harry, the other boys being too docile to need it, and flexed it in her hand, testing its strength. Her face was sad; but she had never shirked a duty, however bitter. She passed a hand across her face, and then straightened herself grimly, drew up the key to the storeroom door, and let herself in.

Isabella was married at the door of Holy Trinity church on the day after Lammas. It was a gray, warm day, and a steady misty drizzle fell from before dawn to after sunset. Isabella cried the whole time, too, as if she were trying to compete with the weather; her eyes were red and puffy, and she was thin and drawn, and looked more than her years, so that Ezra Brazen, when asked if he took his bride, visibly hesitated, as if he thought better of it. Isabella, when asked, spoke harshly and defiantly, but without hesitation. It had taken a week to teach her something about herself, that she might sooner die than marry, but she would not sooner be beaten every day than marry. It had not been the pain so much as the humiliation, and most of all the dreadful waiting, knowing that it was to come, and exactly when it was to come. No, there were some things that were not to be borne.

But she would never forgive her mother. During the wedding feast and afterward her eyes were frequently on Eleanor, burning with hatred and desire for revenge. Eleanor saw it, but shrugged inwardly. Isabella would soon settle down and realize that it was done for her own good as well as that of the family. And if she didn't—well, what matter? She was married, and nothing could change that. Ezra danced with his bride, a little awkwardly because of the high heels he had had fitted to his shoes so that his bride should not overtop him. Whenever he caught her eye, which was not often, he smiled and nodded to her significantly. She did not smile back, for now and then, when he did not know she was looking, she caught him looking at her in a particular way that made her shudder. She didn't like the way he licked his lips.

For the first time in years the face of her long-dead

lover came to her mind, smiling at her across the years, so
dear and desirable and never more lost to her than now.
Oh, Luke, she cried in her heart, why did you have to die?
And, oh, God, what did I do to deserve the fate I have
suffered?

CHAPTER SIXTEEN

Isabella lay in her bed listening apprehensively for the footsteps to come up the stairs. She had been married two months now, and those two months seemed to have lasted longer than all her life before. The bed was a new one of fine carved beech, with new scarlet hangings and a counterpane of sky-blue silk, but it was the only thing about the house that was nice. The whole place had a stale, rancid smell. She had never cared too much for the city, anyway, with its noise and its symphony of stinks—she had always preferred the fresh wind on the moors and its lonely silence. The house smelled as if the city were seeping in through its walls.

The servants, too—they were an old man and woman who had been in Ezra's service for many years, and who did their work silently without ever looking up from the ground, and a grinning boy who turned out to be their son and was an idiot. The servants smelled bad. Ezra bathed only when he was going somewhere special, and he had a stale smell about him. The servants never washed at all, and the smell of them made Isabella's eyes water.

The family was quite reconciled to the marriage. Ezra behaved well when any of them were present, watching his manners at the table and treating Isabella with a politeness that made her want to scream, and Edward had been heard to murmur to Daisy that he turned out to be quite a decent chap. Publicly she had nothing to complain of—but they didn't know, and would never know, what she had to bear.

Every night she lay in bed like this, waiting, as she had waited in the storeroom for her mother to come upstairs with the ferrule and beat her. He didn't beat her, but he hurt her. The first night he had been well drunk on fine wines, drunk enough not to notice her missing maidenhead—for, of course, he must not know that she came to him not a maid. And he had hurt her, badly, so that she had cried out. And he had told her that this was the way it was, and that a woman's duty was to put up with it.

That was when she knew why she was being punished. She was being punished by God and the Holy Virgin for her sin with Luke. For if she had not sinned with Luke, she would not have known what love was really like, and if she had not known what it was like, it would have been easier to bear what Ezra did to her. She had learned not to cry out, for the more she cried out, the more he hurt her—that was what he liked. She did not understand it, but she knew it was so. And he grew more subtle, he had a hundred subtle ways of hurting her—sly, pinching, probing ways. He would place the candle close to the bedside so that he could watch her face while he did it.

"That's the way it is, my chicken," he would croon to her, and she would catch the reek of his breath. "That's how it is for women, that's their lot. You have to bear it, my chicken." And she would whimper, and he would laugh and pinch her again.

Did he suspect, she wondered sometimes, that she had had a lover? Was that why he taunted her, to try to force her into admitting it? She would clench her teeth, sometimes biting her tongue until it bled to stop herself from speaking. She would not give him that satisfaction, nor the satisfaction of seeing her cry. She dashed the tears away from her eyes now, and then caught her breath as she heard the heavy footsteps coming upstairs. Her skin crawled with apprehension, and her palms were suddenly wet. Oh, Holy Virgin Mother, oh, merciful Jesu, help me to bear it, make it be over soon, if it is Thy will.

The door creaked open, and the candle shadows jerked

back and forth across the room. She heard his breathing in the silence. Sweet Jesu, Holy Mother. She wondered suddenly how his first wife had died.

"Are you awake, my chicken?" he chuckled.

The family was all together at Christmas, and celebrated the feast with some enthusiasm as both Daisy and Isabella announced that they were pregnant. There was some surprise and much pleasure at Isabella's announcement, for it had been felt vaguely by everyone that the marriage with Ezra Brazen would not be fruitful. On the whole Ezra seemed less pleased than would be expected and Isabella more pleased; only a person who knew the details of their marriage would have understood it, for the pregnancy meant that there could be no more sexual relations between the husband and wife until the baby was born.

"I'm so delighted for you," Daisy said, hugging her favorite sister. "You must be so happy."

"Well, in a way I am," Isabella said.

"Only in a way? But you love babies—you loved mine, anyway."

"I didn't have to give birth to yours," Isabella pointed out.

Helen looked on sadly, holding little Cecily in her lap. "Some of us would welcome it," he said. "If John and I had been blessed—"

"Poor Helen." Daisy was quick to sympathize. "But you have been blessed—just think, John might have been killed in the wars like poor Thomas and Harry. You should be glad you have him safe and well."

"I am," Helen said. "But I'd be more grateful if I had him and two strong babies, like you." She turned to her sister. "But, 'Bella, you don't look well. You're very thin, and you look tired—are you ill?"

"No, I don't think so. I expect it's just pregnancy," Isabella fended off the question. She looked around, avoiding her sister's eyes and the sight of her husband, who was talking to Eleanor—about business, she dared swear. "It's nice to be home again, anyway. I wonder if Mother would let me come here to lie in."

"I expect so, if your husband wouldn't mind," Daisy said cheerfully. "We'll be about the same time, won't we? But wouldn't you rather be at home?"

Isabella shuddered. "This is home to me," she said tersely, and Daisy, not wanting to stir up any troubled waters, let the subject drop.

That summer, while the Earl of Warwick was negotiating a French marriage for the King, and the King was putting down insurrections in Wales with a pleasant secret under his belt, Eleanor was extending the operations of the cloth business on the flat fields beside Brazen Mill. The acquisition of the mill meant that she was able to have every process of cloth making carried out by her own employees. The wool from her own sheep was taken by packhorse to the various cottages where spinsters worked, and the spun yarn collected the following week and taken to the cottages of the weavers.

The lengths of woven cloth were then collected in the same way and taken up to the fulling-mill, where it went under the water-driven hammers and was then bundled out to the flat field and stretched out on the great wooden tenters to dry and be bleached by the sun. Soon they were processing so much cloth that the whole field was dazzling with the "tents" of white cloth. Once dry, it was taken down and stretched out on the wooden trestles and gone over by hand, any imperfections being picked out with tweezers.

Then, a new set of employees dyed the cloth in great vats, unless it was to be sold undyed or was a fancy weave woven out of predyed wool, dried, teased and sheared it; and then it was collected again and carried to the warehouses, where it was baled, stamped and eventually shipped either by packhorse or down the River Ouse by barge to its eventual purchasers.

The main demand in the area was for coarse, strong cloth, but Eleanor's employees also made some fine cloth, and in particular a small amount of very expensive fancy weave that was exclusive in design and was known in the market simply as "Morland." Eleanor was tireless in business, for with so many employees under her she felt the need to be particularly vigilant against dishonesty. She knew every one of her employees by name, and a good deal about the life history of each, and on her trips around the various work sites she would stop to talk to them, listen to their troubles, and give help where it was needed. In that way she found that she could trust her workmen and women better—they did not want to cheat her.

She rode out almost every day, and was often away from dawn to dusk. On top of this, she also ran all the financial side of the business, feeling that Edward had no head for figures, and, although it was really Daisy's job, she still supervised the running of the house. Edward looked after the farm side of things, supervising the running of the several estates, but even in this province Eleanor could not let well alone, and frequently rode out, now often taking John with her to gain experience, to the other manors to see that everything was running smoothly.

Her energy was enormous. Even Isabella, when she came back to Morland Place in August to lie in and saw how much her mother did, was forced to an unwilling admiration. Daisy sometimes gently hinted that Eleanor did not need to do quite so much, that she could safely leave some things to her and Edward; but only Job really understood that she needed to drive herself the whole of the day in order to stifle that lonely voice inside her. Sometimes, on the long summer evenings Job would go out to her in the herb garden that they had planned and planted together, and sit at her feet and play to her on the guitar while she rested, breathed in the scented air, and looked up at the sky.

She would close her eyes, and he would look into her face and see the lines of sadness there. She was a woman who needed love, who needed to be loved, and her heart was empty, bereft of her husband, of the man she had secretly hungered for, and even of the son she had loved best. And then she would open her eyes and meet Job's gaze, and would smile and place her hand on his shoulder with a mute thanks. Thank you for understanding me, her look would say. Thank you for being here.

Isabella saw them once from a window, and thought that she understood. She was sure now that Job had been her

lover. She imagined it was jealousy over Job that had made
Eleanor so determined to marry Isabella off. It only added
to her bitterness.

It was on a sweltering hot day at the end of August that
Isabella went into labor. Her pains started early in the
morning, and she had panicked and screamed, realizing all
at once that it really was going to happen, and that there
was nothing she could do to avoid it. But as the day wore
on and the pains continued she quietened.

"You won't have it for hours yet," Daisy told her wisely.
She herself was large with child now, and moved with difficulty, but she sat beside Isabella all the same and fetched
and carried for her whenever she wanted something, which
was often. "Don't you think you could walk a bit now? It
would be so much better for you."

But Isabella shook her head and groaned. "I shall die, I
know I shall. Nothing can help me now."

By nightfall she was delirious, held in the grip of a continuous pain and no longer conscious of the passage of
time. She stared unseeingly from one face to another, turning her head over and over from one side to the other,
groaning pitifully and praying aloud for her torment to
end. Eleanor and Anys, stronger in mind than Daisy, got
her to her feet and forced her to walk up and down the
room, but her feet were dragging and it was more a case of
them carrying her than her walking, and it was doing no
good.

"Pull yourself together, Isabella," Eleanor said sharply.
"You must walk, or how will the baby come?"

But Isabella only groaned "I shall die," and slumped
against them.

Two hours after midnight Eleanor sent for the midwife.
"She isn't getting on with it," she told her.

The midwife examined the patient, tutted, and said, "It's
a very big baby, and she's very small. Her first, isn't it?
Has she been walking? No? That's bad. We must see what
we can do."

At dawn Isabella began screaming. She no longer knew
where she was or what was happening to her, she only
knew that there was pain everywhere, that she was being
tortured. She thought she had died and gone to Hell, where

devils were tearing at her with their red-hot fingernails to punish her for her sins. The devils spoke all around her in voices that swelled and boomed, distorted as images in a copper bowl. They had familiar faces, but wicked, evil, tormenting. They tore at her and laughed, peering to see if she would scream. She screamed. "Don't! No! Holy Mother, help me. It wasn't so bad a sin. Forgive me. No more, no more." One of the devils had Ezra's face, and was probing again at the tender parts of her. "She's too small," the devil said in a woman's voice. "We shall have to pull it out." And then he began trying to tear off her legs.

"We'll have to pull it out, or she'll die," the midwife said. "I'll need help."

"Will the baby live?" Eleanor asked.

"I cannot tell, madam. I hope to save my patient, but whether I can save the baby too, I don't know."

"Try to be brave, sweetheart," Eleanor said, wiping the sweat from Isabella's contorted face.

Isabella screamed again, piercingly. It was a horrible scream, almost automatic, like the shriek of something no longer human.

Eleanor shuddered. "Hurry!" she cried. "She suffers."

Cecily was sent away, for she was fainting, and too near her time to witness such suffering, leaving Anys and Eleanor to help the midwife, with two maids outside the door in case they were needed. Daisy went downstairs to be comforted and held by Edward. Job sat by the window, staring out into the morning light, his face gray with suffering. He had always favored Isabella above the other children.

And then the screaming rose to a pitch of demented agony, a shriek of torment beyond human endurance that was cut off abruptly at its highest point. And then in the jangling silence that followed, the small muted wail of a baby. Daisy shuddered in her husband's arms, and began to sob.

"It's all over now," he comforted her.

"She's dead," Daisy said, and no one tried to contradict her. There was something in that last terrible cry that told them so.

It seemed a long time later that there were footsteps on

the stairs, and Eleanor came into the hall, gray with fatigue, a haunted look in her eyes. They all looked up, and Job came across from the window to stand near her, as if he thought she would need his support.

"A boy," she answered the unasked question. "They're both alive. It seems—they—will live." Her head drooped with the effort of having spoken.

"Oh, thank God," Daisy cried, and buried her face in her hands. No one else spoke. Eleanor looked from face to face, and finally to Job, and it was to him she spoke.

"She suffered—dear God, how she suffered. If I had known, if I had known it would be like that—" She meant, I would never have forced her to marry.

"You couldn't know," Job said quickly. "You are not to blame." But he saw she did blame herself, though she would never say so aloud to anyone, not even to him. And for the first and last time in his life, he took her in his arms and laid her head on his shoulder. "You couldn't know," he said gently. And no one thought it odd that he did what he did.

Isabella's baby was named Edmund and was christened at once, though after the first few hours it seemed likely that he would live to be a man, for he was apparently strong and healthy. Four days later, on the first of September, Daisy gave birth with almost insulting ease to a very pretty baby girl, who was named Margaret after Daisy's mother. Daisy was up and about again as soon as was decent, but long after she was back in her normal domestic routine, Isabella was lying on her sickbed, still wracked with pain and hovering between life and death.

Ezra came to visit her and the child, expressed gratification that it was a boy, and anxiety over his wife's state of health.

"I don't think she should come back to York," he said. "I think she should stay here until she's well again. I think it would be dangerous to move her."

"Is it your pleasure to leave the child here, too?" Eleanor inquired rather coldly, for she thought his haste in passing the responsibility for Isabella on to the Morlands was indecent.

"Yes, yes, I think it would be best. My servants are hardly fitted for the care of a baby, and you have a nursery here and trained maidservants. Yes, let the child remain here until its mother is fit to come home again."

In spite of the presence in the house of two new babies, it was an unhappy autumn all around, with Isabella hovering near death in a darkened room upstairs. Then, only two weeks after Daisy's lying-in, John Butler was taken ill, and before the month was out he was dead. He cut his foot while walking around a warehouse, the foot turned gangrenous, and even before anyone had thought of calling in a surgeon to cut the leg off, the poison reached his heart and he was dead. Poor Helen was desolate, for she had dearly loved her kind husband, who had never once reproached her for not bearing him children. Eleanor mourned him sincerely, having learned of his worth during the wars, and everyone who knew him had a tear to shed and a word to say to his widow of how much they had admired him and how much he would be missed. A quiet man, a man of no particular eminence in the world, he had seemed to gather friends wherever he went, and there was no need to hire mourners for his funeral procession—there were hundreds of genuine ones, so many that they could not all get in the church.

And then came shocking news from London: King Edward had married secretly as long ago as May, and had kept the secret until my lord of Warwick had started to explain about the French match he agreed for the King, when it had to come out. Warwick was furious, the Council shocked, and the people, when the news leaked out and became public, were disapproving and apprehensive. For the woman the King had chosen to waste his magnificent self on was a widow five years his senior, a Lady Grey of Groby who had two grown sons by her first marriage, and more poor relations than you could shake a stick at.

Lady Grey's mother, the former Duchess of Bedford, was popularly thought to be a witch, and it was said that she had used witchcraft to snare the King for her widowed daughter.

"Certainly it must have been something," Eleanor said to

Edward when she first heard the news. "He could have had anyone, and he has ended up with a nobody. Her father was no more than a squire who married a rich widow. This Lady Grey has six sisters and five brothers and not a penny piece between them."

"She is supposed to be very beautiful," Edward suggested mildly.

"What's beauty got to do with it? All her clan will be a faction at court. She brings him nothing but troublesome relations as a dowry. Oh, why do Kings seem to be struck with a sort of madness when it comes to marrying? Look at the trouble Henry's Margaret has caused. And I'll wager this Elizabeth of Edward's will be as bad. He should never have married beneath him: a queen has to behave like a queen, not like a flesh-merchant's wife."

"You feel these things too strongly, Mother," Edward said. "She must be a virtuous lady, or he wouldn't have needed to marry her."

Eleanor looked at him witheringly. "No doubt she was well schooled. Men are such green fools. As for feeling things strongly—look what she has done already: she has alienated my lord of Warwick, and he is such a man that a king needs at his shoulder, not at his back with a knife. The country will be split by faction! Oh, why are men such fools?"

"Everything will be all right, Mother, don't worry," Edward said, and Eleanor could only glare at him.

Time healed some of the ills. After Christmas, Isabella was able to go back to Coney Street with the baby, taking two Morland servants, a maid, and a boy with her to help her. Ezra had asked for her back, afraid that he would lose influence over the baby if he left him with his grandmother too long, and seeing how ill she was still, he was anxious to have no fuss, and treated her kindly, giving her a room to herself which she shared with the maid and the baby. The ordeal had left Isabella virtually a cripple. She could stand or walk for short periods only, and would never ride again. She was carried from Morland Place to Coney Street on a litter, a pale, brooding shadow of her former self.

And the quarrel between King Edward and my lord of Warwick was patched over, but there was never the same trust between them, and it was from that time that the latter began to wonder what he had got out of all his struggles to make Edward King.

And to cap it all, a quarrel developed with the King of Burgundy which resulted in his banning all imports of cloth from England. Having put all her resources into cloth manufacture, Eleanor discovered that the markets were closed to her.

CHAPTER SEVENTEEN

In the summer of 1468, the summer the Princess Margaret—King Edward's younger sister—was married to the Duke of Burgundy, Helen and Daisy were sitting in the Italian garden with their embroidery, enjoying the sun and the privacy that allowed them to take off their heavy headdresses in favor of a light linen veil. They were discussing the royal wedding, like almost everyone else in England.

"Two hundred gold crowns," Daisy was marveling. As placid and sweet as ever, she had grown stout since the birth of her last child, and puffed a little when she exerted herself. "It's a terrible lot of money. No wonder my lord of Warwick is against it."

"That isn't why he's against it. He wanted an alliance with France. He's always wanted the King to marry a French princess. That was why he was so furious when Edward married Lady Grey."

"Well, that marriage has turned out all right, anyway," Daisy observed. "Two children already, and another on the way."

"Girls, two *girls*, don't forget."

"And don't you forget that your own mother had three girls before she had a son," Daisy said sternly. "I'm sure the King loves his daughters as dearly as any son."

"Oh, Daisy, that isn't the point," Helen said a little impatiently. "Kings and queens don't have children for the pleasure of it. A king needs a son to prevent civil war after his death."

"Well, well," Daisy said soothingly, reverting to the previous topic, "the Burgundy marriage will be good for trade."

"It hasn't been so far. The Duke still hasn't lifted the ban on English cloth." They pondered for a moment.

Then Daisy changed the subject again. "Talking of marriage . . ." she began.

Helen shook her head. "I know what you're going to say, but please don't."

"But, Helen, why shouldn't you get married again? Poor John's been dead nearly four years, and you're still as beautiful as ever."

"You forget," Helen said quietly, "that I'm barren. No one would take a barren woman to wife."

"But you don't know that you are," Daisy said. "It might have been—well, it might have been John that couldn't have children. You don't know."

Helen looked startled, having assumed, as everyone did, that barrenness was the woman's fault. It was a bold new idea, but even while turning it over Helen knew the answer.

"It wouldn't matter anyway, Daisy. No one would ever believe it, even if we knew it was so. Let's not talk about it." She drew a deep breath and gazed about her. "Oh, it's nice to be home, even if it is only for a visit."

"Why not make it permanent?" Daisy asked warmly. "Oh, Helen, do! It would be company for me, and it would cheer Mother up, after John's leaving home. You know how she hates to let anyone go." John, at eighteen, had recently left home to be apprenticed to one Leonard Byrne, a goldsmith of Gutter Lane in London. It was a good apprenticeship, for everyone knew that goldsmiths were rich and powerful men, and Eleanor was very pleased with the arrangement; but letting go her son reminded her too painfully of Thomas's departure for college, and her temper had been short for days afterward.

"I'd like to come back," Helen said, "but I can't leave Isabella alone in the city."

"Poor thing—how is she?"

"No worse as far as her body goes, but her poor mind is getting feebler. Sometimes she doesn't seem to know me, and sometimes she screams when I come in, as if she thinks I'm the Devil, or something." The two women crossed themselves at the mention of the Dark One's name. Helen lowered her voice. "Daisy, do you know, I've wondered sometimes if all is not quite right about Ezra Brazen. Sometimes I've seen the most *dreadful* bruises and marks on Isabella's skin. Sometimes I've wondered—" She paused, for it seemed too outrageous to voice. She went on, "And that poor child is becoming very odd, too."

"Edmund?"

"Yes. He's nearly four, yet he hardly ever talks, and never moves about much, just sits quietly in a corner staring at you like an idiot."

Daisy's face was distressed. "Oh, Helen, how terrible! I'd forgotten about poor little Edmund. He's the same age as my Margaret, and she's such a bonny child. Couldn't we do something? Listen, don't you think we might get them both back here to live? I'm sure Ezra can't really want to nurse 'Bella, especially if she's—well, wandering in her mind?"

"We could try, I suppose," Helen said doubtfully. "The person to ask is Mother—she can handle anybody. I'm sure if she spoke to Ezra about it she'd get him to agree. Where is she, anyway? I haven't seen her. Is she down at the mill?"

Daisy smiled. "Not today. She's teaching my Thom to ride."

"Already?" Helen laughed. "He's only three, isn't he? Why is she so anxious?"

"Not anxious—it's just that she's taken to him. Really, Helen, from the moment he was born, she seemed attracted to him in a different way from any of the other babies. She cares more for him than she did for her own Richard, and since then she's looked after him, dressed him, talked to him, played with him, and now she's teaching him to ride. I dare swear as soon as he can ride she'll have him hand-breaking his own colt!"

"How strange," Helen said. "I wonder if it's because of his name—she always doted on Thomas, too, when he was a child."

Daisy shook her head. "No, it's something about the child himself, because it was she who wanted him called Thomas, though we never call him anything but Thom. But he must have reminded her of her own boy in some way for her to name him after him."

"Well, let's go and see if she's finished," suggested Helen, for whom to think was generally to act. "Ah, there's Job—he'll know where she is. Job!"

Job paused on his way past with a basket of roses—one of the many odd tasks he found time to perform was cutting flowers for Eleanor's bedchamber—and looked inquiringly at the two ladies.

"Do you know where the mistress is?"

"I believe she's just come in, madam. I think she's in the stable-yard showing Thom how to unsaddle his horse."

"Typical of Mother," Helen laughed. "Thank you, Job. We'll go and find her."

"Undo the cinches—that's right—now pull it off toward you," Eleanor instructed. "No, no, let him do it," she said irritably to a servant who wished to help.

"It isn't necessary, madam," said the servant, who didn't know any better. "I can do it for him. The young master—"

"Leave him be, I tell you, or I'll box your ears!" Eleanor snapped, raising a hand, so that the servant retired hastily. "Not necessary indeed! What kind of a man will he be if he doesn't know how to care for his own horse? How will he know if *you're* doing it right, if he doesn't know how to do it himself? Be off—leave us. I'll see to the horses."

The servant beat a retreat before his grumbling mistress. As Helen had noticed, Eleanor's temper was short these days. She missed John. "Now, then, Thom, put the saddle down, and let me see you lead him in. Pat him, that's right, and tell him he's been good."

"Good boy, Heron," Thom said dutifully, reaching up to pat the hard neck of the horse that towered above him. Then, "Grandmother, why *do* I have to know? If the servants can do it for me?"

"Why, Thom, what a question! What would happen to you then, if you found yourself with no servants around? What if you were called to fight for the King like your

Uncle Thomas, and had to say, 'I can't come, my lord King, for I don't know how to saddle my own horse'?"

"Uncle Thomas was very brave, wasn't he, Grandmother?"

"He was, my child. Brave and handsome and a fine gentleman."

"But he got killed, didn't he?"

"He died in battle fighting at his lord's side. He killed the man who killed his lord, and died beside him, standing over his lord's body," Eleanor said impressively.

Little Thom considered. "I should sooner not die, Grandmother," he decided. "For then I wouldn't be able to go riding anymore."

"We must all die sometime, child," Eleanor said. "And when we die, we want to be able to say to our Maker when we meet him that we made good use of our lives, that we were brave and faithful, honest and loyal, and obedient to the word of our Lord. We want God to be pleased with us, don't we?"

Thom didn't know about that, but he understood the tone of the question and nodded obediently. But he was still thinking. "But, Grandmother, would God be pleased with us if we died like Uncle Thomas?"

"God is pleased when we defend what is right, and when we keep our vows. And if we have to die to do those things, God loves us even more."

Thom did not look convinced. Life seemed to him so full of marvelous things that he was not at all attracted by the idea of dying. Privately he thought Uncle Thomas would have done better not to die, but he loved his grandmother and wanted to please her, so he said, "I should like to be like Uncle Thomas, Grandmother." And that was the right thing to say, because Grandmother stooped down and hugged him, and said in that funny voice, that meant she was trying not to cry, "Thou shalt be like him, Thom, when thou art a man. God bless thee!" Then she straightened up, taking with her that sweet smell of roses that always hung about her, and said, "And now let me see you take off his bridle."

They had just finished with the horses and were turning

hand in hand to go back to the house when they were found by the other members of the family. First they were met by Richard, Ned, and Cecily, who had just been released from their lessons by Master Jenney and were running down to the mews to look at Ned's young kestrel; at least Ned and Cecily were going to look at the kestrel, and Richard was following them as a moth follows a torch. Richard was ten now, and a quiet, studious boy, undersized for his age and tending to be nervous, starting at sudden noises and frequently daydreaming when he should be working or playing. He had a vivid imagination, and was already skilled at writing poetry and songs, and he was much in demand from the girls before bedtime for telling stories about elves and suchlike folk. Eleanor thought it was Robert coming out in him, the love of poetry and music; she saw Robert, too, in the way Richard was attracted to the hardier spirit of his nephews and nieces.

Ned, at nine, was a sturdy, strong-limbed little boy, fair-haired and very like his mother to look at, and with her placid temper, too, though he was as lively and full of fun as he could be. Cecily at seven was more willful than her brother, and if there was any mischief discovered, it was generally Cecily who had invented it. She took lessons with the boys under Master Jenney, for Edward felt a girl should have as much education as a boy, but Daisy complained she was growing up as wild as a young fox, and not at all like a young lady.

Eleanor sided with Edward. "Time enough to be a lady when she gets to ten and we look for a husband for her. Ladylike ways can be learned in a few weeks; Latin and Greek take longer."

Cecily was certainly a beauty, with that fair wild-rose beauty of her mother; little Margaret, who was not yet four, was rosy and chubby enough, but did not yet promise to have quite the same golden dazzle; and Thom, why Thom was like neither mother nor father, but the image of his grandmother, a tall, dark-haired, sapphire-eyed boy with a stubborn chin and a tender mouth. Perhaps that was why Eleanor had loved him so much from the beginning, seeing in him a new chance.

As the children, gathering Thom into their number on the way, ran out of the yard from one side, Helen and Daisy picked their way daintily in from the other side, and accompanied Eleanor back into the house.

"How's Thom's riding coming along?" Helen asked.

"Excellently," Eleanor said happily. "He is very strong for his age, and his balance is perfect. He will make the best rider of them all."

"But surely Heron is too big for him, Mother?" Daisy asked with a mother's anxiety. "Wouldn't it be better to teach him on something smaller—Patchwork, for instance?"

Eleanor sighed. "My dear Daisy, you have no idea at all, have you? Patchwork is a packpony, no better, and as broad as a bed. How can the child learn to ride like a gentleman unless he learns on a gentleman's horse?"

"I'm not worried so much about that, Mother. I'm only concerned that he lives to *be* a gentleman."

Eleanor crossed herself. "Don't say such things. Believe me, Daisy, he's safer on Heron than he would be on a pony that knows nothing but following the tail in front. Trust me. I have brought up eight children of my own."

"Yes, Mother, I know," Daisy said soothingly, seeing the frown begin.

"Actually, it was about one of those children we wanted to talk to you," Helen said.

Eleanor looked from one to the other and suddenly smiled. "You look very serious," she said. "Come then, my daughters, let us sit down and occupy our hands while we talk. There are still a hundred new shirts to be sewn, and none but us to sew them."

"Mother," Helen began when they were seated in the solar busy with their sewing needles, "I've been so worried about Isabella recently, and little Edmund, and I was talking to Daisy about it and she suggested that it might be better if Isabella were brought back here to live. And then I could come home, too, and look after her."

Eleanor did not look up from her work. "Isabella is a married woman," she said. "Her husband alone has the right to say what should become of her."

"I know that, Mother, but she isn't well, and her poor mind is wandering. And Edmund is growing up very strangely. I'm sure he doesn't get lessons, or even proper food. Even if Ezra is his father, he's still a Morland, and he ought to be properly taken care of. And I'm sure Isabella isn't well cared for. Shouldn't we do something? Isn't it our duty?"

Eleanor's needle slowed. "It's a difficult question, child. As to the little boy, if there were any likelihood that he would inherit the estate, there would be good reason to take charge of him, and I do not think Master Brazen would have any objections to it. But there is no chance of that, and it is therefore entirely up to Master Brazen how he brings up his own child." She lifted a hand to stop Helen from interrupting. "Wait, let me speak. It is possible, however, that he might be persuaded to put his child into our nursery just as he might place his child with any wealthy family for his education. Normally that wouldn't be until the boy was at least seven or eight, but in the special circumstances, he might find it a good idea."

"And what about Isabella?" Daisy asked anxiously.

"That is another matter. She is his wife, she is his entirely. He may do as he likes with her—even neglect her, even beat her, if he has a mind. There is nothing we can do, and it would be highly improper for us to suggest that we can take care of her better than him."

"But, Mother—" Helen cried.

"But, Mother—" Daisy cried.

Eleanor set down her work. "It *would* be improper, even if it were true. But don't start clucking like hens before a fox. I think you are right, and I will speak to Master Brazen, and suggest to him that the care of an invalid wife and a small son are too much for him and his *servants*." She said the word with ironic emphasis. "I will go and see him tomorrow. Thank you, children, for the idea."

Ezra Brazen was no match for an Eleanor Courteney determined to get her own way. She swept into the house and swept out again, having arranged for Isabella and the child to be brought to Morland Place by litter the following day, and having allowed him to save face by pretending the arrangement was only temporary. But they both knew that Isabella would never return to the city.

Eleanor was shocked at her daughter's condition. She had never visited Isabella in Coney Street, for their relative social positions demanded that Isabella visit her mother and not vice versa, so she was unprepared for the sight that met her eyes. Isabella lay in a bed between filthy sheets, and had obviously not been washed for many weeks, for she was stinking and had lice in her tangled, matted hair. She was gaunt and haggard, her eyes shadowed and her cheeks sunken, and she talked in an incoherent monotone, her fingers twitching at the soiled bedclothes. Eleanor could not be sure if she had understood what was said to her, or even if she recognized her mother.

"She's far worse than I expected," she said to Edward the following evening, when Isabella had been brought to Morland Place, washed and combed and placed in clean linen in a bed in her old room.

"I'm worried about the child," Edward said. "Edmund's nearly four, and hardly seems able to speak. If you compare him with Margaret—"

"Don't," Eleanor advised firmly. "Give him time—he'll be all right, I'm sure. Master Jenney says he is not stupid, only frightened, and Anys says he showed a proper gratitude and affection to her when she was bathing and feeding him."

"I've never seen a child so thin," Edward said. "It's a vile shame that the child of a Morland should be treated so."

"Well, never mind it now. We have him, and he's safe. I shouldn't be surprised if Master Brazen didn't move away from York altogether."

"What do you mean, Mother?"

"Never mind. We are a powerful family, and there's no use in power unless it's to protect your own." Her eyes narrowed darkly.

"And Helen's coming tomorrow?" Edward asked.

"Yes. She's selling the house, and she'll sleep with Isabella and take care of her."

"Will she turn off her servants?"

"No. I said we could find something for them to do here. I don't like to see a good servant turned out. I think this might be a very good thing for Helen, having Isabella and the child to care for."

"Since she didn't have a child of her own, you mean? Yes, I hadn't thought of it that way."

Whatever it was that Eleanor did, she worked fast. Isabella had only been home a fortnight when the news came that Ezra Brazen had left the county, and he was never heard of again. In later years, some folk wondered if Eleanor had had him killed—she was certainly rich enough to pay someone to do it, though there was some doubt whether she was vindictive enough—but whatever it was she did, she would never speak of it, except to say, "He took on too much when he took on the Morlands. We are the friends of kings."

Brazen's departure without a word to anyone left Eleanor, as Isabella's guardian, in full control of all his assets, the mills, and the land which she was already using, and his warehouse. It was the latter that gave her the idea which she expounded at dinner one morning about a week later.

"Think of the way we make our cloth," she instructed them. "What do we do first? We get the wool spun, and then we take it to the weavers. Then we collect it and take it to the fullers. Then we collect it and take it to the warehouse. Then we collect it and take it to the merchant."

"Yes, of course. But what then?" Edward asked.

"All those journeys. All that collecting and delivering. I should think our wool travels twenty miles before it ever leaves our hands as cloth."

"Perhaps, but I don't see what we can do about that," Edward said.

Eleanor looked around triumphantly, and her eye met Job's. She saw at once that he knew what she was going to say, and it amused him that the others had not understood it yet.

"Well, Job," she challenged him. "What then? Instead of taking the wool to the workers—"

"Take the workers to the wool," he finished for her. There was a silence.

"I don't understand. Does that mean anything?" Edward asked.

"Yes, yes, I see it now," Daisy cried. "Of course, Edward—it's easier for people to move around than wool."

"But—where to?" Edward asked, still puzzled.

"That's my wonderful idea," Eleanor said. "Brazen's warehouse is on the river, and into that river runs the stream over which the fulling-mill is built. So there's really only one journey necessary. We already do several of the processes at the field by the mill, though they are hampered by the weather sometimes. All we need to do is to build a great warehouse, or barn, or workshop there, by the mill, and do everything inside it. If we build it big enough, we'll have room for everything. And our spinners and weavers can come to work there. We'll set up looms there, and these new spinning wheels that are being made in France, and all we need to do is to take the raw clip to the workshop, and then take the ready cloth by water up to the wharf."

There was a long silence while everyone visualized the arrangement.

"Oh, wonderful, Mother!" Helen cried. "It's absolutely brilliant. It will save so much time and money in transportation—"

"And it will be easier to supervise the work and make sure it's done properly," Eleanor added.

"But how will you persuade people to go to work in your workhouse rather than stay at home and work?"

Thom's clear young voice was heard from the lower end of the table. "You could give them more money." Another silence.

"Thom is going to be a great businessman as well as a great gentleman," Eleanor chuckled. "But I don't think it will be a problem. A farm worker goes out to the fields to work, so why shouldn't a cloth worker go to the cloth field to work? After all, some of our workers already do."

"But they have to, because that's where their work is," Edward said.

"Exactly so. And in future, that's where the weaver's work will be, and the spinner's."

"It will cost quite a bit to build this workshop," Helen mused.

"But it will be paid for by the increase in our output of cloth, and by the increase in quality, once everything is properly supervised," Eleanor said.

"Mother, let me give you the money I got for John's house," Helen said. "I have nothing to keep it for now, I shall never have a child."

"Bless you, Helen. I'll take it gladly, and you shall be a partner in the business. And if you do marry again, you will have it back and more for your dowry."

Helen blushed a little, and smiled. "I don't think that will happen. But I'd like to learn about the cloth business, Mother, if you'd let me."

"Of course, dear child. Come with me when I take Ned round, and you can both learn together. We are going up to the mill tomorrow."

On the morrow, Eleanor had planned to take Ned to the mill after dinner, and when the time came she decided it would be good for Richard to go along too. "A man ought to know where his wealth comes from," she said, but the servant she sent to fetch young Richard came back to report he could not be found.

"Nonsense," said Eleanor. "He was at dinner with everyone else. He can't have gone very far. Go again and look for him, and ask the servants who has seen him. He's probably in the schoolroom with Master Jenney."

"I looked there, madam, but Master Jenney hasn't seen him."

"Then look in the nursery. Go, man, don't just stand there!"

Half an hour later it became apparent that Richard was not at Morland Place. "Perhaps he went down to Micklelith to see Elying," Ned suggested. "He likes Elying's stories." A servant was dispatched to Micklelith, and another to Twelvetrees, and when they returned with no news, Eleanor began to worry.

"It isn't like him to wander away. If it were Cecily, now, or Thom— Job, send someone over to Shawe, and ask there. But he could hardly have got so far. It wasn't an hour after dinner that we first missed him. Where could he have gone? Job, send two men round the estate and ask everyone. One of the shepherds may have seen him."

It was almost nightfall when a servant who had been to the city and had only just returned said that he had seen Richard playing by the side of the road near Micklelith that afternoon.

"What was he doing? Who was he with?" Eleanor demanded.

"He was on his own, madam," the servant said nervously, for Eleanor had been known to box a servant's ears when she was anxious or irritated. "He was just sitting there playing with some stones or something on the grass by the road."

"Was no one nearby? Did you not think it strange a child should be there all alone?"

"Well, madam," he said apologetically, "to tell you the truth, I only just glanced at him. My mind was on the friar. You see—"

"What friar? Sweet Jesu give me patience! What friar?"

"There was one of these traveling friars, madam, set up by the side of the road and preaching, you know the way they do. Preaching to passersby. There were some folk stopped to listen to him, so I thought he must be good, and I was trying to hear as I went past, without stopping, you see, madam, because I was on an errand—"

"Never mind your excuses now . . ." Eleanor cried, and Edward interrupted to ask more quietly:

"Do you think Master Richard was listening to the friar?"

"Why—I couldn't say, master. He might have been. He wasn't looking at him, but at whatever he was playing with, if you understand me, master, but—well, now I come to think of it, he was quite close by, and might have been listening, for all I know to the contrary."

"Very well, you may go now, but stay within call. We may want you again." Edward dismissed the servant.

When he was gone, Eleanor stared at him hopelessly. "What do you think?"

"I wonder if someone has taken him away. It has been known to happen," Edward said.

"I never thought I'd curse the day we lived so close by the great road," Eleanor said. "There are such kinds of rogues and vagabonds passing all day. What can we do, Edward. I wish your father were alive! I can't think, I'm in such a way!"

"What about the friar?" Edward suggested slowly. "Folk will know where he is, and he might have seen something, might have seen the boy go, or someone stop and talk to him."

"Yes, yes," Eleanor said eagerly. "Send someone reliable to find the friar. Send Owen. No, wait, I'll go myself. I can't bear to wait here and not know. I'll go with Owen."

She would not be dissuaded, and a little while later she set off with Owen and another man, Jack, to find out where the friar had gone. But all they could find out was that he had gone within the gates, and they could not find if he had come out again.

"He may have gone out by another gate on the other side of the city," Owen said. "Madam, you must go home. Tomorrow at first light we'll go searching again, and ask at every gate. We can do no more tonight."

There followed two nights without sleep, and two days of searching, asking all through the city and at every gate; asking in villages; asking lonely shepherds and field hands, if they had seen a small boy in a green jerkin, or a wandering friar. Eleanor went out with Owen, Job went out with Jack, and Edward took Hal with him, and they went different ways; but no one seemed to have seen either of them. The friar had passed out of the city by Bootham Bar—at least, *a* friar had, though if it was the same one or not, they could not tell. But after leaving the city he seemed to have performed some feat of magic, for they could not pick up his trail.

The third morning came—the Sabbath—and Eleanor decided to go into the city, to mass, and ask at the church, where many people from different areas would be gathered. At mass she prayed to St. Christopher and St. Anthony to help her, and the saints must have been listening, for the third man she asked in the churchyard said, "Why, mistress, there has been a friar staying at the Star Inn these two nights. I know, for I live opposite, and I have seen him standing in the street and preaching. But whether there is a small boy with him or not I cannot tell."

"God bless you for that," Eleanor cried, and, calling Owen, she hurried away toward the inn.

The innkeeper told her at once that the friar was sleeping above the stables, and that he came in from the north on Friday morning.

"Then perhaps he may not be the one we are looking for," Eleanor said in disappointment.

But Owen said, "He may have gone out by Bootham Bar on Thursday and come back in on Friday. There's no knowing with these wandering brothers."

They found the friar having his breakfast in the back parlor, sitting at a bare table and cutting up a hunk of bread with his knife. As soon as they entered he looked up and smiled sweetly and said, "Welcome, welcome. Will you sit down and dine with me? For I have bread and I have the fine ale our Father Adam drank, and enough for all. No, dear lady, don't speak, I know what you have come for. I can see by your eyes you are a mother, and blessed as are all mothers since our Lord took on flesh. He is asleep still, having sat up late last night to hear the talk. We had good talk last night, far into the morning. I knew you would come for him. That was why I stayed in the city, instead of obeying the call that bid me go north among those whom the Word of God barely reaches, and is too often stifled by war and plunder. Yes, of course, he is asleep up there, in the hay, like our dear Lord whom he wishes to follow."

The friar gestured to a wooden ladder that disappeared through the roof, and, while Owen scaled it in great haste, he unconcernedly shaved another sliver off his bread and ate it with slow pleasure.

"One should not eat in a hurry, dear sister, but slowly, to savor every crumb, and remember with every crumb from

Whom it came. To eat is to pray, just as to pray is to eat. Ah, here he is, my small friend."

Eleanor gave a cry of relief as Owen appeared, descending the ladder with difficulty with Richard in his arms.

"Where have you been? Why did you run off like that? I've been so worried," Eleanor cried as soon as she had her breath back from hugging him. Now she wanted to shake him.

"Why, Mother, I've been with Friar Thomas," he said, regarding her with his clear, wide eyes—eyes that were a little too wide, as if they saw more than the things actually before him. "I was quite safe."

"But how were we to know that, you wicked boy? We didn't know what had become of you. Anything might have happened."

"But what could happen to me? God knew where I was. I was as safe with Him as the birds are, and you don't call them wicked."

"It isn't the same thing, Richard. You are not to go off on your own like that. You must have consideration for your family. And where are your shoes?"

"I gave them to a beggar. He needed them more than I did. Friar Thomas goes barefoot. But, Mother, am I to give more consideration to my family than to God? For it was Him that called me."

"My son, our Lord gave you into the keeping of your parents, and He means you to obey and love them until you reach a man's years," the friar chided him gently. "Go where your mother bids you go, and do what she bids you do. God will wait for you. He knows your heart."

"Why did you not bring the child home, brother?" Owen asked the friar shortly.

The friar looked up from his meal. "Who am I to interfere with God's workings. Perhaps he meant you to search, so that you might find more than a lost child," he said.

"Thank you for keeping him with you," Eleanor said briefly, taking Richard's hand tightly in hers. "God's day to you."

"God keep you," the friar replied. He watched the three of them walk out into the sunshine, and a sweet smile crossed his bland face for a moment. Outside the horses were waiting. Owen took Richard up behind him, and they turned and trotted back down the teeming, shadowed street toward the Mickle Lith. Eleanor was thoughtful, and the friar's words echoed in her mind. *Find more than a lost child*? What had he meant?

"Richard," she said as they trotted down the great south road.

"Yes, Mother?"

"Why did you go with the friar?"

"I wanted to find out," he said slowly. "God wants me for something. I wanted to find out what."

It sounded absurd from so young a child. He was not yet ten. Yet it was not absurd. Eleanor felt a kind of awe, for there was, in this child, something that did not come out of her, something special. He had been touched by some finger of light that came from outside. *Find more than a lost child*. Perhaps the friar was right.

A month later Richard was sent to live at St. William's College, a great house that crouched in the shadow of the Minster, to serve the chantry priests in an atmosphere where he could more easily hear the voice of God. It was an ordered community where he would serve at the altar and, if that was what he was called for, begin training to take orders himself. He was young to go away from home, but that strange calmness in him seemed to accept it without any fear. And Eleanor comforted herself that he was still close enough for her to visit him, or for him to come home, if either of them wanted.

CHAPTER EIGHTEEN

Terrible and turbulent had been the days of revolution, but they were over now, and it seemed that peace could now reign undisturbed. Great Warwick and King Edward's mad brother, George of Clarence, had revolted, led on by the hopes of power, the hopes of gain. Those had been terrible days, with King Edward captured and imprisoned, Henry crowned King again, and Margaret of France ruling with Warwick's help.

But King Edward had escaped, helped by his youngest brother, Richard of Gloucester—Richard whose badge of the White Boar bore the motto *Loyaulté me Lie*, Loyalty Binds Me. They had gained the help of their brother-in-law, the Duke of Burgundy, and come back to defeat the Lancastrians for the last time in battle. It was a great victory for York. Richard of Gloucester fought magnificently, despite being wounded; mad George crept back, deserting the cause once it seemed lost, and was forgiven by his brothers; Henry was executed by a King Edward who had learned that his pity could not extend so far as to lose his kingdom for it; Margaret, broken at last by the death of her husband and her son, who was killed in flight, was sent back to France in gentlemanly confinement. And great Warwick, the greatest of the lords of England, was dead, killed in battle against the man he had fought so hard to make King.

Eleanor had never swerved from loyalty to Richard Plantagenet's son, had sent him men and money, and had aided him in his escape to Burgundy. There had been great danger for the Morlands, for York had been a center of revolutionary action, but they had come through it almost unscathed. Almost, for there was one victim. Poor Isabella was dead. Her grip on reality had been fading fast, and she lived more and more in a nightmare world in which she relived the anguish of Luke's death and the horror of her enslavement to her husband. The shouting and marching and alarms of battle had disturbed her poor enfeebled mind more than anyone had realized, and one morning she was found by Job, lying half in and half out of the moat, drowned dead.

No one knew how she had come to be there, for she never left her bed, and was, as far as anyone knew, incapable of walking more than a few steps. Talking about it afterward, Job revealed to Eleanor how Isabella had gone down to meet Luke at a spot close by the place where her body was found, gone down from that same bedchamber where she had spent the last months of her life.

"Perhaps, wandering in her mind as she was, poor lady, she thought she was back in her youth and had to go down and meet him. The noises from without may have seemed to her the signal he used to give. She could not walk very well—it would be easy for her to stumble into the moat, and once in she would not have had the strength to pull herself out."

Eleanor shuddered. "It may be so. We shall never know. But I blame myself very much for it. If I had not made her marry, she could be alive now in some convent, safe and happy."

Job touched her hand. "She was in God's hand. He knew best what should come to her."

Eleanor shook her head, her face tragic. "She could not have deserved such a fate, poor child. I shall never be able to forget."

Helen was dreadfully upset by Isabella's death, too, for she had set herself to nurse her sister, and felt she had failed her. On the night in question, Helen had been at Micklelith, helping look after some wounded soldiers, and had thought, as far as she thought of Isabella at all, that she would be safe enough in a house full of family and servants. All she could do to atone was to take complete charge of Isabella's son, Edmund, and be a mother to him, which she did with a full heart. Edmund had hardly known his mother, except as a shadowy figure, for she was ever bedridden and strange. He was already fond of Helen, so the arrangement worked very well, and he soon began to grow alert and come out of the shell in which he had lived for the first four years of his life.

Isabella's death cast a shadow over every heart at Morland Place. No one talked about it much, but she was never far from everyone's thoughts, and after her burial a brass plaque was put up in the chapel beside the memorial to Thomas and Harry. It read: *"Isabella Morland. 1437– 1469. In God's Hand."*

Once again Morland Place was to play host to a Richard Plantagenet. The first time it had been Richard Plantagenet, Duke of York, and his Duchess Cecily, who had just recovered from the birth of her last child. This time it was that very newborn child, now grown to a young man of twenty years: Richard Plantagenet, Duke of Gloucester, the brother of the King and chief prop to his throne, bringing with him *his* Duchess, the newlywed Anne Neville, Warwick's youngest daughter.

Eleanor had taken a liking to the young Richard when she had seen him at the ceremony of the month's mind for the Duke of York, back in 1461, almost eleven years ago. He had seemed to her then the only one of the brood much like his father, and the solemn-faced, weakly lad who wore the bear-and-ragged-staff badge of the Earl of Warwick then had grown into a serious, mature, and capable man. He was still slight, below a man's height, and thin, but his shoulders and arms had developed great muscle from assiduous exercising. He bore himself well, and even an enemy could not have said but that he had the proper figure of a man and a royal Duke.

And now, having married his childhood sweetheart— much as his father did—he was taking her back to Middleham, the castle where he had spent much of his boyhood and which had been given to him after Warwick's death and disgrace, and they were breaking their journey at Morland.

"The Court, I imagine, is not much to your Grace's taste," Eleanor suggested as they sat down to supper.

Richard of Gloucester shrugged slightly. "I have never been much used to luxury," he said.

His wife added gently, "My lord longs to breathe the fresh open air of the moorlands again. It is where we both feel happiest."

"I can well understand that," Eleanor said. "Since I came to Yorkshire, I have come to feel the same way myself." She liked Anne Neville, too. There was something in her face that reminded Eleanor of her own Isabella, something in the way she just missed being beautiful, with her hair not quite gold and her face freckled and her mouth a little too large. But when she looked at Richard, her face lit with a soft light that made her more than lovely. It was plain that she adored him as much as he loved her.

"There was a time recently when I thought that I'd never breathe fresh air again," she said. "Had not Richard found me—well, at least if I'm ever thrown upon my own resources again, I'll be able to make my living as a cook." She and her lord exchanged a fond smile that was tinged with sadness.

Because of the inclement weather and the Gloucesters' request that there should be no ceremony, they were taking supper in the Winter Parlor, a small dining hall that Edward had recently had built at one end of the great hall. Fashionable people were taking more and more to dining in private in such small parlors, eating in the great hall only on special occasions. Hall life, it was said, was dying. But Eleanor, who had once been so forward-thinking that she had had chimneys built into her new house, was now old-fashioned enough to insist on retaining the hall life except on special occasions such as this. She felt that something was due to the household and servants, that the dining together was an important part of their life. And as she was still mistress of the house, she had her way.

But tonight the wishes of the guests, of course, prevailed; and while the servants, including the Gloucesters' small retinue, ate in the great hall, the Duke and Duchess ate in the Winter Parlor with Eleanor, Helen, Edward, and Daisy.

Since they were so private and cozy, Eleanor made bold to ask, "Would it please your Grace to tell us the story of how you came to be married? We have heard much rumor, and would be interested to hear the true tale, if it would please you to tell it."

Anne and Richard exchanged a glance, and then Anne said, "If you would like to hear it—though some parts are still painful to remember . . ."

Anne had had a turbulent life. She had adored her great and glittering father, and when he had turned traitor to the crown she had been terribly torn, for on the one hand it was impossible to think ill of him, and on the other impossible to conceive of betraying her dear Richard's brother. Warwick had married Anne's elder sister, Isobel, to George of Clarence, promising to make him King in Edward's place, and had wooed Richard with promises of glory. But for Richard one law had supremacy over every other consideration—loyalty to Edward—and he could not be won. So Warwick sought support elsewhere, and, to ensure a second string to his bow, had made an agreement with Margaret of France, and had married Anne to her son, the former Prince of Wales, another Edward.

Anne had been married to him in France, and had found him a spiteful, bragging youth, who had drunk in hatred and conceit with his mother's milk; Anne could only be grateful that Margaret, also hedging her bets, had not allowed the marriage to be consummated, in case she wanted to revoke it later. Then had followed a dreadful sea voyage back to England, during which, in the height of a storm, sister Isobel had fallen into labor and had borne a dead child.

Then had come battle and flight, the terrible news of the death of her father, the grateful news of the death of her young husband, and Anne had been sent with Isobel to the care of vacillating George, who had turned coat just in time to save his skin and his estates. And then the wonderfull moment when Richard came to see her.

"I had always wanted to marry Anne," he said. "When

we were children we used to talk about it—when we are grown up we shall be married—the way children do. Only we meant it. So as soon as I knew she was safe, I went straight to Edward and got his permission to marry."

"But unfortunately, my lord of Clarence objected," Anne said tersely. Richard shook his head slightly, as if to warn her, for George was still his brother, whatever he had done, and it hurt Richard to speak ill of him, however much he had deserved it. But Anne was more robust—she had suffered greatly at Clarence's hands. "We are among friends here, Richard," she said. "Mistress Eleanor was your father's friend."

"My brother, too, speaks highly of you," Richard said to her.

Eleanor smiled. "I am proud that he should do so. I should think it as great an honor if you would regard me—all of my family—as your friends also."

"Of course," Anne said impulsively. "I feel very much at home here, don't you, Richard? Well, to continue with the story—my lord of Clarence felt that as my guardian he should have disposal of the half of my mother's estates that were willed to me. But he wasn't my guardian at all, and when Richard pointed that out, and got the King on his side, George refused to let Richard see me. And when Richard demanded to know where I was, he turned the argument back on Richard and said since he wasn't my guardian, he could not be expected to concern himself with my whereabouts. And then"—she shuddered slightly—"and then, he smuggled me out of the house in the night, and had me taken to the house of a friend of his in London. And there I was disguised as a kitchen-maid and kept a prisoner, beaten, half starved, and perished with cold, sleeping with rats and cockroaches. Oh, the smell of grease and food cooking! It was in my hair, in my very skin! I did everything I could to escape, but he had me watched closely."

Those listening nodded sympathetically. Far worse to be imprisoned so ignominiously than to be kept in a cell, where at least one could retain the outward semblance of gentle birth. And now Anne's face lit with that inner radi-

ance and she reached across and touched her lord's hand
lightly.

"But he found me. I don't know how, but Richard found
me, and rescued me, and took me to St. Martin's le Grand
to the sanctuary there, where no one could touch me."

"And then came the long arguments," Richard said.
"Edward was happy enough for me to marry Anne, and
he'd already granted me most of the estates in question.
But George was badly upset by the matter, and really
thought he was being robbed of what was rightfully his."

It was plain to see that Richard could never find it in
himself to blame his brother, or to attribute his actions to
pure selfishness and greed. He had to convince himself
that George was merely mistaken, or misguided.

"In the end we managed to find a compromise. I gave
up most of the estates—"

"—except in the north. Not Middleham," Anne put in.

"No, not Middleham. We want to live there, always.
And in return, he gave up all claims to Anne."

"You gave up all the estates that should have been
yours?" Edward asked. It seemed a poor bargain. It puzzled him, though he didn't say it aloud, why anyone should
go to so much trouble to placate the Duke of Clarence.

Richard smiled that sudden dazzling smile that lit up his
rather somber face from time to time. "I didn't want them.
I just wanted Anne." He looked at her happily. "We got
married at once, in case anyone tried to stop us. We ought
to have had a dispensation, being cousins, but we didn't
dare wait while we applied for it. We thought we could
always marry again if necessary, but it doesn't look as
though it will be."

"I'm so glad that it worked out at last," Eleanor said
happily. "And you will be living permanently in the north?
That is wonderful. We have need of good government
here—and you have already proved yourself a great governor, my lord."

Richard looked at her steadily from those eyes that,
though gray instead of blue, reminded her so much of his
father's. His father was a general, a soldier, a man of crystal purity; a simple man in many ways, too honest to un-

derstand evil; a man to whom loyalty was the first requis-
ite. It was said of him that no liar could ever meet the
steady gaze of his eyes. Eleanor saw the same things in this
youngest son of his. Though only twenty, he had already
proved himself a soldier and a brilliant general; an administrator of skill and judgment not normally found in a man
of twice his years; a man whose motto of *Loyaulté Me Lie*
was his primary mover; a man whose clear gaze a liar was
not anxious to meet.

"Yes," he said now, "we shall live as much in the north
as we are able. Matters of state will call me to London
from time to time, but I would not wish to live much at
Court. And I think there are others who would not wish me
to be much there."

"Madam the Queen—" Anne began, but Richard
stopped her with a glance.

Eleanor filled the gap smoothly. "The Queen is expecting another child almost immediately, is she not? It is wonderful that the King's marriage proves so fruitful, but the
environs of a childbed chamber are no place for a man. My
husband used to say he wished he could be in Wales while
I was lying in, for he felt as much in the way as a fox in a
hen-run."

Everyone laughed, and the awkward moment was
passed. The Duke of Gloucester had a reputation as a
dour, rather solemn man, but if he was a man of a serious
bent, he showed that night that there was also another side
to him, a merry side that could delight in the ridiculous.
After the supper, dishes were cleared away, and the children, Ned, Cecily, Margaret, Edmund, and Thom, were allowed to come in and meet the illustrious guests. They
were on their best behavior, and showed their gentlest manners to Anne and Richard, who in return questioned them
pleasantly about their lessons and pastimes, and spoke so
naturally and plainly to them that the children soon relaxed
and spoke up frankly in a way that evidently pleased the
guests.

Quite how it happened no one could afterward remember, but half an hour had not passed before everyone,
adults and children alike, were engaged in a riotous game of

blindman's buff that grew so rough and so merry that everyone was exhausted with running and with laughing. When the game stopped at last, because no one had enough breath to carry on, the children took turns entertaining the guests with singing, and finished off with an old favorite, "*Summer Is Icumen In*," which Master Jenney had taught them to sing in harmony. After that Eleanor discovered how late it was, and the night prayers were said and everyone retired to bed with the sweet voices of the children still sounding in their minds.

In the morning everyone was up early, in spite of the late night, for the guests had to be on their way again. Everyone took mass in the chapel and then repaired to the great hall to take breakfast. While they ate, Richard thanked Eleanor for her hospitality.

"The honor is entirely mine, your Grace," Eleanor said, and meant it.

"No formality, I beg you, Mistress Eleanor. I feel as if I have known you all my life—as perhaps I have, in a way."

"Well, my lord, no formality, then. But it is no more than the truth when I speak of being honored. The Lord Constable of England, Chief Justice of Wales, and Governor of the North—who would not be honored?"

"I should think anyone might not feel honor, if the man is not worthy of his titles."

"And you are eminently worthy. I see so much of your father in you—"

"I thank you for that, Mistress Eleanor, and pray I may be worthy always of his name. And now, let us leave complimenting—it makes me feel uneasy. I'm a soldier, like my father, and I can never get used to Court manners."

Eleanor laughed. "In Court, a compliment is followed, so I hear, by a request for a favor."

Richard smiled in reply. "And what are you going to ask me?"

"I beg you to believe, my lord, that I was not paying compliments but simply stating the truth."

"That is good. I have a great liking for the truth. So tell me, mistress, how may I be of service to you?"

They eyed each other, each understanding the other perfectly. "My young grandson, Ned," Eleanor said.

Richard nodded. "A fine, manly boy."

"He has been well trained by our good tutor in his studies, in music and games. He has also learned a great deal about the business that will one day make him a rich man. But I should like him also to be trained in the ways of the great houses, and to learn to be of service. I should be most grateful if you could help him to a place?"

"At Court?" Richard asked.

"I had not looked so high," Eleanor began.

"As a page to the King, he would learn a great deal," Richard said. "And perhaps more quickly than he would learn anywhere else. He seems a boy of strong mind and good conscience; he should come to no harm."

"I should be very grateful, my lord," Eleanor said again.

"It shall be done. I am my brother's representative in the north, and I wish to be of service to you."

An hour after dawn they were on their way, well wrapped in furs against the bitter March winds. Anne sat her horse excellently, another way in which she reminded Eleanor of Isabella. As she exchanged the formal kisses of farewell, Eleanor impulsively hugged the young bride, and was hugged in return.

"God bless you," Eleanor said, tears in her eyes. "You will be very happy together, but no more happy than you deserve to be."

"Thank you, thank you," Anne replied, and then, in a whisper that only Eleanor could hear, "I love him so much."

And a moment later they were clattering out of the courtyard on their way north, and the Morlands were hurrying inside out of the cold to resume their normal lives.

Lord Richard was as good as his word, and in April, shortly after the Queen had been delivered safely of another daughter, Ned departed on horseback for London to take up his service with his King. He was not yet thirteen years old, and though he was well grown for his age, it would have been surprising if he had not shed a tear or two as he left the home he might not see again for many years.

But the prospect before him was so exciting that he could scarcely restrain his excitement, and it was Daisy who wept as the little boy rode away with his escort.

Cecily, unexpectedly, also gave way to tears, and ran off to the herb garden to weep in private, closely followed by her little cousin Edmund, who wanted to comfort her. Coming across them later playing together, Eleanor asked Cecily why she had wept—was it her tender heart?

"Well, I was sorry to see Ned go, Grandmother," Cecily said evasively.

"But that was not why you cried. What then. Come, child, speak up! Why the tears?"

"I wanted to go to London, too," Cecily admitted unwillingly. "I think it would be the most wonderful thing in the world. I wish I wasn't born a girl—boys have all the fun. It isn't fair."

And Eleanor turned away to conceal a smile, but a part of her groaned slightly and wondered if all the problems of Isabella were about to resume in her niece.

CHAPTER NINETEEN

Eleanor finished reading the letter aloud, and looked up at her family.

"Well," she said. "What do you think?"

"War with France," Edward mused doubtfully. "I don't know."

"Why not?" Helen said. "Why shouldn't we take back the lands that are ours?"

"It might not be that easy," Edward said. "I was thinking about trade—how will a war affect trade? Don't forget that we rely heavily on exporting our cloth."

"Oh, cloth! Pooh to cloth!" Cecily cried impulsively. "What does that matter against the glory of England—the soldiers marching and fighting—"

"Enough, Cecily," Daisy said sharply. "Don't forget that soldiers can get killed, and that your brother Ned would be there."

"It's unlucky to talk like that," Helen said, and her hand resting on silent Edmund's shoulder said quite clearly, *Thank God you are too young to go.*

"It's true, though," Daisy said. "Remember—" but she didn't speak the names of Thomas and Harry.

"I shouldn't get killed if I went," Thom cried, jumping up with excitement at the thought. "I should be too clever. I should get my sword out like this—"

"You wouldn't be going anyway," Cecily said scornfully. "You're too young."

"He's nearly nine." Margaret defended her brother stoutly, but he was well able to defend himself.

"I'll *get* old enough to go," he said, "but you'll always be a girl—you can never go."

"Oh I *hate* being a girl!" Cecily cried out passionately. "It isn't fair! I want to go with Ned and fight for the King, and I can't do anything, just because I'm a *girl*."

"You'll do your part," Daisy said soothingly, "you'll do your part when you marry and give your husband some fine sons. That will be your contribution."

"I want to marry a soldier," Cecily said quickly.

"You'll marry whom you're told to," Eleanor said sharply. She already had a match in mind for Cecily, who at fourteen was well old enough for a betrothal, with the possibility of marriage next year. Eleanor had been forming a business friendship with a clothier named Jenkyn Butts, who had two sons and a great deal of gold. It was the elder of these two boys whom Eleanor had chosen as Cecily's prospective husband. Jenkyn Butts was himself a yeoman by birth, but he had married a gentleman's daughter and risen in the world to be called "master" on his own merits. Perhaps because of the similarity of Jenkyn's life story to her own Robert's, Eleanor found him very easy to get on with, and the thought of the closer ties gave her much pleasure.

"It is not fitting that the word 'want' should be so often on your lips," she said now to Cecily, who stared back at her boldly and unabashed. "You will do your duty and obey your elders, and that will be enough for you without *wanting* this and *wanting* that."

"I can't help wanting things, Grandmother," Cecily said. "And I'm sure you wanted just as much when you were my age."

"Be silent! Hold your tongue!" Eleanor said angrily.

Daisy shook her head sternly at her daughter. "You must not answer back, Cecily. You had better go to the schoolroom and read what Our Lord said about obedience, and remain there until you have learned better."

Cecily took her dismissal sulkily and almost flounced from the room. When she was gone Eleanor said, "That child is becoming unmanageable."

"I've wondered recently," Edward said diffidently, "whether we ought to get her a new governess. I've had the feeling once or twice lately that Anys is getting too old to cope with her."

"Nonsense," Eleanor said. "Anys is younger than I am."

"But you are rather a special case, Mother." Edward smiled at her. "Even poor Job is finding it hard to keep up with you, and I have gray hairs in my head. Whereas you—" He surveyed her with admiration. Eleanor was almost fifty-nine, but was still as upright as ever, her figure trim and her hair still black, untouched by any thread of gray; and if she had secret ways of keeping it black, none but her maid knew them. Her eyes were as bright and as sapphire as they had always been, and her energy was as tireless. Anys may have grown stout with age, and puffed when she ran after the girls; Job might complain of stiffness and pains in his limbs when the weather was damp, but Eleanor seemed ageless, untouched and untouchable by the withering finger of time. "Whereas you," Edward said, coming over to kiss her cheek, "never grow any older. No wonder they say the hare is a witch."

"Hush, child, and don't say unchancy things," Eleanor chided him, but she smiled with pleasure all the same. "And now, if we have finished with all the interruptions, we had better get back to the matter of the war. Our blessed sovereign Edward wants money, and asks us of our benevolence to make him a gift of gold. Now, as you and I know, this 'benevolence' is a polite form of tax—there is no question of whether or not we will pay it. The question is only how much we will pay."

"I think we should give generously," Edward said. "We have to remember Ned's position. It will reflect on him if we are niggardly, and it would be uncomfortable for him, since he is in the King's own household."

"I'm glad you feel that way," Eleanor said, "because as foolish as this war is, the King will go, and Ned with him."

"There is one thing, Mother," said young Richard; he had listened silently until now, as was his way. He had always been quiet as a child, and since his six-year stay with the chantry priests he had become more and more a listener and observer, rather than a talker. He had come back now to the family to decide what he wanted to do, whether he wanted to take orders, or join a monastery, or remain in the world. At sixteen, he had grown into a pleasant-looking young man, with a gentle, almost wistful mouth, but eyes that showed maturity and humor. He was no longer a daydreamer. Those years in the cloistered atmosphere of St. William College had brought him nearer the everyday world, rather than taken him farther from it.

"Yes, my son?" Eleanor said. She always welcomed Richard's comments.

"The war may serve to use up some of those energies that are at present driving men to civil strife. Perhaps our lord the King thinks we have more peace at home when we have war abroad."

In January the call came from Richard of Gloucester for men to join the contingent he was to take to France. He had promised to the King, as had Clarence, that he would bring 120 men at arms, including himself, and a thousand archers, and when the message came to Morland Place Eleanor was ready to provide from among her household and tenants three men-at-arms and twenty archers. But even while she was preparing her reply, Richard came to her privately and asked if he might go with my lord to France.

"You, Dickon?" Eleanor asked, almost startled that her gentle son, her youngest, should want to go to war. Why, he was almost a priest, and given entirely to God in his heart, she was sure. "Why do you want to go?"

"I feel that it is something I should do," Richard said.

"But, child, I thought you had dedicated your life to God. I thought you were going to take orders."

Richard walked to the window and stared out at the green hills to the south. "I have thought a lot about my life while I have been in St. William's," he said, "and more and more I have felt that I have not been chosen by God to shut myself away to a quiet communion with Him. I feel that God wants me to do His work, but to do it in the world, where men are and where temptation and wrong are, where good and evil are continually struggling in the

battle for men's souls. I must be out in the world like Friar
Thomas, where I can do the most good. And if I am to
help my fellowmen, I must know the things they know and
experience the things they experience. That's why I want to
go to France. Do you understand?"

The last was asked almost pitifully, as if he half expected his mother to laugh at him. But when he turned to
look at her, her eyes were radiant with love and admiration
for him, and she looked, to him, quite beautiful.

"I understand, my son. I shall tell my lord of Gloucester
that you wish to serve under him. And, oh, Dickon, I'm so
glad! You are the last of my children, and, though I would
not begrudge you to God if He called you to one of His
orders, I'm so glad that it is this way He wants to use you."

And so the letter was sent away to my lord of Gloucester
with the promise of four men-at-arms, including Master
Richard Morland, and twenty archers. At the end of January 1475, Gloucester's chief officer of arms, Blanc San-
glier Pursuivant, visited Morland Place to pay a quarter's
wages in advance to the members of the expeditionary
force at the rate of one pound per day for the men-at-arms
and sixpence per day for the archers, and to arrange for
the soldier's cognizances—each member of Gloucester's
contingent was to wear his white boar badge, no matter
where he came from.

"The muster is to be on the twenty-sixth of May on Bar-
ham Downs, near Canterbury," the Morlands were told.
"My lord will march down by way of York, so you may
join up with him there."

"And has he raised his full contingent?" Edward asked
out of interest.

The herald smiled with genuine pleasure. "The White
Boar is so valiant in combat that men flock to serve him,"
he said. "The contingent is exceeded by more than three
hundred souls."

It was a bright May morning when the household gathered in the courtyard to see the men off on their way to
join up with the Duke of Gloucester. Eleanor passed
among them after the blessing to speak to each one, and
inevitably her mind went back to that morning—Was it
really fourteen years ago?—when she sent her two sons off

to war, never to see them again. Helen, too, must be remembering her beloved husband, who had been with them
on that day, and there were tears in her eyes as she stood
with her "son," Edmund, on the steps of the house and
watched. The men's clothes were bright, their voices cheerful and excited; each wore the badge of the white boar and
was eager to be fighting with that renowned soldier; they
looked forward to excitement, honor, and perhaps plunder
before they marched home again—those that did come
back.

Last of all Eleanor came to her son, who was mounted
on Isabella's chestnut, Lyard, now a mature but still fiery
ten-year-old.

"Dickon," she said, reaching up a hand and resting it on
his thigh. He smiled down at her, more like a friend than
her son. Her son, her last-born, the child Robert had never
seen. "Your father would be proud of you," she said. "Bear
your arms honorably, serve your lord faithfully as your
brothers did. And if God permits it, come safe home to me.
I can't spare you yet, dear son."

"I will, Mother," he said confidently, almost as if he
could see the future and knew what was to come.

"You may see Ned—I hope you may. Give him our
love, and tell him we look to see him when the campaign is
over. And now you must go. God bless you."

"God keep you, Mother." And he gave the signal, and as
Eleanor stepped back the column moved forward and out
of the gates while Thom and Margaret danced along beside
them in uncontrollable excitement and everyone else waved
and cheered from the house steps, before turning to go in.

"I hope he and Ned are together," Daisy said to Edward.
"He will take care of Ned—he's so sensible. One would
never think he was only sixteen."

Harry had been just sixteen, that day they marched
away.

The plan had been that Edward's force—the finest army a
King of England had ever led into France, consisting of
1,500 men-at-arms, 11,000 archers, and a great train of artillery—would join up with that of his brother-in-law,
Charles of Burgundy; but even before the English army

had crossed the Channel it was known that Charles had taken his army off on business of his own and would not be there to meet Edward as arranged. When Burgundy did finally arrive at the English camp, it was with but a small bodyguard and the suggestion that Edward's army was quite strong enough to defeat France alone and that perhaps it would be best if Charles met Edward at Rheims when it was all over to witness the coronation.

It seemed from that point that the campaign was doomed. When the news leaked out to the men, as was inevitable, morale fell sharply. Some thought it would be better to turn around at once and go home; others declared they were better off without Burgundy's men and could fight Louis alone. Ned and Richard discussed the matter as eagerly as anyone. They met fairly regularly, since they were both squires and their masters were brothers and frequently in each other's company.

"I rather hope we don't go home," Ned said. "I know the King does not mean to, but quite what he does mean to do I can't be sure."

"My lord of Gloucester counsels fighting," Richard said.

"Well, if all the commanders were like him, we might have a chance, but as it is—" Ned shrugged, and tweaked at the sleeves of his doublet. Many of his mannerisms were those of the courtier now, and his clothes had a certain edge of fashion over even those his fashion-conscious father wore. The difference between him and Richard was manifest. Theirs was an odd relationship, for Richard was in fact Ned's uncle, and a year his senior, but Ned's being in the King's service and at Court for two years made him seem the more sophisticated. However, they had always liked each other and had been brought up as brothers in the same nursery, so they got on well and were very close.

"Come now, Ned, don't let your tongue run away with you."

"Well, Dickon, you know as well as I do—but you're right. One must be discreet."

"Why are you so anxious we should not go home, anyway?"

"I want to fight. That's what I've come for, and I don't like the idea of having to go home and admit we got this far and then were afraid to go on. Besides, Court life is so—oh, dull, and seething with women. Madam the Queen, and all her brood—and the soft life—I suppose it's being brought up in Yorkshire."

"My master finds the same thing," Richard said softly, making sure they were not overheard. "Madam has no love for him, nor he for her and her ways, so they mouth polite messages to each other a kingdom's length away. One day he will be forced to ride to London, and then—snap!" He clamped his hands together as if catching a fly. "She will have him."

Ned laughed. "You know as much as I do, Dickon, for all that you've never been to court. Well, we are our master's servants, and we will do as we're bid. But if I were the King, I'd fight, and damn the French!"

"Spoken like an Englishman, if not a Christian," Richard laughed. "Come, let's find some ale in this luxurious camp and sing a few songs, and pretend we're back in Morland Place where men are men and not lapdogs!"

"Now you're making fun of me," Ned said, and he was right, of course.

If things were bad, it was not because they could not get worse. By the middle of August the army had marched many miles, made many camps, and even fought a few skirmishes with outflankers, but they had not seen a hair of the French army's head, nor fought a single battle. The English army was beginning to get out of hand, and was straggling far afield. It was becoming difficult to find enough food, for the French King Louis had ruthlessly laid waste his own fields for this very purpose. Duke Charles had frequently ridden into the English camp to eat and drink with the King, but his army remained as distant as Louis'; and it was for these reasons that on the twelfth of August, Edward sent a message to Louis by a released captive that he might be willing to talk peace.

A very prompt reply came from Louis, proposing a peace meeting and hinting at generous terms, and with that in his hand the King called a meeting of his generals—Gloucester and Clarence, Norfolk and Suffolk, Dorset, Northumberland, Pembroke, Rivers, and the Lords Hastings, Stanley, and Howard. Ned, as the King's squire, was in attendance on Edward during the meeting, and he hastened as soon as he could afterward to tell Richard about it.

"King Louis' letter was practically begging for peace," he said, "more or less saying that he would pay us to go home."

"Well, he can't be too happy about an army of this size marching to and fro in his kingdom, even if it doesn't actually fight any battles," Richard pointed out mildly.

"His kingdom indeed!" Ned Scoffed. "He stole it from us."

"And we stole it from the French," Richard said. "Do go on, and try not to let your rhetoric carry you away. Sit down, here; that way you'll be less tempted to declaim." He patted the ground by the camp fire at which they'd met, and with a grimace Ned squatted down, and Richard beside him, and they talked quietly.

"All right," Ned said. "Can I go on now? Very well, then. As soon as the King had finished, the commanders all started talking at once, and from what I could hear most of them were saying what a good idea it was. My lord of Dorset said it would be far better than marching round and round in circles for another month and then being starved out.

" 'Why should we be starved out?' my lord Howard said then. 'There are plenty of supplies inside the towns. We only have to capture them.'

" 'Only capture them,' said Hastings. 'Why should we risk fighting when we can be paid to go home?'

"And then my lord of Gloucester said, 'We have the best army ever seen in this country. There would be little risk.' Everyone grew quiet then and listened. And Hastings said again, 'But why bother to fight? Why not take the money?' And Gloucester said, 'Because it would be dishonorable.' "

The two brothers exchanged a glance. "I'll wager some of them didn't like that," Richard said. "It's rather a hard word to break skulls with."

"You're right," Ned said. "There was a terrible silence then, and everyone avoided Gloucester's eyes. You know how he looks at you—"

"Do I not!" Richard exclaimed. "They say his father had the same way of looking, that makes you feel as if you are made all of glass, and your soul quite visible inside you."

"Yes, I know. Well, someone muttered then, 'It's all right for you, Gloucester. Your troops are well under control, but half the army's practically unmanageable.' And my lord replied, 'That's because they want to fight. They came here to fight, and they're still waiting to join battle.'

"Then the King said quietly, 'I'm in favor of peace, Dickon,' almost as if he were warning him not to cross him. But my lord spoke up boldly, 'So am I, your grace. That's why I say we should fight, and then we could treat for peace as victors, on our own terms.' The King said, 'It isn't necessary to fight,' and half turned away as if that were the end of the matter."

"But my lord didn't let it fall there," Richard guessed.

"You're right. He spoke up again, and you could have heard a pin drop. It was the first time he had ever counseled against the King, and he must really have felt strongly about it. He said, 'The people of England have paid taxes and made gifts to send this army to fight the French. The men came here to fight. It would touch our honor to take the French gold and go home without fighting.' And one or two others agreed, very quietly, in case they should be noticed. The King looked hard at my lord, and then shook his head, smiling a little. 'Very well,' he said. 'Since you feel so strongly about it, we'll take a vote on it.' "

"Don't tell me." Richard shook his head. "I can guess. Lord Richard was alone in his desire for war."

"Not quite," Ned said. "Lord Howard and my lord of Norfolk voted with him. The rest voted with the King for peace, and so it was settled."

"Well, perhaps they are right in the end," Richard said. "What use to have men die? Let them go home to their womenfolk and till the land with all their limbs and raise sons."

"But it isn't honorable," Ned said indignantly. "And if some died, it would be gloriously, for England and the King!"

"Perhaps the only glorious death is the martyr's," Richard said. "For the rest, we must all die some time, sooner or later. It may as well be later."

Ned snorted contemptuously, and Richard added with a smile, "Does it occur to you that you are in agreement with my master and I with yours? Cheer up, Ned! Though you go home with no scars, you may easily get one from a fractious ram once you are home. And you may be drowned crossing the sea, think of that!"

"You may well laugh," Ned said crossly. "But I wish we had fought, all the same."

"You never know," Richard grinned. "We might have lost."

The terms offered by Louis were attractive, and were accepted at once. The English were to withdraw at once and to sign a seven-year truce and trade treaty. In return, Louis was to pay 75,000 crowns at once and pay Edward a pension of 50,000 crowns a year, and marry the Dauphin to Edward's eldest daughter, Elizabeth. The kings also signed a private treaty to defend each other against rebellious subjects within the realm. Duke Charles heard about the treaty and rode in haste to Edward's camp, where he reviled him for making it and refused to have any part of it, before riding away again to join his still distant troops. He had hoped Edward would defeat Louis for him; he had never envisaged an alliance between them.

On the twenty-fifth of August the two armies formed up and marched in ceremonial array to the town of Amiens, where Louis sent a hundred cartloads of wine to the English army, laid out tables weighted with venison pasties and other delicacies, and bid the English soldiers entertain themselves while he entertained Edward. He then opened the city of Amiens to all and bid the soldiers be his guests, offering free food and wine, and giving orders to the citizens to entertain them well.

The soldiers poured into the town in holiday mood, for they had been cheated of battle and plunder, and this was the next best thing—a drunken carouse! Only the camp of the Duke of Gloucester held aloof, pitched at a little distance from the others, and maintaining military order and discipline, the tents properly pitched and guards mounted, with the white boar standard flying over the tents.

Ned sought out Richard. "Come on—aren't you coming into the city?" he cried.

But Richard smiled slightly and shook his head. "You see this cognizance," he said, pointing to the white boar on his chest. "I am one of Gloucester's men."

"That doesn't matter," Ned said eagerly. "Everyone's invited. King Louis himself said—"

"Ah, but my lord said no, and he is the master here."

"*No?* My lord of Gloucester said no?" Ned could hardly believe it. "Why?"

"He said we are soldiers, not plowmen at the Monday fair, and we'll behave like soldiers until we are discharged." Richard did a fair imitation of his master. "And behaving like soldiers means keeping within the camp and under discipline. We are forbidden to set foot in the city, and any man found drunk is liable to a lashing."

"My God!" Ned said in reverent horror. "Aren't the men furious?"

"Little you know about men, Ned, my child," Richard laughed. "The men love him, worship him. 'Old Dick's a harsh master,' they say, 'but he's a soldier, which is more than any of these courtiers are.' This is probably the only camp in which the word courtier is an insult! So go on, my Ned, and have your fun, and don't get too drunk. And watch out that they don't try and knife you in one of those low taverns."

"I'll watch it. I'll steer clear of any low taverns, on your advice. But I wish you were coming, Dickon!"

"I'd spoil your fun," Richard said. "Go on with you! And take care."

The party went on for four days, and it was not long before the other commanders were looking with envy at the Gloucester camp, so quiet and orderly on the flanks of the army. No drunkenness there, no fights, no theft, no women making trouble; the tents did not fall down in Gloucester's camp, the watch was kept, meals were served in the normal way. One or two generals muttered about Achilles sulking in his tent, but Edward publicly praised his brother and awarded him some fine estates to prove that he did not value him less for his opposition to the treaty.

After four days, the Kings were anxious to get on with the signing, for fear that discipline would be lost forever. Edward asked Louis' permission to have the English soldiers thrown out of the town so that he could form them up and march them to a little distance before the ceremony of the signing. The men began to straggle back into camp, some cheerful and relaxed, some haggard with overindulgence, some still drunk, some sick. And then, my lord of Gloucester called Richard to him in his tent. Richard attended quickly, bowed low, and looked curiously at his master. Old Dick's expression was grave, but there was a suggestion of amusement in the depths of those clear gray eyes.

"I am informed by the King that a certain member of his household has not reported back from the city," he said. "Your brother, Master Morland. Someone reported that he was last seen enjoying himself very much with a young woman at the dancing in the public square. This was yesterday evening. I imagine he is still with her. You have my permission to go and find him and stop him, if possible, from making a fool of himself."

"Thank you, my lord," Richard said.

"You are a steady lad, Richard. Be as quick as you can, and use your wits. Go now."

Richard bowed and left, and moments later was cantering toward the city gates on Lyard.

Ned was not much more surprised to be awakened by Richard than to be waking at all. "Oh, my head!" he moaned. "As you love me, Dickon, don't shake me. Am I still alive? What are you doing here?—wherever 'here' is."

"You young fool," Richard said.

"Not so much of that! You're only a year older than me."

"But I've a lot more sense," Richard rebuked.

"Not necessarily," Ned said with dignity. "You've simply never been exposed to temptation." He closed his eyes again. "Besides, being drunk isn't such a great sin, provided you don't do it too often. And it carries with it its own punishment. I feel terrible."

"Ned," Richard said gently, "how much do you remember of the past three days?"

"Nothing," he said blithely, his eyes still closed. "Not a thing. I must have had a marvelous time."

"You don't remember Jocosa?"

"No. Who's she? And where am I?"

"Jocosa is the daughter of one Jean de Trouville, a flesh merchant of this town. Quite a wealthy man, but a vulgar one, despite the 'de' in his name, which by the way he adopted without provocation as being good for trade. This is his house, you are lying in his guestchamber, and Jocosa, your wife, is downstairs."

Ned's eyes flew open. "My what?" He struggled to sit up, and groaned and held on to his head. "I feel sick," he said. "Don't make these awful jokes at this time of the morning."

"It isn't morning anymore, and I'm not joking," Richard said.

"You are. You must be. You said my—I don't even like saying it—my *wife*. I can't be married. I'm in the King's Household. No one in the King's Household can marry without his permission."

"I'm glad you realize the seriousness of your position," Richard said quietly. "I suggest you get up and make yourself as presentable as you can without shaving, facilities for which cannot be got until you get back to camp."

"All right, but for God's sake tell me what all this is about my wife."

Richard helped him to his feet and while he washed his face in the basin told him the story. "As far as I can make out from the merchant himself—whose French is like nothing that Master Jenney taught me, I might add—you proposed marriage to this girl during the course of some dancing in the public square yesterday morning. Apparently the girl had gone out to see the fun and got separated from her chaperon by the crush of the crowd. You came upon her being annoyed by some drunken soldiers and, being just as drunk but more of a gentleman, you sent them on their way and offered to take care of her."

"I like your choice of words—annoyed, indeed! What next?"

"During the course of the fun, which I believe waxed fast and furious, you told the girl what a fine young man you were, and asked her to marry you. She brought you home, and her family welcomed you with open arms and feasted you, no doubt thinking you a fine catch for their daughter."

"My God, I remember now. I thought they were being very friendly—patting me on the back and plying me with wine. I must say I can't remember the girl, but then there were so many girls— You mean, all that merrkmaking was because they thought I was going to marry their daughter? Then everything's all right. You can explain to them it was all a mistake."

"*I* can explain?" Richard said wryly.

"Well, you speak better French than me. It's only because my French isn't too good that the mistake occurred. They'll understand. Anyway they can't hold me to it—I'll be gone soon enough. They won't follow me to England."

Richard looked sadly at him. "I'm afraid there's no question of calling it off."

"What do you mean, Dickon? Come, you can't be so serious as to think I ought to stand by an engagement I didn't even know I made? It wouldn't surprise me if the girl had made it all up. I don't remember her, so she can't be very pretty."

"Pretty or not, you will have to marry her," Richard said. "Last night you—shall we say—anticipated the ceremony. Master Trouville isn't pleased, but he's putting it down to high spirits and love."

"You mean—I'm?" Ned considered, and a slow smile spread across his face. "Did I really?"

"You don't even remember *that*?"

"I remember it, vaguely, but not the girl. It was dark, you see." The smile faded. "There's no way out?" He pleaded.

Richard shook his head.

"What will the King say?"

"Never mind the King. What will my mother say?" Richard said gloomily.

"Sweet Jesu, I'd forgotten Grandmother! She'll flay me alive!"

"Very likely."

"Listen, Dickon, is she very bad, this girl?"

"Not at all. She's rather a sweet thing, so far as I can judge, and reasonably pretty, too, if that counts for anything. But the younger daughter of a flesh merchant, for the heir of Morland Place—it won't do, you know. Mother isn't going to like it at all. But you'd better come down now and talk to the parents. They're waiting."

Ned groaned, but brushed his clothes smooth with his hands, and followed his uncle. "Now I know why we are warned against drink. I'll never touch another drop as long as I live."

The family was waiting in the hall, rather subdued and apprehensive, for they had doubts whether the English soldier with the rich clothes was going to honor his agreement, and there was no way that they could force him to, especially when he would be out of the country in a few weeks' time. Their daughter would then be dishonored, and it would be difficult to find a match for her.

Jocosa herself was in a turmoil, for she had fallen badly in love with handsome young Ned, and had been carried away by that love to anticipate the wedding ceremony, although betrothal was supposed to be as binding as marriage anyway. Her father and mother had been berating her for the last half hour, and she was on the verge of tears because until they scolded her it had never crossed her mind that he would go away without her.

The two young men came into the room, and nervous greetings were exchanged in French on both sides. Ned looked with interest at his "wife" and found to his relief that she was quite passably pretty, plump and dark-eyed, with soft brown curls escaping from her wimple, and a gentle, childish face. She was no great beauty like his mother, but she was far from ugly. He did now have vague recollections of meeting her in the public square, but everything that had happened for the past few days was a blur.

He listened quietly while Richard did the talking in French that was only one grade better than his own. French of the school of Master Jenney was as much a for-

eign language to the Trouvilles as their French was to him.
The father Trouville was tallish and thin—amazingly so for
a flesh merchant—and bald. His skin was that sallow, yellowish color that they had often seen in France. He had a
slack-skinned face and melancholy dark eyes that shifted
anxiously from one face to another. His wife was stout and
greasy-looking, as if she had fed well on her husband's
wares, while starving him; she looked as if she had once
been pretty, but fat had obscured her features, and she now
looked coarse and red. Not Grandmother's kind of people,
Ned thought.

He could understand enough of Richard's French to
catch the gist of what he was saying. He was explaining
that Ned was a member of the King's Household—they
brightened perceptibly at that—and that the King's permission was needed to marry, so that Ned would have to ask
and then come back for Jocosa. He then asked M. Trouville what dowry went with Jocosa, and whether it was
ready to be taken away, since Ned would have to leave
with the army as soon as he was called. Ned didn't understand the answer, and asked Richard anxiously, "What did
he say?"

Richard turned to him. "It's better than I thought. I
thought he would say there was no dowry at all, but he
says that he will give her fifty gold crowns, a suit of
clothes, and a horse."

"Well, that is riches indeed!" Ned said. "But if he had
said no dowry, I could have refused to marry her, couldn't
I?"

"You are already married, don't forget," Richard said
sternly. "If you must do these things, you must pay for
them, one way or the other. I'll tell him we must go back to
camp and will come for Jocosa as soon as we have arranged the matter."

A little while later they were on their way back to camp,
leaving the family still apprehensive, but a little happier
since they now knew where they could send to their daughter's betrothed. Richard took Ned up behind the saddle and
cantered Lyard back to the camp of the Yorkshire men,
and there, on Richard's advice, Ned asked an interview
with my lord of Gloucester, to ask his advice. The two

Morland boys faced the stern general and Ned told his story.

Richard of Gloucester listened attentively and then got up to pace about his tent. "So you wish to marry this girl— or rather, to honor your betrothal?"

"Yes, your Grace," Ned said, subdued by the steady gray eyes.

"You have been foolish, but no doubt you know that. However, I agree that you are bound in honor to this course—and I presume you wish me to speak to the King for you?"

"I had not presumed—your Grace—I hoped—I wanted to ask your advice—" Ned stammered.

Richard Plantagenet's quirky smile lit his face. "You should have asked for that before you went into Amiens, lad. What will your grandmother say, eh?"

Ned made a moue. "I have that hurdle yet to face, your Grace."

"Well, the King is busy at the moment—he is signing the treaty with the French King. Oh, yes, I remained behind." He answered their looks. "I could not be a party to it, not even when it is a *fait accompli*. However, he will be back in his camp this evening, and then I will find a moment to speak to him for you."

"Thank you, your Grace. You are very kind," Ned said fervently. It was well known that Edward respected his brother's advice above all others.

Gloucester turned then to Richard. "You will come with me tonight. It may be your last chance to see your nephew. We shall be marching in a very few days' time."

Ned's interview with the King was brief, and fitted in between state matters. Ned remembered Grandmother's stories of how, when Edward was first King, he was never too busy for small matters.

"I understand you wish to have my permission to marry?' the King said. He was a dazzling figure still, though soft living and overindulgence had blurred him somewhat, and he was more corpulent than he had been when he took the crown.

Ned assented gravely.

The King smiled. "My brother tells me it ill behooves me to upbraid you when I made a secret marriage myself, and one that many people disapproved of. You would agree with that?"

"Your Grace, I—"

"I know, you wouldn't presume. Well, you've presumed to marry this girl, and there's not much we can do about it now, is there? Very well, boy, you may go into the city tomorrow and do whatever you have to do, go through the marriage ceremony, and tell her parents— What's today? The twenty-ninth. Tomorrow's the thirtieth. Well, we shall leave at dawn on the first of September, so tell her parents she should be ready to ride with us then."

"Thank you, your Grace. I am very grateful."

"Off you go, then. I hope she brings you joy, Ned. At least her family will be a good long way off."

And as Ned left the tent, he reflected that the King must be very tired indeed of madam the Queen's relations to allow it to show so openly.

The King called him back. "By the way," he said, "have you wondered what your family are going to think of this? Ah, I thought so. I know how you feel, boy. Don't worry— I'll make it all right with them."

"Thank you, your Grace," Ned said with heartfelt gratitude. They couldn't make a fuss if the King asked them not to.

So on the gray, misty morning of the first of September the English army marched away toward the coast and home. All the commanders except Richard of Gloucester were the richer by large bribes and a promised pension for life. Gloucester was the richer by some plate and a fine horse which he had accepted as a gift when he had made it clear he could not be bribed. The soldiers were richer by experience, and that had to be enough for them. And Ned was the richer by a plump French wife who rode just behind him on a fat white pony and wept loudly and continuously at the thought of leaving her home country forever. The soldiers marching around her made coarse remarks about her presence, but luckily for her only Ned could understand them.

CHAPTER TWENTY

Ned's reception at Morland Place was less stormy than he had expected. This was partly because the way had already been paved by his uncle, Richard. Gloucester's contingent crossed the Channel on the fourth of September, one of the first groups to make the crossing, while the King's own group did not cross until the twenty-fourth. So, by the time Ned and his bride set their feet on English soil the Yorkshire men were already home. Lord Richard himself broke his journey at Morland Place and helped Richard Morland explain matters to Eleanor.

. In fact, though the marriage was a poor match for the heir to the Morland estates—almost a shameful match— Edward and Daisy were more upset about it than Eleanor, for all her energies were taken up with disapproving of the truce and its terms.

"It wasn't for that we gave money and men," she said to my lord of Gloucester. "It isn't going to be popular. I wonder the King could think of it."

"Fortunately, the people will not blame him," Lord Richard said, stretching his legs by the fire. "The people love Edward—they will blame his ministers. I don't doubt there will be some uprisings in the provinces this winter."

"And you will be the better loved for having spoken against it," Eleanor said.

"I didn't like doing it," he told her. "I have never spoken against anything he has done before, but—"

"I know. But you weren't disloyal. He understands that, I'm sure."

"I hope he does. There are always some ready to speak against me."

"While the King loves you, you can afford to disregard the rest," Eleanor said. "And at all events, the people of the north will always be behind you."

"If only I could spend all my life here," Lord Richard sighed. "Here one knows what is right and wrong. There is loyalty asked and loyalty given, faiths are unbroken. The south is all deception and betrayal, fine words covering foul thoughts, a caress concealing a knife. The south is the peat-hag, covered in fine green turf and tempting you to step into it."

He shivered, and Eleanor looked at him curiously. "What is it you fear?" she asked.

"It is hard to say. I am a simple man, and life is so complex. Things are not what they seem, and decisions that ought to be easy to make are impossible. Sometimes even good is not good. Sometimes I'm afraid—some dark, treacherous fate is waiting for me, and I will step into it because I am too simple to recognize the trap." He lifted his eyes to Eleanor, and they were troubled and seeking. "You are wiser than I," he said. "I wish you could help."

"You are a good man," Eleanor said. "No man is more loved, no man has ever been more loved by those who know him. Whatever happens, no one can ever doubt that you act for good reasons; and when you call for help, that help will come."

"I can talk to you," he said, appearing vaguely comforted. "Anne is like you. She looks frail, but she is strong inside, like an apple tree. I shall see her tomorrow, and our little boy. I have missed them so much. Children grow so fast, it is hard to leave them for a day, let alone half a year."

"You will be home tomorrow," Eleanor said, and they both smiled. Home is a good word.

So, when Ned rode into Morland Place with his wife on her white pony a pace behind him, he had no more than a passing coldness and some sharp remarks about the comparative value of fifty gold crowns to endure from Eleanor.

Daisy was tearful, but she could not be severe when faced with the weeping and still terrified bride who reminded her a little of herself, though she had not had so far to come from home. Edward gave Ned a long and severe lecture, and then let the matter drop entirely, for there did not seem to be any point in complaining over something that could not be changed.

So the matter blew over very quickly. Jocosa, once the first strangeness of her situation wore off, became more cheerful, for she was by nature a placid, happy person. She was very much in love with her Ned, and happy when she had him in sight. She began painfully to learn the outlandish language her new family spoke, and Master Jenney helped her as much as he could. She was somewhat teased by the younger children, more than somewhat mortified by the beauty of the females of the family, thrilled and awed by the magnificence of her new surroundings, and bitterly troubled by the cold and damp of the climate. But at the beginning of October, she was able to confirm what she had suspected, that she was with child, and after that her position in the family was assured.

2

"A boy, madam," Anys announced with as much pride as if she were personally responsible for the baby's sex.

Eleanor, who was seated in a bower in the Italian garden, looked up sharply. "Healthy?"

"Certainly, madam." Anys sounded almost indignant. "Both healthy. The labor was an easy one, and the child, though small, is perfect. The mother is resting, but seems not to have suffered much."

"The last day of April," Eleanor mused. "A month early by any reckoning. I wonder—"

Anys knew exactly what she meant. "Never think it, madam," she said. It would not do to wonder if Jocosa had been already with child when the drunken English soldier came so conveniently along.

"It would do no good, I agree," Eleanor said. "Ned is pleased enough with her. But one can't help wondering

. . . However, enough of that. Are they still set on giving it that outlandish foreign name?"

"Paul is a Bible name, madam, a holy saint's name," Anys reminded her.

"It isn't English," Eleanor complained. When one is sixty, one is entitled to grumble a little now and then. " 'Paul Morland.' It doesn't sound well. But I suppose Edward and Daisy are set on it, and I shall have no say in the matter."

Anys smiled a little at this image of Eleanor being forever thwarted at every turn, and said, "The master likes it, madam."

"Poor Robert at least chose decent names for his children," Eleanor said. She looked up at Anys, and saw how gray and bent she was growing, and tears came to her eyes. "Anys, is it really almost twenty years since he died? I wonder if he would know me now."

"He would still love you, madam, as much as he always did."

The two women stared at each other and remembered the years that had gone by and all the things that had happened; and then their reverie was rudely shattered by the sound of children running and shouting just beyond the high hedge.

"What are those children doing?" Eleanor cried crossly. "My children were never allowed to make such a noise— and where are they going without a nurse? Anys, who should be with them? Daisy has no sense of discipline. I don't know what young people are coming to. Well, don't just stand there, Anys. Go and find out what's happening."

It was Margaret and Thom who had made all the noise. Edmund followed them quietly, as he did everything, and they called to him, annoyed that he did not appear as excited as they were.

"Come on, Edmund—keep up! We shan't wait for you! Can't you run any faster than that?"

Edmund could, and did, and the three children ran across the park and reached the safety of the trees.

"Now we shan't be caught and told to go back," Thom said with satisfaction.

"Someone may be sent after us," Margaret said anxiously. "Didn't you see Grandmother was in the garden as we ran past?"

Thom shook his head, and looked worried.

"She did send someone," Edmund told them. "Didn't you see? She sent Anys out to see where we were going."

"Oh, that's all right then," Margaret said quickly. "Anys can't run. She'll go a little way and then go back and say she can't find us. We can stay out until supper time."

"I've got something to show you," Thom said suddenly. He was ten, whereas the other two were eleven, but more often than not he was the leader of their expeditions. They looked at him eagerly now.

"What?" Margaret asked imperiously. "Tell us, or I'll pinch you."

"I was going to tell you anyway," Thom said with dignity, "and I'll wager you couldn't pinch me if I didn't let you."

Edmund looked from one to the other, wondering if there was going to be another quarrel before they got any further, but this time Margaret did not carry out her threat but merely said, "Oh all right. But do tell us."

"No, I won't tell you, I'll show you—but you must be very quiet."

Thom led the way through the woods, leaving the path to plunge into the thicker undergrowth, though an experienced woodsman would have been able to tell that some large beast or beasts had been through this way recently. After a while he signaled them to be silent and crept forward slowly and carefully until they could come up beside him in the shelter of a bush and see two horses tied to a tree a little way ahead.

"That's one of our horses," Margaret said indignantly. "Has it been stolen?"

"Shh!" Thom hissed urgently. "Come on, they're further on."

The three children made their cautious way through the bushes until Thom stopped just past where the horses were tied and they all looked down into the small clearing. Two people were lying on the grass.

"What are they doing?" Margaret asked after a breathy silence.

"They're kissing," Thom said with the proud but anxious air of a showman who does not know yet whether his audience appreciates the entertainment.

"Some of it's kissing," Margaret said doubtfully.

But it was Edmund who spoke what was hovering in the mind of each of them.

"They're mating," he whispered unhesitantly. "Like with the rams in the autumn. I watched it last year. But people do it differently from sheep."

They watched in silence for a moment longer. "It's our Cecily and Henry Butts," Thom pointed out, in case they had missed it.

"But Cecily's supposed to marry Thomas Butts," Margaret said. "I heard Grandmother talking about it to Master Butts last week."

"Maybe you got it wrong," Thom suggested.

Margaret shook her head. "No, I'm sure it was Thomas. Thomas is the elder one, that's how I know. Grandmother wouldn't want Cecily to marry the younger son."

"Then perhaps Cecily's got it wrong," Thom suggested, and they had to be content with that, for at that moment the couple in the grass lifted their heads, thinking they heard something, and the watchers had to freeze, and then quietly creep away.

Henry Butts sat up and brushed a dead leaf from his hair. He was an extremely beautiful young man of sixteen, a year older than Cecily; he was charming and witty, danced like a courtier, and dressed in the forefront of fashion. He would also be fairly rich one day, for he was to inherit his mother's private fortune. The only thing that could be said against him was that he was his father's younger son and that his father's estate would go to his brother.

"Did you hear anything?" he asked Cecily.

She smiled drowsily from the pillow of grass he had made her. "No. Don't worry, we're quite safe here. It was probably the horses moving about that you could hear."

"I'm only worried that if we're caught, something bad will happen to you. I'm not worried for myself."

"Nothing would happen to me. If we were to be found out, they'd just have to let us marry, that's all. I wouldn't be beaten or anything, if that's what you mean. Mother and Father don't beat any of us, and my governess is too old and fat to do it."

"But what about your grandmother? I've heard that she's—well, very strict. And she's very friendly with Father. You know they mean you to marry Thomas."

"Oh, Thomas!" Cecily said with easy contempt. "Who wants to marry Thomas. He's as dull as ditchwater."

"He's my brother, and a very nice person." Henry defended him.

"He's not half as handsome as you," Cecily wheedled, twiddling a grass stem so that it tickled his face. He rolled over and caught her wrists and looked down into her beautiful catlike face.

"You witch," he said. "I believe you put a spell on me, just like the Queen did on the King to make him marry her."

"Only I'm not older than you, and a widow into the bargain," Cecily said. "*Would* you like to marry me, Henry?"

"Of course, you know I would. But my father and your grandmother would never allow it, so it's no use thinking of it."

"There might be a way," Cecily said. "And if there is— You do love me, don't you, Henry?"

"You know that I do," he said fervently, leaning down to kiss her again.

But this time she pushed him away capriciously and sat up. "No, no more now. It's time to go home, anyway. Ned's wife was in labor when I left, and she might have had it by now, so I ought to go back and let them see me—"

"Your sister-in-law in labor, and you just left?" Henry said, shocked.

"Oh, pooh! Who cares for silly old Jocosa or her silly old baby?" Noting his glance of disapproval she added: "Anyway, my being there wouldn't make it any easier for her. I wouldn't be allowed anywhere near the chamber, so I couldn't help. Now don't be so fussy, Henry! Help me up!"

He took her hand and pulled her to her feet, and, having brushed herself off, she snatched his hat from his head and

ran away with it, forcing him to chase her, allowing him to
catch her just by the horses. He embraced her again, his
disapproval forgotten.

"You are a witch," he murmured, staring down into her
face. It wasn't a classically beautiful face, being rather too
broad, the nose rather too snubby and the mouth rather too
wide. But it was breathtakingly lovely all the same, so full
of animation and charm that it appeared beautiful to the
person who loved her.

"Not a witch, but I am a Morland, and I must go home
now or I shall be laced."

In July, a great ceremony was planned in which the bodies
of the Duke of York and the Earl of Rutland would be
exhumed from their resting places in Pontefract and taken
to Fotheringay and there interred with great pomp and
majesty, as befitted the father and brother of a King. My
lord of Gloucester was given responsibility for the affair
and was to be chief mourner, but almost at the last minute
the King announced that he would, after all, be present. It
may have been that he wished to get away from the south,
for there had been an outbreak of the pox in London in
April that was showing no signs of dying out; it may also
have been due to the fact that among the noble guests were
to be included ambassadors from several foreign countries.

Eleanor was invited to the burial mass and feast at Fotheringay, together with Edward and Daisy. Lord Richard
himself gave her the invitation when they met at the Guildhall during one of his frequent visits to York city.

"I understand there will be an embassy from France," he
told her, his eyes twinkling gravely, "in attendance at the
feast. One Guillaume Restout and Louis de Marafin, who I
understand are merchants from the fair city of Rouen, and
with them will be another merchant from Amiens, whose
name escapes me for a moment—"

"Could it be Trouville, your grace?" Eleanor laughed.

"That's the very name. Well, somehow he has managed
to make himself one of the party, by what means I cannot
tell—I wouldn't be surprised if Edward had something to
do with it. He is astonishingly sentimental. And since Foth-

eringay is on the road to York, I am sure he will be glad to accept your invitation to pay you a visit, and see for himself what his daughter has produced."

Eleanor grimaced, and then, "Did you ever see this Trouville? Do you know him? Is he a *very* low sort of person?"

"I never saw him, nor met him," Richard said apologetically, "but I have heard that he is a decent sort of man, an honest citizen at least. And he would not have been allowed to join the party if he had been *very* low. So comfort yourself; if I can accept him as a guest, surely you can?"

And at that, Eleanor was ashamed and begged his pardon.

The *cortége* left Pontefract on the twenty-fourth of July, the bodies being drawn in a magnificent chariot bearing the arms of England and France—as if the Duke had himself been King—and drawn by six beautiful black horses, richly caparisoned. The Duke of Gloucester followed the hearse dressed in mourning clothes, until on the twenty-ninth of July the procession reached Fotheringay. There, the bodies were consigned to the earth at an elaborate mass, and afterward the great feast was held in the castle with the King presiding.

The Duke of Gloucester held himself a little in reserve at the feast, for he was deeply moved by the foregoing ceremony, and wished only to sit quietly with friends, but he did spare a moment to speak to Eleanor and Edward and Daisy and to see them brought together with Jocosa's father. It amused him a little to see the transparent struggle on Eleanor's face between her natural aversion and her natural politeness. It made it even more amusing that Eleanor's French was better than Edward's, while Daisy's was nonexistent, so it was naturally to Eleanor that the Frenchman addressed himself, almost to the exclusion of everyone else. She did still find time to discuss the latest news from London with members of the household; Master Caxton's new printing press that had been set up at Westminster and was said to be able to make as many copies of a book as you wished in the blinking of an eye, and threatened to put thousands of scriveners out of work; and the unabated pox epidemic, which was still claiming lives daily and which was said to have been brought over from France by a merchant ship.

On the thirty-first of the month the Morland party set off for York, and Master Trouville rode with them. He certainly tried to make himself agreeable, and praised the green countryside, the size and fatness of the sheep and cattle, the healthiness of the commoners' children, and the beauty of the women of England. Eleanor privately thought it fortunate that they did not meet with any thieves on the road—there had been much unrest since the army came back from France—or he might have found it hard to praise his daughter's new country.

But whatever she felt about the French merchant, it was touching indeed to witness the reunion between father and daughter, who had never thought to see each other again, and the grandfather's first sight of the Morland heir—Paul was now three months old, and a healthy, wiry baby, despite his small size and yellowish skin. Jocosa had conceived again immediately, almost as if she wished to disprove doubts about Paul's parentage, and this fact impressed Master Trouville greatly. He was immensely proud of the way his daughter had lost no time in getting down to breeding heirs for her new family, and referred to her fertility so frequently that Eleanor felt it verged on the indecent.

On the day after their arrival home from Fotheringay, a splendid dinner was given in Master Trouville's honor, and one or two guests were invited, a few city notables and some friends of the family, including Jenkyn Butts and his two sons. Everything was done in the most splendid style, with liveried servants everywhere under the stern supervision of Job—thin as a rail now, and gray-headed, but still as sharp-eyed and quick to laughter as ever—and musical accompaniment by four instrumentalists and a choir of six boys.

The strong August sun blazed through the colored glass of the hall windows, and as dish after dish was brought on, two small boys pulled ropes to operate an ingenious arrangement of fans, devised by Job, that kept the air moving to keep the guests cool. The doors stood open, and out in the sunny courtyard white pigeons cooed from the eaves and dogs dozed wherever they could find a strip of shade. The hall walls were decorated with fresh green boughs that gave off a sweet woodland scent, and below the boughs the guests talked and laughed in low, clear voices, the brilliant colors of their best silks and linens flashing as they nodded their heads or shrugged their shoulders.

A scene of luxury, a scene of concord, and, if there were any harsh notes, only the habitually watchful Job noticed them, communicating them silently by looks to Eleanor. There was Ned, a proud father now, getting over the shock of his father-in-law, whose appearance he had conveniently forgotten, and looking with a new discontent at his plump wife, whose round, shiny face was made shinier than ever by the plentiful rich food. And there was slant-eyed Cecily, sitting beside her betrothed, Thomas Butts, and talking to him with cool aloofness, while she exchanged sidelong glances of complicity with saucy Henry.

After dinner the guests departed, with the exception of the Butts family, who were staying to supper, and everyone moved out of doors to stroll or sit in the gardens and be cool. Eleanor walked about the herb garden with Jenkyn, talking business as usual. Jenkyn was very interested in Eleanor's system of housing all the processes under the one roof, and they could talk about modification and improvements to the system for hour after hour. Edward went off with Reynold on some business or other; Daisy and Helen and the two Butts boys sat by the fountain in the Italian garden and talked and laughed, and Cecily watched the children bathing their feet in the moat for a while, but soon got bored with that, and slipped away on her own.

Henry Butts shortly afterward offered to fetch fruit from the orchard for the girls and wandered off, and the children slipped away on pursuits of their own and the drowsy afternoon lengthened and seemed timeless. When the family was called in at five o'clock for supper, it was noticed that Cecily and Henry were missing.

"Henry was with us, and he went to fetch us fruit," Daisy said. "I'd forgotten it—he didn't come back. Perhaps he fell asleep in the orchard. It *is* very hot this afternoon."

"Jocosa and I were in the orchard all afternoon," Ned said. "He didn't come there."

There was a brief silence, and then Edward asked innocently, "And where's Cecily?"

Eleanor turned a withering glare on him. She had hoped no one would link the two names before she had had a chance to find out what was going on. But it was done now.

"She went off on her own," Helen said. "I thought she might have gone indoors because of the heat."

There was a short silence in which everyone looked at each other and read the same suspicion in their eyes. Eleanor turned to Job to tell him to send out servants to find them, and at that moment the children, Margaret, Edmund, and Thom came into the hall.

Before Eleanor could stop him, Edward asked, "Have you seen Cecily or Henry Butts anywhere?"

And Margaret had blurted out innocently, "Oh, they're up in the woods—" Her hand flew to her mouth in realization even before Thom, with quicker wits, had punched her in the back to warn her.

"What do you mean, they're up in the woods? You mean they are together?" Edward asked.

"What are they doing?" Daisy asked.

Margaret, turning a guilty red, tried to save the situation. "Oh, just walking. I expect they met up by accident."

Eleanor took over quickly. "Job, send someone up there. And let us sit down to supper. We won't wait for them. Come, everyone, let us take our places."

"But, Mother . . ." Edward began.

Thomas Butts was looking unhappy, Jenkyn Butts furious, and M. Trouville puzzled, as his English was not good enough to follow what was going on.

"Not now, Edward," Eleanor said firmly, but he was for once as firm himself.

"No, Mother, I want to know what's going on."

"I agree," Jenkyn said, glancing at Thomas. "Did you know about this?"

Thomas shook his head.

"Now, Margaret, how long has this been going on?" Edward asked his younger daughter sternly.

Margaret burst into tears. "I didn't mean any harm," she sobbed. "It was Thom who found them."

"Found them? What is this, Thom?"

"We followed them just for fun," Thom said evasively.

"How long have they been meeting?"

"I don't know," Thom said. He looked very uncomfortable, but he was saved from further questioning by the arrival of the two miscreants, red and breathless with hurrying. The servant who had been sent to find them had met them just outside the gates, hurrying home, having just realized that they were late.

"I'm sorry I'm late," Cecily said with great composure, considering the circumstances. "I didn't hear the bell."

"Where have you been?" Edward demanded furiously. Cecily looked from face to face, and then at Henry, realizing that they were found out, though she could not imagine how. But she decided to face it out boldly, saying, "Walking in the woods. It was so hot—"

"Insolent, bold creature!" Edward cried, and then the storm broke.

Jenkyn reviled his son, Edward his daughter, Daisy cried, the children clung trembling to Eleanor and Helen, and Eleanor attempted to stop everyone shouting, alone mindful that they had guests present.

"I don't care," Cecily cried hotly at last. "Henry and I are in love. We want to marry."

"That's right," Henry said, though less certainly than Cecily. He had not quite her care-nothing boldness. "We are pledged to each other."

"You are not," Eleanor said firmly. "Cecily is betrothed to Thomas, and no promises you make to each other can invalidate that. Cecily, come with me. I want to talk to you. No, Edward, let me handle this. And don't forget, I have gone through it all before. Master Jenkyn, I suggest you take your son away for a quiet talk. Helen, look to these children. Daisy, Edward, take the rest of the family to supper, and don't wait for us. We may be some time. Go on now, and don't argue."

Master Butts took Henry out into the courtyard with a look of gratitude at Eleanor for sorting the matter out. Eleanor, having seen everyone move toward the supper table, gestured Cecily to follow her and led the way into the herb garden. There she sat on her stone bench, folding her hands in her lap, her back straight as a broomstick and her head held high and crowned with her great headdress as a church is crowned with a steeple. She was a formidable figure to face, and Cecily stood in front of her looking sulky and defiant, but feeling far less self-assured than she had five minutes before.

Eleanor looked at her in silence for a long time, while more and more of Cecily's courage leaked away. It was a deliberate ploy, and when Eleanor did at last speak, it was quietly but with great authority.

"Have you no sense of shame? You have behaved like a slut, like a tavern-wench, and to do it on a day when we have guests here—to try to shame us in front of guests and in front of your own betrothed and his father—the people who will become your family. Are you insane? You have always been given too much freedom—more than my children ever were—but I would have hoped that you had been taught better than to abuse it in such a way. Have you learned nothing in all these years you have studied under Master Jenney and Anys?"

"I love Henry Butts, and I want to marry him," Cecily muttered doggedly.

"Nonsense," Eleanor said briskly, and so matter-of-factly that Cecily was taken aback. "Love is what a woman feels for her husband. He is not your husband and never will be."

"But we are—pledged to each other—"

"You are not. You are troth-plight to Thomas Butts, and you will marry him."

"Henry and I—we have—" Cecily could hardly say it now and Eleanor saved her the trouble.

"You are precontracted to Thomas. Anything—*anything* —you have said to, or done with, Henry comes after that and cannot touch your betrothal. Do you understand me? Even if you had lain with him, it would be adultery, and not a bar to your marriage with Thomas."

Eleanor regarded her steadily, and under that gaze Cecily's face reddened, and her eyes filled with tears as she realized she had come up against a will even stronger than her own.

Eleanor watched the resistance crumble, and then spoke more gently, encouragingly. "Come, child, where's your pride? You don't want the younger son when you can have the elder! You are a Morland. The match with Thomas is just good enough for you, but Henry— What is he? Besides, the Morland fortune is in cloth, and you can help that by marrying the heir to Master Jenkyn Butts, a clothing merchant. Marry Thomas, and your sons will inherit all his wealth. Marry Henry—" She shrugged. "Henry may be good enough for Margaret," she added, shrewdly, playing on Cecily's jealousy of Margaret's greater beauty, "but you are your father's eldest daughter."

"But Henry—I promised," Cecily began weakly.

Eleanor removed the last stone from the defense. "Henry is even at this moment recanting everything to his father and heartily wishing he had never seen you."

"Do you mean that?"

"Child, I have seen it all before. Believe me, Thomas is the better man, the better match, and the better husband. Do you think I would give you away to anyone but the best? Don't you think I, of all people, know how to value you? Come, come here, my little Cecily, kiss me, that's right. My precious girl—now, don't cry again, we've had all that over with."

"Oh, Grandmother," she sniffed. "I'm sorry. I didn't think—"

"Of course, you didn't. But you will in future. Now, wipe your eyes and pinch up your cheeks, and we'll go in, and you can be nice to poor Thomas. You've nearly broken his heart today, so you must be extra nice to him."

"What about—Master Butts?"

"I'll speak to him. You need never think of this unfortunate affair again."

"Oh *thank* you, Grandmother," Cecily cried fervently, and she looked up at Eleanor with gratitude and love as they walked back together to the house.

CHAPTER TWENTY-ONE

The greenish light of an August evening filtered in to the bough-hung hall, and Cecily, like a wood-maid in her dress of apple-green silk, and her hair braided and bound around her head in a golden crown, sat on a cushion playing the gittern and singing. As her clear young voice lifted, she smiled at Thomas, seated near her, and he looked as ecstatic and content as a dairy cat. The awkward incident might never have happened.

Eleanor and Jenkyn were sitting at a little distance, talking quietly.

"I don't know how you did it," Jenkyn said, "but the surrender appears to have been complete. She eyes him like a yeanling eyeing the tup."

Eleanor smiled, but suddenly into her mind as clear as Jenkyn's voice had come another—her long-dead father-in-law saying to Robert on their wedding night, "Tup her right, and she'll yean thee a bonny lamb!" What strange tricks the mind plays, she thought; he had been dead almost forty years, but I remember the exact tone of his voice.

She put the thought from her and said, "I think it would be a good idea to have them wed as soon as may be. They have been betrothed long enough—best wed them before any other temptation crosses their path."

"I agree," Jenkyn said. "I know we shall not quarrel about terms, mistress. Her dowry is generous, and I shall make as generous a jointure. They are a pretty young couple, and it would not become us to do anything less well than the best."

"They are content," Eleanor said. "Shall we have a wedding before the month is out?"

"Aye, it will do. What do you say to the thirtieth of August?"

They agreed upon this, and then Eleanor turned a thoughtful eye on Henry, who was leaning against the chimney corner and watching his erstwhile love with a morose eye.

"What of that young man?" she asked, drawing Jenkyn's attention to him. "There's one person who isn't happy with the present arrangement."

"Yes, we must do something for him, or he may be tempted to stray into forbidden pastures. What say you to another marriage? The other young maid is a likely girl, and Henry will have his mother's estate."

Eleanor looked across at Margaret, who was playing tables with Edmund while Thom looked on. She was as fair as a rose, but the curve of her cheek was the smooth round curve of a child's.

"She is only twelve years old," Eleanor said. "She is too young to be wed."

"Maids are married younger than that," Jenkyn pointed out.

"I know that, but I believe fourteen is soon enough to start to match them and Margaret is very much a child still, younger in her mind than Cecily was at the same age. No, that will not do—and yet, something must be done with Henry."

Jenkyn was a little put out that Eleanor refused to consider a second match, and he had a suspicion that Eleanor thought the match not good enough. However, there was nothing he could do about it.

"Perhaps," he said, "it would be best to remove Henry entirely from her influence. I have been toying with the idea of making use of Henry in the business, for I do not like to see a boy with nothing to do but enjoy himself and look for trouble. He is sixteen, and well old enough to work for his living."

"What had you in mind?"

"My factor in London is growing old, and I doubt not will soon be past his work, though he is an excellent man and has served me all his life. Suppose I send Henry down to London to work with him and learn his business so that he can gradually take over?"

"An excellent idea," Eleanor said. "A complete change of scene for him will soon drive Cecily from his mind."

Jenkyn looked at her slyly. "And in London he may perhaps find a rich young girl to marry," he said, hoping he might scare Eleanor into snapping up the eligible Henry before it was too late.

But Eleanor countered this coolly. "I fear not, Master Butts. In fact, judging from my own experience, the opposite is more likely to happen. My own son, John, was sent to London to be apprenticed to a goldsmith some years ago, and I have heard recently that he is wed to a woman of low circumstances and no money at all. He has even written me to ask for help, which I refused, of course. So I fear you must warn your son against such women before you send him, else you might acquire a daughter-in-law not at all to your taste."

Jenkyn Butts looked grave, but his eye was roguish. "My commiserations to you, madam," he said solemnly. "I wish I may have more luck with my son than you had with yours."

Eleanor knew she was being baited, but she merely smiled; she knew she had nothing to fear from Jenkyn, or she would never have admitted anything so damaging as John's unfortunate marriage.

Master Trouville remained at Morland Place for the wedding, and a fine occasion it was, too. Edward and Daisy made up by its splendor for having been cheated of the wedding of their son and heir, and Ned, knowing this without being told, looked askance again at his sallow, plain wife, already large again with child. Cecily wore a surcoat of cloth-of-gold over a cotte of primrose silk, and the hall was decorated with great bronze marigolds, golden colors chosen to suit her golden, purring beauty. She looked like a lovely lioness, scarcely tame, and Thomas appeared hardly able to believe his luck as he stood beside her and put on her finger the great gold ring set with rubies that Jenkyn had had made for her in London. Jenkyn also gave her, on her wedding day, a fine necklace of pearls alternated with small gold beads, and a bright bay palfrey already broken to carry a woman. He would not let it be said that anything was done on a small scale.

Master Trouville left for home on the day after the wedding feast, tearfully embracing his daughter, whom he could not hope to see again—he could not expect another such occasion to arise to bring him to England. Jocosa wept so much, Eleanor told her quite sharply to stop or she'd sour her baby's temper. Henry Butts left for London on the same day, and he and Master Trouville were to travel together, making up a party with two English merchants bound for Calais and some Burgundian woolmen going home before the winter. Their going caused Eleanor a sigh of relief, for Cecily's capitulation had been so sudden she could never be sure that the girl wouldn't break out again in a fever, all the more virulent for having been forced inward.

Christmas that year was quiet, because Jocosa, who was near her time, was unwell, apparently suffering from the cold and damp to which she had never managed to adjust. There was also the sad news that Clarence's Duchess, Isabel Neville, had died in childbed on the twenty-second of December. Eleanor knew this would make it a sad Christmas at Middleham, too, for Anne of Gloucester had been fond of her sister, and had already lost too many relations to spare any more.

Then, on the thirtieth of December, exactly eight months after the birth of Paul, Jocosa went into labor, and in the last hours of the day brought forth another son, a small, frail boy who christened at once by Master James in the name of his father.

Anys, who was nursing Jocosa, was very unhappy about this outcome, saying to Eleanor, "She has failed twice to carry to term, and it is likely that this is a fault with her and will always happen."

"What of the child?" Eleanor asked.

"I'm afraid it will not live—it is so small and weak. If it were summer, it might be different, but I fear the cold will carry it off in a little while."

Cecily, who was staying with her husband and father-in-law for the Christmas season, showed an unexpectedly kind streak by sitting with Jocosa for many hours, and trying to cheer her with talking and reading aloud out of *The History of Troy,* printed at the Sign of the Reed Pale in Westminster by Master Caxton's printing press. This volume, one of the first printed books and therefore very expensive, was Thomas's Christmas gift to his wife, and had been obtained and sent to Morland by Henry, now well established in London. Cecily was very proud of it, and glad to have an opportunity of showing it, even to the poor audience of Jocosa. But also she was now pregnant herself, and felt a good deal of sympathy with her sister-in-law, whom before she had scarcely considered worth a thought.

Jocosa did not recover quickly from this birth as she had from Paul's, and she was further set back by her distress when, on the third of January, her baby boy found the struggle for life too much for his puny body. The winter was pratically cold, and even with a fire roaring in the grate, and a fur rug on the bed, Jocosa could not seem to get warm. She lay shivering and miserable, cheered only by the visits of pretty Cecily, and heartily wishing she had resisted that temptation to revel with the handsome English soldier in the streets of Amiens.

In January came the news that Charles of Burgundy was dead, leaving only one daughter, his sole heiress, Mary. This was grave news, because the cities of Flanders were the keystone of English trade, particularly the cloth trade, and Burgundy had been an ally of England and an enemy to France. At once King Louis announced that all the lands of Burgundy had reverted to the French crown, and prepared to invade the country with his armies to make sure it did.

If it happened, it could paralyze English trade. The King called a meeting, and Richard of Gloucester rode hotfoot to it from Middleham. Edward was in the city when the entourage passed through, and brought back the news to Morland Place that there was still another danger in the situation, which as yet was known to but a few people—George of Clarence, recently widowed, was already negotiating for the hand of Mary of Burgundy. It was another of his mad but dangerous schemes for stealing his brother's crown.

"One day the King is going to realize that there is no end to that man's folly," Eleanor predicted. "There comes a point when even brotherly love gives out, and I am only surprised that the point hasn't yet been reached."

"I understand Lord Richard hasn't heard the rumor yet. I suppose no one dares tell him, for it will break his heart when he hears of it," Edward said.

At the end of March, the cold spell broke at last, and with the sudden advent of warm weather Morland Place was shrouded with fog for days on end. Jocosa was still convalescent from childbirth, and Anys privately confided to Eleanor that she wondered if Jocosa would ever be fully well again. She seemed seized by a melancholy that had seemed to quench her normal quite good humor. Ned slept apart from her, and though this was done for her wellbeing, it only seemed to depress her more. The truth was the only thing that had made England pleasant for her was her love for Ned, and now she thought that he no longer loved her, there was nothing in life to please her.

The warm, foggy weather brought with it the usual outcrop of coughs and colds, but also, more seriously, a renewed outbreak of the pox that had ravaged the south last year; but this time it was closer to home. It started in Coventry, and traveled north, and at the beginning of April it entered Morland Place and attacked the weakest member of the household. It was not noticed at first: Jocosa, always weak and fretful, was not noticed to be more weak and fretful than usual. It was only by accident that Eleanor discovered what was wrong with her. She had come into the room where Cecily was reading to the invalid to tell her grand-daughter that it was time to get ready to go home.

"Your husband will wonder why he bothered to marry you if you spend so much time here," she said cheerfully, and then turned to Jocosa. "And how are you today, *ma fille?* You look better, as if you have some color in your cheeks." And she stooped to brush Jocosa's hair back from her forehead. "But you are burning hot!" she exclaimed, and laid a hand across the forehead, and felt the telltale small lumps under the skin, like onion seeds felt through thin cloth.

Her face turned pale, and Cecily, seeing her expression, cried out in fear, "Grandmother, what is it?"

Eleanor laid her finger to her lips—Jocosa must not be alarmed—and she removed her hand from Jocosa's head with a significant look.

Cecily repeated the gesture, felt the lumps, missed the significance for a moment, and then, as it dawned, her eyes widened, and her hand flew to her throat.

"Sweet merciful Jesu!" she whispered, and her hand made an automatic sign of the cross. "The pox," she whispered, her eyes wide with horror. "My baby! I've been with her all the time. Oh, Grandmother—"

"Shh!" Eleanor warned as Cecily's voice broke out of the whisper. "She must not be upset. Go outside—I shall come to you."

"What is it, *Gran'mère?*" Jocosa asked, realizing that something was wrong.

"It's nothing. Rest yourself. Cecily feels unwell, that's all. I will send Anys in to you. Lie back, don't fret yourself."

Jocosa turned her flushed face uneasily on the pillow, but she was already too feverish to understand properly what Eleanor was saying. She murmured in French, her English abandoning her at the first onset of sickness, and hardly seemed aware that Eleanor had stepped quietly out of the room. She found Cecily in tears outside.

"Oh, Grandmother, what can I do? I'm bound to catch it—I've been with her all the time! And my baby, I'll lose my baby! Oh, why did she have to come here? Why did I sit and read to her—the ungrateful French bitch. Why did Ned have to marry her, instead of some decent English girl? Oh, what shall I do, what shall I do?"

"Be quiet, Cecily, or I shall strike you," Eleanor said sharply. "There is no reason why you should get the pox. You are young and healthy—Jocosa is sick and weak. And there is no reason why you should lose your baby. But you must certainly not go home—you would only spread the infection. You must remain here until the danger is past. I shall make you up a draft straight away, and you must keep away from Jocosa and from the rest of the family. In a week it will be safe for you to go home. Now go down and send Anys up to me, and then go and sit in the winter parlor till I come."

Cecily went, braced by her grandmother's astrigent tongue. But it was not Anys who came up to her, but Helen.

"Anys isn't feeling well," Helen said. "She's gone to lie down, so I thought if anything was wrong with Jocosa you'd prefer me to one of the maids."

Eleanor told her the situation and they looked at each other with their fear naked between them. "Anys, too," Eleanor said quietly. "I pray not. Dear God, I pray not."

"We must all pray," Helen said. "Mother, will Cecily catch it?"

"I don't know. There's a good chance—she's young and strong. But—I don't know. Helen, you must go away from this room. I'll nurse Jocosa, and Beatrice can help me. I don't want you to catch it."

"No, Mother," Helen said firmly. "I'm the best qualified to help you, and you know it. Don't worry, we'll manage between us."

Eleanor looked at her with a deep affection. "How strong you are, dear Helen," she said. "Help me, then, if you wish. I am glad you're here. Now we must make plans. The children must be kept away, and someone must go for the doctor—"

A terrible quiet fell upon Morland Place as the sickness took up residence and did its awful work. Eleanor isolated the sick women in the hope of preventing further outbreaks, and with Helen and Lys and her own maid, Beatrice, did all the nursing of the patients. It seemed at first that they were successful, but on the third day two more servants were sick, and on the fourth day Cecily discovered the spots on her own skin and ran screaming to her grandmother for help as a child will cry, *Make it not to be!*

The doctor was encouraging. "This is not the worst sort of pox," he said. "There is a good chance for those young and strong, like the young mistress; but I'm afraid the old and weak cannot withstand it. And—the young mistress may lose the baby. Do not tell her so—the shock would surely bring it about."

On the fifth day, Jocosa died. She had been only half conscious for more than two days, muttering in guttural French as if she thought she were back at home in Amiens, and sometimes calling out for Ned. Ned, of course, was not there, but at the other end of the house with those who had not succumbed to the sickness, and it was only when Master James came back from the sickroom that he learned he was a widower. He bowed his head, and accepted the prelate's comfort meekly. He was saddened, for he had had some affection for his wife, and his son, not yet quite a year old, was now motherless. But he could not help also thinking that it was perhaps for the best, and that he would be more careful in his choice of a second wife than he had been in the first.

The news of Jocosa's death was kept from Cecily, for even while her sister-in-law was breathing her last, Cecily was in labor. It was a long and hard labor, but Helen was there to hold her hand and encourage her. Cecily was not a good patient, and screamed a good deal louder than Jocosa had on either of her occasions. When Helen tried gently to quiet her, for fear of disturbing the other sick ones, Cecily only cried out angrily, "What do you know about it? You never had a child! You don't know how bad the pain is!"

And Helen could only continue, sadly, to hush her. After a labor of eight hours, just before dawn, Cecily's baby was born. It was a boy, and it was dead. Cecily wept despite her exhaustion and would not be comforted. "I want to go home," she cried. "I want Thomas. I want to go home."

Eleanor was still firm in her rule that the infection must not be spread, but Cecily was making herself sick with crying, and at last Eleanor consulted the doctor.

"She has only a light infection," he said. "Few spots, and no fever, and I believe she has already past the worst of it. If she feels well enough, and if her husband is willing, it may be as well if she goes home. But once home, she must stay home, and not go out in the streets or visiting, until the last spots have been gone five days. Tell her so, and make sure she understands."

So Thomas came and fetched his wife away, and she clung to him as one drowning clings to the only safe rock. He held her closely, obviously as much in love with her as ever, and Eleanor remembered wryly how she had not wanted to marry him, had passionately declared she would have his brother. Well, marriage had changed her. "Pray God she may conceive again soon," she murmured as the young couple went away. There was nothing as good for making you forget a dead child as another live one.

Anys died the same day. She was fifty-seven, and had been unwell recently, her stoutness making her breathless and giving her pains in the chest. She had had dropsy, too, which had made it harder for her to walk, and though she made a valiant struggle against the pox, and had seemed to be recovering, she died quite suddenly. The doctor said that it sometimes happened that way, that the heart just gave up beating for no apparent reason.

The loss of her friend and companion of so many years almost overcame Eleanor. The whole household mourned her most sincerely, for she had been much loved. She had nursed all the Morland children for three generations, shared their play, and taught them manners; she had been through all the crises and triumphs of the family, and if Morland blood had run in her veins, she could not have seemed closer to them all. Eleanor sat beside her bed for a long time after her eyes had been closed for the last time, remembering the scenes of her life that Anys had shared since she had assisted at the birth of Anne over forty years ago.

Anys had given her life to Eleanor, even to the extent of never marrying, though she had once been a pretty and lively girl. Eleanor had thought at one time that Anys and Job would marry, but it had never happened. Job would be grieving too at the loss of his friend. They had grown up together, all three, Job, Anys and Eleanor; no one could take the place of that dear friend and faithful servant.

The light was almost gone from the room, and there was work to be done. Eleanor gave one last, long look at the stout gray-haired old woman who had been that little round-eyed girl at Anne's birthing, and her eyes filled with tears, the last tribute she could pay to one who had served her so long and so faithfully. Her throat was tight, and she could not speak for it.

"Good-bye, dear friend," she whispered through the pain in her throat, and, turning, she went out, closing the door behind her.

Outside in the passage she found Helen, who had been looking for her.

"Mother, I don't feel well," she said, and a little sigh escaped her as her eyes met her mother's and read the message there.

On a blustery day in late April, Helen was laid to rest beside her husband in the family plot. A fine misty rain wet cheeks already running with tears, and the wind tore the tentative petals from the blossoming trees and flung them, bruised, on the dark earth. Her brothers, Edward and Richard, leaned together for support as they wept; Daisy gathered the sobbing children around her, children who so soon after losing their dear nurse had also lost their beloved aunt. Eleanor stood a little apart, her face unmoving; but Job, standing at her shoulder as always, knew of the pain inside, and as she swayed a little he let his hand touch the hand that hung by her side, and knew that she had felt his offer of comfort.

But saddest of all was the sight of the bewildered twelve-year-old boy who had lost the woman he had called Mother. Edmund hardly remembered Isabella at all; for the last eight years of his life, Helen had been his mother, the one to whom he went for praise or consolation, the one to whom he sang his songs and told of his adventures of the day. The other children might mourn Anys as their closest friend, but Edmund had had only one allegiance, only one person ever to call his own, and that was the woman they were laying now in the wet, black earth.

Life would never be the same for him. Daisy would

mother the two motherless children, and Eleanor had already arranged to promote Lys to the position of governess. Death was a part of life, and life went on, leaving the loved ones behind to pass into memory, but Edmund would never forget this day nor the loss it represented.

2

The country reverberated all year with the mad exploits of George, Duke of Clarence, so that even those who had thought they could no longer be surprised by anything he did were amazed by each new piece of folly. He was widely known to be a drunkard, and the more kindly disposed put down much of what he did and said to an excess of Malmsey wine; others thought he was wicked through and through and only wondered at the King's patience.

Eleanor believed the Duke was literally insane. "There is no sense to the things he does," she said. In April, for instance, he sent armed men to break into the house of a woman who had been a maid to Isabel Neville and drag her away. She was given a form of trial by Clarence's men, and then hanged for poisoning her mistress. In May he spread rumors that the King practiced black magic and poisoned anyone who disagreed with him. Also in May he started a rebellion in Cambridgeshire to put himself on the throne, and in June renewed his plot to marry Mary of Burgundy and take the throne by force of arms.

It was a surprise to no one when King Edward summoned his brother to appear before him, accused him of treasonable acts, and had him arrested and taken to the Tower. The only surprise was that it had taken him so long. The question remained, What was to be done with him? It seemed that he was incorrigible, and if let loose, he would only start his madcap scheming again. On the other hand, to hold him indefinitely in the Tower would not only provide malcontents with a focus but also cast a shadow over Edward's life.

In October, Richard of Gloucester rode to London for the first time in a year and a half to plead with Edward for Clarence's pardon.

"He simply cannot believe anything bad of his brother," Anne Neville told Eleanor when they met in York at the Hallows' Eve mass. "It doesn't matter how often George does something unforgivable, Richard goes on forgiving him. Look at the way he behaved over my mother's estates: they were willed half to me and half to Isabel, but he let George have them all without a murmur. He's too gentle, too forgiving. When I chide him, he simply says we shall all need forgiving one day—as if that were an answer."

"What do you think the King will do?" Eleanor asked.

"I don't know," Anne replied, shaking her head. "In one way, I hope he does forgive him again, because it would do something terrible to Richard if Edward did have George executed. But on the other hand—"

"We're none of us safe while he's free to make mischief," Eleanor finished for her.

Anne nodded. "And George wouldn't hesitate to have either Edward or Richard killed if it suited him. *He* hasn't any old-fashioned ideas like family love or loyalty—but it's no good telling Richard that."

Eleanor could see that, while she was worried, Anne Neville was really proud of her husband's integrity, and loved him all the more for it. "However, I have a feeling this time he won't get off. Madam the Queen hates him—she blames him for her father's death, you know—and now he's actually in the Tower she will do all she can to make sure he never leaves it."

"How much real influence does she have over the King?" Eleanor asked.

Anne shrugged. "He loves a quiet life, and she nags. Look how he virtually insulted Mary of Burgundy by offering her the Queen's brother to wed. That was only because the Queen urged it."

"She refused quickly enough," Eleanor observed.

"Even more quickly than she refused George. But it shows that the Queen *can* make him do what she wants. Richard's gone to plead for him, but the Queen hates him almost as much as she hates George, so I don't suppose he will have much effect, for all that Edward loves and trusts him." She shivered. "I hope it's all over soon, one way or another. I hate Richard to be away. I only feel safe when I have him here at home, in the north where people love us and don't do dreadful, inexplicable things. Oh, I know people here aren't perfect—they do bad things, too, but at least one can understand why they do them."

But Anne's wish was not fulfilled. Richard remained at Court all through the winter, was there at Christmas, and was still there in January 1478 when his nephew, the King's younger son, Richard, was married to the six-year-old heiress of the Duke of Norfolk. Richard pleaded for his brother's life; and in the other ear the Queen urged her husband to take his brother's life. Parliament met to hear the case, and Edward pronounced that he would forgive his brother if he submitted himself and asked for pardon; but Clarence refused to step down, and his presence became a threat to the safety of the realm. On the seventh of February, Clarence was found guilty and the sentence of death was passed upon him.

Even then, Edward hesitated. Richard's pleas redoubled—he could not, *could not,* kill his own brother. It looked as though mad George might get off at last. But the Queen sent word to the Speaker of the House, who presented himself to the Lords and requested that whatever was going to be done should be done at once; and on the eighteenth of February, Clarence was executed within the Tower.

Richard of Gloucester waited no longer. The Woodville Court left a bad taste in his mouth, and despite his unswerving love for his brother and his nephews and nieces, the death of George was a bitter blow to him, and marked his loving heart with a deep scar. He asked his leave of the King, and rode hard for the north.

He stopped one night at Morland Place, and spent the evening talking to Eleanor, pouring out his confusion and grief into her sympathetic ear.

"I shall never go back," he said. "Unless I am called there specifically, I shall never go to London again. I'll stay here in the north, at Middleham, and live quietly with Anne and Edward. Thank God I am not important enough to the throne to be needed there. I have my work to do here, and I do it well, I believe. Edward knows—he understands. He gave me Middleham because he understood the way it is with me. I believe, I believe if he could go back and choose again, he would not choose her. God knows she's been a good wife to him, borne his children; but she is a bad woman, and she has his ear. She makes him do things he'd rather not think about. I think it's more comfortable for both of us if we do not meet again very often."

After a long time, he had talked himself out and was quiet. He raised his clear gray eyes to Eleanor and said, "You are a good friend, to listen to me so quietly. I would rather say it all now, for it would hurt Anne so badly. Do you mind?"

"No, my lord, I don't mind. I am glad to be of service to you."

He rubbed his eyes wearily, and his mind jumped back to his dead brother. "We were brought up together, you know—he and I and Margaret. We never saw Edward and Edmund—they were at Ludlow. It was always George who decided what we should play. He led us into mischief and we followed him—even then he was always doing what he should not. I don't know why he was so wild. Our mother always disciplined us firmly, and our father, when he was home, was a strict and godly man. Of course, you knew him, didn't you? How could he have a son like George?"

Eleanor did not answer, knowing it was not required. It was only required that she should listen.

"Father entrusted us to Edward's care. He said, promise you will take care of them, and he did. He used to come and visit us in our lodgings. How could he kill his own brother?" His eyes filled with tears again.

"It was the drink that did it, you know—he drank and drank until his wits were addled. Poor George, he couldn't help it. It was wine that made him do such mad things. Wine was George's folly—all the rest followed from that. And it led him in the end to the block."

He rubbed his eyes and stared into the fire. "I left London as soon as I could. The talk was everywhere—it was as if the walls were whispering about how the House of York eats its own flesh. The Londoners have a joke about

George—they say he drank so much Malmsey wine, he finally drowned in it. An epitaph for a drunkard, eh? They've a sharp wit, the Londoners. Drowned in a butt of Malmsey, that's what they say of him. What an epitaph for a King's brother!"

BOOK THREE

THE WHITE BOAR

CHAPTER TWENTY-TWO

Corpus Christi. The city of York had been crowded since the day before yesterday, for people came from miles around to watch the pageant procession that began at dawn and went on, by torchlight, long after dusk. The villages near to the city would be like Pompeii while the celebrations were going on; while every lucky houseowner who lived along the pageant route would have hired out his front parlors, sometimes for as much as nine or ten shillings, to folk who wished to watch the pageant without being jostled in the street.

The Morlands were going to watch from Jenkyn Butt's house, which was conveniently situated on the Lendal, almost opposite St. Leonard's hospital. They had all come—Eleanor, Edward and Daisy, Ned, Margaret, Thom, Edmund, and little Paul, who was four years old. The servants, too, and all the retainers and tenants were in York for this, the favorite festival of the year. Only Richard was missing: he had left home over two years ago, walking out with nothing but the clothes he wore, saying that he was going to walk all over England and "speak to the people." Eleanor had not tried to dissuade him, but she had been desperately sorry to see him go. She had been glad, in a guilty sort of way, when he had come back from St. William's College with no desire to become a priest or monk, and had hoped he would settle down at Morland Place, marry and raise a family. She had borne thirteen children, and only one of them was left at home—it seemed hard.

Jenkyn and Eleanor were both, of course, members of the clothiers guild, and of the separate Corpus Christi guild of which the Duke and Duchess of Gloucester were eminent members, and they had contributed largely of time and money to the staging of the pageant; but Jenkyn had paid a separate and quite substantial fee to have the carts stop outside his house for a performance of their scenes from the Bible. This was because Cecily had just laid in of her second child, Alice—her first, Anne, was two, having been born only a few days after the execution of the Duke of Clarence—and she would not otherwise have had a chance of seeing the pageant.

There were to be fifty separate carts, drawn by horses and curtained to hide the nature of the scene until the moment they arrived at each station, each the responsibility of a guild and each performing some sacred story. They marshaled on Toft Green, by the Mickle Lith, and wound their way slowly through the streets all day, stopping at each "station"—marked out by a display of banners bearing the city's arms—to perform their scenes. As the actors refreshed themselves, between stations, liberally with the food and wine supplied by the Corpus Christi guild and the Mayor, the scenes, even the serious ones, grew merrier and merrier as the day advanced.

Preparation was taken seriously, starting in Lent when the city's best actors began auditioning the men of the different crafts to find the most skilled at acting and declaiming. The costumes and props, stored in a warehouse on Toft Green, had to be looked over, costumes repaired or replaced, gilding and paint retouched, new parts copied out and song-sheets replaced as they grew too thumbed to read. The Corpus Christi guild supervised all this, and fees were collected from all the rich people in the town, along with special penalty fees from anyone who worked at a craft whose guild did not perform on the day. With the rich costumes, the gold paint, the actors' fees, the refreshments, and so on, it was an expensive business to stage a pageant of fifty wagons.

The scenes were allotted to guilds with a kind of logic where possible: the shipwrights and mariners were performing Noah's Flood, with a gread deal of hilarity from the "animals," who wore huge, elaborate animal heads of wood covered with cloth or fur, and who made a point of being extremely difficult to drive into the ark. The fishmongers were portraying the sea of Galilee and Christ walking across the water to join the fishermen; the master vintners—of which Luke Cannyng's father was still a member—were performing the miracle at Cana, the turning of the water into wine, a scene at which there was inevitably much sampling but which, owing to the sobering presence of Our Lord as a character, grew more and more solemn as the day went on until the wedding looked more like a funeral. The goldsmiths—the richest of the guilds—always did the arrival of the Three Kings from the East, and dressed the kings so richly and splendidly that they rode on separate horses alongside the wagon between stages and were cheered almost like the real King himself.

The ordnancers did a very popular scene in which the devil popped out from a trap door in the floor of the wagon to tempt Christ in the desert, with firecrackers fizzing and banging all around him; the butchers did the Gadarene swine, a scene that always ended in a number of bruises and cuts as the swine allowed themselves to be driven without care for life or limb off the side of the cart; the tailors were performing Joseph's wonderful coat, and the coat itself was so magnificent it dazzled the eyes and so heavy that Joseph could hardly remain upright under it. Whatever was done, it was done to the limit of logic: Herod and Judas were so magnificently wicked that the audience sometimes got carried away and tried to climb up on the wagons to assault them; God and Abraham were so beautifully noble and dignified that it moved you to tears to watch them.

The clothiers were doing the casting out of the moneylenders this year, and, as with all the guilds, rehearsals had been going on since Lent. Any actor who forgot his lines was likely to be fined, even though there was a man paid to sit behind the curtains and prompt. The first stop on the route was at the house of one Master Wykeham, where the Duke and Duchess of Gloucester and their closest friends were watching, refreshed, as guests of the Mayor, with an array of dainty food and good wine that should easily last them until sunset. Here the actors generally put on their most earnest and sincere performance; the clothiers' scene was done with such energy that one of the moneylenders was flung right off the pageant wagon and lay like one dead for five minutes until he was revived with some good ale.

The second call was Jenkyn's House, which was so near to Wykeham's house that the children, by running down to the corner of the Lendal, could see both performances, which they did when their favorites came by. The crowds in the street were huge, but it was a festival of such good humor that no one worried about the children being out among them. In between wagons, the family talked and sang and laughed and made merry, and feasted. Jenkyn and provided two dozen loaves of fine white bread, five fat capons and five fat pikes, a pipe of wine, baskets of pippins and oranges, and boxes of sweetmeats and comfits and ginger.

Cecily had laid in only a week ago, and so had to stay in her chamber, but Daisy and Eleanor and Margaret spent much of the time with her, and everyone, including the proud father, paid her a visit. Margaret was wildly excited by the pageant, for she found life at Morland Place rather dull and longed for the greater excitements of city life, for a sight of rich people and perhaps even members of the Court. She often confided in her sister that she would love to live in London, where, she believed, every day brought some fresh view of the King and Queen and their sumptuous lives.

"I used to feel like you," Cecily said placidly. "I used to think there was nothing more to hope for in life, but now I've a husband and two children, I know better. I'm happy here with dear Thomas and Anne and Alice, and it's all I could ever want."

"It's all right for you," Margaret said restlessly. "You live in the city, with everything going on outside your own window. And besides, you've got your husband. I haven't got one yet, and how am I to meet the right people stuck away at Morland Place?"

"How do you think I met Thomas? Grandmother comes into the city often enough to pick out the right husband for you, never fear. Anyway, dear, you can always come and visit me here. You know I'd like to have you much more often than you do come."

"I know, but it's not the same," Margaret complained, and then her attention was arrested. "Oh, look! Who is that absolutely marvelous man? Look at the fur on his coat! Oh, he sees me! He's lifting his hat to me!" Margaret simpered and blushed and fluttered her fingers at the unseen passerby, while Cecily was scandalized.

"Margaret! Come away from that window at once! Behaving like a wanton, and from my window! What will people think? You'll get me a bad reputation. Come away, I say!"

"Oh, don't be such a spoilsport, Cecily," Margaret said, though she did leave the window, mainly because the man had passed out of sight. "You had fun before you were married, with H—"

"Hush! Don't dare mention it!" Cecily cried out, discomforted. "What can you be thinking of to say such a thing."

"Well, it was true, I saw you—"

"How can you be so cruel as to bring up my wickedness when it was all over so long ago and everyone's forgiven me?"

"I don't think it was wicked—I think it would be fun."

"I won't listen to such scandalous talk anymore. If you can't behave—" Cecily was almost in tears, and Margaret hastened to soothe her, for she didn't want a fuss, and the view was better from Cecily's window than the parlor.

"Oh, all right, Cecily, I'm sorry. There, don't cry. Shall I fetch up some comfits for us both? Or some fruit?"

"Yes, all right, do that."

"And you won't cry anymore? There's a dear, I won't be long." And pretty Margaret tripped away.

Downstairs, Eleanor and Jenkyn were talking over a cup of watered wine, while the rest of the family stood by the windows waiting for the next wagon and discussing the ones that had gone before.

"—nine children," Jenkyn was saying, "and four girls and two boys surviving. You can't say she hasn't done her duty."

"I don't," said Eleanor, "but at what cost?"

Edward, by the window, overhearing, called out, "Never mind Mother, sir, she has a natural dislike of all Queens. I remember how she used to revile the last one!"

"Hush, saucy boy," Eleanor said, and turned back to Jenkyn. "You know the cost as well as I do—that family of hers; and coming between the King and his brothers; and she is nobody really, for all that she parades her mother's ancestry. As if anyone could be proud of being French; her uncle, Jacques—"

"Lord Jakes, the Londoners called him," Jenkyn remembered with a smile; "Jakes" was London slang for "privy." "The Londoners have no reverence for anyone. But she has done a lot for the Court, you know. In the late King's time it was a disgrace to the country. Foreign ambassadors used to carry such tales away with them. But you should hear what Henry says now—it is one of the most magnificent and cultured in the world, for all that the King is very firm about economy."

"That is her low breeding, trying to cover up for itself," Eleanor said obdurately, but her interest was diverted. "Does Henry go to Court, then?"

"Quite often," Jenkyn said proudly. "He provides cloth to many of the eminent people there, including the Queen. She does use such a lot that it is very good business to be friendly with the Queen, and as my factor—"

"He is doing well?" Eleanor asked. She did not want to hear too much more about Elizabeth Woodville. "You are pleased that you sent him to London?"

"Very well. He has five sub-factors under him, and some of those have sub-factors under them, too. He deals with the greatest of our customers and is received everywhere most flatteringly. He dines out, I believe, most evenings of the week and receives gifts from most of the notable people in London."

"Well, that must be gratifying for you," Eleanor said, and at that moment, as if by design, Margaret came in for the sweetmeats for Cecily and herself.

"How pretty that maid has grown," Jenkyn said softly.

"Yes, we are very proud of her," Eleanor said. "She is as pretty as her mother was at the same age."

"At her age? Yes—you must be thinking now of a match for her," Jenkyn said innocently. Eleanor did not answer, knowing how his mind was running. "I believe we once discussed the possibility of a match between her and my Henry."

"Did we?" Eleanor said vaguely. "Well, that was a long time ago. The maid was too young."

"She is not too young now."

"But I am loath to let her go. There is no hurry. She will not lack for a husband if she stays at home a while longer." The truth was that Eleanor already had a match in mind for Margaret in one of the gentlemen at Middleham, but she did not want to tell Jenkyn that. She did not want to offend him, for the alliance between the two families was fruitful, and besides, she liked Jenkyn and got on well with him. So she evaded the issue: time enough to tell him of the match when it was a match. Henry was a tempting proposition, but not as tempting as a gentleman from the household of the Duke of Gloucester.

"The tie between our families has proved so successful," Jenkyn tried next, "that I would not be unwilling to create further ties." He allowed a hint of wounded feelings to color his voice.

Eleanor flashed him a brilliant smile, a smile that could still make a man feel shy and call up a memory of her former beauty. "Nor I, Jenkyn," she said pleasantly. "Nor I, indeed. Ah, look, the next wagon is approaching—let us go and watch. Come, now, children, make a place for us!"

Everyone pressed forward to the windows, of which there were fortunately enough for everyone to get a view. Thomas Butts lifted up his small daughter, Anne, and set her on his shoulder to watch, and then, seeing that Paul on tiptoe could only just see over the windowsill, he lifted him up, too, and set him on the other shoulder. The two children looked at each other across Thomas's head and exchanged a shy smile, and it gave Eleanor an idea.

When the wagon had moved on Eleanor and Jenkyn returned to their more comfortable places. Paul and Anne, being set down by Thomas, wandered over to a corner where Anne had a toy horse and began playing quietly together, shyly at first, but soon chattering freely to each other. Two-year-old Anne was a very forward child, and so four-year-old Paul did not find it too much beneath his dignity to play with her.

"I have been thinking," Eleanor said, "about what you said concerning closer ties between our families."

"You have?" Jenkyn said eagerly. "You mean—mistress Margaret—"

"No, not that. I have been observing a tie that seems to be making itself." And she looked pointedly in the direction of the two children playing in the corner. Jenkyn followed the direction of her eyes, and his face lit with comprehension. It lit also with pleasure, for this was a match far better than between Henry and Margaret, two younger children of not very much importance. If Cecily and Thomas had no son—which was always likely, for she had borne only two live chilren in four years of marriage, and both were girls (girls always survived more easily than boys)—little Anne would be the heiress to all Jenkyn's estates. Paul Morland, eldest son of the eldest son of the eldest son of Eleanor, was undisputed eventual heir to the Morland fortune. If these two children were to wed, it would weld the two estates indissolubly together.

The suggestion was, moreoever, a great compliment to Jenkyn. The social position of the Morland family was far higher than that of the Butts family, and Paul Morland's marriage was a matter of much more importance, therefore, than that of Anne Butts, even if she did turn out to be the heiress. Paul Morland would one day be a very important person, and for Eleanor to suggest that he should reach that position already betrothed to Anne Butts was an honor for Jenkyn he had not looked for; and also convinced him that Eleanor's reason for not wishing a match between Margaret and Henry was really that she wanted Margaret at home for another year.

What he did not know, of course, was that Eleanor found the prospect of the distant mating between the two children much less daunting than the imminent one between Margaret and Henry. She was also quite capable of dissolving a betrothal between Paul and Anne if and when it suited her. A betrothal was, in the eyes of the church, as binding as marriage, and could not be broken; but if you were rich enough or powerful enough, you could disregard it and quieten any uneasy consciences with gold, or buy a papal dispensation for any further match. Kings did habitually break contracts of child betrothals; so did Eleanor.

The children continued to play together happily, unaware of the machinations that were going on around them. Eleanor and Jenkyn did some hard talking, and before the day was out agreed on a betrothal, to be carried out as soon as the Corpus Christi celebrations were over.

"And the marriage to take place as soon as Anne comes to a woman's years?" Jenkyn asked hopefully. That would be when she was twelve.

"Not until she is fourteen," Eleanor said firmly. "I do not agree with maids being married until they are fourteen."

Jenkyn agreed to this, and Eleanor was content. The marriage could not take place for twelve years, and anything could happen in twelve years.

The following day was the more serious part of the celebrations—the day given over to the procession of the Corpus Christi guild. The procession formed at the church of the Holy Trinity—the one by the Mickle Lith at which the Morlands had got married and buried since Eleanor came to York—and walked from there through the city to the Minster. It was a solemn, spectacular, and dignified procession. First went the cross-bearer and the choir singing the processional hymn, followed by the representatives of the trade guilds, each trade displaying its banners and symbols, with the company of clothiers by tradition walking last of them. Here Edward had his place, a fine, tall figure in his padded and fur-trimmed long gown, a great bonnet with a jeweled brooch, and a two-inch-broad gold chain across his chest.

Walking behind the trade guilds came the religious guilds, such as the guild of St. Catherine and the guild of the Holy Name, and with them walked a representative

selection of the folk their work supported, old people and
orphans and cripples.

Then came the central part of the procession, headed by
the Corpus Christi guild itself, with its cross and standard,
and the most notable members walked behind the cross to
represent it. The Duke and Duchess of Gloucester walked
here in solemn dignity, as did many eminent people of the
town. Eleanor had her place, magnificently dressed and
erect and proud, as if her years were half what they really
were. Jenkyn Butts had a place here, too, though somewhat
further back than Eleanor.

The Corpus Christi guild acted as escort to the central
and sacred part of the procession, where, under a golden
canopy carried by four priests, a litter was borne past bearing the shrine of silver encrusted with gems that housed a
beryl vase containing the Sacred Elements. Behind this
came the second choir contingent, the prelates and eccle-
siastics, and behind them the chief officers of the city and
other notable citizens. Brilliant with banners, dazzling with
torches and tapers and crosses, glittering with rich clothing
and adornment, the procession moved slowly through the
packed streets, singing the hymns of praise. The spectators
knew the hymns as well as the choristers, and joined in
with a will, the music lifting their hearts in praise and joy
for the Father who made them and brought them safely to
this glorious June day.

The route of the procession was strewn with rushes; every house along the route was decorated with arras tapestries, hung out of the window and nailed to the front beams,
and every doorway was wreathed with greenery and loops
of plaited flowers. At the street corners the city's banners
had been erected, and their posts were decorated with
vines and ivies, and over the heads of the people the blue
sky seemed to rock with the clamor of bells—every church
bell in the city was rung without pause, giving tongue like
brazen hounds as the procession wound its way towards
the Minster.

There high mass was sung, and afterward some renowned preacher gave a sermon. After the members of the
procession were inside, the general public could crowd in

and try to get a place, and there were always so many people in the city that day that the last comers could only stand outside the great doors, unable even to see the glimmer of the candles on the altar, and having to imagine the words of the sermon, but able after all to kneel and stand with the rest, and to sing with the rest when the time came.

In the evening, various supperfeasts were held, the chief among which was the Lord Mayor's, at which Richard of Gloucester and Anne Neville were guests. It was to this feast that Eleanor went, while Edward and Daisy and Jenkyn Butts went to the feast given by the company of clothiers, which was the second richest of the guilds, next to the goldsmiths. There was always a good deal of rivalry between these two guilds as to who should give the best feast, and so food and wine and entertainment of the best were always to be had at both, and an invitation to one was the security of a good evening.

The Mayor's feast was a little more reserved and dignified, though the provisions were in no way inferior. Richard and Anne were personally very popular, and it was traditional that they should move around during the feast and talk to as many people as possible, rather than sitting still on the dais to be looked at. Eleanor watched them while she waited for her turn to come, and noticed, with affection, how many people they seemed to know by name, and what small matters were brought to their attention for praise or for remedy: small on a national scale, that is to say, not small to the person involved. But no matter was too small for my lord of Gloucester's personal attention— that was one of the reasons he was so loved. His brother Edward had the same facility: it was said of the King that he knew all the main people in every city and town in the country, and many of the smaller people, too.

Lord Richard came to Eleanor as to a personal friend and he gave a wry little smile, saying, "Now, Mistress Eleanor, what problems have *you* for me to solve?"

"No problems, your Grace," she smiled back, "and no questions either, other than to know how you and your lady are, and little Edward—the Earl of Salisbury, I should say."

"Edward is good enough," he said. "We are old friends,

are we not. Well, Anne and I and the children are happy and healthy, though Anne is thinner than I would like to see her—but then she was always thin." They both looked to where his Duchess was talking to another friend a few paces away. She was thin, it was true, but she had a healthy glow in her face and her eyes were bright and clear.

"She looks well," Eleanor said.

"God be thanked. We are to go to London as soon as the celebrations are over, did you know? My sister Margaret is coming for a visit. It will be good to see her again."

"I'm sure it will," Eleanor said. "When was the last time, your Grace? I suppose it must have been in France?"

Richard made a wry face at the thought of that campaign. "Yes, that's right. In 1475 at St. Omer."

"And is it a family visit this time?"

"I suspect not. I suspect the matter is marriage—Maximilian's son to one of my nieces—but we shall see when the time comes." Mary of Burgundy had married Prince Maximilian of Germany, and it was to him Richard was referring. "But enough of that—what of you, Mistress Eleanor? How are your affairs going? Can I be of service to you?"

Eleanor looked at him doubtfully. She knew from experience that when he asked if he could be of service, he meant it literally, and there was something she wanted. On the other hand, it seemed hard to be bringing up business at such a time. She hesitated.

"Ah, I see there is something," Richard said shrewdly. "Come then, out with it."

"I hesitate to mention it at such a time—" Eleanor said.

"Come, mention it—everyone else does," Lord Richard said. And then, seeing she thought he was angry, added gently, "You had better speak now, for I leave at once for London to stay until the autumn, and then I doubt not but we shall have a campaign against the Scots, so you may not see me again until next year."

"Well, sir, in that case—it is about my grandson Thom—the best of the boys, I believe, counting my sons and my grandsons. I had hoped that you might find a place for him in your household."

"But of course, my dear Eleanor, I am glad to do so! The north needs hardy young men, and I am glad, truly glad, to have a hand in training them. I know we shall not quarrel about his board and allowances, so shall we agree that it is settled? He shall come to me when I return from London."

Eleanor agreed, hastily and gratefully, but there was no time then even to express her gratitude fully, for there were others who had to be spoken to, and Richard must move on. But Eleanor knew he was a man of his word, and that Thom, who had been fifteen at the beginning of that month, was settled for the next few years. It was the best training he could get for whatever life would send him.

2

The letter was a long one.

> *I promised you, Grandmother, that I would be a good correspondent, and perhaps my zeal may even wear out your interest.*

There was little hope of that, Eleanor thought. Even the smallest detail of Thom's life at Middleham Castle was of the greatest possible interest to her, but paper was costly, and her appetite was likely to exceed Thom's budget.

> *As to the castle, it stands on a steep slope above the village, looking down on the little river and backed by the high moors. It is gray, massive, and ancient. They say it is the largest keep in England, and has been here three hundred years, and within its walls there is a village more complete than the one below on the green slope.*

> *It is harsher land than we know around York: our moors are soft parklands to the moors here in Wensleydale; and such people as we meet from hereabouts are harsh, too, though I believe they are godly, earnest, and very loyal. However we do not have much to do with them: the steward, chaplain, and governor are the men who rule our lives here.*

> *There are several other boys with me, to be trained,*

as I shall be trained. They are from noble families and mostly younger than myself, but no one makes any difference between us, and we are all as likely to be beaten for our sins. My lord and my lady are very devout, and so we are, too. Their son, whom we call my lord Earl, is a merry lad of seven and very quick at his lessons; his cousin Edward, my lord Warwick is less so; but both study and work with us in the same way.

We rise at five in the morning and go to mass—in summer I am told we rise at four or dawn if it is earlier—and then break our fast in the great hall on bread, meat and ale, along with all the officers, grooms, ushers, esquires, clerks, and servants of the household. Then we go to our studies under Master Governor. Thanks to the good teaching of Master Jenney, I am well up in my studies of French, Latin, Law, Mathematics and Astronomy. Thanks to you, Grandmother, I excel my companions in music, singing, and dancing. But a good deal of our time is devoted to the courtly arts, in which I am, at least, no worse than the others—in declaiming, penmanship, knightly conduct, etiquette, courtesy, and codes of war. These things we must know if we are to live at court, which most of the boys expect to do, or serve as an esquire to my lord or the King.

We dine at ten, or at nine thirty in summer, in the great hall, and my lord and lady preside, so there is no talking allowed until the nap is drawn. Then in the afternoon we put on our armor and ride out into the fields to learn the martial arts. My good bay, Barbary, is the best horse of any of ours, and I am proud of him and love to tell the others that you trained him and fed him from your hand, and he helps me greatly to "ride cleanly" in my harness, for his paces are so good.

We have to learn to fight on horseback and to joust, but also to fight on foot and handle the sword, dagger, and battle-ax. The mock tournaments are fought hard, and many of the lads smaller than I have scars from them. No doubt I shall get mine soon. The times I like best are when we go hunting or hawking, for here I can show what I know, and justify my years of seniority. The hunting is good here, though sometimes I am tried by the necessity of following etiquette when I would wish to be pursuing the prey my own way.

At four we go in for supper, very weary and aching, as you can imagine, and then we sing and play the harp and dance and play games until nine, when we retire to our dormitory to sleep. Through all my days, I keep thinking of my lord living here as a boy and doing the same things that I do, making the same mistakes, perhaps, and feeling the same triumphs—and the same aches. You know, Grandmother, how slight my lord is, but when you see him in his shirt, which we do when it is our turn to wake him in the morning, you can see that his shoulders and arms, particularly his sword arm, are massive with muscle, which he got doing these very exercises which make me ache so each day!

The greatest honor is to be chosen to go with my lord on border-raiding parties against the Scots. The Scots are very unpopular hereabouts, and to call another person a Scot in anger is an offense punishable by law by a large fine! My lord is known affectionately as "The Reever," which is a name given to those lawless folk who live on the border and get their livelihood plundering farms. Next year, we are told, there will be war proper against the Scots, and then we will all have the chance to show our prowess in arms. I am determined to be good enough by then.

I have no more paper, so pray, Grandmother, give my humblest duty to my Father and Mother and tell them I am living as good and godly a life as can be got by the exercise of my Will over my Nature! Nor have I contracted any secret marriages yet. And my fondest love to you, Grandmother, and be sure I think of you daily. Your affectionate Grandson, Thomas Morland.

The light was almost gone by the time Eleanor had finished reading the letter. She put it down in her lap and leaned back against the paneling—she was sitting in the window-

seat of the solar window to get the last light—and avoided
the curious eyes that rested on her as the rest of the famly
waited to hear what Thom had got to say. She knew that
Daisy was peeved that Thom should write to her rather
than to his own mother; she would have to read the letter
out eventually; but for the moment, let 'em wait. She
wanted a moment or two with her own thoughts, while her
head was full of the images Thom's letter had conjured up.

To avoid the fixed gazes she closed her eyes, feeling the
cool air from the windowpanes on her cheek. Much of the
life Thom described was familiar to her, for she had lived
in a castle in her girlhood—Corfe Castle, with Belle and
Lord Edmund—and had witnessed the training of young
sprigs of nobility alongside the children of the family. Suddenly her mind took her back to that summer day, long
ago, when she sat in the window-seat with her fine-work
and dreamed of the man she wanted so much to marry;
that summer day when her life had changed abruptly and
forever, in the soft, green lands of the south that she had
never seen again. . . .

She must have dozed off for a moment, for she came to
her senses abruptly, with the knowledge that there was
some kind of disturbance in the house, though, befuddled
for a moment, she could not determine what it was. Then
she realized that the door of the solar had opened and Job
had come in at perilously near a run, moving as fast as his
stiff limbs would allow, and obviously greatly disturbed.

"Madam," he cried, "Mistress Eleanor!"

Eleanor struggled to full attention, but before Job could
say anything else he had been followed into the room by a
stranger. A tall, gangling man, it was, with barley-pale hair
and beard; a great bushy beard, and hair that had last been
trimmed, it seemed, with a knife; a dusty, travel-stained
stranger in a long gown of coarse brown wool and feet bare
in monkish sandals, despite the chill of the season.

There was a moment of stunned silence as everyone
wondered who the stranger was and how he dared march
into the family's private quarters in that way. And then he
spread his hands, and his teeth showed white in his beard
in a great grin, and he said to Eleanor simply, "Mother!"

Eleanor was across the room in a second and her arms

were around the man tightly, despite his dirty clothes. "Rich-ard," she cried. "Oh, Dickon, you came back!"

"But of course I did, Mother. You should have known I would, sooner or later."

"Oh, my son, come in, come in. Tell us what you've been doing all this long time."

Now everyone was crowding around him, eager to greet him after his two-and-a-half-year absence, and to make him welcome. Only Job stood back a little and tried to catch Eleanor's attention. When he finally managed it, she saw the doubt on his face and asked apprehensively, "What's the matter, Job? What is it?"

"Madam—" he said helplessly, with a small gesture to-ward the door.

Richard laughed and swung around. "It's all right, Mother. Job's just reminding me that I didn't come home alone. I've brought someone to meet you—my wife."

"Your wife?" Astonishment in every face.

"Yes, I married her last Eastertide in her own country. She comes from a long way away, north of the border, so far away that they do not speak English there at all. But I have taught her a little English since we have been on the road. Come in, Constance!"

And in the doorway, between the still-anxious Job and the genial, beaming Richard, appeared a small, slight girl, dressed in an outlandish woolen plaid, one end of which was drawn over her head. The garb reached only just past her knees, and her legs and feet were quite bare; her hair was dark and a tangle of curls, her dark eyes peered at them shyly like a wild animal's from under its matted thatch.

"My wife, Mother, everybody—Constance."

So that was why Job was so unsure. She was nothing but a barefoot gypsy. And she was very evidently pregnant.

CHAPTER TWENTY-THREE

The stir caused by the arrival of Richard and his wife did not soon die down, though at first everyone was too stunned and surprised to make much comment. Eleanor, however, took the first opportunity to speak to Richard alone and question him of the circumstances of his marriage, and the nature of his bride.

"Constance isn't her real name, of course," Richard said airily. They were taking advantage of a mild morning to walk in the herb garden. "You couldn't pronounce her real name, but translated into English it means something like constancy, so I chose to call her Constance. She doesn't mind very much."

"But who *is* she, Richard? Where did you find her? Who are her parents?" Eleanor asked, keeping patience with an effort.

"She is Constance Rhuaid. I found her on the northwest coast of Scotland. And her father is a tribal chieftain," Richard answered, not without an inner amusement. "Does that satisfy you?"

"Of course it doesn't," Eleanor said crossly.

"Of course it doesn't, Mother. You are the guardian of our dynasty, and very properly anxious that we shouldn't sully ourselves with inferior blood. Like Scots blood."

Eleanor found herself remembering that line from Thom's letter, saying that to call someone a Scot was an insult punishable by law. "But how could you do it, Dickon? A gypsy, a barefoot gypsy!"

"*How* could I do it? Very easily, as it happened. I found their village in need of some simple medical aid, which I provided. I was invited to stay with the chieftain indefinitely. During the course of my stay, I was very much taken by Constance, who is the chief's youngest daughter, and he, in gratitude, proposed I marry her. Which I did, by their own rites."

"By their rites? Not in a church?"

"Certainly by their rites—very curious ones they were, too," Richard mused.

"Thank God!" Eleanor said, clasping her hands together in relief. "Then the marriage isn't lawful, and can be disregarded. Her people won't object, even if they ever find out. We can find a safe place for her somewhere, I dare say, with some light work to keep her occupied—"

"Mother!" Richard stopped her in mid-flow, not angrily, but firmly. "She is my wife and is expecting my baby. She is not a servant, a mistake, or a doxy. She is my wife."

"Nonsense, Richard," Eleanor said briskly. "No one could possibly hold you to it. If you weren't married by a priest, the marriage isn't lawful. Where's the contract? What's her dowry and her portion? You see—"

"Make your mind up to it, Mother, she's my wife. Her dowry was her fortnight spirit, her portion was a share of my bread and my lot. She came with me without hesitation, to walk with me through the land and meet God's people and talk to them about their lives and their thoughts. She's a wild, sweet, fiery thing, with a tongue of pure flame and a heart as innocent as a roe-deer's. I thought you would be honored to meet her, would learn something of her. I hope I was not mistaken in you."

"Honored, to meet a penniless peasant girl, a Scot into the bargain?" Eleanor said indignantly. "You insult me, and you insult this house to bring her here pretending she's your wife. She can't live here, except as a servant, and that's for sure."

"Oh, we aren't going to live here," Richard said calmly. "As soon as the baby's born, we'll be off again."

"Oh, Dickon, don't speak hastily—I'm sorry if I offended you. Perhaps we can think of some way round the problem. There's no need for you to go. Don't be hasty, child, I beg you."

"Mother," Richard said with a smile, "it isn't anything to do with you. I never intended to stay—I only came to visit you all, and to find shelter for Constance to have the child. I always meant to go on again afterward."

"But, Dickon, why? You've been wandering for long enough, surely. Can't you settle down here now? There's plenty for you to do—and I dare say we can get used to the girl in time. She must learn our ways, and you must marry again properly, but after that—"

"No, Mother. I'm sorry if it upsets you, but that isn't my life, it isn't my way. I don't want to be a country gentleman, or a clothier, or a merchant."

"Then what do you want to be? You once said you thought God had called you for special work. Don't you think that now?"

"I do, He has called me. That is why I have to go on walking, meeting people, asking questions, listening to the answers. I don't know yet what God wants me for, but I know that this is what I have to do in the meantime. I have to learn something before I can be of use. I have to learn what people are, and what they want, and what they fear, and what they are capable of."

It was outlandish, it was unchristian, it was not right. These were not the thoughts of a true son of the Church; a true son lived a normal, godly life according to the dictates of the Catholic religion, heard mass daily, read the Bible, and did what the priests told him. He did not tramp the country barefoot in the company of a Scottish tribeswoman. Even the wandering friars heard mass and taught from the Bible. But how could Eleanor say all this to Richard. She looked sideways at him, with his great bushy beard and strange light eyes, and wondered if he was mad.

"I don't understand," she said at last.

Richard stooped and kissed her broad white forehead. "Mother, that's the first honest thing you've said—I honor you! I don't understand either—none of us do. That's why we have to ask questions, and seek, and wait. And that's why I can't stay here."

Eleanor's lip trembled, and she allowed it to show. "You will leave me, then, though I only have Edward left after you? It is hard to be a mother—"

"Mother, don't try to look weak and helpless. You are the strongest, fiercest, most indomitable woman I have ever met in the length and breadth of this island. It wouldn't surprise me at all if you turned out to be immortal! Now, let us enjoy the time we have together. And give me your word that you will be nice to your new daughter-in-law while you have the chance."

Eleanor shuddered at hearing that creature called "daughter-in-law," but she said, "Well, I'll do my best. But she must try to learn our ways while she's here. I can't disrupt the whole household for one new member."

"She'll learn—she's young enough and flexible enough. She's not yet fourteen, you know."

"Merciful God," said Eleanor mildly.

Constance's baby arrived a week after they came to Morland Place, and took everyone by surprise, since she didn't seem to be able to give any idea of when to expect it. After a short and apparently easy labor she gave birth to a small baby boy, dark-haired, dark-eyed, and dusky-skinned—"Like a monkey," Daisy commented disgustedly.

Constance scandalized everyone by appearing downstairs only a few hours after the birth, and would not seem to understand that she was supposed to keep to her chamber for a week, and then be churched before she could join normal company again. It was also positively indecent how little she made of the process of giving birth, appearing to expect to behave quite normally as soon as the baby was breathing.

"Just like an animal," Daisy said. "You can imagine her dropping it in the field while she works, like a sheep. It's unnatural."

Richard was as pleased and proud with Constance's behavior as with the child. He thought it a "bonny thing" and decided, despite all opposition, to call it Elijah.

"Elijah Morland," Eleanor sighed unhappily. "It isn't likely." But she had given up protesting, and now, despite her love for her last-born child, was only anxious for them to be gone so that life could resume the normal tenor of its ways.

The only person who really liked Constance was Ned, who took a great interest in her and spent long hours talking to her in the evenings.

"She's really interesting, you know," he tried to tell his parents. "She doesn't speak English very well, but she manages most intelligently with the little she knows. And she's such a lot to talk about. She's been telling me all about her ancestors and the battles they fought against other tribes. They've got some marvelous stories about ancient times and the great heroes of antiquity."

"Yes, we've seen you talking to her, hour after hour," Daisy said, crossly. "You might remember she's a foreigner and someone else's wife, and treat her with a little more distance. You're setting a bad example to Margaret."

"Oh, don't worry, Margaret hates her, she'd rather die than talk to her."

Then Ned discovered she could ride, and was forever neglecting his duties to take her out on to the moors.

"She pines for the open air," he explained to his irate parents. "She hates being cooped up in the house."

"Then let Richard take her," they said. "You have work to do; and it isn't right that you should be seen riding alone with her. Besides, she rides without a saddle, which isn't decent, and with her legs bare like a trollop."

"She can't ride with a saddle—she doesn't know how. She rides so well, she can handle any horse, however difficult. She'd be wonderful at breaking them in, you know."

His enthusiasm knew no bounds, and Richard, when appealed to to stop the riding escapades, only laughed and said it saved him from getting on a horse, which was an exercise he could do without, having got used to traveling on his own two legs and not wishing for more legs than God gave him. Daisy and Edward could only look forward to the time when they would leave, and thank God privately that the visit was to be only a visit and not a permanency.

The unseasonably mild weather broke just before Christmas, and Eleanor thought that they would stay until the spring. She was getting used to Constance now, and managed to be thankful at least that she and Ned were riding out every day and bringing back fresh game to supplement the diet of salt meat and stored vegetables, which always grew monotonous in January and February. But at the end of January, despite thick snow on the ground and a freezing wind, Richard and Constance departed from Morland Place on foot, as they had come, with their six-week-old baby, Elijah.

They took with them nothing but a little bread and salt-fish to last them a couple of days on their journey, and a length of coarse woolen cloth to wrap around themselves at night. During the day, Richard wore it around his shoulders. No one tried to stop them going, but there was a sadness all the same as the family gathered at the door to watch them set out, making small dark tracks through the great expanse of snow.

"Such a strange thing," Daisy said, turning to go in. "Well, it's a good job they've gone, really. She'd have disrupted the household terribly, and I daren't think what influence they'd have had on the children." She sounded as if she were trying to convince herself.

Eleanor remained a moment longer staring out into the white wilderness, her eyes distant as if she were trying to understand something, or hear something beyond her reach. Then she sighed and turned also.

"We shall never see them again," she said.

2

In the autumn of 1482 Eleanor and Jenkyn Butts agreed to terms for a marriage between Margaret and Henry, who were by then eighteen and twenty-one respectively. It was an advanced age for them to be still single, especially when their marriage to each other had first been mooted six years ago; but Eleanor had been trying for higher matches for Margaret, and Jenkyn was content to have Henry unmarried, and working for him in London, always expecting that in the end Eleanor would agree to the match.

In December, Henry rode from London to spend Christ-

mas at Morland Place and to celebrate his marriage. It was
the first time he had been home since he had been sent to
London to keep him out of Cecily's way, and there were a
number of curiosities seething before his arrival. He rode in
two days after St. Nicholas's day on a fine horse, accompanied by a manservant, and dressed so richly and fashionably that even Eleanor was, unwillingly, impressed.

"Perhaps the match is a little more even than I expected," she murmured to Edward.

Edward, who considered himself the arbiter of fashion in
Morland Place, felt his nose was about to be put out of
joint. "He has more colors on him than a popinjay," he
muttered ungraciously.

Henry's manners, however, were so pleasant and courteous and charming that he won all the family's hearts to
him within a very short time. Margaret thought him the
handsomest and finest gentleman she had ever seen, and
positively preened herself over her good fortune. He was
especially charming to her, as behooved him; he was secretly relieved that she turned out to be as pretty as she
was, for he had secretly wondered if she had remained unmarried because she was in some way unmarriageable.

There was some tension when Thomas and Cecily rode
over for Christmas, with four-year-old Anne and two-year-
old Alice, more than one person wondering what would
happen when the ex-lovers met. Thomas and Henry
greeted each other with unreserved pleasure, Henry and
Cecily with a cool touch of the hand and a formal kiss.
They regarded each other for a moment with curiosity, and
then moved apart. There was nothing there between them.
Henry wondered how he could ever have been bewitched
by this plain, contented housewife, who looked so much
like her mother, even to becoming stout with childbirth.
Margaret was much, much prettier, and more vivacious.
Cecily thought Henry unnecessarily brightly dressed, probably a popinjay in character as well as in looks, unreliable,
and nothing like the man her dear husband Thomas was.
So the moment passed in the most satisfactory way. Their
former love was dead, and could be buried and forgotten.

Henry was full of talk, about his work, of how successful
he had been, about London, about the Court.

"Tell us about the King," Margaret demanded like an eager child. "Is he really handsome?"

"Oh, yes," Henry said airly. "At least, he was once, and he can still charm you and make you forget that he is overweight and overtired and well past his youth. He works tremendously hard, still, and then stays up all night drinking and wenching into the bargain, though he's been ill a lot recently, and things have been a little quieter."

"What does the Queen think when he goes wenching?" Margaret asked daringly, avoiding her mother's eyes.

Henry smiled, showing his white teeth. "Oh, she doesn't mind. She introduced him to most of them. It's being Queen that she likes, not being the King's wife."

"Is she beautiful?"

"Like a snow maiden," Henry said. "Beautiful and white and cold. Her hair is as bright as gold and her eye as frosty and sharp as an icicle. No one ever crosses her, not even the King, and she keeps as much state as an empress."

"Her family are much in evidence, I suppose?" Edward asked, hoping to turn the conversation to less scandalous lines.

"They are everywhere. It's called the Woodville Court, even by the foreign ambassadors. But her nose has been put out of joint recently," he chuckled. "The King's brother has been paying a visit, and he is guest of honor while London rings with his praises over his conduct of the Scots war. No one can say enough in praise of Gloucester, and the Queen has to grit her teeth and bear it. She hates him worse than the ague, though I'm sure no one knows why."

"Evil always hates good," Eleanor said quietly. "It sees it as a threat."

Henry shrugged. "That may be so—I can't say. But the King is delighted to have his brother at Court, and spends most of every day with him, talking over old times and making plans for the future. And the Queen grinds her teeth and stamps about her apartments like a caged ferret, and sends her spies to try and find out what the royal brothers are saying to each other!"

The young people laughed, though the older ones looked grave.

"Has my lord of Gloucester brought a large train with him?" Eleanor asked.

Henry turned his winning smile on her. "I know why you are asking that, and I had meant to tell you at once that your grandson is among those attending my lord of Gloucester. We did meet once, shortly after their arrival in London, and I would have asked him to dine with me but there was no time before I left for York. But you will be glad to know he is well and sends you all his duty and love. He did very well, I understand, in the war, and is highly thought of by my lord, though he is too modest to do much more than hint at it. He showed me his wound, though, got in battle; a very impressive scar it will make, too. The length of the forearm."

"Thank God he is well and safe," Eleanor said. "The wound is healing?"

"Oh, perfectly, I assure you. He seems a young man of lively temper, and is valued by his master to cheer him when his mood is dark, which I believe happens often. My lord of Gloucester may be a very worthy man, but he is not one to enjoy the gaiety of the Woodville Court."

"Gaiety with virtue he could enjoy," Eleanor began sternly, "But—"

"I'm sure you're right," Henry interrupted smoothly. "But really there is a great deal to be got out of the Court, if you can pick your way between the factions. Men of true learning, men of wit, men of genius; a love of beauty, of art, of knowledge. The Queen may be a cold tyrant, but it is her influence that has made our Court the envy of Europe."

He had Eleanor in a cleft stick here, for she naturally wanted to acknowledge that the English Court was the best in the world, while she did not want to allow any credit to the Woodville woman.

While she was struggling with herself Henry went on, "By the way, I have some more news for you—this time about your son."

"My son?" Eleanor said.

"Richard?" Edward asked quickly.

"No, no, your son, John. It is just a rumor, and may fall

short as well as long, but I did hear from a reliable source that he is contemplating marriage again." Eleanor's expression was stern. "I understand that his first marriage did not quite meet with his family's approval, but this time his choice has settled on a Devonshire woman, a widow of substantial means."

"Her name, sir, do you know her name?"

"No more of her at all than I have told you, I'm afraid. It is merely a rumor, as I have said."

"She might perhaps be known to my daughter Anne," Eleanor explained. "If I knew her name, I might write to Anne and ask her. Perhaps I will write anyway—John may perhaps have communicated with her. If this woman is respectable and rich, we can forgive him for his first mistake."

Henry thought it very likely John Morland did not want forgiveness, but he kept his thoughts to himself.

"I hope at any rate to have made myself acceptable to you with this news of your family," he said.

"I should have preferred news of Richard to news of John," Eleanor said, and then recalled her manners. "But we are most truly grateful to you, and when you next see Thom I beg you will give him our love, and tell him we hope his master will spare him soon for a visit home."

"I can tell him so myself, Grandmother," Margaret said, smiling blushingly at Henry.

By Our Lady, Henry thought, she is prettier than any other woman at Court. With new, fashionable clothes she will do very well. I shall be much envied.

And had Margaret been able to hear his thoughts, she would have been as well pleased with Henry.

The wedding was celebrated on the second of January, and Margaret dressed in crimson velvet with deep borders and sleeves of white fur looked as pretty as any winter bride could. Henry gave her a white dog, a tiny thing with long silky fur and a pushed-in face, which was said to have come all the way from China; and a magnificent necklace of rubies and pearls. Cecily felt the smallest stirrings of envy, for though her husband was the elder of the sons and would inherit his father's estate, Margaret's husband had a competence of his own and lived a far more exciting life, which it seemed Margaret would share.

"I can't wait to go to London and see the Court and the Tower, and see the King and Queen and all the rich and noble people there. Henry has promised me he will present me at the first opportunity. And I am to have new dresses, you can't imagine how many, and everyone will come to dinner with us, and—"

Cecily listened with stony patience while her sister's voice ran on. She could not forget that it had always been her desire to go to London, to live with the excitements of the big city. Society in York was too quiet for her taste. And though she loved Thomas, she was remembering now that Henry had loved *her*, and had promised *her* he would take her to London.

"Yes, yes, I've heard all this before," she interrupted her sister.

Margaret opened her eyes wide in innocence. "Why, Cecily, you can't be jealous, can you? When you have such a lovely home, and Thomas and the girls—" she said provokingly to her sister.

"No, of course I'm not jealous," Cecily snapped. "*I* shouldn't want to go to Court and have to be polite to the Queen—to that Woodville creature." She corrected herself in imitation of Eleanor. "You know what Grandmother says—"

"Oh, pooh! Grandmother! She only likes to say how much she hates the Queen so that everyone will remember how friendly she used to be with the King," Margaret said. "You can wager your pearls that if she met the Queen she'd be just as nice to her as she could be."

"She would not!" Cecily said hotly. "She loves my lord of Gloucester and hates his enemies. And since he is our patron, you ought to have more loyalty to him."

"Oh, I'm as loyal as may be," Margaret said carelessly. "But I don't see why one mayn't be loyal to him and still be polite to the Queen. After all, we don't *know* that she is his enemy. She's never done anything to harm him." She narrowed her eyes. "Anyway, you'd jump at the chance to go to London even if it meant kneeling before the Queen every day for a week, so you needn't sound so virtuous."

And after that a coolness sprang up between the sisters.

Shortly after the wedding came bad news; Maximilian of Burgundy had made peace with Louis of France, giving up certain lands to him and signing a treaty not to help the English anymore. Louis's son, the Dauphin, who was betrothed to Princess Elizabeth, was now to marry Maximilian's daughter, and with Princess Elizabeth jilted, the pensions Louis had been paying to Edward and the English nobles stopped. It was a bad blow, especially since Burgundy was the major trade link between England and Europe; and with the French in control of the coast, invasions of England were to be feared for the future.

But just before the end of January, some better news followed: Lord Richard, for his great services to the King, was to be given hereditary Wardenship of the West Marches, which made him virtually autonomous prince of a great county palatine stretching from York up to the borders of Scotland. It meant, to Eleanor, that Richard would be safe at last, ruling over a small kingdom within the kingdom, strong enough to be safe from any enemy for as long as he lived; and also that the north would have his strong and just government over it, to change it from the semilawless place it still was, to a part of the civilized country.

The pleasure of that news almost outweighed the worry of the other news; almost, but not quite, for the loss of England's only ally left her helpless against France. Word came that the King had been badly shaken by the news, which came on the day before Christmas Eve—so much so, that he had not been able to join in any of the Christmas revels, which had, of course, been avoided by Lord Richard as a matter of course. It must have been a dull Christmas.

Nothing, however, could dim Margaret's anticipation of London and the Court, and she grew more and more excited as the time drew nearer for her to depart with her husband. They were to leave on the day after Candlemas in order to get to their house in London before Lent began, for Margaret would have to take up the running of her household and make sure that supplies were ordered in time.

"But don't worry too much," Henry had whispered to her privately. "Almost anything can be got in London if you have gold enough, and *I* have gold enough."

"Better not tell Grandmother that," Margaret giggled. "She wouldn't like the idea that a poor housewife wouldn't be punished for her unthriftiness."

And, at the last minute before they left, Cecily broke her cool reserve and flung her arms around her sister and begged her to write to her.

"I long to hear about your life in London, and I may never see you again. Promise me you'll write, Meg, do!"

Margaret too began to cry. "I will, oh, I will. I'm sorry if I was horrid to you, Cecily—I didn't mean it. I shall miss you very much. And we will meet again, soon. Henry and I will be rich enough to ride up and see you often, and you must come down and visit us, too, and then you'll be able to see the places for yourself."

"I don't suppose that will ever be," Cecily said sadly, "but if you'll write to me, it will be almost as good."

Then the sisters embraced one last time, and Margaret and her husband and their attendants set off on the long journey to London.

CHAPTER TWENTY-FOUR

On an evening early in May, Thom sat with his sister Margaret, and her husband, Henry, in their house in Bishopsgate Street at a late supper. That day Thom's master, Richard of Gloucester, had called together both Houses of Parliament and the city magistrates, and had publicly administered to them a solemn oath of fealty to their sovereign lord King Edward, fifth of that name, a boy of twelve. It was the end of a passage of hectic action and terrible dread, which had had the people of London, in particular, quaking in their shoes. The people were now relaxing with a sigh, beginning to think that life might go on normally after all.

"They say," said Henry, breaking a silence, "that Lord Howard has sent home thirty of his retinue. That's a sign that he thinks everything's going to be all right."

"It's the same all over the city," Margaret said. "What with all the nobles up here for the coronation, and everyone with their armed guard, it's been impossible to find lodgings anywhere. But there were streams of men going out of the gates this evening."

"What do you think he will do next?" Henry asked Thom. "The Lord Protector, I mean."

"Form a Council," Thom said, watering his wine to a delicate pink. "That's obvious. As to who he'll choose, I'd say he'll keep more or less the same men as the late King had. They were good, sober, honest men, most of them."

"With one or two notable exceptions," Henry said drily.

"Rotherham won't be chancellor again, not after handing the Great Seal over to the Queen. But he was always the Queen's man."

"That woman!" Thom said, exasperated. "I haven't heard the full story yet of why she bolted into sanctuary—"

"And we haven't heard your story yet," Henry said quickly. "Have some more wine and tell us from the beginning. Then we'll tell you what happened here. I can't believe it's only three months since we left Morland Place after our wedding. It seems like years."

"I know what you mean," Thom said. "It was only the end of February when my lord said good-bye to King Edward and we left for Yorkshire. We thought then that none of us would see London again for years, if ever. And now he's dead. He was only about forty, wasn't he?"

Henry nodded. "It was so sudden. He caught a chill out fishing with some friends and went to bed and never got up again. No one knows why he should have died. He just seems to have given up."

They exchanged a glance heavy with meaning. Finally Margaret voiced the terrible word. "Poison?"

"I can't think it could be that," Henry said. "He hadn't an enemy in the world. Who would do it? No, I think it was just his time, that's all. But what a mess it left us in. The last thing he did was to tell everyone he left my lord of Gloucester Protector of the kingdom, and the first thing madam the Queen did when he was dead was to start planning to seize the new King and have Gloucester murdered." He shuddered. "I tell you I thought then of taking Margaret for a holiday at Morland Place, for all that we'd only just arrived here. You never knew such confusion!"

"It wasn't confused at Middleham," Thom said. "But it was terrible enough. We'd only been home a month when a messenger came with the news. My lord was grieved. He really loved his brother, you know, and it hurt him that he hadn't known in February that he was seeing him for the last time. I think it was a good thing in a way that he had something to worry about, because all his life he'd followed King Edward and served him, and I think he'd have felt lost if the crisis hadn't arisen."

"So he knew straightaway there was trouble?" Henry asked.

"Oh yes—the letter, you see, was from Lord Hastings, not the Queen or the Council or anyone official. It said the King was dead and had left everything to my lord's protection, and warned him to secure the new King's person and get to London as soon as possible. I think he must have guessed the rest. He wrote to the Queen and the Council and to the new King's household in Ludlow, and all the time there was worse and worse news coming in from Hastings and nothing from anyone else, except Buckingham's man, who rode in with an offer of a thousand armed men. We all knew that if the Queen once got power she'd not rest until my lord and lady and their son were dead."

"So why didn't he ride south with an army?" Margaret asked. "That's what I'd have done. I wouldn't have left it to chance."

"How could he?" Thom asked. "Talk sense, Meg. That would be an act of provocation, and make it look as if he were trying to grab something he wasn't entitled to. No, he had to behave as if everything was normal, and ride south with a few gentlemen, all in mourning, to meet the King on the road in his official capacity. Rivers had said they'd meet at Northampton. I just can't understand that man, by the way."

"Rivers? Why is that?"

"Well, he must have known what the Queen was up to—I mean, there he was bringing the boy King to London with a great armed guard—a thousand men, I think it was—and yet he sent the politest letter imaginable to my lord to suggest meeting on the road. You'd think he'd have ridden hotfoot for London and ignored my lord's letter. And then when he gets to Northampton, instead of meeting as arranged, he sends the King and the army on to Stratford and waits for my lord alone. I just can't understand what he was up to."

"Vacillating, I'd say," Henry said. "Probably isn't wholeheartedly with the Queen, and was trying not to offend either party. But what happened when they met?"

"Oh, he told my lord that there wasn't enough room in

Northampton for the King's men and my lord's men, and that was why he'd sent the King on to Stratford. My lord didn't say anything to that, but he gave him a stony look, and then invited him to supper. They were just beginning when Buckingham rode in, and he joined them and—it turned into a sort of party." Thom reflected on that strange evening. "One or two of us were in attendance," he said. "There was this small inn room, with the table and benches in the center, and candles all round the walls. And there were the three lords, eating and drinking and talking and laughing; like a place out of the world, out of time it was; you'd think they hadn't a care in the world."

"They didn't mention the situation then?"

"No, not at all," Thom said. "They just talked like friends. Lord Rivers, you know, is a learned, witty man, and Lord Buckingham is vivacious, and the talk was wonderful. My lord didn't say much, but his eyes went from one to the other, and he smiled a little, and you could see he was enjoying it. When Rivers wanted to break it up and go to bed, my lord kept him back talking for another hour. It was as if he couldn't bear for the evening to finish."

"Perhaps he didn't want to think about what he was going to have to do," Margaret said. "Perhaps he really liked Lord Rivers and wished he didn't have to arrest him."

Thom shook his head. "I don't think so. I think he admires Rivers for some things, but he doesn't really like men unless they are truly virtuous."

"They say Rivers wears a hair shirt under his rich clothes," Margaret said. "That's virtuous, isn't it?"

"He liked his brother of Clarence," Henry pointed out, "and you can't say he was virtuous."

"No, but he was his brother, and that excused him. Anyway, the next day at dawn he had Rivers's lodgings surrounded and arrested him as he came out. Then my lord and Buckingham rode to Stratford and caught the King just mounting to ride on. It was extraordinary," he reflected. "There was my lord with only a few unarmed gentlemen, and there was the King with Lord Richard Grey and Sir Thomas Vaughan surrounded by a thousand armed men, and yet no one even so much as interrupted my lord while he was talking, let alone tried to stop him."

"And what did he do exactly?" Henry asked.

"He took the King inside his lodgings again and explained what had happened. You could see the King didn't believe him—he's been brought up since infancy by his mother's relations, and they tell him only what they want him to know—but he had to accept it. My lord said that he would serve him truly and protect him and there was nothing he could do but say thank you. Then my lord had Grey and Vaughan arrested too, told the soldiers all to go home, and rode back to Northampton with the King."

"Did the soldiers go without a fuss?" Margaret asked.

"Oh, yes, they just wandered off. They'd no leader, you see, and my lord is always good with soldiers anyway. They all knew him by reputation if not in person. And once we were back in Northampton, we just settled down to wait until Hastings sent word it was safe to bring the King to London. So everything went off peacefully. No battle, no deaths, just a few quiet arrests and it was all over."

"It wasn't like that here," Margaret said. "Everything was confusion and shouting."

"When the news came in about the King being taken by the Protector," Henry said, "you should have seen the panic amongst the Woodvilles! They ran round in circles like chickens, clucking and squawking and pecking at each other. The Queen's a stupid woman, as well as unprincipled—if she'd sat still and done nothing she might have made a job of denying everything. But she and her son the marquess rushed about dragging people out of bed and trying to raise an army against the Protector; but of course no one wanted to know, and when they realized that, they rushed for sanctuary."

"At Westminster," Margaret added. "You should have seen the panic that was going on there, all by torchlight, while the poor sanctuary attendants stood about wringing their hands. She was dragging everything she could lay hands on into sanctuary—furniture and plate, tapestries, boxes of clothes and jewelery—"

"And don't forget the royal treasure from the Tower," Henry said wryly. "She wasn't going to leave that behind."

"She took that as well?" Thom asked, shocked.

"Oh, yes," Margaret said. "She had her men break a

hole through the sanctuary wall so they could hand the stuff in quickly before anyone arrived to stop her. There were the princesses weeping and running about trying to save their little treasures from being damaged or broken: Princess Cecily with her bird in a cage and the little Duke of York holding the Queen's hand and staring about him as if the world had gone mad."

"You could forgive him for thinking it had," Henry said. "Because, of course, of all the fuss as Westminster sent the wildest rumors flying about, and even before dawn there were people fleeing the city by boat and others arming themselves and barricading their homes. Oh, it was the maddest night."

"What did you do?" Thom asked.

"We rode home, telling everyone we met on the way to do the same, and just sat tight and waited for my lord of Gloucester to arrive. We knew we had nothing to fear from him. And, of course, as soon as day came, Hastings sent out messengers all over town to tell everyone that there was no danger, that the Protector had rescued the King and was bringing him to London, that the Woodvilles were finished, and everything was all right. And when the Protector rode in without an army, everyone realized they could trust him, and lined the streets cheering."

"I heard," Thom said. "I was riding just behind him. They were booing the Woodvilles too."

They paused a moment, thinking of the wild scenes they had witnessed over the past few weeks.

Then Henry said seriously, "There's still going to be some resistance to him, you know."

"From the Woodvilles?" Thom said. "But surely—"

"There are a lot of them, and not all of them have been accounted for. But I wasn't meaning that. There will be those who aren't happy to serve under a man like him. Virtue isn't universally popular, you know. The unscrupulous men who would do well under a corrupt government won't like him. They won't get on fast enough under a government that rewards virtue only."

"It won't matter as long as the majority of people appreciate that he's good and he's strong. There'll be plots—

there always are—but they won't come to anything. And
then when the King comes of age—"

"You said the King doesn't like him—what of that?"
Henry asked.

"He'll learn to. Separated from the Woodvilles, he'll
come to realize his uncle loves him, and can be trusted."

Henry shook his head. "I wish I had your faith. You're a
little like him, Thom—simple and trusting. I've lived some
years in London, and close to the Court, and I've learned
that most things are not simple—they're terribly complex—
and most people can't be trusted unless what you ask them
to do is in their own interests anyway."

"You're a cynic." Thom laughed. "As you say, you've
been too long in London. Some good Yorkshire air would
blow all that out of your head."

"Unfortunately, it's in London, not in Yorkshire, that the
problems are going to arise," Henry said.

"Well, till they do," Margaret put in, "let's be cheerful
and celebrate the fact that I'm seeing my dearest brother
again after—What is it, Thom?—three years. Let's have
some more wine, and bring in the sweetmeats."

"We should be able to see much more of you, while your
master is at Crosby Place," Henry said. Crosby Place was
only a five minute walk away from their house.

"I hope so," Thom said, "but somehow I think we're all
going to be kept very busy over the next few weeks.
There's a certain event in the offing—"

"The coronation, you mean," Henry said, smiling. "Yes,
that had slipped my mind, strange as it may seem."

"As soon as the date is fixed, we'll all be run off our
feet with the arrangements," Thom said.

"And we'll be run off our feet with all the orders for
cloth," Henry added happily. "It's sad to lose the old King,
but a coronation is certainly good for business!"

Busy though the times were, everything went smoothly at
first. Richard of Gloucester was confirmed in his appointment of Protector by Parliament, the young King was
moved into the royal apartments at the Tower with his
household, and the new Council was appointed, consisting

mainly of the members of the old Council with a few changes that were universally approved of. One change that was not wholly popular was the appointment of the Duke of Buckingham to a prominent place in the Council. Richard was impressed by the way Buckingham had rushed to his support instantly on hearing of the death of the old King, and liked his cheerful, ebullient character. Others, especially prominent members of the old Council like Hastings, were not so impressed. They thought Buckingham was an upstart, a pushy, flamboyant man who would oust them from the center of government and monopolize the Protector's ear.

But for the present things moved smoothly. Richard sent, at the first opportunity, for his wife, and Anne arrived in London on the fifth of June and took up residence at Crosby Place. Their son, Edward, remained at Middleham. He was considered too fragile to make the long journey or to risk the unhealthy airs of London.

Thom witnessed the tender reunion between his master and mistress, and noticed an immediate improvement in his master's spirits. He was close to the Protector for much of the time, for Richard was essentially a lonely man, and liked to keep those he felt his friends close by him. Thom could ask nothing better, and since his own temperament was a lively and cheerful one, he was often able to lighten his master's mood when his multiple cares pressed too heavily on him.

On the same day that Lady Anne arrived in London, the orders were given out for the coronation to take place on the twenty-second of June. This meant there was less than three weeks to get everything done, from the choosing of the squires to be knighted for the occasion to the planning of the seating at the banquet afterward. Richard sat up late into the night dictating and signing orders while his attendants thought longingly of their beds, to which they could not go until their master retired to his. Finally, Thom plucked up the courage to murmur into the Protector's ear as he came to the end of a batch of papers.

"My lord, there is so much to be done tomorrow. Might it not be best to take some sleep now? The Lady Anne retired long ago."

Richard's head came up, and his gray eyes—shadowed with weariness now—gazed into Thom's for a moment before his face relaxed and some of the grim lines softened.

"Perhaps you are right, my friend," he said. He laid down his pen and stretched achingly. "And of course, you all want to get to your beds, too, don't you?"

"I thought only of you, my lord," Thom said protestingly.

"Of course you did." Richard smiled. "No, I believe you, in this case. You are my friend, are you not? It is good to have people around that one can trust. There are so many, many enemies. The south was always like that—a great spiderweb of intrigue, and always from the people one would expect it from least."

"Who this time, my lord?" Thom asked softly. He had an idea—rumors were rife in the seething atmosphere of the city, and it was not hard to sift out those that contained a grain of truth.

Richard's eyes were piercing. "What have you heard, Thomas?" he asked quietly.

"It is known who visits the King, my lord, apart from yourself. And it is known also that a certain lady has been visiting the Queen in sanctuary, a lady who has no reason to love her," Thom said cautiously.

Richard looked impatient. "Rumor, Thom? Have these people no names? Come, tell me what you have heard. There are none here we cannot trust." There were only a handful of attendants present, all trusted members of the Protector's household.

Thom swallowed nervously. "My lord, it is well known that my lord Hastings visits the King when you are not there."

"My lord Hastings is a member of the Council and a friend of my late brother, the King," Richard said impassively. "Go on—who is the woman you speak of?"

Thom knew that he knew—it was the substitution of "woman" for "lady" that gave it away. "Mistress Shore, my lord," Thom said. "It is said that she volunteered to be a messenger to allay her feeling of guilt toward the Queen." Jane Shore had been the late King's mistress, and was now Hastings's. It all fitted. Richard sighed and bent his head.

"I believe you are right. I have heard this myself. Do not speak of it to anyone—the secret must not pass these walls until we are ready to act."

"My lord, I believe that they will strike soon," Thom could not resist adding. "They must, at any rate, act before Parliament assembles on the twenty-fifth—"

"Yes, I know. Be assured I understand the position. But *we* cannot act until we know what they intend. That is why no word of this must escape this chamber. But why should he do it? I had believed he was loyal—and he was Edward's friend—" Richard murmured wearily. It was a heavy load to bear. Hastings had never loved the Queen, hating all her brood as upstarts, and hating her in particular as a rival for the King's ear.

"He knows that the King dearly loves his mother and her relations, my lord," Thom suggested. "If he wishes to have control of the King, he must be friendly with her."

Richard nodded, but said nothing for a moment, apparently plunged in gloom.

Then a curiously grim smile crossed his features, and he said, "I wonder why men *want* power? If they could see me now, bowed down as I am with work and worry and fear of plots, would they not be content to let me have the pain for them? I never wanted power, but it was my responsibility, and I have never stepped back from responsibility. It would be so much easier now to step down and give them what they want—but I cannot do it. I have been handed a sacred trust, and I *will* carry it out, though it cost my peace of mind—though it cost my life." There was a brief silence, and then he stood up abruptly. "But you have already reminded me that I must go to bed, and still I am keeping you up. Very well, then, I will go now." He caught sight of Thom's anxious face and patted his shoulder gently. "Don't worry, my good friend. God sees us, and He will never send us more than we can bear."

Thom watched him go toward his chamber, a small but erect figure, a soldierly man on whom authority sat with the ease of accustomedness. That may be, he thought, but some can bear more than others, and you, my lord, will pass our breaking point.

* * *

Friday, the thirteenth of June. An unlucky day, a day on which mariners would refuse to set sail, on which the cautious would avoid, in any way, tempting the forces of darkness, and would take extra care in all their doings. A meeting was called in the Council room at the Tower of a section of the Council, consisting of Hastings, Stanley, Morton, Rotherham, and Buckingham, Howard, and one or two of Richard's principal advisers.

Richard himself had been more than usually reserved since he rose before dawn, and from the stern set of his face those nearest him felt that something unusually unpleasant was in the offing. Thom was among the henchmen who accompanied him to the Tower, but they were not, of course, allowed into the Council room while the meeting was in progress. When they arrived at the door, Thom was surprised to see a group of armed guards approaching from the opposite direction; and glancing at his master's face, he realized that they were here at Richard's command. So this was it, Thom thought—the moment had come. The rest of the Councillors were already within, and Thom reached for the handle of the door to let his master in, but Richard stayed him with a gesture and turned to the captain of the guard.

"You remember your orders?" he asked.

"I do, sir," the captain replied smartly.

"Good," said Richard, but by his face it was anything rather than good. He looked deeply anxious and unhappy, and his gaze passed from face to face unseeingly as his henchmen and the soldiers watched him sympathetically. Finally he seemed to make up his mind, squared his shoulders, and moved to the door. His eye met Thom's.

"Stay by the door," he said to him. "Listen. When you hear me shout treason, fling the door wide and stand back so that the guard may enter."

"I understand, my lord," Thom said. He had no right to say more, but he tried to express with his look all his love and sympathy for his beleaguered master as he opened the door to let him into the chamber. Thom had a brief view across his master's shoulder of the richly clad councillors seated around the table, saw them rise to their feet and heard the muted whisper of conversation cease as the Protector entered, and then he drew the door shut again.

It did not take more than a few minutes. The door was thick, and normal conversation could not be heard from without; but Thom, with his ear to the oak, heard a sudden scrape and bang, as if someone had leapt to his feet overturning his chair, and then a thud, and the word angrily shouted—Treason! The word seemed to bite into Thom's heart so that as he flung open the door he himself shouted "Treason! Treason!" as if it were he that were betrayed. The faces turned to the door, Hastings and Stanley were on their feet, daggers in their hands. It was Stanley's chair that had overturned. Morton and Rotherham were white-faced, Morton with anger and Rotherham with fear. Buckingham was waving his fists in the air in a kind of triumph. Howard looked grave.

But as the soldiers ran in past him to seize, two to a man, Hastings and Stanley, Morton and Rotherham, Thom's eyes were fixed on his master's face.

"Take Lord Stanley to his lodgings and let him be detained there," Richard said quietly to the waiting captain. "Secure the other three within the Tower."

"Yes, sir!"

The prisoners were marched out between the guards, and it was all over. But at what cost? Thom wondered, for he could never afterward shake from his mind the memory of that expression on Richard's face, an expression not of anger or triumph or indignation, but of bitter, bitter grief.

That same day, a few hours later, a full meeting of the Council was convened to decide what to do about the conspirators. Hastings was condemned to be executed, and not even the Protector spoke up for him—he felt the betrayal too deeply. The other three were to be detained in captivity for the time being; but the three prisoners who were taken at Northampton—Rivers, Grey and Vaughan—were also to be executed, for they were too dangerous in their close relationship with the Queen, to be left alive.

Hastings was executed the following Friday, the twentieth of June, at which time Morton, the next most dangerous of the conspirators, was taken to Brecknock to be imprisoned at one of Buckingham's castles. Rotherham, who was considered weak and ineffectual, was released, and Stanley remained in his own lodgings under constraint. At that same meeting, it was decided that the Queen must no longer keep the King's brother, the young Duke of York, as a political hostage at Westminster, and on the Monday morning, the sixteenth of June, the Archbishop of Canterbury collected him and escorted him to join his brother in the royal apartments in the Tower.

London settled down again to await events and to prepare for the coronation, which had again been postponed. It had not long to wait. There was a meeting of the inner Council on the eighteenth, after which there was seen to be frenzied activity around Crosby Place and Baynard's Castle, a stream of visitors coming and going, long discussions, and grave faces. Something was definitely going on, but even Thom, as he told Henry and Margaret when he supped with them, had no idea what it was.

"It's being kept very quiet, whatever it is," he said. "But it's certainly something very big, very important indeed."

"What sort of something?" Margaret asked curiously. "Another plot?"

"No," Thom said hesitantly. "I don't think so. The Protector doesn't look angry or unhappy, just grave and worried. I've heard a rumor—" He paused, and then went on hurriedly, "No, I'd better not say anything. If it isn't true it's too—no, no matter. I'll keep my peace until I know."

And Margaret and Henry had to be content with that, tantalizing though it was.

On Sunday the Protector rode to Paul's Cross to hear a sermon given by a friar, Ralph Shaa, the brother of the Lord Mayor of London. With him went his wife, and all the leading magnates, and even before they heard the first words, Thom had guessed that this was more than just a sermon, that it was to be in the way of an announcement. There was an atmosphere of subdued excitement, and Lord Buckingham was red in the face with it like a child at Christmas. He laughed a lot and made jokes to his master as they rode side by side, Buckingham on his handsome chestnut, Richard on his great stallion, White Surrey.

Thom, riding his own Barbary a pace behind with the other henchmen, saw his master wince once or twice, as if he felt it was no time for joking. But he did not, as he never did, try to restrain Buckingham—one of the reasons Hastings had hated him.

As was customary, the friar announced the text of his sermon first, and Thom drew a sharp breath as he heard it—"Bastard Slips Shall Not Take Root." Then the rumors were true! The friar went on to praise the Protector's father, who had fought and died for the House of York, and then to praise the Protector himself, talking of his character and career, mentioning his great deeds, and saying that he was a man worthy in himself to be a King.

There was a pause as the preacher drew breath for the essential part of his harangue. Thom glanced at his master's cold profile: not for anything would Richard reveal any emotion at this point. The Lady Anne was biting her lip, and her thin face was so white, it looked almost transparent. Buckingham was looking gleeful, Howard quietly pleased. There was no doubt they all knew what was coming next.

"In truth," the friar continued, "it has just been discovered that, as he is worthy by his own character and deeds to sit upon the throne of England, so is the Protector entitled by God's law and the law of the land to that same crown."

In the silence, the jingle of a bit could be heard as a horse tossed his head restlessly, and further off the throaty cooing of a pigeon sunning itself on a roof. Buckingham giggled nervously, and changed it into a cough; no one else made a sound.

"It has been discovered," the friar cried in a ringing voice, "that when our late sovereign Edward the fourth married Dame Elizabeth Woodville, he was already married and troth-plight to one Dame Eleanor Butler, daughter of the Earl of Shrewsbury. The marriage with the present Queen is therefore unlawful, and the children begotten upon her are illegitimate. Thus, with the children of King Edward set aside by reason of this illegitimacy, and the children of the late Duke of Clarence disabled by their father's attainted blood, Richard of Gloucester, the Lord Protector, is the sole true heir of York, and therefore the rightful King of England."

So that was it! It was all very clear now. Edward, the blond giant, the indefatigable lover, who had made a secret marriage with Elizabeth Woodville in order to get her into his bed, was then only repeating a ploy he had already used to get an Eleanor to submit to his caresses—for if a woman was virtuous and a man wanted her, what could he do? Many gentlemen of the Court had used the troth-plight to trick virtuous women. Lesser people could put aside such holy and binding contracts, for little depended on them. But a King could not. A King's offspring must be beyond reproach—and Edward's fine litter was not.

The crowd dispersed quietly, talking softly among themselves. There was surprise on some faces, Thom noticed, but no disbelief or disapproval; and open relief on others. Even those obdurate enough to disbelieve the story would be happy that there would be, after all, no minority, with all its accompanying strife, bad government, and bloody struggle for precedence. Buckingham spoke a few words to Richard, bowed, and went away on some business. The Protector and his wife, followed by their attendants, rode home in silence, their faces shut tight.

At Crosby Place, they dismounted, the horses were led away, and they went in, walking up the stairs to dinner.

Thom was close behind them, close enough to hear the Lady Anne say to her husband in a quiet voice, "Then it was true?"

"It was true," Richard said. There was no triumph in his voice, only weariness. "Bishop Stillington told me about it last week—he performed the ceremony. That was why Edward had him imprisoned all those years ago—to shut his mouth. I never understood that at the time."

"Then Edward—but of course, he knew all the time. How could he do it? How could he hope to get away with it?"

"The lady in question was dead. Only Stillington knew, and if he was warned to say nothing—there was no harm. It would have been all right if he had not died leaving young Edward a minor. Had he lived a few years longer, the boy would have succeeded and could have decided what to do about Stillington himself."

"Then why did Stillington keep silence all these years, and speak only now?" Anne cried.

"He couldn't speak while Edward was alive—he had been warned. And now—he said he felt he must speak, so that a bastard should not take the crown that was rightfully mine." Richard made a wry face. "He need not have been so jealous of my possessions."

"What will the Queen think?" Anne mused.

"Oh, she knows already," Richard said. "I heard the full story. George somehow found out about it, and made a point of letting the Queen know that he knew. He always hated her, and once he learned the secret of the precontract he was sure of being King afterward. That was why she had to make sure he died." His voice was bitter—he had suffered dreadfully over the death of his mad brother. "Edward was not blameless, I see now. It was in his interest, too, and George had given him plenty of excuses. The Queen whispered in his ear, and in the end he had to do it. That was why the execution was carried out in private, in case George should take it into his head to address the crowd on the subject."

There was a silence. They had paused on the landing by the door to the chamber and turned to look at each other. Richard took her hand and caressed its slight fingers, looking down tenderly into her frail white face, trying to read the look that was in her steady eyes.

"Anne," he said, "what else could I do? God knows I don't want to be King. God knows it's the last thing I would do to you, to burden you with this unhappy crown, my hinny, but what else could I do? The boy can't be King. I could perhaps reverse the attainder against George's boy, but he is only a child, too, so what good would it do? And besides, he is not a good boy, he's weak and vacillating." He stared at his wife almost desperately, and his voice rose a little in appeal as she said nothing, but merely looked at him. "I don't want this, but I don't have the right not to want it. It's my duty and my responsibility. It's more than that—it's just a fact. Anne, what else could I do?"

And she gave a quivering sigh at last, and let her gaze drop. She looked down at her hand imprisoned in his and then lifted it so that his fingers came to her lips, and she kissed them and put her cheek against them.

"No, there was nothing else you could do, I see that. We must make the best of it we can."

She stared at the ground with a small troubled frown, and Thom saw her lips form the word "Edward" before she straightened up and led the way into the chamber. He often wondered afterward whether she was referring to the King who had died, or the boy King who was to be deposed, or her own small son who would one day now be King. And as he passed into the room behind her, Richard said softly, "Your father would be pleased, anyway."

On the following Wednesday, Parliament met to discuss the matter, but by then they had already made up their minds, and it was only a matter of recording for the parliamentary rolls their unanimous decision to ask Richard to take the throne. So on Thursday the twenty-sixth of June, the Lords and the Commons formally called upon the lord Protector to accept the crown of England, and on his formal acceptance they hailed him with great acclaim as King Richard the Third.

The news flew through London like fire, and was greeted almost unanimously with great joy. The evils of a minority were after all to be avoided; they were to have a King who had already proved himself an able administrator, a brave general, and a just and virtuous man. With the great fortune left behind by the late King Edward, and the Council of wise and capable men, a new golden age was about to begin, and already people spoke of him as "Good King Richard."

That evening Thom had supper with Henry and Margaret, and got very, very drunk. He celebrated with them the wonderful good fortune that had come to the country, but just before his forehead struck the table and he passed out with the excess of good wine, he wept for his master and mistress, and the peaceful life in Wensleydale that they loved and would never know again.

CHAPTER TWENTY-FIVE

The news was received at Morland Place with great joy and some surprise. Eleanor quickly recovered herself and declared that the hand of God was visible in the way things had worked out, and that she had known all along that Richard was more fit to be King than his brother. Edward and Daisy accepted that with a private smile, and Edward went so far as to say he was surprised by the story of the precontract.

"Can it really be true?" he wondered.

"It's probably just made up for the occasion," Daisy said, more to provoke her mother-in-law, who sometimes annoyed her, than because she really thought so.

"Of course it's true," Eleanor said scornfully, "and it just serves that Woodville woman right. Using her body as a snare for the King, just because he was a King. If she had done all openly, the precontract would have come to light, and the problem would never have arisen."

"Rather hard on her all the same," Cecily said—she and Thomas had ridden over on hearing the news. "I mean, to hold out for marriage, and then to discover it isn't marriage at all. After all those years and ten children—"

"Rather hard on the poor lady who *was* his wife," Thomas added, seeing Eleanor about to explode in wrath at the idea of any sympathy being offered to the Woodville woman in her house. "What happened to her, by the way?"

"She went into a convent, and died there, I believe," Edward said.

"Why on earth didn't she say something when the King married again?" Cecily wondered. "Even if she didn't want to be Queen, you'd have thought she'd want to stop anyone from making a false marriage."

"Perhaps she didn't want to upset the situation," Edward suggested. "She died, apparently, in 1468, and the King only married in 1464—she may have been too ill or too tired to care by then. And remember, he'd been married for six months or so by the time the story got out—a bit late then for declarations."

Cecily looked unconvinced, but her husband said, "If anything points to the story being true it's the similarity of the cases—both widows, both older than him, both beautiful and virtuous—"

Here Eleanor snorted derisively. "—and both secretly married. One wonders how many other 'wives' of King Edward are scattered about the country."

"Probably," Daisy said, "if the Queen's mother hadn't been so ambitious, she'd have ended up obscurely in a convent like the other poor lady."

"Better for her if she had," Edward said rather more forcefully than usual. "Imagine how she must feel having lived nearly twenty years in sin and having borne ten bastard children, and only finding it out when she has been accustomed to being Queen and lording it over creatures like Jane Shore."

"I don't think we should feel too sorry for her," Eleanor said. "Thom says in his letter that she knew about it at the time the Duke of Clarence was executed, and she went on to have two more children afterward. If she had been truly virtuous, she would have avoided his bed from then on, but she probably thought the story would never come out and that she was safe being Queen for the rest of her life. Ambition when it isn't governed by good principles is a dangerous thing."

There was a silence, there being no answer to that.

Then Thomas said, more cheerfully, "Well, the coronation I hear is set for the sixth of July—that's next Sunday. He's certainly not wasting time."

"All the arrangements have been made long ago, for young Edward. It's only a matter of adjusting them a little," Edward said. "But it's a pity that we hadn't more notice, or we could have gone down for the occasion and stayed with Henry and Margaret—"

"But, Papa," Cecily cried, her face lighting up, "we could still go, couldn't we?"

"There isn't time," Edward said. "It's a ten-day ride to London."

"No, Papa, no it isn't. It needn't be. You know very well it can be done in five days if we ride hard. The roads are good at this time of year, and we could do forty or fifty miles a day easily. If we started off tomorrow morning we'd be in London by Saturday night. We could just do it."

"It's foolish, Cecily," Edward said, but she interrupted him hastily.

"No it isn't, it isn't foolish—it's a wonderful idea. How often do you get a chance to see a coronation? And this is the coronation of our own good lord, our own Duke of Gloucester, who has slept under our roof and eaten our meat—"

"Cecily's right," Eleanor said suddenly.

The young woman turned eagerly to her new supporter. "You'd go, wouldn't you, Grandmother?"

"If I were your age, I certainly would. What you say is right, and I could only wish I were thirty years younger. But I'm too old and stiff to ride so far so fast. But you, Edward—you're a young man in comparison with me."

"There!" Cecily said triumphantly. "Who will go, then? You will, won't you, Thomas? And Ned will and cousin Edmund— Where is he? Let's ask them."

"They're over at Shawes," Edward said, "but I don't know really—"

"I can't go," Daisy said firmly. "I'm too stout to ride fast. If there were time to ride slowly, I would like to go, though. So why don't you go along, Edward? See Margaret and little Thom again, and bring us back all the news and let us know exactly what everyone wore and did."

Edward did not take much more persuading. He had not been away from Morland Place for many years, and never as far as London, and the thought of seeing Lord Richard's coronation was a strong temptation. When Ned and Edmund rode back from inspecting the Shawe Estate that afternoon the idea was put to them. Ned was immediately enthusiastic, but Edmund only shook his head and said no in his quiet way, without vouchsafing any reason. Cecily tried to press him, but Eleanor stopped her and told her to leave him alone. Edmund had always been a little strange, and she would not have him annoyed by his more vivacious cousin. The rest of the day was spent in hurried preparation as the best horses were chosen for the journey, clothes selected and packed, food prepared and servants told off— for a Morland now could not think of performing a journey without attendants.

So the next day the house was astir at three o'clock for first mass, and at five o'clock the horses were brought to the door, and Edward, Thomas, Ned, and Cecily mounted up.

"Give my love to Thom," Eleanor instructed.

"Give our love to everyone," Daisy corrected her. "And try to remember every little detail to tell us when you come back."

"We will, we will," Cecily cried. She waved to her two daughters, who had been brought over the day before to stay in the Morland nursery until their parents returned, and then turned her horse, and they were trotting out of the yard in the early sunshine.

"I wish I was going with them," Eleanor said quietly as she turned to go in. "There are penalties in being old, after all."

Her hand was taken by seven-year-old Paul. "Don't be sad, Great-Grandmother," he said. "I'm staying with you, and so is Anne. We can have lots of fun, too."

Eleanor smiled down at the dark-eyed, sallow-skinned little boy, who was so much a foreigner in his own family, and to whom one day everything she had worked for would belong.

She smiled, and stooped to kiss his forehead. "I'm not sad, child. I'm glad you're staying with me. Shall we go out into the garden and pick some herbs for Jacques for dinner?"

"Yes, and I'll take them in to him afterward," Paul said eagerly. "Can Anne come?" He took his little cousin and betrothed by the hand.

"I know why you want to take the herbs in—you think Jacques might find you a little cake for your trouble! Ah, yes, don't deny it, for I know it's true. But it does you credit that you want to share with Anne, and so you may go, and bid Jacques give you three cakes—one for your cousin Alice as well."

And Paul, who cared not at all for his cousin Alice, smiled happily and walked at his great-grandmother's side out into the sunny garden, his life bounded by the pleasing prospect of a promised cake, and Anne staying with him, perhaps for several weeks.

The party from Morland Place reached the gates of London just before curfew, and were stopped and questioned by the guards on duty. By their rusty sallets and strong accents the guards were known to be northerners, and on hearing that the Morland party was from York, they became friendly and talkative.

"Here for the coronation, are you? That's right—you only just made it in time. Ten o'clock curfew, by the King's orders. He don't want no trouble in the streets like there was in the last King's time. No quarreling, no stirring up old feuds, and no attacking foreigners or Woodvilles."

"Wouldn't mind breaking that last rule," the other guard grinned. "I'm King Richard's man—always have been. I wouldn't mind having a crack at some of madam's tribe. Still, that's what we're here to stop—marched in las' Monday to keep the peace. Where are you folks heading for? You're late for lodgings—you'll probably have to apply to the King's harbingers to find you beds, and even then I don't know that there'll be anything better than a hen-roost for you."

"Oh, that's all right," Cecily said, before anyone else could answer. "We're going to stay with relatives—my sister and her husband. My brother's in the King's service—he's one of the henchmen."

"Is that right?" said the first guard, impressed. "Well, think of that! Pass on, little lady, pass on, and the gentlemen, too. All right, Jack. The word of the sister of the King's henchman is good enough for us, a'n't it?"

At the house in Bishopsgate Street there was a delighted reunion between Edward and his children. The Butts brothers shook hands solemnly, Cecily and Margaret embraced, Ned slapped everyone on the back indiscriminately, and Edward smiled proudly with tears in his eyes while Margaret's little white Chinese dog ran around and around in circles like a child's toy on a string, yapping without a pause.

"Oh, it's so good to see you all," Margaret sighed when they had calmed down a little. "What a pity Edmund wouldn't come, too. Why wouldn't he?"

"Oh, you know Edmund," Ned shrugged. "But where's Thom? I thought he'd be here, tonight of all nights."

"I doubt if he could have come even if he'd known you were coming," Henry said. "He's one of the King's henchmen, and his duties will keep him occupied tonight."

"He's terribly important now," Margaret bubbled irrepressibly. "You simply can't imagine—he's first in attendance of all the boys and—oh, what a pity you weren't here earlier! You missed the procession through the city today. It was marvelous, and Thom was chosen as one of the seven henchmen to ride right behind the King in the procession. We were by the road watching, weren't we, Henry? And I'm sure he saw us, only he couldn't wave, of course—"

"I should think not, indeed," Edward smiled. "Calm down, child, you're chattering like a popinjay."

"But it was so exciting! And Thom looked so handsome—he looked the best of them all. He had on this marvelous crimson doublet, and his gown was white cloth-of-gold, and his hose—"

"I'm sure they don't want to know about Thom's hose at this very moment, dearest," Henry interrupted her gently. "They've had a long journey, and I'm sure they'd sooner have something to eat and drink."

"Oh—yes, of course, I'm sorry." Margaret was halted at last. "I'll call our steward."

"And you had better consult him over finding beds for our guests," Henry added, then turned to his guests. "Once the coronation's over we'll be able to put you up more com-

fortably at the inn next door, but for the moment there isn't
a bed to be had at an inn in all of London, nor, I'll warrant, in any village from Greenwich to Chelsea. We may
have to make do with mattresses on the floor for a couple
of nights."

"That's all right." Ned waved away the consideration
with an airy hand. "What matters is that we're here, and
after the ride we've had, I wouldn't care if I had to sleep
standing up. Do you realize we only started out on Tuesday
morning?"

"Really? Why did you leave it so late? Oh, of course,
silly of me; you wouldn't have had the news much sooner
than that, would you? I've been so busy I'd forgotten how
quickly it all happened."

"You've had a lot of extra orders for cloth, I should
imagine?" Edward asked, his mind on business.

"You never spoke truer, sir," Henry said proudly. "I've
been seeing Master Curteys daily—he's the Keeper of the
Wardrobe, and a very civil man. He hinted that the King
has told him to put business my way, because of his friendship with Grandmother Morland, and I've done very well
out of it. On budge alone, can you imagine it, he wanted
nearly seventy thousand powderings, and at twenty shillings the thousand—"

"Remarkable!" Thomas exclaimed.

It was clear that he and Henry and Edward were preparing for a long discussion on cloth and prices, and Cecily
and Ned exchanged a glance. They were not the least interested in business.

"How is it, Master Henry, that you don't ask after your
nieces?" Cecily cried out, changing the subject. "What sort
of an uncle are you?"

"And your nephew, sir," Ned chimed in with mock af-
front as Henry stopped in mid-sentence.

"And what about Thom, when shall we see him?" Cecily
went on.

Ned shook his head at her. "No, no, Cecily, it's a bad
policy to start two hares at once. Now, you see, he does not
know which to go for."

Henry laughed. "I see you two haven't changed. Well,
well, I'll ask about my nephew and nieces by and by, when

Margaret comes back. And as for Thom—we hope he will be able to join us tomorrow, after the ceremony. We are having a supper feast here to celebrate, and we hope he will be able to join us once his part in the ceremonial is over. He is serving at the royal banquet, but if his turn is the first or second course, he should be able to be with us by eight or nine o'clock."

Margaret returned at that moment, followed by servants bearing trays of food and wine.

"Ah, here we are," Henry said. "Now we can all sit round the table and talk about the family news while you refresh yourselves. Father—would you like to say grace for us?"

The streets were thronged the next day, from dawn onward. The people were all dressed in their best clothes, and a cheerful good humor prevailed, even though as it started to get hot the crush was uncomfortable and tiring. The sun shone down out of a brazen sky, and only near the river was there a breath of air to cool the sweating crowds who waited for a glimpse of their new sovereign. Every peer of the realm was in attendance—it was the best-attended coronation in the history of England—and in addition there were so many notables of the gentry invited that there would not be room inside the Abbey for more than a handful of the commoners.

The Morlands secured themselves a good place on a temporary platform between Westminster Hall and the Abbey where they could survey most of the river of red carpet that lined the way between the two places, and along which the procession would pass. At last the glittering parade came to the roaring accolade of the crowd—first the royal heralds with their trumpets, then the musicians and singers, and then the priests bearing the great cross, abbots in their dull black and white and brown, bishops as richly dressed as any worldly lord.

The great peers came next bearing the regalia—swords, scepter, ball, cross—all glittering with jewels—and then the newly created Duke of Norfolk, who had been Richard's friend, John Howard, carrying the fabulous crown itself, the great crown of St. Edward with its purple velvet, gold, and magnificent gems. And then came King Richard himself.

He walked barefoot under the canopy of estate, which was of cloth of gold and held aloft on four poles covered in gold leaf. His long gown was of purple velvet, furred with ermine, his doublet of cloth of gold decorated with the white roses and golden suns of York. The cheering rose to a crescendo.

"He looks so noble!" Cecily cried, tears of joy and excitement running down her face. "And so serious. God bless him!"

Margaret was less reverent. "Those are the barons of the Cinque Ports holding up the canopy," she offered.

"I know that," Cecily said. Then, to Henry, "Is it true they are allowed to keep the cloth and the poles afterward as their fee?"

"So I believe," Henry replied.

"Who's that holding the King's train? The big blond man?" Thomas asked.

"That's the Duke of Buckingham," Henry told him.

"His clothes are almost more gorgeous than the King's," Edward remarked.

"Ah, here comes the Queen now," Henry said.

"Isn't she beautiful with her hair all down her back like a girl?"

"She's lovely!"

"Do you know who that is, carrying her train?" Edward said.

"It's Lady Stanley, isn't it?" Margaret answered.

"Yes, but do you know who *she* is?"

"Who? Should we know?"

"She's Margaret Beaufort," Edward said. "The niece of our Lord Edmund Beaufort who married the bastard son of Queen Kate de Valois."

"Really?" Cecily stared. These were names out of history—Queen Kate, Henry the Fifth's wife? Was it possible?

"Amazingly good of the King," Ned commented, "to allow such a notable Lancastrian the honor of bearing the Queen's train."

"He wants to end all possibility of quarreling," Henry said. "He's been trying this past week to reconcile everyone. That's why everyone was invited—and they've all accepted, so it must be working. Lord Stanley was a member of the Hastings conspiracy, but the King pardoned him and let him free, and now Lady Stanley's bearing the train."

"She's a dangerous woman," Edward began, but his voice was drowned by a shout from Ned.

"There's Thom! Look, there! I say, isn't he magnificent? He sees us, I'll swear he does. Thom! Hi, halloo, Thom! Over here!" Ned waved excitedly.

Thom, of course, didn't look up, but the family were thrilled at having witnessed his part in the great procession. Now they were all into the Abbey, and though the doors were left open, the crowd could not see what was going on. However, a running commentary passed through the crowd from mouth to mouth, and their own knowledge of the general procedure kept them abreast of what was happening. A special service was said first, and then the King and Queen went to the high altar and, stripped to the waist, stood bareheaded to be anointed on head and breast with the chrism. Then the robes were put on them, and they were crowned by Cardinal Bourchier, the King's uncle.

Music then burst forth from the organ, and the choir sang the Te Deum, which could be heard outside, for the crowd kept a reverent silence. When finished, the High Mass was said, and the King and Queen took communion. And then the service was over, and they came out again into the sunshine, to a fanfare of trumpets, the sacred chrism still wet on their heads. Music burst forth, the organ playing and all the King's musicians vying with the clamor of every church bell in London. The crowds cheered themselves hoarse as the procession made its way slowly back to Westminster Hall. The King and Queen smiled and waved as they walked along the red velvet carpet, and the people threw flowers under their feet, and called blessings on them, and wept for happiness.

When the procession had gone into Westminster Hall, the Morlands left their stand and began to make their way home. It was past noon, and none of them had dined. The royal banquet would begin at four o'clock and go on into the night, but it was not something that spectators could witness, and so for them the public part of the coronation was over, and the private celebrations began.

"I do hope Thom can get back to join us," Margaret said as they collected their horses to ride home. "Is his horse up here, or will he have to come by river?"

"Oh, it'll be at White Hall," Henry said. "Don't forget he rode behind the King yesterday. If he serves the first course he should be free by about six o'clock."

"What does he have to do?" Cecily asked curiously.

"He stands behind the King on the dais," Henry said, "and any time food or wine touches the King's lips, he and another page have to hold the cloth of estate over his head. There are attendants to do the same for the Queen."

"He has the better part," Margaret said. "There are two other pages who have to lie facedown in front of the King the whole time. They won't get to see anything."

"They won't mind that," Henry laughed. "I'll wager there are a hundred boys in the city who'd give their right arms for the honor, facedown or not!"

"I dare say you're right. Oh, Henry, they say the conduit in Cheapside is going to be running wine—shall we go and see?"

"What do you think, Father, Cecily? Some of the guilds will be roasting oxen in the street, and there's bound to be music and dancing—shall we go?"

"Oh, yes, do let's!" Cecily cried. "It would be such fun." The others nodded in agreement.

"Right," Henry said. "We'll leave the horses at home and walk down, and we can go back to supper afterward, at about five o'clock."

Midsummer was not long past, and when Thom rode through the city at half past eight it was still light, but nonetheless torches and flares had been lit at the street corners, vying with the light of the fires that had been lit to roast the oxen and pigs. London was holding a party to which everyone was invited. Wine ran in the conduits for everyone, and there was roast meat and bread enough, besides the pies that the piemen had been selling and now, under the influence of all the free wine, were giving away.

Fiddlers and pipers accompanied the couples dancing on

the streets, girls in their best dresses, with flowers in their hair, and lads red in the face with trying to outdo each other in the leaps. Children and dogs ran about, getting under the dancers' feet and stealing hunks of meat from the hands of people too drunk to care. On the river everything that would float was bearing parties of merrymakers, and lanterns on poles hung from the sterns danced a reflection in the smooth-flowing water, while their song and laughter echoed to the green banks as they drifted by.

Thom rode without haste, enjoying the sights as he went. Once or twice a girl leaning out from the overhanging pentice of a house would try to ruffle his hair as he passed, or would throw him a flower and ask him to stop and bear her company. He grinned at them and rode on. He was a handsome youth, and with the glamour of a rich household clinging to him, he had grown used to being propositioned by girls.

There was a warm welcome waiting for him at the house in Bishopsgate Street, and hugs and kisses from his father and brother and sister, whom he hadn't seen since he went away to Middleham nearly three years ago.

"Come, Thom, take off that awful old cloak," Margaret said, fussing around him. "Where on earth did you get it from?"

"Oh, it was the first thing I could pick up—I think it belongs to one of the porters—but I had to have something to cover up all this crimson satin!"

"Why, you're still wearing your coronation clothes!"

"Hush, Meg, don't let everyone know! I took off the golden gown—I think I'd have been clapped in the Tower if Master Cosyns found I'd taken that out of the robing room—but I took a chance on the doublet and hose, otherwise I'd never have been here. Cecily, you're as blooming and pretty as a June rose. How wonderful to see you! When did you decide to come? How is everyone—how are Mother and Grandmother? And the children? Didn't Edmund come, too? Oh, well, I suppose someone has to look after the business. And how are dear old Job and Master Jenney and everyone? Oh, you can't imagine how I've missed you all!"

"Your grandmother sends you her special love, Thom,"

Edward said when he could get a word in. "And your mother—she'll be so proud when she learns you had a place in the procession."

"Thom, sit down, take a cup of wine. You have a long way to go to catch up with us," Henry said cordially. "Tell us about the banquet—it must have been a magnificent sight."

"Not when you're face down on the dais! It's all right, I'm only teasing! Meg, do take this dog away, I'm sure he's trying to gnaw my ankle like an old bone."

"We've all missed you at Morland Place—it's seemed very quiet without you."

"Blissfully quiet, I should think, without Margaret and me to torment you all and lead you a merry dance. Master Jenney thought us so wicked, we were beyond redemption. Dear old man, how is he?"

"A little grayer, a little stiffer," Edward said. "He falls asleep sometimes over his lessons. If Paul weren't such a dutiful child, he'd be running wild all over the country, for I'm sure Master Jenney couldn't stop him. But, bless the boy, when the master wakes up, there he is sitting as quiet as a mouse waiting for him."

Thom laughed loudly at this. "Imagine Meggie and me waiting for him to wake!" he crowed. "That child must be an angel."

"No better than Papa was when he was that age, I'll be bound," Cecily said.

"We were much more strictly brought up," Edward confessed. "And Ned was—but your grandmother relaxed her vigilance a little over you younger ones."

"How grateful I am," Thom said. "Ned must have worn her out."

"I was the soul of virtue, wasn't I, Father?" Ned said indignantly, and the laughter that followed was interrupted by a loud knocking at the street door, audible even to them in the upper chamber.

"Who on earth can that be?" Margaret said.

Henry went across to the window and looked out, but it was dark now, and whoever it was was hidden by the shadow of the pentice. There was a lengthy pause, as if there was some debate going on downstairs, and then the steward appeared and addressed himself to Henry.

"A man is below, sir, and wishes to speak with you."

"What sort of a man?" Henry asked cheerfully. "Whoever it is, tonight of all nights we should invite him in and give him a drink. Who is it, Matthew?"

"A strange sort of man, sir, a vagabond almost, except—" Matthew paused doubtfully, and went on: "—except he *says*, sir, that he's madam's uncle."

At those words Ned leapt to his feet. "Richard!" he shouted. "It must be Richard! Bring him up. Henry, let him be brought up, for I truly believe this must be my father's brother, Richard."

"Bring him up, Matthew," Henry nodded, and the steward went out. "What is all this?"

"My brother, Richard," Edward told him. "Don't you remember him? He was at home before you went away to London, Henry, but shortly afterward he went a-wandering like a friar and he's only been home once since then."

"Yes, of course I remember him now," Henry said. "You and he were in France together, weren't you, Ned?"

"We were—God pray it is him—"And at that moment Matthew appeared at the door again and ushered in the "vagabond."

Richard was wearing much the same sort of coarse gown he had the last time he came home, girded about the waist with a rope. His beard fanned out over his chest, its ends bleached almost white by the sun. A cloth bundle was tied to his staff, and he carried a small baby in his arm, while a ragged child of two or three stood beside him, staring up at the assembled company with the dark, solemn eyes of a monkey.

"Dickon!" Ned cried, and ran over to him and embraced him. "It is you! How wonderful to see you."

"Ned, my dear Ned." Richard seemed almost dazed. "But what are you doing here? And Edward, and little Cecily and Thom—I didn't realize—I didn't know."

"Richard, come in," Margaret said. "Matthew, bring a cup and more wine for my uncle. Here, let me take the baby from you."

"Where's Constance?" Ned was asking as Margaret came forward to relieve Richard of his burdens. Richard seemed not to know quite what was happening; he looked from one face to another, and they saw now that his face was pale under the dirt of the roads, and that he was very thin, though his great beard and long curling hair disguised it from a distance.

"Give me the baby," Margaret said again, reaching out her hands.

Richard's eyes met her own. "The baby's sick, I think. That's why I came—I think it needs nursing, and I don't know what to do with it."

"Dickon, where's Constance?" Ned asked again, anxiously this time.

Richard looked at him, his eyes haunted. "She's dead. Constance is dead. She died on the road two weeks ago. She was never really well after Micah—the baby—was born. So I thought I'd come here. But she couldn't make it. She died near Reading, and the monks buried her."

"But how have you been feeding the baby?" Cecily asked, bewildered.

At the same moment, Margaret exclaimed, "This baby's nothing but skin and bone! I believe it's starving!"

Edward took over quietly. "Richard, you had better come here and sit down, and Matthew will bring food for you and—I suppose this child must be Elijah? Come here, child—don't be afraid, we are all your friends." The dirty-faced mite clung to his father's rough gown and spoke not a word, the great dark eyes moving apprehensively over the faces of the strangers. "Margaret, something must be done with that baby. Do you have a reliable woman?"

"Yes—let me see—I suppose Mary is the best, and she has children of her own," Margaret replied.

"Very well, then. Matthew, let this baby be given to Mary, and let her feed it and wash it and see to it, and bring word to your mistress as soon as you can if Mary thinks the child is ill or only hungry."

"Yes, sir," Matthew said, and he took the little scrap gingerly into his arms, and walked out, concealing an expression of distaste at this unstewardlike duty. He returned shortly without the baby but with a tray of bread and meat

for Richard, and a bowl of hot gruel for the ragged child
and told them that Mary was caring for the baby and
would report to them when she had done.

Richard and his elder son were soon sitting at the table
devouring the food that was put before them with every
evidence of a hunger that was not a day old nor yet two
days old. The rest of the family gathered around in sympathetic silence to wait until Richard seemed willing and able
to tell them what had happened. He seemed to revive
greatly with the food, and the dazed expression gradually
faded from his face, leaving him more alert and more unhappy.

Thom tried to lighten the mood by saying, "I can't imagine how you could be hungry tonight of all nights, when
they have been roasting oxen in the streets."

"Are they? Who? Why?" Richard asked. "I didn't see
anyone—I kept to the small alleys. But I thought there
were rather a lot of people about."

"Oh, just a few people, out celebrating the coronation of
our sovereign liege King Richard the Third," Thom said.

"Is it today? I had forgotten. I've lost track of the days
of the week, the months of the year—since poor Constance
died."

"What happened, Dickon?" Ned asked gently. "Can you
bear to tell us? Poor Constance—I liked her very much."

"Yes, I remember you did, Ned—you used to take her
out riding—you were good to her. It would have been happier for her if I had never left Morland Place—she might
be riding with you now on the moors. She was happy—" He
broke off, obviously deeply moved. The ragged child huddled closer to him and tugged at his sleeve, and he patted
the small hand, accepting the offered comfort.

"What happened?" Ned prompted again. He and Richard had been brought up together like brothers, and no
one else was close enough to him to dare to prompt him to
speak from his evident grief.

"There was another baby," he said at last. "Last year—
the winter before last. It died before it was born. She
slipped it like a frightened ewe, when the snow was on the
ground. We were in Wales then, a cold place to winter in,
and she was cold afterward, as if the cold had entered her

in place of the child, and she couldn't get warm again. So we started to come south and east, to the warmer country. We were in the Cotswolds a long time—I helped with the lambing—and then we moved on. It was in Salisbury that she told me she was with child again."

He paused, and Henry pushed the wine-cup into his hand again, and he took a mouthful and seemed revived a little by it. He went on: "She was always strong and quiet, like a mountain pony. She walked easily, even though the child was growing big inside her, she walked easily. Her feet were light, they hardly disturbed the dust. We wintered near Winchester, and then came on, and got slower. She didn't seem so well, and when we got to Reading we stopped. The baby was born there, at the end of May, and we moved on, but she wasn't well. She complained of pains, walking hurt her, she said. And then she got a fever, and in two days it consumed her, and she was dead."

He rubbed a hand over his face, as if he wanted to rub away the memory. His face was contorted with grief. "The woman—who attended her—the midwife—said—"

"What?" Ned prompted.

Richard drew breath harshly, as if he were sobbing. "She said I had no right to make my wife wander with me, if I could do better. She said . . . she said it was I who killed her."

"But it wasn't your fault," Ned cried. "Women do die in childbirth sometimes."

But Richard wasn't comforted. He put both hands over his face, his words muffled. "The woman said she needn't have died, that she died because she had to go on walking too soon. If she had had the baby at home, she wouldn't have died."

There was no other sound in the room but his harsh sobs. The child, Elijah, was crying, too, but he made no sound, the tears rolling silently from his eyes and making clean tracks through the dirt on his face.

At last it was Cecily who got up and put her arm around him. "It wasn't your fault," she said. "You don't know— she might have died anyway, even if she'd had the baby at home. Women *do* die in childbed—it's God's will. Hush

now, there, there. You're tired, I expect, with walking on
an empty stomach. Why don't you go to bed and rest?
That's right. And the little boy—come, Elijah, that's right.
You'll come with me, won't you? I'm your cousin, Cecily.
Will you take my hand? That's a good boy—come, then.
We'll go upstairs—"

And talking gently, soothingly, she led them both out,
holding the child by the hand, and with her other arm
around Richard's waist. The others watched in silence until
they had gone, and then quietly shut the door behind them.
No one wanted to talk. The scene they had witnessed was
too painful.

"Poor Constance," Ned said, at last, "and poor Dickon!
But he'll get over it in time, and every one of us has to die
some time. Don't let us allow our celebration to be spoiled.
Perhaps it will have a good ending—perhaps he'll come
home now, and that will please Grandmother."

"Ned's right," Thom said. "Let's be cheerful if we can.
This is a glorious day for England."

So they sat an hour more, talking quietly and pleasantly
among themselves before retiring to bed, but each of them
had the problem of Richard in his heart, and the image of
him in his mind.

Over the next few days they all to some extent addressed
themselves to the problem. Rest and food soon restored
Richard to his normal wiry health: the baby proved only to
be undernourished; and the older boy was wonderfully
transformed by a little of that care he had lacked all his life.
Cecily took charge of him, burned his rags, washed him,
fed him, and fitted him out with new garments, and he
turned out to be quite a handsome little boy. His hair was
not black as it originally appeared, but a very dark auburn,
like the color of a fox's coat, and Cecily took great delight
in brushing and curling it, and choosing cloth the right
color to complement it. The child was very shy, and would
scarcely speak a word, but gradually became more at ease
with Cecily, though any other member of the family had
the effect of sealing his mouth tight in an instant.

One by one, the family tried to sound out Richard on

what he intended to do, and one by one they discovered that he had no plans other than to carry on as he left off, and that as soon as the baby was pronounced out of danger.

At last Cecily lost patience and cornered him, saying, "These children are coming back with me to Morland Place."

Richard looked mildly surprised. "I hadn't intended to go north right away," he said. "I was thinking of going farther east, into East Anglia. I believe the people there are quite different from anywhere else in the country."

"You may do as you please, Richard," Cecily said impatiently. "Go east or to any other point of the compass, but the children are coming with me to York."

Richard shook his head. "No, my dear, no. I don't think you understand. My boys stay with me. I might perhaps make a visit home later on, next year or the year after, but—"

"Oh, do talk sense!" Cecily cried. "You can't take these children with you on the road again. How are you going to feed the baby? You almost starved it to death once—are you going to try again? What are you going to feed it on? And what will you do in the winter? You'll have two of them to carry then, for Elijah won't be able to walk in the snow."

Richard looked thoughtful. "I must say that I have been worrying about the baby. I can get milk when I pass dwelling-places, but babies seem to get hungry so often, and then there are long periods when I am not near any place of men. It is difficult."

"It isn't just difficult, it's impossible! A baby needs regular feeding and a warm cot, or it will die, and that is the truth, Richard. Do you want your baby to die?"

"No, of course not. Well, perhaps you are right. Maybe it would be better for you to take Micah with you—"

"Both of them. I'm taking both of them."

Richard grew firm in his turn. "No, not Elijah, I can't part with him. Why, he has been with me from the beginning. He went on the road when he was only a few weeks old, and—besides, if you took him I might not see him for years. He would forget me—"

"Then you had better come back to York as well, and settle down there with the children."

"Oh, no, I can't do that. I have my work to do in the world. I can't neglect the call God has sent me."

"Uncle Richard, just look at that child," Cecily said. "He's growing up, he needs a home and a proper upbringing. He ought to be doing his lessons. Do you want him to grow up ignorant and wild like an animal? He'll never be able to take his place among civilized men if he doesn't have an education."

"Civilized men are quite willing to talk to me," Richard said with dignity.

"You were brought up in a proper home," Cecily pointed out. "You *chose* your life, but have you the right to choose the same lot for the children?"

"It is the best lot there is, to be chosen to do God's work. I have a responsibility—"

"Perhaps you have," Cecily said abruptly, "but how can you feel a responsibility to other people when you neglect your responsibility to your own family?"

Richard looked at her, and his eyes opened a fraction wider. "You don't believe in my work, do you? You don't believe I was called?"

Cecily's blue gaze did not waver. "Frankly, no, I don't. I think you do it because you enjoy it. But that doesn't alter the fact that your children need a proper upbringing."

Richard thought about it. "I can't give up this life," he said at last. "I can't live in a house again—I'd suffocate. No, I can't come home yet, not just yet. Let me take the children for a little longer—just until the end of summer. Then I'll come to York."

"I have said you may do as you please. But I am taking the children to York with me."

He sighed. "If it must be, it must be. But it is hard to take a man's children from him."

"You needn't be parted. You can come, too."

"Not yet," he said, almost desperately. He stared past her out of the window like someone imprisoned. "Not yet. Take them, then. Perhaps I'll work my way north instead of east. If I find I can't do without them. Take care of them, and don't let them forget me. I'll be back." He stood up and went to the door.

"Where are you going?" Cecily asked, startled.

"Away," he said, as if surprised. "Back to my life."

"Just like that? And now? Without saying good-bye?"

"There is no reason to stay longer. And I would rather not have to say good-bye to my children. It hurts less this way." And he turned and went out.

Cecily ran to the window, and a moment later she saw him come out into the street, carrying his staff and nothing else. He looked up and down the street, and then walked hurriedly eastward. Cecily watched in astonishment until she could see him no more. She couldn't help feeling she had been put upon, for now she was going to have to explain to the others that he had gone without a word, and was also going to have to tell Elijah that his father had left him.

"Why *me*?" she said aloud, crossly. "Why is it always *me*?"

CHAPTER TWENTY-SIX

Eleanor was more than a little surprised when the party returning from London at the beginning of August brought with them two new children for the Morland nursery. She was not, however, entirely displeased; for Paul, like his father before him, would be sent away in a few years time to be brought up in the King's household, and then these babies of Richard's would keep the house lively. There had never been so few children in the nursery, and Eleanor was suddenly made aware by how thin a thread the Morland fortunes hung. She decided then and there that she must look around for suitable wives for both Ned and Edmund, and must speak to the King about a match for Thom.

For the time being, however, she had little spare energy for worrying about filling the nursery, for, along with the city officers and the leading citizens of York, she was busy with the preparations for the King's visit at the end of the month. Almost immediately after the coronation the King had deemed it politic to go on progress, since he was well known only to his citizens in the north, and he expected to reach York on the thirtieth of the month. York was very much the King's city, and wanted to be sure that the welcome he had there outdid anything any other city could show or had ever shown to any King in the history of the world.

For Eleanor, the event would have the added joy of being the means to meet her favorite grandson again. For many days after the party arrived back from London she had them telling her over and over again every detail they could remember of the coronation and Thom's part in it, and she looked forward to hearing from Thom himself about all the parts the spectators could not witness.

On Saturday, the thirtieth of August, the King and Queen and Prince Edward made their state entry into the city by the Mickle Lith, bringing with them a great train of nobles and bishops and officers of the household, all splendidly attired. The little Prince was so frail that he could not ride, but was borne in a chariot, and on either side of him rode his young cousins: Warwick, Clarence's son; and Lincoln, son of the King's sister, Elizabeth. The mayor, aldermen, chief officers of the city, and chief citizens met the cavalcade outside the gates to conduct it in, and Eleanor made herself one of this party. In a crimson gown and mounted on a black horse, she was well conspicuous, and after the mayor and aldermen she was the first to give the King and Queen welcome.

"This is the happiest day of my life," she said with tears in her eyes.

Richard smiled at her. "Perhaps of ours, too," he said. "Coming to York is like coming home."

Thom was riding close behind the King with the other henchmen, now under the Mastership of Sir James Tyrrel, a long-standing friend of the King's, but he and Eleanor could only exchange a loving glance—it would not have been etiquette to talk now. The cavalcade moved on and into the city. As Eleanor rode under the barbican of the Mickle Lith, she glanced up and remembered that terrible day when the head of her beloved Richard of York had been displayed there, bloody and dripping and crowned with a mocking circlet of straw.

The wheel turns, she whispered in her heart. You should have been King; but here now is the best of your sons, the son of yours likest to you, and bearing your name. He is King, and will be the best king this land has ever known. Rest easy now, beloved: all is well, the pattern is worked out.

Within the gate they were met by a huge crowd of cheering citizens, all dressed in their best, and a display of banners showing the suns and roses of York, the falcon-

and-fetterlock of the King's father, and the white boar that was his own special device. A series of pageants were performed as the royal couple rode through the city, and every street was decorated with tapestries and banners and green branches. Finally, when they reached the minster the mayor made a speech of welcome and presented the royal pair with gifts from the city.

Richard replied, expressing his gratitude for the welcome they had received.

"So welcome have you made us feel, that we wish to honor this city especially. We have recently created our dear son, Edward, Prince of Wales and Earl of Chester, and we now intend to carry out the ceremony of investiture here, in York, to show our great pleasure in the city and people of York."

A great cheer went up, for this was an honor indeed. A day a week hence was appointed for the ceremony, and orders were dispatched to Master Cosyns in London for the sending up of great quantities of cloth and rich stuffs for the making of ceremonial costumes.

The week passed in a series of official ceremonies and public and private dinners and suppers as everyone in York hastened to do honor to the King and Queen and to receive honor themselves. With the investiture to be organized, Thom was, like the rest of the household, too busy to make a visit home just yet, but Eleanor was able to see him in his position of great honor when he attended to the King at a private supper to which she was invited. They had time, then, for a pleasant talk, and Eleanor chatted also to the King with an ease that made many onlookers jealous. But Eleanor at sixty-seven had a presence and dignity about her that made it possible for her to do things lesser mortals could not.

Richard openly admired her and complimented her on her beauty, and it was not insincere. The bone structure of her face was beautiful, and framed in the fine white linen of her wimple it was like a carving in alabaster; but her eyes were very much alive and still bright blue, and she wore a surcoat of peacock-blue velvet that emphasized their color.

"You must have seen a great deal of change during your life," Richard said to her.

"Indeed, I have. When I was a girl the country was in chaos, lawlessness and poverty everywhere, great tracts of land uncultivated, farms left empty and untenanted. Now there is peace and order. The country is prosperous, trade is good, luxuries abound, we have a good and stable government, and the farms are being worked."

"The north is still wild, much of it," Richard said, "but we are slowly bringing it to order. I have plans for that—the north has its own problems, and I believe it should have its own Council to deal with them. London is too remote. I shall set up a Council of the North, and I think I shall put young Lincoln in charge of it. He is a good, steady lad, and loyal to the family. He can take charge of Warwick, too. He may be a steadying influence on him."

This is what I have dreamed of all my life, Eleanor thought. My sons died to make your father King, but to have you here shows they did not die in vain. This stern, soldierly man with the level gray gaze and the pure, loving heart was all that Richard of York would have been.

Once the ceremony of the Investiture was over, Thom was able to come home to Morland Place for a week and discuss his plans for the future.

"I want to stay with the King," he told his father and mother, to Eleanor's entire approval. "I am one of the seven leading henchmen now, and I'm sure the King will offer me a post in the household pretty soon. You can always be sure that if you serve him well, he'll reward you well. And he has mentioned to me that he will think about finding a match for me as soon as everything's settled down."

"Well, that's wonderful, Thom. It sounds as if your future is really settled," Daisy said. "The only pity is that you'll be so far away in London—we'll hardly ever see you."

"I may not necessarily be in London," Thom said. "There will be positions to fill up here. The Queen and the Prince of Wales will be going back to Middleham soon, and I could be sent there. Or, as you know, there's to be a household set up at Sheriff Hutton for Warwick and Lincoln. There's talk of sending the other two princes, the late King's sons—my lord Bastard and my lord of York—to be brought up there as well. I could be given a duty there. But I hope not. I'd be sorry to be far away from you, but I want most of all to be with the King, and I hope I get a post in his household, and then I'd always be with him."

"Spoken like a true Morland, Thom," Eleanor applauded.

"Oh, Mother," Daisy sighed.

"Never mind, Daisy. There is a loyalty that comes before family," Eleanor said sternly, "and Thom understands that. However, it's a different matter with Ned. His duty is to marry again and beget some more children, and we're going to see he does it. He's too like you, Thom, in that—too fond of paying attentions to ladies he has no intention of marrying."

Thom grinned engagingly. "Not much of that goes on in King Richard's Court, Grandmother, I assure you. Ned has far more opportunities than I."

In October, the idyll was abruptly shaken. The archconspirator, Morton, had hatched another plot, and this time had talked the vainglorious and weak-headed Buckingham into helping him. Buckingham's head had been turned by the glory of being Richard's right-hand man, he had accumulated wealth and honor since befriending him, and now he felt power was not enough.

He saw himself as another great Earl of Warwick, a kingmaker, and like Warwick before him, he found the subject of his first attempt a little too full of integrity for his own liking. He wanted someone weaker, more easily swayed. Morton, with his efficient ring of spies stretching over England and France, provided him with the answer. Not the former boy King—the country would not, could not accept him now he had been shown to be a bastard; but someone else whose bastardy was rather more remote.

The Morlands discussed the news. "Henry Tidr?" Eleanor said with blank amazement.

"He calls himself Tudor now—thinks it sounds more regal, I suppose," Edward said.

"But who is he?" Ned wanted to know. "What claim has he to the throne?"

"He's the son of Lady Stanley," Edward said. "Don't you remember when I pointed her out to you carrying the Queen's train at the coronation?"

"And he has no claim to the throne at all," Eleanor said savagely.

"He claims it through his mother," Daisy said more evenly. "She is supposed to be the last of the Lancastrians."

"She is the daughter of the eldest son of the house of Beaufort," Edmund pointed out, "and since there are no sons left alive, she is the heiress—for what that counts."

"Precisely, Edmund," Eleanor said. "For what that counts. The Lancastrians are descended from John of Gaunt, but the Beauforts are his bastard children by his mistress. They are disqualified by bastardy from ever having anything to do with the throne. My lord Bastard has a better claim to the throne than they, and he has no claim at all."

"This Henry has a bend sinister on both sides, then?" Ned said. "Didn't you say, Father—"

"That's right," Edward said. "His father was Edmund Tidr—"

"Who was the bastard son of Queen Kate and her Welsh dancing-master," Eleanor finished. "Buckingham must be mad. The country would never accept him even if they could defeat the King's armies."

"There are a lot of Lancastrians left in the country," Edward said cautiously, not wanting to upset Eleanor too much.

"Not enough," she snapped.

"And then there are the Woodvilles—"

Eleanor stared. "Why should they help?"

"Madam Elizabeth knows that her son can't be king now—but she might not object too strongly to her daughter being queen."

Eleanor understood immediately, and her face twisted with disgust. "Marry Princess Elizabeth to the Tidr and put them on the throne? Oh, what a wonderful thing that would be for the country! A bastard Queen and a bastard-sprung King, ruling under the thumb of Buckingham and

Morton and supported by French soldiers! Dear God, it's a
wonder to me that the earth doesn't open up and swallow
them, for they are not fit to live who would think of a plan
like that."

There was nothing to worry about. The rebellion lasted less
than a month, and was defeated. Buckingham and one or
two other prominent men were executed, but Morton escaped to France, where he joined with Henry Tidr, who
had sailed about the Channel for a couple of weeks and
then gone back to France when he heard the rebellion was
failing. The country, having held its breath for a while,
settled down again happily and the King and Queen were
back in London in time for Christmas.

In January, Parliament assembled to do its proper work,
and much emphasis was laid on the maintaining of law and
order and the dispensing of justice. In March, the former
Queen, Elizabeth Woodville, finally consented to leave
sanctuary and take up residence at Court with her daughters. Richard forgave her for her plotting, and gave her a
pension, and treated her daughters well, promising to find
them suitable husbands when the time came, and to give
them dowries. The bastard princes were sent up to Sheriff
Hutton to join the household of their cousin, the Earl of
Lincoln, where they would be brought up as king's sons
should be, following much the same routine as Richard
himself had as a boy at Middleham. There, they would be
in the company of Clarence's son, Warwick, as well as
their cousin Lincoln, and also young John of Gloucester, a
bastard son of the King's from the days before he married
Anne. It was a pleasant place, and a healthy spot where all
the lads could grow up strong and learned and able to handle their weapons, dance, converse, and make courtly love,
and generally become good and useful members of the
Court.

And then, when everything was looking happier, Fate
struck a terrible blow; early in April, a messenger from
Middleham rode through York on his way to the King with
the terrible news that the Prince of Wales was dead. The
messenger found the King and Queen at Nottingham,
where they had set up Court for the summer, intending to

go further north later in the year to visit their son and the other household at Sheriff Hutton.

"It was terrible," Thom said later of that day. "I was not there when the news came, but as soon as I heard it I went to the private apartments, though it was not my turn of duty. The attendants were standing in groups, staring at each other in helpless shock, not knowing what to do, and everywhere there was a terrible hush. The Queen was kneeling on the floor, her arms wrapped round herself, rocking back and forth as if she was in pain and making terrible cries, like a wounded animal. Not weeping, but crying out. It was her only child, and she could never have another.

"And then the King came in. I could not bear to look at his face. He dropped to his knees beside the Queen and put his arms round her, and held her until the veins stood out in his neck, but he never made a sound. And then the Queen started to scream." He paused, his eyes shadowed with that terrible scene.

"She was almost demented with grief. The little boy, it was said, had been ill only a short time, and had died of the belly-gripes, and one of her women told me that she had visions of the child calling for her and his father in his pain. He died on the ninth of April, the same day as King Edward had died. The King took to his chamber and remained locked inside for almost a week, seeing no one, while all the time the only sound in that silent place was the Queen weeping endlessly; in the end, you hardly heard it, it became part of you, heard only in your bones, like the sound of the wind moaning round the house in winter."

At the end of the month, the King and Queen and the nucleus of the household rode north for the Prince of Wales's funeral and then to Middleham for a short rest, and it was there that Thom was given leave to go home to Morland Place for a visit.

"And how is the Queen recovering from the shock?" Daisy asked him.

"Not well," Thom said. "She looks very ill and tired, and thinner than ever. She was always frail, but I think the shock has made her worse. The child was never strong, but they didn't anticipate his death like this."

"If it was the belly-gripes, they always come suddenly, sometimes with no warning at all. That's why they are sometimes mistaken for the symptoms of poisoning," Eleanor said. "I remember your grandfather telling me how his brother died of them. But it's terrible to lose a child like that, particularly when it's your only child."

"And the Queen can't have another, the doctors have told her. That's another reason she weeps so—she feels she's let him down. He tries to comfort her, but there's little he can do. Except," Thom paused, "I heard him apologize to her once for making her Queen. I didn't really understand, but I think he meant if she hadn't been Queen she could have stayed with the boy and looked after him."

"It wouldn't have made any difference," Eleanor said sadly, shaking her head. "Nursing can't help with the belly-gripes. They come suddenly, and kill quickly."

Shortly after Thom's arrival news arrived from London that Margaret had given birth to her first child, a boy whom they had called Henry after his father. The news cheered the family a little, for still Ned had not been provided with a wife. A messenger arriving later in the month, however, brought news of another match: the letter was from the King and was addressed to Eleanor.

I had not forgotten that service which you asked of me last year, in the matter of a wife for your grandson my good servant Thomas, and a young woman has now come to my attention who I think would be admirably suited. She is Arabella Zouche and is one of the Queen's ladies, and the daughter of a gentleman who lives near Nottingham. She is a cousin of Lord Zouche of Coventry, whom you know and who is a gentleman for whom I have a great regard.

If you are content in this choice, I pray you bid the boy's father come with him to Nottingham when he rejoins us there, when he may meet Master Zouche and discuss the matter. If you can agree over the terms, which I doubt not but you can, the bethrothal can take place at once.

"How kind of him to remember, and to take that trouble in the midst of his own grief," Daisy said, more struck by this than by anything the King had ever done.

"He is the King," Eleanor said, "and a king must stand outside the man and the father and continue to function even through a storm of grief. But it *is* kind, all the same. Who is this girl, Thom? Do you know her?"

Thom's cheeks were a little red. "Well, yes, I do know her—a little, that is. She is one of the Queen's attendants, not long come to Court. She came when the Princesses were taken in, to swell the numbers, but she's a good girl and likely to become one of the Queen's personal ladies."

"An honor, then," Daisy said anxiously.

Edward smiled and said, "I think the King is acting for his own good as well as ours. If he marries one of the Queen's good girls to one of his own good men, he doubles the likelihood of keeping them both close. How old is she, Thom?"

"I believe—fourteen or fifteen—I'm not sure," he said. "She's very pretty—she has golden hair and her eyes are lovely, a sort of smoky gray-green color—"

Ned laughed uproariously. "He knows her 'a little,' he says—but how he gives himself away! How long have you been courting her, Thom? And how long is it since the King noticed?"

"I haven't—I didn't—well, I mean—" Thom stammered, only making Ned laugh the more.

"You see, Grandmother, this isn't so much an honor for the family—it's a desperate attempt by our lord the King to save Thom from getting into trouble with this green-eyed goddess."

"Nothing of the sort—!" Thom expostulated, and Eleanor tapped him on the wrist laughingly.

"Don't you know when you are being teased, Thom? Have done, Ned! Now, Thom, tell us something about her—not her hair and eyes, child, but who is her father? Has he money? Is she an educated girl?"

"She's a very good girl all round, Grandmother. She plays and sings beautifully and dances like an angel, and she often helps out Princess Cecily with her lessons, so she must be learned. And we like all the same books and the same poems, and she rides better than I do, and—"

"Yes, yes, I understand that she is utterly perfect," Eleanor said. "But now, about her family?"

"I don't think she has a mother," Thom said slowly. "I've never heard her mention a mother, anyway. She often speaks affectionately of her father, though. I don't think they have much money, but her father is a gentleman born, and they have a coat of arms."

"Well, we do not lack for money," Eleanor sighed, "and so that the boy is contented I don't suppose it much matters."

Daisy was stung. "You are very lenient with Thom, madam, to be worrying whether or not he is content with the choice. I don't remember you conditioning for that when other matches were being discussed."

"Now, Daisy," Edward warned, too much in the habit of obeying his mother to be easy at hearing her criticized.

Eleanor looked at stout Daisy witheringly. "When a match is suggested by the King, it is well enough even without money, and if the match is well, why should the boy not be content? After Ned's choice and my son Dickon's choice, we should all be glad Thom is bringing the daughter of a gentleman of coat-armor into the family."

"I only said," Daisy began hotly, but she was interrupted by a whoop from Ned.

"Let me congratulate you, Thom, my dear brother, on being about to be wed to the girl of your choice! I shall have to do something along those lines myself, for I can see now that I am letting the family down. Grandmother, I wish to apologize abjectly for all these years I haven't been wed—I understand now why you've kept chiding me."

"You're a saucy boy, Ned. I don't know which of you is worse, you or Thom. But you remind me of my duty—I must find a wife for you and for Edmund, and quickly."

Daisy, whose nose was a little out of joint, said peevishly, "Edward is the head of the household, Mother—it's his duty to find the boys wives, not yours."

Eleanor didn't even answer this, but merely froze her daughter-in-law with a glance and said to her maid, "Go to Job and find out that the King's messenger has been looked after. And tell him we will be coming down to supper presently."

Daisy didn't know when she was well off, and now said, "And that's another thing—why do we have to take every meal in hall? I don't know anyone who still eats in the great hall, and certainly nobody of fashion does, except on the great feasts. We have a perfectly good winter-parlor—"

"While I am alive," Eleanor said with icy dignity, "we will eat in the great hall. It is a tradition that goes back to the beginning of time, and I shall not be the one to break it. When I am dead, you may please yourself—but remember that the people you disdain to eat with are the people on whom your wealth depends. They—and the sheep."

"Bravely said, Grandmother," Thom said irrepressibly, threading a hand through her arm. "We'll have Reynold fetch the sheep up in no time—I should think most of them will fit into the hall if we pack 'em tight—and then we'll say a special grace before dinner: 'I thanke God and ever shall—' "

" 'It is the sheep has payed for all'!" Ned finished off the rhyme that had been repeated to them since their infancy.

Eleanor allowed the two young men to escort her to the door. "I'm glad you remember it, my children," she said, laughing back at them.

Edward and Cecily exchanged a glance. Edward head of the house? Not while Eleanor lived!

Supper was never an elaborate meal unless there were special guests—just bread, meat, and ale—but it was always pleasant, for Eleanor liked to have music played while they ate, and all the children were present, even the youngest, in this case Micah, brought down in his nurse's arms under the watchful eye of Lys, the governess. Master Jenney was no longer with them, but had retired and was living with other pensioners at Micklelith House. Paul had a new governor, a bright young man called Huddle, who got on very well with his young charge, who was now eight and had recently begun to teach Elijah, who was three and a half.

After supper the family remained in the hall and carried on their recreations while the household members occupied themselves with little tasks—needlework, leatherwork, woodcarving and the like. Eleanor liked this peaceful time, when all her family was around her, and there was pleasant talk, games and mumming, or singing and dancing to pass the time.

She was just saying to Edmund, "I really am glad that Cecily brought Dickon's two children back. In two years at the most Paul will be sent away, and then what could we have found for Master Huddle to do? As it is he'll have Elijah well along by then and Micah just beginning." And she saw Job coming toward her from the outer door, a curious expression on his face, and even before he had spoken she knew what it was.

Job was not going to be caught at a loss this time. With as much formality as if he were announcing a lord, he said, "Master Richard is here, madam."

"Bring him in, Job, at once. Why is he waiting outside?"

"He wasn't sure if you'd want to see him, madam."

"What nonsense! This is his home, he may come here any time he wishes."

"I'll bring him," Job said.

A moment later, Richard was standing before her, ragged and empty-handed as usual, but without his usual confidence.

"It's strange, Dickon, how you always arrive at the right time," Eleanor said calmly. "I was just thinking about you, and talking about your sons."

"Are those my children?" he asked unbelievingly, looking at the two bonny black-eyed children who stared at him across the room. He had not seen them for a year, and they had grown a great deal.

"Of course," Eleanor said. "You know, I almost think I can conjure you now by thinking about you. You are real, aren't you? Not some wandering sprite?"

"I'm real, Mother, but I feel as if I've been wandering all my life. I didn't mean to come here tonight, but I came near and I could see the lights burning, and suddenly I wanted to be in here with you all. I knew this is where you'd be—I could see the scene in my mind's eye. It hasn't changed in my lifetime. But then, when I got to the door I became afraid. I suddenly thought, 'I've done nothing, ever, for my family. Why should they welcome me? I've almost broken my mother's heart—why should she want me back?' And then, the dogs barked, and Job came out, and so I sent my name in."

"I want you back, Dickon," Eleanor said. "This is your

home." And she held out her arms, and the tall man seemed to crumple. He fell to his knees, and buried his head in his mother's silken lap as if he were a child again. "Dickon, my dearest boy," she murmured.

"I've come home, Mother," he said, and his words were muffled by the silk of her surcoat.

"It was mainly Cecily who changed my mind," Richard was saying. It was later that same evening, and he had had a hasty wash and put on some of Edward's clothes, and was now sitting on the floor beside his mother, leaning on her knee and talking. His own son, Elijah, was sitting on *his* knee, staring at him and keeping a tight hold on a fold of his gown, as if he were afraid his father would disappear again.

"She said that I had not fulfilled my responsibilities," he said, "and all the time I was wandering I kept thinking of that, working it over and over in my mind, until at last I thought she was right. But by then I had told myself that you'd never forgive me, so the best thing I could do was to disappear out of your lives forever."

"It always did take you a long time to think out things other people know without thinking," Eleanor said.

"Well, now you're here, you've no need to fear you won't be welcome," Edward said. "There's always too much to do and not enough people to do it, especially with Thom away at Court all the time, and Edmund having to be at Shawes several days a week."

"And I'm not able to do as much as I once did," Eleanor said. "I get a little stiff if I'm in the saddle all day. You could make yourself useful by taking charge of what Jenkyn calls the 'factory.' I have a good overseer there, but the men and women work better if they know you're keeping an eye on them."

"If I can, I will—but you'll have to refresh my memory about it all," Richard said. "It seems a long time since I worked on that end of the cloth-making process."

"What do you mean?" Daisy asked. "What end have you worked on?"

"Sheep shearing and lambing," he said with a grin. "That's how I earned my keep, working sheep. I've lambed 'em and dipped 'em and sheared 'em and counted 'em and killed 'em. Maybe it would be better to promote one of your farm hands and put me to the job I'm good at."

"You'll be just what we need at the factory," Eleanor said. "You get on with the common people, and they'll like that. I was always good at the 'common touch' but Edward's hopeless."

"Oh, Mother—"

"Well, you are, Edward. You're too much of a gentleman, you're too shy with them."

"You're a gentlewoman," Edward pointed out.

"Yes, but I had a lot to do with your grandfather when I was first married," she said, "and that did a lot for me. One thing, though, Richard, you'll have to dress like a gentleman at least. They won't respect you at all if you appear like a rogue monk—and neither will I. You'd better go into York tomorrow with Thom and see the tailor. Thom has good taste, he'll guide you right. And spare no expense, Thom."

"Those are the kind of orders I like, Grandmother," Thom said, grinning.

"I'll go, too," Ned said quickly. "I need a new short gown."

"You've work to do," Edward said sharply.

"It'll keep," Ned said easily. "Thom won't be here for long, you might let me share his company while I can."

"Don't use me for your arguments," Thom said, waving him off. The brothers smiled at each other.

"Besides," Daisy said, "why do you want another new gown? You have the blue one—"

"But it doesn't go with my yellow hose, Mother. You said yourself I looked a fright beside Thom."

"You're doing it again!" Thom protested.

"This visit sounds as though it's becoming troublesome," Richard said. "Perhaps I'd better go alone. I want to visit Cecily and Thomas anyway, so perhaps Thomas will come with me to the tailor."

"Oh, that's a good idea," Ned said. "Thom and I both have to see Cecily, don't we, Thom?"

"Do we? Oh—yes—of course we do. Very urgently. So we'll have to go."

"I don't know what you two are plotting," Eleanor said, "but after all, as you say, it isn't often Thom is home. I dare say I can manage your work, Ned, while you're away. But you go into the city too often, and neglect your work."

"I won't so much in future, I promise, Grandmother. You'll see," he said mysteriously, and she left it at that.

"What was all that about?" Thom asked his brother in bed that night. He whispered so as not to disturb Richard and Master Huddle, who were also sleeping in the room. "All that about urgent business?"

"Oh, that was a brilliant plan of mine. I was wondering how to get into town tomorrow without appearing too obvious. We'll see to Richard's clothes, and then dump him at Cissie's and say we'll call back for him. Then you'll come with me. I'll need you."

"What for?"

"You'll see, Thom. It's very exciting, and very secret. You'll support me, won't you? Grandmother's going to be really furious."

"I'd sooner face a mad bull than Grandmother in a rage, but—well, I suppose I'll back you up. What is it? It's nothing bad, is it?"

"No, it's not bad, it's wonderful. Well, you'll see. Good old Thom, I knew I could rely on you."

The three young men rode into the city as soon as the gates were open the next day, and went straight to the Master Tailor, who generally served the Morland family. They were received with the politeness that was due to valued customers such as themselves; but Thom, who was a noticing sort of person, felt that the tailor's journeyman was scarcely civil, and eyed Ned with a kind of dislike, almost hatred. Ned behaved in his usual jaunty manner, and between them he and Thom chose the cloths and advised on the cut, as Richard was turned this way and that, measured and draped, as if he had no life of his own but were a stuffed effigy.

"Well," Ned said at last, "that seems to be everything. You'll have those things made up at once, won't you, and send them to Morland Place when? Tomorrow?"

"All but the damask doublet, Master Morland," the tailor said obsequiously. "That damask takes some matching, you know, and you wouldn't want a botched job, would you, now?"

"Certainly not," Ned agreed with a man-of-the-world air. "Very well, take your time over the damask. My uncle can wear the silk until it's ready."

"Yes, sir, of course. You'll have it before Friday, Master Morland, sir, that I promise you. Good day to you, gentlemen."

Outside Ned wiped his hand across his forehead. "Phew, it was getting hot in there, wasn't it?"

"There were some red-hot looks being thrown at you, anyway," Thom said cheerfully.

"Not so loud, for God's sake," Ned hissed at him, casting a glance at Richard to see if he'd noticed, but apparently he wasn't listening. "Now, uncle," Ned said to Richard teasingly, "if you can heave your poor old bones on to that horse, we'll help you round to Cecily's. It isn't far—only on Lendal."

They were there in ten minutes, and Richard had only just had time to embrace Cecily and ask after the children, when Ned tugged at Thom's sleeve and said loudly, "Cissie, Thom and I have some very urgent business we have to attend to now. We'll leave Richard with you and call for him again later—is that all right?"

"Well, I suppose so," Cecily said, slightly bewildered. "But will you be back for dinner?"

"I don't know. What's the time now? Half past eight? And you dine in an hour?"

"No, at ten o'clock," Cecily said. "We don't have to keep such early hours in the city as you do at home."

"We might be back by ten, I hope so. Anyway, we must go now. Good-bye, we'll be back later."

"Now, will you tell me what it's all about?" Thom asked patiently when they were outside. "Where are we going?"

"To horse, to horse!" Ned shouted excitedly as he mounted. "We're going to church!"

"To church? What for?"

"To get married," Ned called over his shoulder, for he

was already ahead and trotting before Thom down the street.

"Not me?" Thom yelled after him, spurring his own horse into a trot.

"No, not yet," Ned grinned back at him. "I'm the lucky one. Come on, we're late!"

At the door of the tiny church of St. Crux they stopped, and Thom followed Ned's example in jumping down from his horse, giving the reins to a nearby urchin to hold with the promise of a coin for his trouble.

"It's all right, we aren't late—she isn't here yet," Ned said happily. A small knot of passersby began to gather at the sight of the two richly clad young men.

"You aren't afraid she won't come?" Thom asked curiously.

"Oh, no—she'll come all right."

"Who is she? Can you tell me yet?"

"I thought you'd half guessed it this morning," Ned said gleefully. "Don't you remember at the tailor's—the journeyman who was glaring at me fit to kill?"

"Yes, I remember him—don't tell me you're going to marry him?"

"Of course not, ass! It's his daughter."

"Ned, you aren't serious?"

"Of course I'm serious. We've been troth-plight for months, but we kept it secret. I was terrified to tell Grandmother. But now she's with child, and so the time has come to take the plunge. Her father thinks I've been hanging round her with evil intentions, and so he glares at me, but doesn't dare do more for fear his master turn him off for frightening away his best customer. But I dare swear if it went on any longer he'd waylay me one dark night and have my ears and nose."

"But, Ned, why her?" Thom asked, baffled.

"Hush, here she comes! You'll see why now."

A small figure was hurrying toward them from the Shambles, wrapped in a cloak of thin wool with a hood that was drawn up, unseasonably for the hot summer weather. Ned went to meet her, caught her by the hands, and then brought her to Thom as she put off her hood and let the cloak fall open. Yes, I see why, Thom thought. She was a slender and beautiful girl, with dark curling hair covered by a simple thin linen veil, an exquisitely white complexion, rosy cheeks and lips, perfect teeth, and brilliant dark eyes. She looked to be about thirteen or fourteen, and she gazed up at Ned with evident adoration.

"Thom, this is Rebecca. Rebecca, my dear brother, Thom, whom I'm sure you will shortly come to love almost as much as you love me. I say *almost* in the hopes you'll take that for a warning and not fall in love with him like every other girl who's ever set eyes on him."

"God's day to you," she whispered shyly, holding out her hand to him.

"God's day to you, Rebecca," Thom said, and stooped to kiss her on both cheeks. He felt that Ned was making a big mistake, but it was obviously too late to do anything about it.

"Take off that awful cloak now, child," Ned commanded her. "You have on the surcoat I sent you—ah, yes, that's much better."

Under the concealing wool cloak, she was wearing a surcoat of fine lapis-blue linen, and she also brought out from the concealing folds a circlet of white June flowers, which she placed on her hair over her veil.

"Now, then, we can proceed. Hullo, Master Clerk, are you within? Ah, there you are. Now, sir, do your duty as I bid you, and you shall have the fee I mentioned, and a pair of new candlesticks for your altar into the bargain."

The withered old cleric came out from the darkness of the church, blinking in the sunlight as if he had spent all his life in there, like an owl in a burrow. His clothes were old and threadbare. It was obvious that he made no very great living out of St. Crux.

"I don't like to do it without the father's permission," he faltered.

Ned looked stern. "Now, then, master, we've been through all that. You know that her father doesn't care for her, and I do, and I'm far richer and far better a person to please than he is. Besides, would you have the bairn brought into the world without the blessing of Mother Church? Don't blush, my flower, he knows all about our haste and anticipation. That's what finally swayed him, wasn't it, sir?"

"It was, master," the cleric said sighingly.

"Then let's be done. Come, have you your book? Good. Then away!"

The cleric read the ceremony in his halting voice, Ned produced the ring and put it on Rebecca's slim white finger, and the thing was done. Marrying at the door, they took no mass.

"Never mind," Ned told his bride, kissing her, "you shall have everything hereafter that your heart desires. Come, Thom, you shall kiss her too and wish us well."

"I do, with all my heart," Thom said, shaking hands with his brother. Then he kissed Rebecca and said, "God bless you. I hope you will be happy, and have many sons."

The little crowd that had gathered laughed and applauded, though one or two of them muttered about gentlemen making free with poor girls and bringing them to shame. Thom felt it was necessary for them to go somewhere, but quite where he did not know. Suddenly he had an idea.

"Rebecca, I must buy you a bride-gift! I haven't anything for you, because I didn't know I was coming to a wedding, but we'll go now and look around and you shall choose anything you like."

"Good idea, Thom. Here, boy, bring the horses! There's a penny for you. Now, Rebecca, let me lift you up onto the saddle—thank God you're only a feather, for I'm shaking so much I don't know what to do. Now, then, hold tight to his mane—that's right—and off we go."

Thom had the idea Ned was grateful to him for getting them by an awkward moment. They rode down to the stalls in Stonegate and after some looking and much blushing, Rebecca was induced to choose a slender gold bracelet, very plain and fine, which used up all Thom's allowance for that month and the next. Then they made their way back to Lendal to Cecily's, aware that it was past dinner time. Ned was glad enough that it was, for he felt the arrival would be eased by being an interruption to dinner.

They stopped before the door, and Ned, glancing up, saw a face look down from a window and rapidly disappear.

"We've been seen," he said. "Now for it."

There was little anyone could say. The deed was done, and it was none of their business to object to it. They tried to be nice to Rebecca, who was terribly shy and nervous, aware that the storm was still to come, when they should ride home that afternoon. Cecily got Ned to one side later on and asked him a few questions.

"How did you meet her, Ned? She told me she lives in the Shambles, and I'm sure there's no one down there you know."

"It was in the tailor's I met her," he explained. "She was there one day bringing a bite of dinner to her father. I fell in love with her at once. That's why I've had so many new clothes this year—I had to find some reason to be there. But her father was suspicious."

"Why didn't you tell him you meant to marry her?"

"You don't know him. He'd have gone straight to Grandmother and sold her the information for the highest possible price."

"At the cost of his own daughter's happiness? Surely he'd rather have her well married?"

"Not he! He hates poor Rebecca. She was his daughter by his first wife, and his first wife was a Jewess. He married her to get hold of her father's business—her father was his master—but when her father died he found he'd left everything to another daughter to keep it out of his hands—Rebecca's father's hands, I mean. So he hated his wife and he hated Rebecca even more. He's married again now, and poor Rebecca has a terrible time at home."

"Well, it's all very touching," Cecily said, "but I don't know what Grandmother's going to say."

"She wanted me to get married."

"Not quite this way," Cecily said grimly.

"Come home with me, Cissie, and make it all right."

"Not me! But Richard will put in a word for you, won't you, Richard?" Cecily said, seeing her uncle approaching them.

"If you like," he said equably. "I can't see what else you could have done, since she's with child. But it gives me such a queer feeling to look at her—she's so like Constance."

"So she is! I hadn't noticed," Cecily said. "Was that why you chose her, Ned? You were very fond of Constance, weren't you?"

"I don't know. I hadn't thought about it. But I didn't really choose her. God chose her for me, and put her in my way. I couldn't turn her down after that, could I?"

"If that's the argument you are thinking of putting to Grandmother, I advise you to think again," Cecily said. "Stick to the simple fact of the coming child."

"Oh, well." Ned sighed. "I'm not the first at any rate. Richard did it and got away with it. And she was awfully mellow about Thom's young lady. I'll just have to trust to luck."

Cecily sighed. "You'd have done better to trust to good sense from the beginning," she said. But it was not said unkindly.

CHAPTER TWENTY-SEVEN

Daisy wept, Edward stormed and shouted, but worst of all had been Eleanor's dead-white coldness, anger in which there had been a little of hurt: that had been the hardest to bear. Eleanor ruled her household with a hand of iron, and she was beloved because of it. Edward had been for setting the marriage aside and buying a dispensation at whatever cost, but Eleanor, unexpectedly, opposed it.

"No," she said. "Let him live with his own error. It will not do to set her aside if there is a child. That would only mean trouble in twenty years time, strange young men appearing and claiming. We must accept this—girl. And Ned shall learn as he grows older the penalty of loose behavior, of following his own will in disregard of his parents'."

After that she went out into the herb garden and walked up and down for a long time. Thom watched her out of the window, saw Job go up to her and walk two turns with her, talking, and then leave her again, dismissed, it seemed, by a small wave of the hand; and when he had gone it seemed there was a slight droop in the normally proud carriage of that beautiful head. Thom could not bear her to be unhappy. He hurried down and went out to her.

Without a word he took her hand and placed it on his arm companionably, and, fitting his steps to hers, he walked with her, up and down. Her head was up again, for she would not let anyone see her less than erect, but her face was closed and cold.

At last Thom said, "Don't be unhappy about it, Grandmother. What's done is done."

"But such a girl, Thom! A nobody! How can he have such small pride, and he the heir to the whole estate? We have failed somewhere in bringing him up. I know Richard behaved badly, too, but Richard was always strange, and since he was the youngest it didn't matter so much. But for Ned to be so undutiful— he cannot care anything for us at all."

"He does care, Grandmother. He is deeply sorry to have offended you—"

"Then why did he do it? He is sorry to have been found out, I dare say, but not sorry for his deed."

Thom sought for an answer that would satisfy her. "It would be a sign of weakness in his character if he regretted the deed now, don't you think, Grandmother? It would be a sign that he had done it rashly and without thought."

"In what other light can you view such a—marriage?" Eleanor asked scornfully.

"It began with a rash act, of course," Thom said thoughtfully. "He fell in love, which was rash, and he courted the maid, which was more rash. But when he thought of the consequences of his deed, he felt that he had to face up to them and stand by the girl who was, after all, his wife by then in the eyes of the church, and marry her properly and bring her home to Morland Place even at the cost of losing your approval, which is a great cost to him, truly, Grandmother."

Eleanor looked at him skeptically. "Do you call that responsible behavior?"

"Yes, I do," Thom said boldly. "He could have taken his pleasure lightly and abandoned the girl to suffer—to starve and certainly to be cast out by her father, perhaps to die. He could have done that. Many men have done it. Many would have done it in this case. But he didn't. Having done wrong, he did not compound the wrong, he took up his burden bravely and faced his family's wrath."

"Why are you his advocate?" Eleanor asked. "*You* are not like him, Thom. You would not do such a thing."

"I'm not his advocate, Grandmother. It's just that I think I understand him, and I don't want you to be unhappy."

"Unhappy?"

"I don't want you to think he did what he did because he didn't care about you and the family and the Morland name. He does care, very much."

"And you think loss of Ned's regard would make me unhappy?" Eleanor said stiffly.

Thom pressed her hand against his side and smiled at her. "It did, dearest Grandmother. I know when you're not happy, even if no one else can guess it."

Eleanor smiled at him fondly in response. "Someone else did," she admitted.

"Job?"

"How did you know?"

"I saw him from the window. What did he say?"

"Much what you have said, but less forcefully, more deferentially," she said.

"He loves you very much, doesn't he, Grandmother?"

Eleanor raised an eyebrow. "He's been with me since he was scarcely more than a child." It was hardly an answer, and she reverted to the problem in hand. "The worst thing is that Ned should have done it twice. I might be able to believe your excuses if it were only once—but twice!"

Thom thought quickly. "Who does that remind you of?"

"What?"

"Someone else made two secret marriages—someone you cared for. Who was it?"

Eleanor stared. "What can you mean, child? You cannot mean King Edward?"

"Yes—he made two unfortunate and secret marriages. Both to women not suited to his rank, with whom he fell in love. And Ned was in his Court, was a page to him for three years."

"Are you trying to tell me that he behaved that way because his master behaved that way?" Eleanor asked, astonished.

"It isn't as ridiculous as you may think, Grandmother. Everyone admired King Edward tremendously, and anyone who was near him was as much in love with him as if he cast a spell on them. Now, when you're a page, you tend to copy your master's behavior—you know that, don't you? That's why you are at pains to find a good master for your children; for that very reason, that you expect them to follow his example. So what more natural in Ned than that he should have grown an amorous and romantic side to his nature at the expense, perhaps, of a little of his moral nature?"

Eleanor thought about it. "I believe you may be right," she said at last. "I forgave him for his first mistake because the King himself asked me to. I wonder if you may be right?"

They walked a couple of turns in silence, each absorbed in his own thoughts.

Then Thom said, "At all events, Grandmother, it will at least mean a few more bairns for the nursery, and that should please you. And next year when I marry my Arabella—"

"I pray that I may see your babies one day, Thom. Though I am glad that you should have a place at Court, I am sorry in that it means you cannot live here at home."

"But we shall come and see you often," he reassured her. "You know that the King loves the north, and I dare say he will often visit York, and spend some time at Middleham each year, too. So I shall be often near enough to come and visit."

"I hope so, my dear child, I hope so," Eleanor said. She paused and turned toward him, and on an impulse cupped his face in her hands, his beautiful, high-cheekboned face with the dark blue, speaking eyes. This was the child with whom she had walked hand in hand in the orchard; the child she had taught to ride, placing him with her own hands astride his first pony; the boy she had taught to sing and play the gittern; the young man she had placed at Court, whose career she had watched with pride. "My dear Thom," she said. "When your grandfather came south to court me, his father brought gifts with them, fine cloth and engraved cups and other valuable things. But your grandfather brought me a pup from his own bitch, the pick of the litter. There is always one pup better than the others, better in every way. The pick of the litter—" She kissed his forehead. "God bless you, child."

She released him, and they walked on again in silence, companionably, and once again hand in hand.

* * *

Rebecca was miserable. The terrible scene when Ned had brought her home was bad enough, but what had followed was worse. The grandmother, from whom she had expected to fare worst of all, in fact was easier to cope with because she just ignored Rebecca and went her own way as always, but the mother—the mother was after her all the time, chiding her and criticizing her and bullying her. She discovered quite soon that Rebecca could not read nor write nor reckon, and decided that she was useless, and told her so.

"How you ever thought you could be mistress of such a great house I don't know! How are you to keep the accounts if you cannot reckon? How are you to order the household's needs if you cannot read or write? Why, the servants are better educated than you are! How do you expect them to respect you and obey your orders?"

Useless to try and tell her that she had not expected anything—that she had married Ned because she was asked, because she was in love and with child, and to get away from an intolerable home. Daisy would not listen to her shy stumblings. Sometimes Rebecca thought she was being punished for her sin; sometimes she wished she was back home, sleeping in the garret and running errands for her father and stepmother, and being cursed. Here there were far more things she could do wrong, and a tongue-lashing from Daisy was worse, somehow, than a blow from her stepmother or a beating from her father. The pain of the latter was soon forgotten. The former haunted her memory and made her more nervous and more clumsy still.

If Ned had supported her, it would have been easier to bear, but he had to be out a lot of the time. He told her he would have to work extra hard to placate his parents, and so every morning he would ride off on some business or other and not return, sometimes until supper. And in the evenings, after supper, there were so many things he liked to do that she could not do. She did not know how to play chess or tables, and the card games that she knew were not the ones he knew. She could sing, but she didn't know the same songs, and she could not play a musical instrument or dance.

She had been brought up alone, and did not know any of the games they played, and it was hard to learn the rules because they played so spiritedly and boisterously and could not be bothered to explain the rules to an outsider. An outsider, that's what she was in truth. She spent most of her days alone now. Daisy, having discovered that she was a good plainwork needlewoman (though she had not learned much of embroidery), set her each day a huge task of plainwork—shirts and sheets and other linen—and put her in one of the linen storerooms alone to do it. So, Rebecca sat all day alone in an empty room sewing her way through a heap of linen until her fingers were sore, looking from time to time wistfully out of the window at the sun and the green fields, and earning no praise even if she by some superhuman effort finished the day's task.

In the evenings she sat, an onlooker in the hall, while the family played and amused themselves. At night, in bed, Ned sometimes made love to her, but that was not as it had been before their marriage, for they had to do it quietly now because they shared a room; and he did not do it every night, sometimes just turning his back on her and going to sleep without a word. And then when she had been there a month, she discovered that she was not pregnant after all—it had been a false alarm, and Ned was furious and accused her of tricking him, and after that he would hardly speak to her or kiss her or make love to her, ignoring her, coldly, as if she didn't exist.

It was no wonder, then, that she was miserable, and alone in her workroom she sometimes wept silent tears that her love had brought her to such misery. One day, just before supper, she slipped out of the house and wandered into the orchard, and there she sat down beside a tree and wept bitterly. And then she felt a hesitant hand stroking her head as if to comfort her. Ned! she thought. He loves me after all—he had come to stop me crying and take me in his arms! She lifted her tear-stained face and turned, catching at the hand, trapping it between her own. And she dropped it quickly, with a gasp. It was not Ned, it was his cousin, Edmund.

"I—I thought—" she began, and then her misery engulfed her again and the tears welled out of her eyes. Edmund sat down on the grass beside her and regarded her quietly, letting her cry until the worst of it was over, only stroking her head or shoulder from time to time, as one might soothe a small hurt animal. At last she grew calmer, and, sniffing and hiccuping, she sat up a little and looked at him. His face was a Morland face, but somehow just missed the usual beauty of the Morlands. His features were not quite regular, slightly asymmetrical. His eyes were a little too pale, and not as spectacularly large as Thom's; his hair slightly lighter, a nondescript brown. He had no great beauty, and was so quiet and uncommunicative that he seemed to have no great character either. He did his work quietly and well, and amused himself by reading.

"Why are you so unhappy?" he asked her now. His voice, too, was rather flat, as if he wished to efface himself even when he did speak. "Is anyone unkind to you?"

"My mother-in-law," Rebecca said quickly. "She is unkind. And everyone here despises me because I am not educated or from a wealthy family. Even Ned despises me, and wishes he hadn't married me. And I wish," she said passionately, "that I had not married him!"

"Why did you?" Edmund asked in the same quiet, incurious voice.

"Because I loved him," she said. Edmund waited, and she added honestly, "and to get away from home."

"Weren't you happy there?"

"No."

"Did you not love your parents?"

"My mother is dead. I have only a stepmother, who hates me, and a father who never wanted me from the beginning. What about you? What happened to your parents?"

"I never had a father at all," Edmund said, "but I had two mothers."

Rebecca thought this was a joke and gave a quizzical smile.

Edmund did not smile, and went on, "My first mother drowned in the moat over there."

"Oh!" Rebecca was not quite sure, from his expression,

how she ought to react to that so she said, "How did it happen?"

"She fell in love with one of the swans that live on the moat. She used to feed him by day with scraps from her own plate, and by night he used to swim to the edge of the moat and change into a human being, a fairy prince, and my mother would meet him there, and they would walk and talk together all night until the moon set. And as soon as the moon set he would change back into a swan, leaving my mother behind, brokenhearted."

Rebecca was staring at him, with her mouth open. She had never heard anyone talk like this.

"One day, she consulted with a witch, asking if there was some charm that would release him from the spell so that she could marry him. And the witch happened to be the very witch who cast the spell in the first place, and she was jealous of my mother and wanted to punish her for falling in love with the prince. So she told her that the prince could never be released from the spell, but that she could give my mother a vial that would change *her* into a swan, too. And my mother said, 'Give it to me then, for that way I can be with my love forever. Swans mate once for life—we shall never be parted.' And the witch gave her a vial of liquid and said, 'When the moon sets and the prince turns again into a swan, drink this down, and follow him. As soon as you step upon the water, you will change into a swan'."

He paused, looking sideways at Rebecca. Her tears had dried on her face, and she was utterly absorbed in his tale, her sadness forgotten. "What happened?" she asked, breathlessly.

"The witch had tricked her. The vial was filled only with plain water. So when my mother drained it off, and stepped on to the surface of the moat, it broke under her, and she fell in and drowned."

"Oh!" A breath caught in distress. "And what happened to the prince?"

"He remained a swan, and he never left the moat or mated again. He is there still—you may see him if you care to—swimming around and around sadly, mourning his lost love until he dies."

"Oh, how sad," Rebecca whispered. And then she realized that it had been a story. "It's—it's just a tale, isn't it? Why did you tell it me?"

"To stop you being sad. And I did, didn't I?"

"Yes—why, yes, I'd forgotten all about—"

"All about yourself?"

"Yes. I sometimes used to tell myself stories—when I was sleeping in my garret, and the rats used to run along the rafters, and I was afraid. I'd try to tell myself a story to stop myself thinking about them. But I'm not very clever, and I don't know many stories," she finished sadly. "So it usually didn't work."

"I do that, too," Edmund said, "but I think other people's stories are better than my own."

"But how do you get people to tell you them?" she asked. She didn't feel shy with this member of the family, for he spoke so plainly, and with no haughty look, just as if she were one of them.

"I read them in books," he said, "which is the way folk long dead tell their stories still."

"Oh!" A little cadence of disappointment—she had hoped to be told a secret that would help her.

"Why oh?" he asked.

"I can't read nor write," she said sadly. "I never was book-learned."

Edmund smiled suddenly. Few people ever saw Edmund smile; Rebecca, seeing it for the first time, wondered how she could ever have thought him plain, for his smile lit his whole face. "I could teach you," he said.

"Could you? Could you really? But I'm not very clever," she said. "Is it very hard?"

"At first it is, but after a while it gets easier, and then easier, until it's as easy as speaking." He let the book he was holding fall open—he had been reading in the orchard when the sound of her crying had drawn him over to her—and held it out to her. She stared in wonder at the page covered in tiny black marks.

"Is it true?" she whispered in wonder. "Can you really look at those marks and say what they say?"

"Really," he said, smiling.

"The same every time?"

"The same every time."

She looked up challengingly, and pointed to a set of marks. "What does that say?"

He looked. *"Pilgrimages,"* he said.

She stared in wonder. A set of squiggles, almost a random pattern, but he looked at it, unlocked it with his magic, and drew out a word, a thought, a whole set of associated ideas. Pilgrimages. It really was magic. Could her own eyes, which saw only black patterns, ever be taught to look through that solid paper and ink to the crystal treasures behind? It seemed impossible. She raised her eyes to his face again, wonderingly, and her fingers stroked the page of the book tenderly.

"Could you teach me? Truly? It seems like magic."

"I can teach you," he said. "I will. Truly." His eyes were looking into her with such a great meaningfulness that suddenly she felt her heart fluttering, and the soft blood stole to her cheeks. Her lips parted slightly with her quickened breath. Edmund continued to look at her, and he placed his hand over her hand as it rested on the book and began to stroke her small slender fingers.

2

The country was at peace, and content, under a just and prosperous rule, but there was sadness at the Court, for all the superficial gaiety of the Christmas season. The Queen had been ailing since the death of her son, and the true nature of her disease now came to be discovered. Thom wrote:

My poor mistress, though dressed in the most gorgeous of gowns, could be seen to be failing fast, and her illness was only emphasized by the presence at her side throughout the celebrations of the Princess Elizabeth, a golden-haired beauty dressed as magnificently as the Queen herself. The King remained near my mistress all the time, and though he played the host as well as he was able, his great misery could not but be felt through it all. The only moment of relief came when a messenger brought news— in the midst of a revel—that the Welshman will surely invade our land this summer, and the King cried out,

"Thank God for it!"—for here at last was something that could be done.

After Christmas, the Queen took to her bed, and as if to make the worst even worse, her doctors told my lord that the nature of her disease—the wasting sickness—was contagious, and that my lord must avoid her bed and even her presence, except for a brief visit. My lord cried out in agony that he had lost everything, that his son had been taken from him, and that now his wife too was slipping away, leaving him alone and in darkness. He went to his room then, and for weeks stirred not abroad, doing the work of the King but refreshing not the Man at all. Still he could never forget that he was King, and ordered even such small things as a new set of clothes for my Lord Bastard to be sent to him in Sheriff Hutton. He appointed his son John of Gloucester to be Captain of Calais, and when it was then rumored he would legitimate the boy and make him his heir, he made a public proclamation that my lord of Lincoln was to be his heir, and after him the Earl of Warwick. Everything must always be done correctly, even then.

And then March came, and the Queen died. It was a terrible day. I remembered my master's words—that he was left alone in darkness—for as she lay dying, the sun went away, though it was broad noon, and a terrible, unnatural darkness came over us. It is said it covered the whole land, and therefore you will have seen it too, and felt the horror that it struck into our hearts. The people in the streets knelt down and prayed for mercy from Heaven; the beasts in the fields cried with terror and huddled together.

And in that dreadful darkness the Queen died, and the King cried out and wept most dreadfully, and we thought that the end of the world had come, and that we would never see the sun again, but would perish in the dark like our mistress.

The sun returned for us, but not for him. I believe he is in that darkness still, for there is no light behind his eyes as once there was. Scarcely was the Queen dead when rumor began to be bruited abroad that he was glad she was dead so that he could marry the Princess Elizabeth, his niece. May they be accursed in Hell who could say such a thing!

My lord called together a meeting of all the chief men in Westminster, and told them publicly that he had no intention of marrying the Princess Elizabeth, nor ever had. The Princess herself was so grieved at the loss of her mistress, whom she loved, and the cruel rumors, that my lord sent her to Sheriff Hutton to be with her brothers and her cousins for a while to cheer her.

And now my poor master, who never cared for hunting, rides out daily hunting and hawking to distract his mind. I believe if it were not for the great strength of his will and his duty, that he would lose his mind, for never did a husband love his wife more, or need her presence as much.

English spies abroad brought the news of the Welshman's activities, news that he was gaining support from the King of France, who was providing him with money and men for an invasion in the summer. Morton was with him, his uncle Jasper Tidr, and the Earl of Oxford. If he came, he might find some support in Wales, and in the southwest where there were still some Lancastrian families ambitious enough to help him. England would have to have an army ready in case he tried an invasion, and heralds went out to the rich people of the land to ask for money. Not gifts, this time, they were told to be sure and point out, but loans, which the crown would repay. Few people were asked for more than fifty pounds. The Morlands and one or two other wealthy families gave a hundred pounds; and there was the usual promise of armed men, two men-at-arms and twenty archers.

"If it comes to a battle," Richard Morland said, "I want to go and fight, Grandmother."

"I, too, by God," Ned said eagerly.

Richard was bored with life in one place; Ned had always been bored by a life of virtue, and since he wasn't in love with his wife anymore, he had nothing to keep him. So the promise was four men-at-arms. In June, the Court once again moved to Nottingham as a conveniently central place from which to initiate the defense of the realm if it should be necessary, and the King set that realm in a state of readiness, ordering the sheriffs to be ready to come to arms at a moment's notice.

Then, at the end of June, Lord Stanley came to the King and asked permission to retire to his own estates to rest. From the moment of the discovery of Hastings's plot, he had not been out of the King's sight; once released from confinement and pardoned, he had been made a Steward of the Household so that he should be under the King's eye all the time. His unstable character was a watchword; he had changed sides so often it was said he didn't know from one moment to the next which way he was facing; and the King had made sure he would not be able to do anything without its being known.

Now, on the eve of the expected invasion, he asked leave to go. His wife was the invader's mother. This would be the moment to clap him under guard until the battles were over.

But the King hesitated.

"Your Grace—sir—you can't let him go!" his advisers cried. "He will go straight over to the other side."

"He says he will be better able to rally his men to our defense if he is at home," Richard said. "And that's true."

"He is also better able at home to rally them to the Tidr's defense," Lovell pointed out.

"That is also true," Richard said. "But I will give him leave."

"But why? Why, your Grace? Why not just lock him up for a while?"

Thom knew the answer before it came, and though he admired the man who could say it, he felt a twinge of anxiety all the same.

"A man can only give his loyalty," the King said. "It cannot be forced from him. If Stanley wishes to betray us, we shall fight him as well."

So Stanley rode away, and the country settled down under the hot summer skies to wait. In Nottingham the King rode out and hunted in the great forest, and Thom rode always near him, helping with the hawks, carrying for the King the handsome falcon he had bought from Morland Place in the spring. His master was as serious and courteous as always, but there was a closed-off well of grief in him that Thom longed to assuage, and which made him loath to be from the master's side for a moment. He slept when the King slept, and at all other times remained within sight, close to him as a hound presses close to his master when the thunder growls and a storm draws near.

July turned into August. The King and his close attendants hunted in Sherwood Forest, staying overnight sometimes at Bestwood Lodge, and it was here that a sweating, dusty messenger on a lathered, exhausted horse found the King on Thursday the eleventh of August. He had ridden the last lap of a relay of messengers, bringing the news from Wales that the Tidr had landed with his French mercenaries and had set foot in the realm at Milford Haven on the previous Sunday, the seventh of August.

The armies gathered near a village called Sutton Cheyney on the twenty-first of August, perhaps ten miles from Leicester and two miles from Market Bosworth, and pitched their camps on a clear but sultry evening. The English army was on the high ground to the east, the Tidr's French army on the plain to the west; and to the north, between the two, was Lord Stanley's contingent. He had refused to muster at Richard's request, as had been expected, but he had not yet joined the French. Changeable as ever, he knew that no one in England gave a plucked hen for the Welshman's chances, and despite his promises to his wife, he was holding off to see which way the battle went before joining in. Richard was so forgiving he felt that even if he scuttled over at the last moment he would be all right.

As darkness fell, the King called his commanders to him for the eve-of-battle consultation, and the tactics decided upon were that John Howard, the Duke of Norfolk, should advance straight along the plain, while the King and his contingent held Ambien Hill to the northwest, thereby keeping Stanley's men from swooping down on Norfolk's flanks. The third division of the army, the men under Northumberland, the King discounted, though not openly. Northumberland had been slow to answer the call to arms, and it seemed probable that he would not fight at all on the morrow. He had fought for Richard's father and Richard's brother, and he was tired of fighting the Crown's battles. From now on, Percy was for Percy only; that was his attitude; so Richard placed his own men a little to the north and west of Northumberland's, just as if they were not there.

The meeting broke up, and the commanders went to their tents, and the King walked about the camp a little. Thom watched him, trying to gauge his feelings. The King passed one or two groups around fires, glancing at the faces of the men sharply, here and there asked to inspect a sword-edge or feel the spring of a bowstring—the things a general did. The men greeted him cheerfully and respectfully. Behind his back they called him "Old Dick" or "Maister Dickon," the sort of names men gave to a master who treated them fairly but worked them hard. They were glad to be fighting under him, the premier general in the known world. The Tidr had no chance.

Passing on, the King stood at the edge of the ridge and looked across the plain at the French camp. The lights of their fires pricked the velvet darkness like the tails of fireflies; it was quiet here, outside the circle of the English camp, so quiet you could almost believe you could hear the Frenchmen talking, little murmurs of sound traveling across the plain and on the small sweet breeze upward to the hill. Was that the sound of a horse whinnying? A ring of iron on stone—a cook-pot being set down, perhaps, or a sword sharpened?

The King's gaze turned then toward the smaller lights of Stanley's camp, and Thom saw the expression of his master's face, in profile now, harden, as his brows drew down. What would Stanley do? The only thing that can wound a King is treason—all else he accepts as his burden. A little breeze lifted the King's crest of silky dark hair, fluttering it, and he shivered. Thom moved up beside him.

"Will you take a little wine, your Grace, and go to bed?"

Richard turned abruptly at the voice, and for a moment, before he controlled himself, there was a desperate empty grief in his face that wrenched at Thom's heart. Then it was gone, and it was the soldier, grim but confident, who addressed his henchman.

"We have the better position," he said. "And we have the better men. God will decide the issue. If we lose tomorrow, it will be the end of England—she will suffocate and die under a French despotism."

"We will win, sir—we must win," Thom said.

Richard stared at him for a moment, and then recollected himself. "We'll go and look at the horses, you and I," he said, laying an arm over Thom's shoulder, "and then we shall both sleep. It will be a long day tomorrow."

A little while later they parted, and the King retired to his tent. Thom could not sleep, but wandered about the camp like a benevolent spirit. He longed to get at the enemy, and his ferocious eagerness cheered those who spoke to him. But in his heart he carried an ache for his master that was like a barb lodged in his flesh. What had he been thinking there on the ridge? Not of the battle, he was sure. Perhaps it was of Anne and his son. What else could make him look so desolate?

Before dawn the camp was astir again, officers waking the soldiers, cooks rekindling the fires and making breakfasts, grooms feeding the horses and rubbing them down. In his tent the King, white-faced and weary from lack of sleep, was dressed in his gilded armor by his pages, and as the chief men gathered in front of his tent he emerged, Thom walking behind him, carrying Richard's healm over which was fitted a golden crown, the slim circlet designed for wear in battles only. Around him were others of the henchmen and esquires-of-the-body, wearing the white boar cognizance; and the royal heralds, their tabards quartered with the royal dignities, the leopards of England and the lilies of France; nearby a groom held White Surrey, curving his great neck and fidgeting with excitement, his rich caparisons fitting him for the bearing of a king. But it was the general, not the King, who came from the tent, his expression showing neither fear nor hope, his eye moving about, scanning his own men and then the sky, gauging their mood and the likelihood of rain. Thom remembered how often his grandmother had said he was like his father, his father who before him had been the greatest general in England. It was Richard of York who stood before them that day, and who mounted White Surrey, and put on his circleted healm.

Quietly, the army moved to its places, the royal army, including the eighty or so members of the King's own personal command, moving westward along the ridge to Ambien Hill, Norfolk's contingent spreading themselves over the lower slopes, and Northumberland remaining back at Sutton Cheyney to repel Stanley if he should attack. The Welsh-French rebel army was drawn up in three groups on the plain. The numbers of the two sides were almost equal; but if Northumberland did not bring his men in, and Stanley fought on the Welshman's side, Richard would be outnumbered almost two to one.

The rebels began the attack, edging toward the base of the hill and firing with small artillery. Norfolk's men under his banner of the silver lion answered with arrow fire and there were small losses on either side. The rebels under Oxford's "star with a fiery tail" fell back a little. Trumpets sounded, the rebels advanced again, and with a great clash the two lines met. Up on the hill Richard watched the battle, dispatching reinforcements wherever the English line seemed likely to be weakening, and slowly the rebels were forced back. In the center of the English host, Jack of Norfolk fought grimly with his son Surrey beside him, and further along, Lord Ferrers and Lord Zouche, the cousin of Thom's betrothed, swung steel at the enemy's heads, maintaining the flanks. The rebel trumpets sounded again, they fell back and reformed at their standards, and after a short lull the battle began again more fiercely.

A messenger came running up the hill—one of the scouts Richard had set at the outskirts of the field—to say he had spotted the pretender, and, having had him pointed out, Richard could see the Welshman mounted within a group of about five hundred men, apparently a reserve, holding back from the battle. Almost at the same moment news arrived that both Jack of Norfolk and Lord Ferrers had fallen. There was no time for personal grief. The King sent reinforcements to the line, and a messenger to call Northumberland into battle. Back came the answer— Proud Percy would sooner remain where he was "in case the Stanleys attacked," he said.

Catesby, one of the King's secretaries, called to him,

"Sir, we should retire—nothing has been lost yet. If we withdraw, we can gather more men and fight another day."

"No," Richard said. "The issue must be decided here—today."

"The Stanleys will attack at any moment—" Catesby began.

But the King waved him away impatiently. "My healm," he called to Thom, and Thom came forward to close the visor for him. "We ride to seek Henry Tidr," he said.

A cheer went up. Behind him were all the men of his own household, his esquires and pages, his henchmen, the nobles and sons of gentry who had served him and loved him all their lives. Thom glanced back at them. He saw Francis Lovell, whose tunic bore his device of a running hound; John Kendall, the King's secretary; Ratcliffe, Ashton, Constable, the Staffords; good Sir Robert Brackenbury, the Constable of the Tower, who had ridden hotfoot with a contingent of London men to be at the battle by his master's side; the other henchmen, and the pages, some of them hardly more than boys. In all, perhaps eighty men, to ride against Henry Tidr's five hundred. But they were enough. If they could kill the Welshman, the rebel army would have nothing to fight for and would scatter and run. And Stanley would scurry to put himself on the right side again. It was their lives for the victory.

Yelling the battle cry, Richard spurred White Surrey down the hill, and his men plunged after him, cheering wildly. They were his, his own men, bound by a loyalty nothing could alter. *Loyaulté Me Lie.* Thom drove Barbary hard, his eyes on the slight figure waving a battle-ax whose head was crowned with gold; dust spurted up from the horses' hooves; above them fluttered the three standards, the quarters of England, the cross of St. George, and the White Boar of Gloucester. Across the plain they galloped, giving tongue like hounds, under the very noses of the red-coated men of Stanley's army straight toward that group of waiting horsemen clustered around the Welshman and the red dragon banner.

Horses reared and screamed, whirling axes caught the brilliant sun and flashed like fire, yells of anger and pain

shook the air, and the dust was covered with blood. Now a
sea of flesh was cloven before them, blows ringing sometimes on plated steel, sometimes sinking yieldingly into
flesh and bone. Lovell and Sir Robert Percy were up by
Richard's side, Thom was at his other shoulder with Ratcliffe close behind him, and foot by foot they were cleaving
their way toward the beating heart of the rebels, that whey-
faced, straw-haired Welshman who sat shaking with fear
on his horse, watching death coming for him inexorably.

Only yards from the pretender, the King himself hewed
down the standard-bearer, and the red dragon was trampled in the dust; and then Ratcliffe screamed above the din
of battle and pointed, and the King's men saw the red-
coated men of Stanley's contingent riding at them from
their flank. So Stanley had joined battle at last! Ratcliffe
and some others turned aside to face the new threat, but
now Richard's men were falling on all sides. His own
standard-bearers were down, while still he fought on, so
fiercely that he was separated from his own men by the
force of his attack.

"Treason! Treason!" he shrieked, and Thom, hearing
that desperate, wounded cry, felt his heart lurch up into his
throat. "Treason!" Gasping for breath, his eyes wet, Thom
flung himself forward toward his lord, seeing, through the
thicket of weapons that surrounded Richard, the golden-
circleted helmet and the arm still swinging the bloody ax.

"My lord!" Thom cried, his voice parched with dust. He
caught a glimpse of a white face, and felt sure his King
had heard him; and then a mighty blow seemed to explode
inside his head, and he fell. A dozen weapons hacked
through the King's armor then, and with a terrible cry he
too gave up his life, falling beneath a battering sea of blows
only feet from his enemy, his lips parted still in that word
that spelled death to his heart.

The battered and bloody remnants of the army of the last
English king fled north and south. The men of York, including the Morland contingent, were still on the road: the
duty of calling them out had been Northumberland's, and
he had not performed it, so that they had not heard of the
muster until late on Friday, the nineteenth. They had

marched before dawn on the twentieth, but by ten o'clock on the twenty-second, when the battle was all over, they had not even reached Leicester. They turned and rode home, their hearts racked with grief and shame.

On the twenty-third, at the same time as one John Sponer, an officer of the Mayor's Council, was telling the news to the mayor and aldermen in the Council Chamber in York, a dusty and bloody refugee reached Morland Place, seeking shelter, and bringing the same terrible tidings.

The family gathered in the hall, their faces stricken, to hear what he had to say. Eleanor herself knelt beside him and bandaged an ugly wound in his arm, while Daisy and Rebecca washed the dust from his face and lifted a cup of wine to his lips. As soon as he had his breath back, he began to cry, his thin shoulders shaking helplessly. He was one of the henchmen, his white-boar cognizance reddened with blood, not all of it his own. He had served with Thom, though was junior to him. In stumbling words he told the story of the battle, tears running freely down his cheeks, when he reached the crisis of his narrative.

"Thom—what of Thom?" Daisy interrupted him as he told of traitor Stanley's intervention.

"He fell—he and the King—almost at the same moment."

Daisy gave a hoarse sob and put her hands over her face; Eleanor only stared, her face white and set, her eyes burning in their sockets like blue torches.

"There were so many swords," the boy sobbed. "You couldn't see them for the swords. And when he was down, every man hacked at him, the treacherous dogs, hacking at his dead body; though they had been so afraid of him in life, they shook in their shoes at the thought of him. Oh, my lord King!" He stopped, unable for the moment to go on.

Eleanor's fingers were still on the bandage, arrested at that moment as if her heart had been stopped, and would never begin again.

At last the boy continued: "Maister Ratcliffe was dead, too, but Sir Francis called us back, those of us left alive. We got to the hill and stopped there. We saw the Traitor take off the King's helmet and hold it up, and then he took the crown from it and put it on the Welshman's head. And I thought my heart would break, but there was worse to come. Oh, worse." He faltered.

Eleanor whispered, "Go on."

"We fled on the road to Leicester, but after a while I got to feeling faint from my wound, and I couldn't keep up, so I dropped by the roadside, and hearing soldiers coming, I crawled into a ditch and hid. I saw it was the Welshman— still wearing my King's crown, may God rot his filthy heart in him—and his troop. Frenchmen and Welshmen, cursing and blaspheming, crowing over the victory a traitor won for them, the gutter curs—"

"Hush—leave off cursing, child," Eleanor said. "It isn't fitting. Remember—" She could not finish—remember who is dead.

The child drew a shaking breath. "Oh, mistress," he whispered, "we heard him cry out when they slew him. I don't think I shall ever forget that, waking or sleeping, until death takes me, too. And those filthy curs had stripped him naked—not even a clout to cover his loins, and flung him naked across a pony like a dead hart. And they derided him as they rode, and one of them tied a rope round his neck, and called him a felon."

The listeners drew their breath with horror.

"An anointed King," Edward cried in a cracking voice.

"They would not dare—" Daisy rocked back and forth, groaning like a woman in labor, and Eleanor bit her lip until the blood came.

"Blasphemy," she whispered, her eyes wide. She crossed herself. "Oh dear God alive, what will come to us now, when such a murdering dog as this can defile the body of an anointed King? Dear God, shall we all die? Oh, Richard, Richard—"

"They passed close to me," the boy said, "but I wasn't afraid anymore that they'd find me. Death would have been pleasant to me then, when I saw my master, more wounds on him than a man could count, and every wound like a mouth crying out 'Treason! Treason! Oh avenge me!' " He began to sob again.

"Stop, no more," Edward intervened, afraid that the

women would be driven to a frenzy. "Let be now, rest yourself."

"Let him weep," Eleanor said. "A hundred years of weeping would not shed enough tears for this day's deeds. Our gentle King is dead, and a vile-born Welshman wears his crown, and tomorrow, who knows what terrible things he will do."

Later, the Morland men who had been too late for the battle rode in, their hearts burning with shame and anger that through Northumberland's treachery they had failed their master. Later still, the records of the city of York for that day were entered up. "This day," the entry read, "was our good King Richard most piteously slain and murdered, to the great heaviness of this city."

The following morning the young henchman resumed his pointless journey.

"Where will you go now?" Ned asked him.

"Back to Wensleydale, where I come from. And then—I don't know. My lord of Lincoln is King now. I'll wait for him to call us to arms."

Ned shook his head. "If he has not already fled, the Welshman will have him captured and killed. The Court at Sheriff Hutton is bound to be his target—everyone is there, everyone who has a claim to the throne. The Welshman won't leave them alive to challenge him. Lincoln, Warwick—even King Edward's sons—he'll murder them all."

"Well, if that's so, I'll get across the border and wait my time," the lad said. "But one thing is certain—I shall have my revenge on one person—Northumberland. As soon as the battle was over he went and knelt to the Welshman, God damn him. If I have to wait until my life's end, I'll pay out proud Percy!"

"Well if you do," Ned said. "God go with you. I would I had been you, for all that you saw. I'd rather be you, or even my poor brother, than to have to live all my life knowing I was not there to fight."

"It's no blame on you," the lad said. "Good-bye."

"Good-bye. God speed you."

CHAPTER TWENTY-EIGHT

Henry Tidr, or Tudor as he now insisted on being called, entered London in September, and received there, shortly afterward, the contents of the household at Sheriff Hutton, whence he had dispatched an armed force after the battle. The captives included Warwick, John of Gloucester, my lord Bastard and his brother, Margaret of Salisbury, the Princesses Elizabeth and Cecily, and Lincoln's younger brothers. Lincoln himself managed to escape across the sea to his aunt Margaret in Burgundy. The Princesses were put into Henry's household; the male heirs he imprisoned in the Tower until he decided what to do with them.

He had himself crowned on the thirtieth of October, a coronation to which few who were invited cared to come, and on the third of November he called Parliament to pass an act making him King by right of battle. The Parliament made two other significant actions. The first was to attaint King Richard and twenty-eight peers of treason—thus confiscating their estates for the Treasury—by the novel expedient of dating Henry's reign to the day *before* Bosworth. This meant that Henry was King on the day of the battle, and everyone who fought against him was therefore a traitor. There was a terrible outcry, both in Parliament and in the streets of London, when this was heard, and some men even dared to speak against it in public, for if such a thing could be done, there was no surety for any man in his actions.

The second action was to repeal the Act of Titulus Regius, the Act that had pronounced King Edward's children illegitimate and made Richard King. It was, against custom, ordered to be repealed unread, and all copies of the Act burned, on pain of death. The significance of this passed the commoners by, but the peers and the gentry understood well enough.

"He means to marry Princess Elizabeth," Edward remarked when the news reached York.

"Of course he does," Eleanor said scornfully, "and by reversing the Act and making her legitimate, he hopes to get a firmer grip on the throne he stole. But you forget one thing."

"What is that?"

"If he makes her legitimate, he makes them all legitimate—all her sisters and brothers. Which means—"

"Of course! My lord Bastard is automatically made King again. King Edward the Fifth."

"Edward, you must be stupid, or you would not say it in that joyful tone," Eleanor said sourly. "Don't you see, he will have to kill them now?"

Edward's face darkened. "Yes, I see. I'm sorry, Mother. What do you suppose he will do? He can't execute them. There's nothing he can accuse them of."

"He'd find something, I dare say—but a trial would only remind the people that he *was* King. No, it's my belief he'll have them quietly put away. They'll just disappear quietly one day and never be heard of again."

"And the others?" Edward said. "Warwick? Lincoln's brothers?"

"He has them mewed up safe enough for the time being. But I think he will be rid of them, one by one, as the opportunity arises, and all those whose blood is more royal than his."

In January, Henry Tudor married the Princess Elizabeth, who was held in much affection by the Londoners, and much pitied for having to wed the Welshman. Margaret and Henry were still in London—Margaret was now expecting her second child—and they both witnessed the procession on the wedding day and thought the Princess looked very unhappy. But then the Welshman's mother had come to Court, and anyone who met her had no doubt as to who was really going to be Queen to the Tudor. She had forsworn Traitor Stanley's bed in a religious vow in order to be free of him to take up her residence there, and Stanley spent most of the rest of his life on his estates.

Ned made a business trip to London in the spring and stayed with Margaret and Henry, and conveyed to them Eleanor's fears about the fate of the new Queen's brothers.

"We have wondered the same thing," Henry said. "In truth, we don't much like being here. Margaret feels contaminated, and I feel too vulnerable, but we think we ought to stay until the baby is born—it's a long journey when Margaret's so far gone with child. But as soon as we are able to travel, we'll put the business under the subfactors and come home. There's not much business to be had out of *this* Court—the Welshman dresses like a shepherd and makes the Princesses mend their clothes. And even if they wanted my business, I don't know that I'd be inclined to deal with them."

"I'm only sorry for the poor Princess," Margaret said sadly. "It must be terrible being married to your uncle's murderer, who has all your family locked up, and lives like a husband with his mother."

"Now, Meg," Henry warned.

"Well, he doesn't treat the Princess like a wife, does he?" Margaret said. "No one goes to see the poor thing, while his mother sees all the envoys and spends hours in consultation with him that no one must disturb."

"Well, never mind it—we shall soon be gone. The baby's due in June. We should be able to leave in July, and be home by the end of the month."

"In time for Grandmother's birthday," Ned said, smiling for the first time in that conversation. "She'll be seventy in August, you know, and we thought we'd have a special celebration for it, a great feast and lots of the kind of music she loves."

"Good idea. Well, we must certainly be home in time for this," Henry said. "How is she, by the way?"

"Oh, you know Grandmother—she never changes. But I

think she's lost a little weight since last year. She seems—I don't quite know—sort of brittle, like a cornstalk. But then, she *is* very old."

"She's the oldest person I know," Margaret said cheerfully. "And that's certainly worth a celebration."

"When you do come," Ned said, "don't forget not to refer to the Welshman as 'King.' She won't have it said, not even in jest, and her tongue isn't any blunter since the King was killed."

On a hot, still day in mid-June, Margaret laid in of her second child, a fine big boy whom they named Richard. And on that same day—the seventeenth of June it was—a terrible rumor made its whispering way through London. The day before an officer of the household, Sir James Tyrrel, had been given a general pardon—that is to say, a pardon for all offenses whatsoever committed before that date—and an order to receive the keys to the Tower from the Constable for one night. It couldn't have happened in the King's time. Brackenbury, who had perished at Bosworth field fighting for his King, would not have given up his responsibility without knowing why: but under Henry Tidr, one did what one was told without asking questions, and the new Constable was a man of his own household.

And on the seventeenth, the little trickle of rumor fled like a fire before the breeze westward through London from the Tower toward Westminster, that Prince Edward and the Duke of York had disappeared. It was murmured very low. For one thing, nobody knew quite what the Welshman was capable of against anyone who crossed him; and for another, no one wanted the poor Queen, Princess Elizabeth that was, to hear it.

Henry kept it from Margaret as long as possible, not wishing to disturb her while she was in childbed, and when she did hear, he knew he had been right.

"I want to go away from here," she said passionately. "I keep thinking of the poor Princess. I don't want to be here when the rest of them begin to be hustled away. I want to go home to Yorkshire where the air's clean and one knows who is loyal to whom."

"We will go, then, just as soon as we can. Hush, now, hinny, don't fret, we'll be gone in a month. And besides, it may just be rumor. You know how rumors grow out of nothing."

It comforted her a little, but on the sixteenth of July the rumor seemed confirmed by the issuing of a second pardon to Sir James, along with a grant of the Constableship of Guisnes, to which place it was announced he would be traveling at once. And two days later Margaret and Henry and their month-old baby and year-old son, Henry, together with the principal members of their household, not forgetting Margaret's Chinese dog, rode out of the sad city of London in which the poor Princess Elizabeth was confined to a captivity that would last her whole life. They took the old Roman road north-eastward, trotting briskly through the July haze, and it was like a flight, an escape from a dark prison back into the sunlight.

The birthday feast was magnificent, more than fifty dishes finding their way to the table, including a whole roast peacock decorated with its own feathers, its great tail cunningly fixed erect, and a pie whose crust was modeled in the shape of a castle with small flags flying from its turrets. There was no hare served, of course, but there was a marvelous subtlety in the shape of a pure white hare sitting up on its hind legs and boxing off a falcon that was trying to capture it. It was a work of art and of culinary genius, the hare being, of course, a compliment to Eleanor; but she wondered afterward how much cunning there was in the choice of subject. A hare fighting off a falcon? Did someone order it that way, because the falcon was the symbol of Richard of York, her long-dead secret lover?

It was something to think about during that day. Her family gathered around her happily, for she was the heart and head of the household, a proud old queen ruling her kingdom with a rod of iron tempered with love and justice. Of her own children only Edward and Richard were there—Anne could not travel so far, the journey would have been too much for her; she was over fifty now herself, and had borne many children, and Eleanor had never seen her since the day she went south to be married.

But there was pleasure in looking at her grandchildren: Edmund, quiet and steady as he had always been; Ned and his wife, Rebecca, who was greatly improved since Edmund had begun teaching her to read, and was now pregnant again, though Ned pretended to be surprised; Cecily and her Thomas, and Margaret and her Henry, happy and prosperous married folk, the backbone of England. And in the nursery were little Elijah and Micah, also her grandchildren, five and three years respectively, and doing well under Master Huddle, throwing off their disadvantageous beginning.

Then there were her great-grandchildren, beginning with Paul, now ten years old, the flower of the House of Morland and its pride. There would be no place for him now at Richard's Court: he would not serve a king, but it was hoped he would be able to join some other noble household for a few years, perhaps that of the new Duke of Norfolk, Jack of Norfolk's son. He was a handsome, able, likable boy, very much like his father, except that he was a little steadier. Like Thom, perhaps. And finally there were the Butts children, Anne and Alice, Henry and Richard, children of good parents who would be brought up in the good old-fashioned way, and lend their cousinly blood to the Morland family to strengthen it. Anne was to marry Paul—Eleanor had no qualms about that now. Perhaps Rebecca would have other sons and daughters who would marry the other Butts children. It was good yeoman stock, and she was glad to have it in the family.

The family brought up their presents to give to her, the finest gifts each could afford and find, some truly valuable, others valuable because they were given with love. From the grandchildren there was a magnificent arras hanging for her chamber, a wonderful thing picturing the Garden of Eden, filled with every kind of flower and a number of beasts both real and mythical: pansies, lupins, wallflowers, gillivors, roses, bluebells, stocks, buttercups, and daisies bloomed in that tapestry garden under the hooves and paws of unicorns, leopards, horses, foxes, sheep, griffons, a cameleopard, a white boar with a gold collar, stags, hounds, and wildcats. In the center a white hare hopped blithely over a sprig of heather that had somehow strayed in off the moors, and while the air overhead was bright with flying birds of every jewel hue, in the branches of a tree above, a white falcon was chained by his fetterlock to the bough.

It was a wonderful piece of work, and Eleanor pored over it and exclaimed and wondered for some time. There were other gifts of jewelry, furniture, plate, books, and cloth, but it was to the arras she turned again and again, delighting the family with her own pleasure.

When the feast was over the musicians played and sang while it was digested, and there was a play performed by the servants on the theme of an old local folk legend. Then the musicians struck up again for the dancing, and Edward solemnly led his mother out to head the first line of dancers. Ned danced with her then, and afterward Paul insisted that it was his right as eventual heir to lead her out, but after that, she grew pale and breathless and had to sit down.

"I am too old to dance so fast and so often," she said. "I shall enjoy watching you, children. On with the dancing!"

She resumed her seat on the dais, and smiled happily in reply to Job's anxiously raised eyebrow, and he came forward to fill her cup again and murmur that she must not overtire herself.

"I am very well," she said. "You take care of me too well for it to be otherwise."

He touched her hand slightly as he straightened up, a little gesture that would appear accidental to anyone else, but in which he had grown skilled over the years. No one but him had filled her cup at dinner for longer than anyone could remember. His own birthday gift to her, a tiny engraved ivory ball which opened to reveal a similar, but smaller, ball inside, and then another, and another, was hanging on a chain from her ceinture beside her missal, and that was the best compliment she could have paid him.

"The family is looking wonderful, is it not," she said to Job as they watched the dancers stepping and springing to the music. "Indestructible, like the whole family of the animals of the field. The children playing like lambs, the older ones grazing peacefully on their own pastures. Whatever the Welshman does or tries to do, he cannot defeat us."

"God pray he cannot, madam," Job said. "He thinks to rule us like a French king in France, with taxes and fear."

"But he shall find we are made of a stronger and better material," Eleanor said. "I have been worried and afraid since our King was killed—"

"I know it," Job said.

"But now I feel strangely peaceful, as if I knew that nothing could ever harm us," she said. She turned her still beautiful eyes up to meet his. "Some of us may die—all of us will die one day—but the family goes on. Don't you feel that?"

He nodded, having no words.

"I had such a dream last night, Job," she said. "Such a vivid dream. I was running over the moors, over yonder towards Shawes, running so fast and fleet and free, as if I were on four legs, not two. Perhaps I was. And then there came a strange voice in my head from nowhere, and it said, 'You can fly if you wish. Let me show you,' and I seemed to be lifted up into the air, and I traveled through the air without any effort, as if I were borne on the wind. And I looked down and I saw Morland Place and all the lands spread below me, and the sheep grazing in their hundreds, thick as snow over the pastures, and people coming and going to the house, passing in and out, dozens of them, family and servants, all going about their proper work unhindered. Then I flew away, on and on, and this same feeling came over me, this feeling of peacefulness that I have now." She paused.

"That was a strange dream, mistress," Job said.

"But a good dream," she added.

"Yes, a good dream."

"Now, Grandmother, you must be rested enough to dance again," Thom said in her ear.

She turned, startled—no, not Thom of course, it was Ned. He sounded so like Thom at times.

"Yes, I am rested. Take my hand then—but not too quickly. Remember how old I am."

"That is what we're here to remember, Grandmother," Ned said cheerfully. "But in truth, you look so young that I think either you must have been lying to us, or else you're a witch and will never grow old."

"Go along with you," Eleanor said, laughing. "Anyone could tell you learned that sort of flattery at Court. Your grandfather once said the same thing, that I never grew old, but that was nearly thirty years ago, and I don't think he would repeat it if he saw me now."

"Then I would have to challenge him to a duel for insulting you. Oh, Queen of this night and Queen of my heart—" He began a flourishing bow.

"Stop it now, Ned, you make me laugh too much. It isn't seemly."

He kissed her hand. "Anything you do looks seemly, Grandmother. You are a true queen."

The dancing went on until late in the evening, and it was almost midnight when the servants finally put out the torches and the family went up to bed. Ned and Richard carried the arras up to Eleanor's room and hung it temporarily with nails over the old one. "We'll fix it for you properly tomorrow," they said, "but it shall be the first thing you see in the morning when your curtains are drawn."

"Thank you," she said, "and bless you. Bless you all, my children. I have had a very happy day."

"I hope you won't be too tired in the morning," Richard said. "I want you to ride with me to the mill, remember. There are some things that I think need your attention."

"When was I ever too tired?" Eleanor said. "When something has to be done, we do it."

But when her maid went to draw the curtains around her bed at five o'clock the next morning to get Eleanor dressed for early mass, she stared for a moment at the sleeping face, and then went to wake the master. For all her haste, Job was there first, feeling for his mistress's pulse and listening to her breathing.

"Overtired, too much dancing last night," was his verdict. But his eyes met Edward's anxiously, and he said, "It may be best to call the doctor."

The doctor said much the same thing. "But at her great age, there is no knowing. She has a stout constitution, and with rest may be as good as new. I cannot yet tell. Call me if you feel it is necessary. Otherwise, I will call tomorrow."

Eleanor woke around nine o'clock, and the first thing she saw was the children's tapestry, and the second thing was Job's face, close to hers, his misty eyes staring in hope and expectation.

"Mistress," he cried. "Eleanor—I was afraid—I've been here since this morning—"

"What o'clock is it?"

"After nine. You danced too much last night and tired yourself," he said. "You must rest and regain your strength. I'll send for your dinner—"

"Mother—" Here was Daisy pushing past him.

"Help me to sit up a little," Eleanor said. She was very weak and could not stir for herself. They lifted her and propped her with pillows. She saw that her maid and Rebecca were also in the room, sitting on the window-seat quietly. "I feel so weak, like a little child," she said. "Pray you, move away from the window so that I can see out. That's better. No, Job, no dinner. I am too tired. Just be quiet, let me rest."

She directed the women to sit down, and bid Job stay beside her, "In case I want to send for something. You are a quieter messenger than these women."

"Yes, madam. The doctor—"

"Hush, I don't need the doctor. I'm just tired. Job, I had that same dream again last night, the one I told you about. I was out there on the moors—see, you can see them from this window. Out there the air is so fresh and clean, and the light is so strong, I couldn't get used to it when I first came north. But now, it's like the breath of life to me. Even the heather smells different from the heather in the south, and the bees make a different noise, and the flowers grow differently.

"I used to talk about going south again as going home, but this is my home now. I never want to leave the moors and the north. I shan't ever. Richard loved it here. And Thom knew how to love it. I'm glad Richard had Thom with him at the end. And I'm glad, now, that Thom died— yes, don't be shocked. Because how would it have been to live on and his master dead?"

She was silent for a while, gazing out of the window; then her eyes moved around to the tapestry, and she studied it again, and smiled. The nimble hare in the center had been sewn with great cunning so that it was as lively as a real hare, and there seemed to be a smile on its face. The fox, beyond it, was looking at it, creeping from behind that tall clump of grass, but the hare was jumping over the sprig of heather with no care in her heart, and smiling at Eleanor across the room as if to say, "I know he's there, but he can't touch me." And there's the white boar, and a white rose, and the falcon, and the sun up above in his splendor. All the emblems of York. Our house has been bound up for so long with the fortunes of York, they are woven into the tapestry of our lives as they are woven into this tapestry. Whoever ordered it so knew the truth, and did right.

"Job," she said after a while, "you always knew about Richard, didn't you—Richard of York, I mean."

"Yes," he said softly.

She reached out a hand—a feeble hand that would hardly lift from the bedclothes, and he gave his own to it. Her fingers closed around his. "I'm sorry," she said. "Did you mind very much?"

He shook his head, unable to speak.

"Poor Job," she whispered. "No one else ever knew, did they?"

"No," he said. It was the answer she wanted. She sighed—a contented sigh—and closed her eyes. He risked a look at her. Her face was as white and perfect as a cameo, and her hair that was tumbled over the pillows luxuriantly was still jet black—her vanity had never permitted her either to allow it to become gray or to admit that she did not allow it. Job's eyesight had been failing for years, and there was an advantage to it, for now to his misty vision she looked just as she had when she was a girl and he had first fallen in love with her.

She opened her eyes again and smiled at him, and his lips trembled. He was an old man, and it was too easy to cry; but understanding was in her eyes, and she looked away toward the window and the moors again, and her fingers squeezed his slightly.

"Open the window," she said. "Let me smell that good air as well as see it."

Rebecca got up quietly to do it, and Job watched her, afraid to look at his dear mistress, whose face was turned away from him now to save him embarrassment.

"That smells good," she said softly. She took in a deep breath, and let it out, sighingly.

Job waited to hear the next breath drawn in, but there was only silence, and when he looked down, he saw those white, slender fingers slowly relax and uncurl under his hand. Tears flooded his eyes, and he opened his mouth to speak, and then closed it again. No, let him have her to himself for a moment longer. It made no difference to them, and once they knew, they would take over, and there would be no place for him.

So the old man sat on at the bedside, his hand touching that of his dead mistress, and his misty eyes gazing out of the window toward those wide purple moors where the white hare would leap forever, and would never grow old, and never die.

The powerful and passionate saga of THE MORLAND FAMILY will continue with The Dark Rose, the second book in Dell's exciting new Morland Dynasty series.

The Dark Rose is set against the wonderfully colorful and turbulent background of Tudor England. When the novel opens in 1512, King Henry VIII rules the land and Eleanor's great-grandson Paul presides over the large household at the beautiful and sprawling Morland Place. In the years ahead the Morland's fortunes are seriously threatened and the proud family bloodline torn by a bitter rivalry. Paul's beloved niece, Nanette, becomes maid-in-waiting to the ill-fated Anne Boleyn in Henry VIII's royal court, and is swept into the grand and flamboyant intrigues of English court life. Finally the promise of happiness lures her back to Morland Place, where a loving Paul awaits her. But the passionate bond that links these two will soon be cruelly shattered.

With all the power, romance, and historical richness of *The Founding*, Cynthia Harrod-Eagles's *The Dark Rose* triumphantly continues the compelling epic story of the Morland Dynasty.

Here is a preview of *The Dark Rose*, to be published by Dell in June 1982:

They passed between the great hedges, and there at last it was dark. Nanette could hardly see Paul's face, and there in the aromatic darkness he stopped and turned to her, and she felt herself beginning to tremble.

"I thought I would never find another human creature to love," he said. "But sometimes when you cut down a plant, it begins to grow again, in spite of you. It puts out buds, and the buds are stronger than the first growth was." He took her hands in his and lifted them to his lips and kissed them, first one, then the other. "Why do you tremble?" he asked. He slid his hands up to her elbows. "Are

you cold?" He passed them around her body and took the
last step to her that brought her against him. She felt the
hard muscles of his thighs against her legs, felt the warmth
of his body, the sweetness of his breath stirring her hair,
and she was overcome with the desire to yield to him. She
pressed against him avidly, her face tipped back as instinctively as her arms went up around his neck. She could not
see his face except as a white blur, but her mind's eye supplied the warm dark eyes, the lean features, the full, sen-
suous lips. For so long she had repressed the wild urges of
her passionate nature, fighting them as her religion bid her,
and now she had no more strength or will to resist. She was
young and healthy, and she wanted to be made love to,
here, among the scented shadows, and by this man whose
sexuality made an almost tangible aura around him.

"Nanette," he said, dazed by her response.

"Yes," she said, not wanting him to talk, reaching up on
tiptoe, her lips parted for him.

"You were the one who brought that second spring to
my heart. I love you, Nanette."

He kissed her, and the world went away, and they were
spinning through a warm black void where there was nothing but themselves, the touch of their lips and hands, the
taste of each other, the smell of each other, the sound of
their breathing, and the pulse of their blood. Thought fled
before sensation. They sank to the ground, and Nanette
was aware only of the fragrance of the grass crushed beneath her, the coolness of the air around her bare head as
her headdress was discarded, the scent of the yew hedges
that framed them, the warm weight of her lover against her
legs. Though armored above, a maid's body was as defense-
less below as a mouse's belly; the warm, strong hands on
her legs, caressing her thighs, spanning her waist, were
rousing her to a pitch of maddened excitement, filling her
with a desire she did not know how to appease.

An awkward fumbling, and then the flesh touching hers
was different, and the urgency lanced through her like
lightning. Instinctively she knew what to do; and though
she could not make any sound—no groan or cry would escape her frantic mouth, which seemed to suckle on his
tongue—in her mind she cried, yes, yes, now!